DEVIL'S LAIR

After the violent death of her husband, Callie retreats to a cottage in the grounds of an old mansion in Tasmania. The place is a balm to her shattered nerves, and the locals seem friendly, particularly horseman Connor Atherton and his siblings at the nearby property, Calico Lodge. But the mansion has a sinister past, one associated with witchcraft and murder. As Callie is threatened by odd events in the night, and strange dreams overtake her sleep, she begins to doubt her own sanity. What's really going on beneath the surface of this apparently peaceful town? As events escalate, Callie starts to realise that the mansion may hold the key to unlocking the mystery, but the truth might have as much power to destroy as it does to save.

SPECIAL MESSAGE TO READERS

THE ULVERSCROFT FOUNDATION

(´ ... ... 73)

for

r(eases.

s Eye

Great
en
and
ology,

roup,

Books should be returned or renewed by the last estern
date above. Renew by phone **03000 41 31 31** or
online *www.kent.gov.uk/libs* Royal

Y(ation
7.

I you
or

:t:

THE ULVERSCROFT FOUNDATION
The Green, Bradgate Road, Anstey
Leicester LE7 7FU, England
Tel: (0116) 236 4325

websit(C161050832 ion.org.uk

SARAH BARRIE

DEVIL'S LAIR

Complete and Unabridged

AURORA
Leicester

First published in Australia and New Zealand
in 2019 by
HarperCollins Publishers Australia Pty Ltd

First Aurora Edition
published 2020
by arrangement with
HarperCollins Publishers Australia Pty Ltd

A catalogue record for this book is available
from the British Library.

ISBN 978–1–78782–402–7

Published by
Ulverscroft Limited
Anstey, Leicestershire

Set by Words & Graphics Ltd.
Anstey, Leicestershire
Printed and bound in Great Britain by
T. J. International Ltd., Padstow, Cornwall

This book is printed on acid-free paper

To the family who always were, and the treasured people who become it. Especially a much-loved grandma. Thanks Angie x

1

Callie leant against the solid warmth of her husband and sipped her coffee. From the back deck they looked over the sparkling pool to the long, neat rows of vines and the sun rising over the lush green mountains beyond their estate. Birds sang their first songs of the day in the blue gums that dotted the grounds, while the sweet scent of daphne caught on the warming breeze. Dale rested his head against hers. Callie could feel her eyelids drooping as the tranquillity seeped into her, even as the coffee slid down her throat.

'Quiet day today?' Dale murmured.

'Yeah. You?'

'Not so much.' He played with a curl of her hair, letting it slide through his fingers. 'How did I end up with such a beautiful wife?'

She lifted a hand and tucked the auburn curl back behind her ear. 'What do you want?' she said with a laugh.

He smiled against her forehead. 'Do you think you could update the prices on the wine catalogue for me? It needs to go out.'

She contemplated the request, took another sip of her coffee. 'Sure. Do you think you could bring one of those 2008 vintage merlots back after work to fix the headache it's going to give me?'

He chuckled. 'Deal. We're a pretty great team, you and I.'

'I think so.' Rosellas flocked to the grass by the property gates, catching her eye and reminding her, 'I think I want to put in another garden bed where that tumble of rocks sits near the front gate. It could look really great with the right plantings.'

'I was going to take them away with the backhoe.'

'You've been going to do that for the last five years.'

'Things keep getting in the way.'

She tipped her head back to smile at him. 'Right. So, I should plant it out.'

'You can take the girl out of landscaping, but you can't take the landscaping out of the girl.'

'I don't think that makes sense.'

'I think you're right. Go ahead. It'll look spectacular.'

'Great.'

'Paisley's back today, right?'

'Yeah. Should be. If she's managed to tear herself away from Tassie.'

'It's a nice part of the world.'

'Maybe we should find time to zip down there one of these days. You could show me where you grew up,' she suggested.

'I think we've got enough to do, don't you?' Dale asked.

As though in agreement, the office phone rang. Callie groaned, untangled herself from the warmth of her husband and walked through the pair of glass doors to the cosy kitchen, snatching

2

the cordless off the bench. It was unlikely the call would be business at seven in the morning, but habit had her answering, 'Highgrove Estate, may I help you?'

Silence. Then a mumbled . . . something. Dial tone.

'Have a nice day,' she grumbled as she replaced the handset on the charger. She picked up Dale's mail, which was stacked by the phone. He was hopeless with correspondence. Unless she put it in his hand the mountain would only continue to get higher. A black envelope amid the more businesslike white collection caught her eye and she pulled a face. That one had been sitting there for close to two weeks. She carried it out along with the rest and dropped them in front of him.

'Oh, ta. Who was on the phone?' he asked.

'Wrong number, I think.' She sat down beside him. 'What's the black one?'

A flicker of irritation flashed across his face. He shrugged, got to his feet. 'Just something from an old school friend.'

'Who is this old friend?' she pressed, because his reaction was odd.

'Not someone I want to renew ties with.' He dropped a kiss on her forehead. 'I'd better get moving.'

'Do you have to start this early today?' She caught him behind the neck before he could straighten, pressed her lips to his. 'I could make breakfast . . . or . . . '

'Witch,' he groaned, removing her hand before kissing her fingers. 'You know I do. And you

3

need to look over that catalogue.'

'Hmm.' She sulked into her coffee.

'I'll make it up to you later.' He leant in and kissed her until her toes curled. 'We've got forever to look forward to lazy breakfasts.'

'Okay . . . But take your mail!' She reluctantly finished her own coffee as he scooped up the letters and his cup and disappeared into the house. She heard his car start up, the engine noise fading as he headed down the drive towards their winery. She stretched, took one last appreciative look over the grounds, over what they'd achieved in just five short years. Forever, she thought, sounded just perfect.

★　★　★

Callie started on the catalogue right away, eating a slice of toast as she altered prices and checked her calculations. Assuming her assistant, Paisley, did get back today, she'd have her give it a final once-over before sending it out.

She scanned emails and online bookings, and paid the latest assortment of bills, then, satisfied the office work was under control, decided to reward herself with time in the garden. She snatched her cap from the stand by the door and tucked her hair up underneath, then walked out into the sunshine. After a quick trip to the gardening shed, she pointed the wheelbarrow towards the wide, winding drive lined with rose hedges. Most of the roses were finished and required deadheading. White blooms looked so lovely, but the brown mess that was replacing

4

them did not. She worked quickly, humming to herself.

'That's quite a job you've got ahead of you,' a friendly voice remarked.

'Mrs Bates, good morning,' Callie said to the woman staying in room five. 'How are you enjoying your weekend?'

'Everything's perfect, dear. Which is why we come back every year — well that, and to restock the wine cellar,' Mrs Bates said, eyes full of fun.

'Are you sure you wouldn't like me to make you some breakfast this morning?'

'We're eating on the fly, but I'll take you up on one of your delicious omelettes tomorrow.'

'No problem.'

'The gardens always look so beautiful here. You do a remarkable job.'

'I enjoy it,' Callie said. 'Landscaping used to be my job but then I married and — ' she smiled, added a little lift of her shoulders, ' — plans changed.'

'Well, I just think that's wonderful. A husband to love you, a beautiful home and business, and all these incredible gardens to play with. You're living a fairy tale!'

'I pinch myself occasionally,' Callie agreed. 'How is Gerard doing?'

'Getting fat!' Mrs Bates said of her son. 'Being one of the top food critics in the country certainly doesn't help the waistline! Did you happen to catch his review of that new restaurant down the road from here?'

'Yes,' Callie said and bit down on her grin. 'It was a little rough.'

'It was abysmal,' Mrs Bates corrected. 'I told him he would have been better off coming here.'

Callie laughed. 'For bacon and eggs?'

Mrs Bates chuckled and gently touched a still fresh flower. 'I do love these roses. I have a few at home. Haven't managed to find one quite as incandescently white as this one, though.'

'These are Icebergs. Make sure I give you some cuttings before you leave.'

Mrs Bates's face lit up. 'I'll do that. Thank you. Oh, here's my ride,' she said as tyres crunched behind them. 'Never let it be said women take all the time in the shower. We're off to McWilliam's to stock up on their muscat. Marvellous stuff.'

Callie sent the couple a friendly wave as they drove away. What would she and Dale be like together at that age? Still happy? In love? She hoped so.

Her gaze fell on the pile of earth and sandstone that would soon become her next garden. She planned it in her head, mapping out what would go where. Some pretty groundcovers would crawl among the cavities in the smaller sections of rock, spilling over them in vibrant splashes of colour. Brightly coloured flax could fill the deeper holes. She'd include deciduous trees: a lime green robinia, and perhaps something red — a prunus? — to go with it to provide some shade in summer. There was a perfect spot for a pond in the low corner, so she'd measure it out.

Callie had worked her way around most of the drive when she heard the hum of a car engine.

She looked over her shoulder. A dusty silver Audi crept along the otherwise empty road. At the gate, the driver touched the brakes, once, twice, then drew the car to a stop. Idled.

She wasn't expecting new guests today, but she pulled off her gloves and tossed her shears on the pile of cuttings in the wheelbarrow. Smile in place, she moved around the hedge and approached the car.

'Hi, can I help you?'

The woman was too thin, dressed in casual clothes that spoke of a good fashion sense and a healthy bank balance. But even through the woman's designer sunglasses Callie could see the edgy stare in the eyes framed by untidy bottle-blonde hair. The woman's hands clutched the steering wheel, and one leg jigged up and down in a nervous staccato. 'I'm looking for — '

A quick beep from behind them made Callie look up. Paisley had pulled into the drive. She waved. Callie sent her a distracted smile and returned her attention to the woman now staring into her rear-view mirror.

'Looking for?' Callie prompted.

The woman's eyes darted back to Callie and her head shuddered from side to side in an erratic negative action. 'Doesn't matter.'

The car jerked forward. 'Hey!' Callie jumped out of harm's way, then watched the car speed off down the road. 'What the hell?'

'What was that about?' Paisley called.

'No idea. But there was something wrong with her.'

'Who?'

'The maniac driver I've never met before.' Callie sighed and shook her head, glad her toes hadn't been run over, and walked over to Paisley's Pajero. 'How was your trip?'

Her assistant's mouth twisted. 'Eventful. Got time to hear about it?'

'Yeah, I could do with a break,' Callie decided, with one last glance back at the road. 'I'll catch up with you in the office.' She followed Paisley's car through the gates, picked up the wheelbarrow and steered it down the drive. By the time she put everything away, Paisley was on the phone, so she went through the office and into the house, made some cold drinks and took them back.

'If you want coffee, I'll go get you one. I felt like something cool.'

'All good, thanks.' Paisley made a note on the computer, then took a glass, sipped, and smiled. 'Everything run smoothly while I was away?'

'Of course. I've just updated the wine catalogue. You probably should do a last check.'

'I'll do it now.'

'I think Dale was hoping you'd run straight over to the winery and help him when you arrived. He's got a lot on today.'

'Then I'll be quick with the catalogue.' She flicked through it. 'We don't have any check-ins today?'

'No. I think I might go tree shopping. I want to play around with the front area by the gate.'

'The boulders,' Paisley guessed. 'I knew you'd get to that one day.'

Callie smiled. 'Dale's all for it.'

'So he should be. You love it, and you're damn good at it. This whole place looks like a magazine cover.' The computer pinged with a new email and Paisley read it.

'What is it?' Callie asked when Paisley's brow shot up.

'Next door has put another offer in writing.'

Callie pulled a face as she took a long sip of her lemon sparkling water. 'The place is not for sale. Besides, Dale hates them and would rather die than see them turn this place into a hundred-room concrete monstrosity. I'm inclined to agree.'

'It's a lot of money.'

'Hmm.'

Paisley turned the computer monitor around. 'Look at it.'

'Fine.' She looked, and choked on her water. 'Wow.'

'Yeah. Wow.'

'And no.'

Paisley nodded. 'Good. I like my job here. Had to show you, though.'

'So . . . Tasmania?'

Callie regretted the question when Paisley's eyes lost some of their spark.

'It was freezing, as you'd expect at this time of year, and my welcome wasn't a hell of a lot warmer. You know Dad and I haven't been in each other's company much over the last few years.'

'But he asked for your help, didn't he?' Callie asked, confused.

'No, Ned told me Dad needed my help,' Paisley said. 'They are two very different things.

9

And he's right. Dad's having trouble managing out there. He's always been fine on his meds, but dementia's kicking in and he keeps forgetting to take them. His moods are all over the place with the bipolar and he's paranoid someone's out to get him because of the schizophrenia. He had a fall recently and whacked his head. Luckily, Ned turned up to mow the lawns. It's only going to get progressively worse. He won't be able to stay out there on his own forever.'

'They have a good relationship, don't they? Can't Ned convince him to move into care?'

Paisley leant back in the office chair. 'Ned can't cope with the heavy stuff. He has the emotional strength of a wounded deer, and his IQ isn't exactly up there, either. You know the story.'

Callie nodded slowly, remembering Paisley's parents had taken Ned in because his mother was very young and didn't want him. 'Your mum was a psychologist, right?'

'At the asylum down there. Pretty much ran the place — and ran Dad. If they'd stayed together, everything would be a lot different.'

'Mmm.' Callie silently wondered how Eileen Waldron could have worked with the mentally ill all day then come home to a mentally ill husband and raise someone else's child with issues of his own. An amazing woman. Though she'd left, eventually. Perhaps she'd had nothing left to give.

'Anyway,' Paisley continued, 'I've organised for a community nurse to check in on Dad a couple of days a week. That should buy him some more time.'

'Well, that's something.'

'Best I can do. Dad's digging his heels in, refusing to leave, and honestly, packing up would be completely beyond him. He's a hoarder. Not as bad as some of the ones you see on the TV but he's got fifty years of stuff in piles around the place — rubbish everywhere.' She chewed on a fingernail, thinking. 'I might have to try and get down there a bit more regularly to tackle it. I'll need the money from the house to fund his care so it's going to have to be done. Otherwise no one will ever buy the place.'

'If it's as lovely as you say it is, surely someone will see past a bit of mess?'

A hint of wistfulness touched Paisley's expression. 'A huge old home on acres, right on the River Derwent. Completely buried in junk as old as it is. Tell you what,' she said brightly, 'why don't you buy it as an investment property?'

'Ha. No. Sorry.'

'It'd make a gorgeous bed and breakfast. If we clear away a foot or two of mess in the kitchen we might even find some of the original pots and pans.'

'As much fun as that sounds,' Callie replied, 'I've already got my hands full. And speaking of — you'd better look at this catalogue before Dale realises you're back.'

'Can do,' Paisley said, spinning her chair back around to the monitor. 'I've also got to go over the new artwork for it with Dale. I sent some ideas across before I left last week but I bet he hasn't looked at them.'

'I bet you're right.'

'I'll make a note.' Paisley pulled up another screen, frowned. 'I think I forgot to tell you the couple coming in tomorrow requested a bottle of bubbly and a cheese platter on arrival. They're celebrating a wedding anniversary.'

'That's okay, I'll do a supply run this afternoon. We're now officially out of that quince paste and low on the triple brie.' She glanced up. 'Uh-oh,' she teased as Dale's car stopped out the front. 'Sprung.'

Paisley groaned good-naturedly. 'I'll go through the rest at lunch.' She got to her feet. 'I'll see you — Hey, that car's back.'

'What car?' Callie followed Paisley's gaze out the window to where the silver Audi sat. 'It's that woman again! What the hell could she possibly want?'

'Dale's heading over,' Paisley said.

They both watched from the office window as Dale approached the car, leaning in the driver's window. There was some sort of conversation. Then the car slowly pulled away. Dale's expression was exasperated as he removed his cap and dragged his hand through his hair.

'That's weird,' Callie muttered, and went to the door to meet him as he came back. 'Who was that?'

'In the car? Just a lost tourist,' he said. 'Hi, Paisley. I need you at the winery.'

'To look at the artwork for the catalogue or go over my advertising proposal that you've no doubt forgotten about?' Paisley asked.

'You'll be surprised to learn,' Dale replied smugly, 'that just last night I marked up some ideas. It's all back in my Dropbox folder.'

'Surprised is an understatement. Thanks, boss. Will I go ahead and order the material?'

'Not until you've taken in the comments I made — and I've seen the new costing.' His grin was there, Callie noted, but there seemed to be an underlying tension from speaking to the woman on the drive.

'Dale, that woman you just talked to was here earlier. She looked upset when I spoke to her.'

'You spoke to her?'

She didn't expect the snap in his voice.

He turned to Paisley. 'What did she say?'

Paisley shrugged. 'Don't look at me, I didn't talk to her. Cal?'

'She was jittery and upset. I think she was looking for something but I didn't get a 'lost tourist' vibe.'

'More like a lunatic vibe!' Dale took a calming breath and wrapped Callie in a hug. 'I'm sorry — I didn't mean to jump down your throat. I didn't want to worry you, but she was strange. I don't think she'll come back. But if she does show up again, call me.' He straightened and looked her in the eyes. 'Don't go near her again, okay?'

'Ah . . . Sure.'

With a nod, he let her go. 'You right if I pinch Paisley?'

'Go ahead. I'll need her back after lunch.'

As they left, she looked past them to the gate and the road beyond. Was the stranger likely to come back or had Dale scared her off for good?

2

Paisley dropped her bag lightly on the desk. 'Morning.'

'Hi,' Callie said, jumping to her feet. She'd been waiting for Paisley to arrive so she could go out. 'We have three couples turning up this afternoon and because Dale ended up keeping you all day yesterday, I didn't have time to pick up the stuff for that fruit and cheese platter for the wedding anniversary.'

'Want me to go get them?'

'No — thanks. I'll do a full shop while I'm out.' Callie grabbed her jacket from the back of her chair and swung it around her shoulders.

Paisley took a water bottle from her bag and placed it on the desk, before taking off her coat. 'So Dale's not in today?'

'Playing in the backhoe. They're prepping the south paddock.'

'How is it coming along? Will it be ready for planting next season?'

'Hopefully. We'll see.'

'I've costed out his suggestions for the promotion. I was hoping he'd okay it today.'

'He'll tell you it's not until September, not to stress,' Callie said.

'Yeah. You know when he okayed the Mother's Day one?' Paisley said. 'Ten days before Mother's Day.'

Callie grinned. 'And yet you pulled it off.'

14

'I feel so taken for granted,' Paisley said dramatically. 'You'd better grab me a nice triple brie while you're out to make me feel better!'

'You can share it with me this arvo by the pool. It's a gorgeous day. I'll open one of our chardonnays to go with it.'

'I can't get you in that pool in summer, let alone winter.'

'No.' And she never would. 'But it's nice to sit by it.'

'Agreed.'

Callie was still smiling as she drove into town. She did all the running around she needed to and made time to call in at the nursery to order the trees for the new project. Then she turned the car towards the Hunter Valley Cheese Company.

The place was busy, and a minibus was held up at the entrance waiting for a car to reverse out. As she scanned for a spot she noticed the outdoor tables held a good scattering of tour group couples and families. And —

Surprise then disbelief had Callie accelerating around the minibus then awkwardly pulling up further along the road, bumping the gutter distractedly before coming to a messy stop. She looked in her rear-vision mirror, then adjusted it until she got a better look at what she hoped she hadn't seen. But she had seen it. Dale. *With that woman*.

Unwilling to believe the mirror, Callie spun around in her seat and peered over the headrest. She'd know Dale anywhere and though the blonde's face was obscured by distance and sunglasses, she was sure it was the same woman. Who else could it be?

Reasons and excuses skidded through her mind but none stuck. None of them made any sense. What was going on? Had Dale lied about not knowing the woman? Had they met since yesterday? As Callie watched, Dale lifted his hands from under the table, placed them over the woman's and ducked his head towards her. Callie's stomach lurched. Nothing about that gesture screamed, *We just met.*

She started to shake. Even as she told herself she didn't have the first clue what was going on, she struggled to deny the most obvious reason for this that came to mind.

The pair leant back as they sipped drinks, then the woman reached for Dale again.

The lurch in Callie's stomach churned into one long, nauseating roll.

Her phone rang and she fumbled to answer it. 'Yeah?' she asked, her voice hitching in her throat.

'Don't forget the — what?' It was Paisley.

'I'm at the cheese company.'

Paisley's voice turned sharp. 'Callie, what's wrong? Have you been in an accident or something?'

'I could be overreacting,' Callie said. 'It's just — no, it's not nothing. They're holding hands, Paisley. They're talking all *close* and *intimate*.'

'What? Who?'

'Dale! And that *woman*!'

'What woman?'

Several seconds ticked by as Callie kept watch.

16

She couldn't take her eyes off them.

'Ooh. The car woman? Are you sure?'

'Are you kidding?'

'Okay, sorry. Of course you're sure. Shit. Okay, just . . . stay calm. Let's approach this rationally. There must be an explanation. Where are they?'

'One of the outside tables.'

'Do you really think Dale would risk doing anything underhanded out there? Everyone knows him.'

Paisley had a point and yet, there he was. 'One way to find out,' Callie said. She'd rather do almost anything than approach them, but she needed to know.

'Wait!' Paisley snapped. 'You can't confront them while you're as upset as you sound. If you storm over there and there's a perfectly acceptable explanation, you're going to look stupid and everyone's going to think you're a nut.'

'Okay, granted. But — ' She looked down at her hands and clasped them tightly. 'God, I'm shaking — a minute ago I wanted to run and hide. Now I just want to go over there and demand answers. Why would he go behind my back like this?'

'*And,*' Paisley continued, 'if you storm over there and there's not an acceptable explanation, you're still going to look stupid and everyone's going to feel sorry for you. Do you really want either scenario flying around town tomorrow?'

Not an acceptable explanation? Could it really be possible Dale was cheating on her? Not Dale, no. Their marriage was so perfect. But as Callie watched him with that woman, doubts crept in. Damn it, why did Paisley have to make so much sense?

'So what I just . . . leave them here?'

There were a few seconds of silence, then: 'Tell you what. Come home. I'll shoot out there and 'accidentally' run into them, introduce myself to the woman so I can find out who she is — and suss out Dale's reaction to me finding them there.'

Callie took some deep breaths. Paisley was right; she was in no state to confront anyone. 'Okay. Okay. I'll be there in ten.'

She was there in five. The drive home had done nothing to calm her down. Dale had said yesterday that he didn't know the woman. He'd lied. If there was a reasonable explanation, why would he lie?

Paisley came out before Callie could get inside. 'I'll let you know,' she said, then she was in her car and reversing out of her spot, tearing away.

Callie unpacked the groceries, trying to focus on drawing up the layout for her new garden. One of the expected couples checked in and — damn — she realised she still didn't have the cheeses she was meant to buy. It didn't seem important now.

When the phone rang she pounced on it.

'Sorry, Callie. Are you absolutely sure the woman was with Dale?' Paisley asked. 'I couldn't see them anywhere. I checked the café, did a drive around looking for his car then went out

18

via the new estate and there he was, working with Gavin. He certainly looked as though he'd been there all afternoon. Still in the work clothes he'd been in this morning.'

'He was in them when I saw — ' She broke off as a car sent gravel flying in the driveway and jerked to a stop. Callie stood slowly. 'Ah, Paise? That woman. She just arrived.'

'She's there? Sit tight. I'm two seconds out!'

The woman got out of her car and ran towards the door.

'What do you want?' Callie demanded.

'Where is he?' the woman asked.

'Where is Dale? You should know, you were just with him!' Callie heard the edge of hysteria in her voice and willed herself to keep it together. 'Who are you?'

'I'm not supposed to talk to you.' The woman's head was shaking from side to side almost like a tic. 'I need to see him.'

'Wait!' Callie grabbed the woman's arms and held her back as she prepared to walk behind the desk and into the house.

The woman took two steps back and twisted her hands together in front of her. Everything about her was nervous energy and urgency. When she swayed, Callie thought she was going to fall over.

'Would you just stop! You need to calm yourself down.'

'I have — I have some . . . ' The woman shakily delved into her bag. Most of the contents, including a pill container, spilled out onto the floor.

'Bloody hell,' Callie muttered as the woman scrambled to open the container and popped a pill in her mouth. Callie bent to pick up more of the woman's things. Her hand hovered over a folded black envelope. 'Is this Dale's?' She unfolded it and saw the name Lisa, before it was snatched back.

'No. No, it's mine.' The woman shoved it inside her bag.

'What is it?'

Lisa snatched Callie's hand much as she had the envelope. 'I'm sorry,' she whispered again. 'You seem to have such a beautiful life. I don't want to wreck that. But it's all a lie.'

'What?' Callie said, her vision tunnelling.

Paisley burst through the door. 'What the hell?'

Lisa's distressed stare moved from Callie to Paisley. 'I can't do this anymore. I just can't.' When she again made a grab for Callie, Paisley leapt between them.

'Hey!'

'My cat's dead! I need to tell. I need to end it.'

'End what?' Callie asked.

'All of it.'

'Okay,' Paisley said, unimpressed, 'I'm not sure what you're on, but you and your dead cat can go be on it somewhere else.'

'But I need to — '

'What you need to do, lady, is leave,' Paisley ordered. 'Or I'm going to call someone to remove you.'

Something akin to confusion crossed Lisa's face before her eyes widened. 'Of course. Okay.

20

Of course. I'm sorry.' With a nod she ran back to her car. She drove away, wheels spinning.

'Did she hurt you?' Paisley asked, checking Callie over.

With a quick shake of her head, Callie dropped into her chair and stared at the floor. She hugged her arms around herself, rubbed her hands up and down against the emotional chill the woman had left in her wake. 'I never question what he's doing, where he goes, what he's up to. I've never seen her before yesterday. Have you?'

Paisley shook her head. 'No. What did she say to you?'

'Just that she was sorry, but my life was a lie.'

Paisley's expression softened. 'Callie . . . that woman was far from stable.'

Callie's head shot up. 'But she knew Dale, and he told me he didn't know her. He had lunch with her, when he was supposed to be somewhere else. She talked about lies. And he's lied to me.'

'We don't know anything yet.'

Callie walked to the fireplace and plucked a photo of their wedding day from the mantelpiece.

Paisley put a hand on her shoulder and squeezed it. 'Talk to Dale.' Her phone rang, but she ignored it. 'Just talk to him before you start jumping to any wild conclusions, okay?'

Callie drew in a deep breath. Nodded. She was prone to leaping to worst-case scenarios, but she wouldn't do that with her marriage, with the man she loved and trusted. 'You're right. I should — '

The phone rang again. Paisley swore and checked the screen, then rejected the call. 'Come and sit down, I'll get you a glass of something. Take the edge off.'

'No, I don't think drinking is a good idea at the moment. I need to think. Calmly.'

'Damn it!' Paisley exclaimed when her phone rang again. She silenced it once more and smiled apologetically at Callie. 'Sorry. It's Ned.'

'Go, I'll be fine.'

'Are you sure?'

At her nod, Paisley gave her a hug. 'I'll be at the winery. If Dale comes in I'll let you know. In the meantime if you need me, call. I'll be right back.'

'Thanks.'

'If he comes here first, let me know how it goes.'

Callie paced, unable to settle. Paisley rang three times, and three times she'd refused her offer to lock up and come back. When she got tired she sat, staring into space and thinking about the possibilities. Why wasn't Dale back? She felt sick, her stomach rumbling, making the churning worse. She forced down a sandwich. When the clock hit nine o'clock, she poured herself a glass of wine. At midnight, she caved and called him. He didn't answer. Nor at twelve-thirty, or at one. Was something wrong? Could something have happened to him? Around two in the morning, another thought crept in. Was he with Lisa?

He couldn't be. He'd never shown the slightest hint of being interested in anyone else.

So where the hell had Lisa come from? When had they met? Callie had known Dale forever. Of course, Dale was quite a bit older than her, but he'd let her tag around with him and his mates when she'd been small, and had looked out for her. They'd been close for so long, moved in all the same circles. When their relationship had developed as adults it was such a natural progression no one batted an eyelid. Callie liked to think it was meant to be. Maybe that was the problem — too much, too soon. Had Dale simply gotten sick of her?

She went upstairs to the bedroom. The bed, with its pretty cream-coloured linen and big, soft pillows, looked anything but inviting. The lace-curtained windows that, of a day, displayed a stunning view over hills and vines, framed only a void as dark as her mood. The whole room, the whole, warm, comfortable room, felt suddenly unfamiliar. Cold.

★   ★   ★

The vibration of her phone on the bedside table had Callie stirring from sleep. It was still dark, rain pattering lightly, and she turned to see Dale's side of the bed was empty. Not quite awake, she reached for her phone and turned off the alarm. She had guests to cook for. Head aching and eyes swollen, she dragged herself up, stood for a moment and pulled herself together. She couldn't afford to think. Just the idea of thinking had new tears springing up behind her eyes.

A noise downstairs caught her attention as she headed for the shower. Someone was moving around. Dale? She wrapped her thick robe around her and silently tiptoed down the stairs. A quick glance outside revealed the outline of his car against the overcast early morning. Another sound: the slide and clink of the filing cabinet closing. What was he doing?

She stayed where she was, plastered against the wall of the staircase while she rallied the courage to face him. More muffled noises, the humming of pipes in the walls. The downstairs shower was running. Needing to keep herself occupied while she gathered her thoughts, she put on coffee. She sorted out the breakfast orders, because regardless of what happened next, the guests would still need to eat.

She wondered what Dale had put in the filing cabinet. It had to be something he didn't want her to see. And why would he shower downstairs before announcing he was back?

She listened. The shower was still running, so she quietly went into the office. She knew which drawer to check: the bottom one. She tried it and wasn't surprised she couldn't get in. Dale kept the key on him with the excuse that all their most important paperwork was in there and she'd never thought to question him over it. Now she was questioning everything. She knew how to get in — she only had to lift out the drawer above. She'd figured that out when she'd needed their passport numbers once.

Removing the drawer was awkward, noisy. After every clunk she stopped, checking for the hum of the shower. When the drawer was finally free she dived in through the space and rifled through files, finding only paperwork. The folders scraped loudly as she slipped her hands underneath them, worrying at any moment Dale would be in the doorway. Then her fingers brushed something cold and hard.

She lifted it out. A thumb drive.

Confused, she flicked open her laptop, inserted the drive and waited impatiently for the system to boot up. While it worked at preparing itself, she slid the drawers back together, relieved when she found it easier than getting them apart.

'Come on . . . ' she muttered to the laptop as the file folder popped up on screen. She hovered the mouse over the folder to open it. Then she heard the water shut off with a clank.

'Shit. Shit. Shit.' She clicked anyway, too close to give up. Thumbnail images appeared.

She sank like a stone to the chair. Stared.

What was this? What the hell was this? She clicked on the first photo to enlarge it, pressed her eyes tightly closed then opened them. A chill that froze her like ice washed over her and pierced the fog of her clouded mind. It was the woman — Lisa. At least, she was pretty sure it was her. She was dead, staked to the earth, arms and legs outstretched. A red circle surrounded her, candles posted around it. Her clothes, her body, were ripped to shreds. Everything was damaged. Everything was broken. Somewhere under the tangle of hair that covered her face, Callie got the impression of wide, staring eyes, a mouth open in a scream.

'No.' It came out as a whimper. This was too much to take in. How could she possibly process this? She dragged her eyes from the image and stared, unseeing, out the window as her mind raced for an acceptable explanation. Maybe Dale had gone back to see Lisa a second time and found her like that. Callie nodded in desperation. He would have called the police — could have been there all night trying to help, to find out what had happened. Yes, that was sure to be it. He'd explain. He wouldn't want to, but he would. He must be upset, exhausted. He'd need time to gather his thoughts before talking to her. That would be the reason for the downstairs shower.

Callie got her feet under her and walked unsteadily to the kitchen. Because she was bone-deep cold, she tossed another log on the dying fire. The table still held her wineglass, a plate and the remaining half of a bottle of chardonnay, sitting by a fruit bowl. She should tidy them up. She realised her legs were shaking, so she leant on the chair.

Her husband was not a murderer, she told herself again. She would *know*. He was a kind, generally considerate, brilliant man. What had been done to that woman would challenge the limits of a crazed psychopath. And why the photos? And the thumb drive? If he'd done it, taken pictures, why take the time to store them on a drive? She had this all wrong. She had to have it all wrong.

'You're up.'

Dale's voice startled her. He stood behind her,

26

a towel around his waist. Scratches marred his cheek and a garbage bag was clutched in his hand. He walked past her to the fire, and tossed the bag in. The plastic shrivelled and, with a whoosh, the material within ignited.

'I didn't think you'd be cooking yet,' he said with a smile marred by tension. 'Early breakfast orders?'

'What?' She dragged her eyes away from the fire with difficulty. 'Where have you been? What happened last night?'

He joined her at the table and placed his hands on her shoulders, a kiss on her forehead. 'Sorry if I worried you. You knew I was working late. I fell asleep at the winery.'

'But — your face. And the — '

'And the what?' Dale's expression changed from calm and apologetic to intense, his eyes looking straight into hers. It stopped her in her tracks.

He turned to fill the coffee cups. 'I woke up about an hour ago, went to call you and realised I didn't have my phone. I'd been out to the new estate yesterday and decided I should check I hadn't left it on the machinery parked out there for the paddock development. On the way back, a damn roo jumped out in front of the car. It was still alive so I tried to help it but it attacked me trying to get away. Scratched my face. Made a hell of a mess of my clothes.'

A kangaroo? She studied the marks on his face, tried to believe an animal could have put them there. The image of Lisa on the ground wedged itself firmly in Callie's mind. It had been too dark to make out anything around the woman, but there was grass and dirt. Lots of it. Much like where they'd dug up the far paddock to plant out the new rows of vines. Callie swallowed the bile rising in her throat as every reassuring excuse she'd come up with faded.

He's killed her, her mind screamed. *Oh, God, no, he can't have killed her!*

She pasted on a weak smile. 'That's all good then.'

'You sure you're all right, Callie? You look a little pale.'

'Fine.'

'Good. I need to get dressed.' He stepped back, and his smile was there but it lacked warmth. 'Could you rustle me up some toast?'

'Sure.'

With trembling hands she took out the bread and made herself throw him a quick smile as he left the room. She needed to find the explanation that fit. *Any* explanation that fit other than the one she couldn't, *wouldn't,* consider. Dale was not a murderer. The photos would make sense. Somehow.

Her laptop. She envisaged it sitting open on the desk. If he — Damn it. She needed to move. She raced into the office, slipped the thumb drive into her pocket.

'Callie?'

She spun around to see Dale staring at her darkly, blocking the doorway. She tried for a smile, but noticed he wasn't staring at her. He was staring at the image still open on her computer.

28

'You saw that and didn't tell me?' he said, his voice quiet. 'What were you going to do?' he asked, his eyes finally moving to meet hers. 'Dob me in?'

Her head shook vigorously. 'No! Dale, of course not, just — tell me you didn't have anything to do with this!'

He swore and snatched the computer. 'I didn't want it to turn out like this. I'm sorry. No one can know about this, Callie.'

What did that mean? Her heart gave one large thud and then seemed to stop altogether. She couldn't breathe for the tight band of worry clenching at her chest. Did she know this man at all? She ducked around him and ran through the door.

He lunged, got a hand on her.

'Let me go!' she screamed.

'Let me explain!'

A bright shock of rage slipped past the fear. She pointed at the laptop in his hand. 'There's no way to make that better!'

With a growl, he dragged her with him to the kitchen, then pitched the laptop into the fire to join the clothing. It smashed and began to melt.

'Callie!' Paisley thumped on one of the twin glass kitchen doors, eyes wide. 'Callie? Are you okay?'

'No!' She used the distraction to rip her arm from Dale's grasp and dodge past him. He lunged again, got a hand on her robe and dragged her back. She grabbed the table, couldn't hold on but pulled the tablecloth off. The glass, bottle, plate and fruit bowl all shattered on the floor. 'Let me go!'

'Don't go out there!' The words ended on a violent curse as Dale slipped.

Paisley was still desperately pounding on the glass. Callie needed to get to that door, flip the lock. She felt Dale's hand around her ankle as she leapt, then the pain of slamming onto the floor as he pulled her foot out from under her. Her hand landed on the broken wineglass and she grabbed it despite its jagged edges and kicked free, lashed out with the glass as he roughly dragged her back. Felt the jarring of it as it lodged in his cheek.

Callie stared, horrified. The shattering of the door as Paisley lobbed something through barely even registered. Dale got up, staggered, reaching for her, then slipped again. This time when he went down, his head cracked with a sickening thud against the bench. He didn't move, didn't get back up. She wondered why she couldn't see, and didn't realise she was sobbing.

Paisley rushed in, got hold of Callie when she would have collapsed.

'Callie, are you okay? Are you hurt? What happened? I can't believe what I just saw.'

'That woman was dead. And he wouldn't deny it was him. He just said no one could know.'

'What?'

'That *woman*! She's dead. Murdered. And he was scratched and he burned his clothes and there were pictures . . .'

'Okay, okay.' Paisley dragged her to a chair and clasped her fingers in her hair. 'We need to call the police.' She pulled her phone from her

30

pocket, then stared past Callie back out the door. 'Callie! Do you have anything to tie him up with?'

'Tie him up?'

'Until the police arrive. Do you have anything?'

'Maybe in the garage.'

'Go and look!' Paisley's shocked eyes moved back to Dale. 'Go and look.'

Callie got up, then doubled over with nausea at the sight of blood spreading on the floor around her husband. 'What if he doesn't wake up?'

'Seriously, Callie? What if he does? Go out to the garage, get some tape or cable ties or something. Now! Not that way!' Paisley ordered when Callie somehow moved her legs and would have left through the kitchen. 'Go through the back. I'm calling for help,' then into the phone she said, 'Yes, I need an ambulance and the police . . .'

Callie ran blindly outside, barely noticing the rain that had started to fall, swiping uselessly at her face, eyes stinging while she fought for every breath she dragged into her lungs. She scanned the garage shelves, knocked most of their contents to the ground as, hand trembling, she struggled to find what she needed. Then she found three cable ties in an almost empty pack. They would do. Still fighting hysteria, she made her legs take her back inside.

The first thing she noticed was Dale wasn't moving. Paisley was bent over him, every muscle taut.

'He doesn't look right.'

The expression on Paisley's face as she dropped back from Dale to sit on the floor all but answered the question Callie was too afraid to ask. The breath clogged in her throat again, dissolving the strength in her legs. She dropped down beside her friend, drew her knees up to her chin and tried to breathe.

'He's dead, isn't he?'

The soft words were barely discernible even to herself over the monotonous drumming of rain on the kitchen roof. The scene became dreamlike. The horror of the previous few minutes was incongruous with the tidy, brightly lit space, the comforting fire burning in the hearth and the lingering scent of coffee.

She glanced sideways when her friend took a while to answer.

Paisley raked her fingers through her long, blonde hair. 'Looks like.' Then, with a heavy sigh: 'Hell.'

A hysterical laugh broke from Callie's throat, loud and sharp in the quiet space. 'I just accused him of being a murderer. Then I did this. I'm as bad as he is.'

'Was.'

'What?'

'As bad as he was. Except you're not.'

Callie clamped one shaking hand in the other. The fire snapped, shooting out another spurt of brightly dancing lights as the laptop continued to dissolve.

The damn laptop. She should have shut it down. Shut it down, or run away. Not this. Anything but this.

'It doesn't matter. This isn't real. I'll wake up in a couple of hours and he'll be alive. Right beside me.'

Her stomach threatened to turn inside out as reality crept in on a wave of revulsion. Without really wanting to, she looked at her husband's prone figure. He'd fallen in an awkward, unnatural position, almost like he was running, horizontally, but his head was backwards, in a *The Exorcist* kind of way. And the back of that head was dented, bloody. The wineglass stem buried in his cheek glinted under the kitchen light. The pool of blood had stopped a centimetre or so from where she sat hugging her knees next to her best friend, on the polished floorboards.

'It can't be real,' she repeated, just a whisper, and began to rock.

Outside, the wailing of a siren was faint but the flashing red and blue lights cut through the wall of falling water. 'So . . . you should probably tell me the whole story pretty quick,' Paisley suggested. 'So I can back you up.'

'Back me up?'

Paisley stood, and with one last, horrified look at Dale's body, moved to the door. 'Cops are going to want to know why he's dead.'

'Oh, God.' As the shaking became tremors that rocked her whole body, Callie's head fell onto her knees. 'Because I killed him. I killed my husband.'

3

Central Highlands, Tasmania, 2019

'There!'

Connor spun his horse around, his gaze following the line of Logan's outstretched arm towards a copse of thick scrub, which moved as one cow swivelled and pushed against another. More strays. Connor's legs squeezed against his horse's sides and the eager gelding bounded forward, up the slope of the culvert.

'Careful,' Logan warned, manoeuvring his horse down the slippery, leaf-littered terrain towards them. 'That's pretty uneven ground.' But as Logan's horse hit firmer ground it too fought for its head, sensing the chase.

'If we can spook them out of that rut, we won't have to go in after them and risk the horses,' Connor said.

'Risk the horses?' Tess scoffed from behind him. 'If cattle can get in there, Flash can.' To prove her point, she ducked in front, cutting him off, her mount popping over a fallen tree and diving into the cows' cover. The cattle bounded out, scattering around the riders and regrouping to head down the trail at a trot. Within seconds, as though resigned to the trek before them, they dropped back to a steady walk, forming a line to follow the easiest route down the mountain.

'Show off,' Connor said.

'Chicken,' Tess called back.

One of the cows moved off the track, deciding to make a break for it. Connor bumped into it, his horse pushing it round before chasing it back to the small group.

'Not bad!' Logan called out. 'For a chicken. Tend to forget you've got it in you. You spend too much time behind a desk these days.'

Connor silently agreed, but there was nothing that could be done about it if the guesthouse was going to keep running. 'Someone's got to do the real work!' he shot back.

The view across the mountains to the home paddocks below made him smile. He loved it out here. To his mind, there was nowhere more beautiful than Tasmania's wilderness. He could have ambled back, savouring the sights, breathing them in, but his stockmen Mick and Ned had turned up with a couple more stragglers, and his horse was jogging. The morning had been an easy one and the energetic animal underneath him had his own blood pumping. 'Hey, Tess, you reckon you could get this mob down with Ned and Mick?' he called.

Tess's 'pfft' was accompanied by a roll of her eyes. 'Without them. In my sleep. Why?'

Connor sent Logan a grin. 'Beat you back to the yards.'

Logan picked up the reins and nodded. 'Cross country or trail?'

'Give me a break.'

'Beat you both!'

Tess's horse bounded between them, their sister perfectly balanced over her mount as the striking sabino mare bolted off the track and disappeared into the bush. He'd known there was no way she'd settle for wandering back with the stockmen; she was one of the best damn riders he'd ever seen — and competitive as hell.

He laughed. 'Cheat!' His horse danced on the spot, eager to follow, and his legs barely brushed the gelding's sides before it shot forwards after her, Logan's horse at their heels. They navigated logs and dips, skirted the steeper country and felt the splash of freezing water kicked up by Tess's mount in front of them as they hit the bottom of one slope, raced through the shallow creek and up the other side. The ride was exhilarating and the smile on Connor's face was wide even as, true to her word, Tess beat them both. He and Logan did what they could to give her a hard time, because that's what brothers were supposed to do when they're beaten by their little sister, but she gave back as good as she got and as they walked the horses the rest of the way to the yards to allow them to cool down, it occurred to Connor that that was the most fun he'd had in a long time.

'Are we sorting the cattle as soon as the stragglers get back?' Tess asked Logan.

'No, Connor and I want to use them with the new rehab group tomorrow.'

'Sounds good to me.'

'It'll work out well,' Connor said.

He gave his mount a pat and was thinking of heading back to the stables when Tess said, 'I forgot that was starting. I was going to ask you to take five tourists out on the kayaks tomorrow at

11. I'm taking the shuttle run out to Cradle Mountain.'

He thought about that. 'I'll get Kaicey to do it.'

'That's what you always say when something comes up,' Tess said. 'You know we pay her to be our receptionist, right?'

Logan moved his horse up beside Connor's. 'You know, if you paid Kaicey a bit more you could change her job title to, I don't know — assistant-everything-we-can't-fit-in, since you won't get an actual assistant because you seem to enjoy being tied to your desk every day.'

Not this again, Connor groaned silently. 'Most of the year, I'm fine.'

'Uh-huh.' Logan jumped from his horse and tossed the reins over a railing. 'Except you're not fine and this is the quiet part of the year. It's been more than a year since Dad died, and Rosie's taken off with Nat for who knows how long. They both used to do a lot more around here than we realised. You're working long hours. Why not take some of the pressure off?'

'I'll think about it,' he said. 'But changing things when they're just starting to do well seems like tempting fate.'

Logan chuckled. 'And taking on a new group of young crims isn't doing that?'

Connor had wondered the same thing the first time they'd run the program as part of a plan Corrective Services was utilising to reduce the rates of reoffenders, providing them with opportunities for rehabilitation, personal development and community engagement. His

37

sister-in-law Indy had pitched the idea to him, and it had worked out so well. 'I hope not. Last year it made a difference, you know that,' Connor said. Then, spotting the others coming in the gate, he called, 'Hey, Ned! Push them into the far yard with the rest of the herd. We'll sort them later.'

'No worries, boss!'

'I've got to run. You got this?' he asked Logan.

'Yeah. No worries. See you after.'

Connor headed off, taking in the scenery as the horse's easy stride chewed up the couple of k's between the cattle yards and the stables. Mountains, sky — space. There were trails you could ride for days, pretty spots to stop or camp. They'd done so enough times as kids. It had been too long since he'd been out there, too long since he'd felt free enough to take the time. Maybe he'd think about what his brother and sister had said after all.

At the stables he dismounted and gave the big bay stockhorse a pat.

'Connor, hi.' Larissa, Logan's stable hand, appeared from somewhere inside.

'How's it going?'

'Great.' She took the reins. 'I'll cool him down.'

'Thanks.'

'No problem.' She looked up at him with a shy smile. 'Did you get all the cattle in?'

'Hopefully. Logan should be back soon.'

'Okay. See you.'

Conner nodded, smiled, and started towards the guesthouse. He knew Larissa had a bit of a thing for him, but it'd pass. She was barely out of her teens. He was pretty damn sure when he was her age, thirty-three had seemed a lifetime away. But the years had passed in the blink of an eye, despite all the shit he'd been through. Hopefully when Larissa did find someone, it'd turn out a whole lot better than his attempt had. Jules. Jeez, the thought of his once fiancée, of what had happened, still hollowed out his stomach and left a bad taste in his mouth.

He reached the guesthouse steps, walked through the glass doors that slid open in welcome and headed straight for reception. He needed to fill Kaicey in on what was going on later today, but she was on the phone. He waited impatiently, earning a quick, nervous glance from her.

'I can't talk about this right now,' she said into the receiver. 'I'll call you back. Michael! I'll call you back!'

Connor's impatience turned to concern as he took note of Kaicey's tone and the lack of colour in her cheeks.

She put down the phone slowly, closed her eyes, then opened them, plastering a smile on her still pale face. 'Sorry about that.'

'Is everything all right?' Connor asked, though it obviously wasn't.

Kaicey shrugged it off. 'Friends and dramas — you know.'

'Okay. I wanted to make sure you knew the skills program for the drug rehab kids starts tomorrow.'

'Yep. All the paperwork's here in this folder.'

She waved it at him and dropped it back on the desk.

Of course it was. Kaicey was just that efficient. 'Great.' He considered bringing up the idea of a promotion then caught sight of the clock behind her. He was running behind already. With a curse, he took the stairs to the first floor two at a time.

★ ★ ★

It was a damn shame. Michael Smythe had received his black envelope almost two years ago so he'd hoped he was in the clear, but no, he supposed it shouldn't really have been too much of a surprise to walk out and see his dog — what was left of it — mutilated and swinging from the big old fig tree, one or two feet from his kids' brightly painted cubby house. He sighed heavily and looked back at the house. He'd come out for a smoke, left the kids eating Froot Loops in front of the morning cartoon show, and going by the upstairs light, his wife had retreated to the bathroom to get ready for school drop-off and her shift at the local BP. Busy. Good. Best they didn't see this. He cringed at the thought of getting Buddy down without making a hell of a mess. No, it wasn't much of a surprise, but it was a nasty one.

After one last desperate drag, he flicked the cigarette from a hand that wasn't quite steady, crossed the yard and rattled around in the three-by-six tin shed he stored just about everything in until he found his utility knife.

'Oh man,' he breathed as he sawed at the rope and let the dog drop. It made a sound he'd rather forget. He pulled the body behind the tree just enough to shield it from the house and went inside to make sure everyone was ready to clear out for the day.

He quietly mentioned Buddy's passing to his wife, mumbling some unintelligible reason for the death when the tears turned up and threatened to ruin her mascara. He knew she wouldn't push for details, not while the kids were around. Better to tell them tonight, after school. He helped them out the door with backpacks and afternoon instructions, reminded them to go to after-school care. And when the car turned out of the street he made a quick call, donned a pair of overalls and a shovel and found a spot for Buddy under the murraya bush. Though he'd never have admitted it, he shed a tear, said a few silent words of thanks for the dog that had helped raise his kids.

As far as punishments went, it hurt. But that was the point. He was just damn grateful it wasn't one of his kids in the cold earth. Maybe he should have gone further away than the pretty seaside town of Burnie — interstate might have been a better idea. No point worrying about that now. He wasn't exactly ashamed of what he'd done back then, though some would say it was wrong. Greater good and all that. He leant the shovel against the old oak and reached for a cigarette.

He caught a movement in his peripheral vision. Another pair of hands grabbed the shovel, sending it slicing through the air. Before he could react, the sharp edge buried itself in his skull. He dropped like a stone, but he didn't die.

Several times over the next couple of hours, he'd wish that first blow had killed him.

★ ★ ★

When the kids got home and raced outside to play with Buddy, they were spared the sight of their beloved family pet swinging from the tree. Instead they found their father.

4

Hunter Valley, New South Wales, 2019

Callie disinterestedly pushed salad leaves around her plate, her fork squeaking against the china in annoying little spurts. Just the thought of putting anything in her mouth was enough to make her heave. Eighteen months since Dale's death. Eighteen bloody months and there were still days she expected to wake up at any moment from the nightmare, expected Dale to walk through the door alive and well so they could attack that garden bed by the front gate, get on with their forever. But every day the nightmare only got longer, worse. *Please, God, just let it be over.*

'Hey.' Paisley put a hand over Callie's to still her jerky movements as the squeaking of the fork on the plate got louder and louder. 'Let me take it away.'

'I'm sorry,' Callie said. 'I just can't . . . '

'I get it. It's no big deal. Why don't you take one of those sedatives the doctor prescribed and try and sleep?'

Callie nodded, because the only rest she got from the nightmare was oblivion. 'What are you going to do?'

'I'm going to talk to Mum, then maybe have an early night too.'

'Is everything okay with her?'

'Why do you ask?'

'It's just that the whole time I've known you up until this last year, you barely ever talked about her. In the last few months, you've mentioned her a lot. I guess I just didn't think you spoke.'

'We've always had a difficult relationship. I suppose everything that's happened has made me think about things differently. I'm trying to make things right. I don't know. We'll see.'

'That's great, Paisley. You should have told me.'

'I wasn't not telling you on purpose. There's just been so much going on.'

Callie nodded and went back to fiddling with her fork. 'Out of everything, all of it — the arrest, remand, hearings, trial — this is the worst. Why can't the jury just make up their minds?'

'They will.'

'I thought they would have by now. They can't have been impressed with my testimony. The prosecution ripped it apart, you know that.'

'It wasn't that bad.'

'I felt so stupid — I panicked. I stumbled over my words. I didn't even make sense.'

'And your lawyer came back with a closing argument that used that distress to your advantage. That's what the reporters are saying, right?'

'At least you were good. You didn't waver at all.'

'Try not to overanalyse. It's only been two days. Don't do this to yourself. Sleep.'

'Maybe we should go over what's got to happen.'

'We've talked about it,' Paisley said gently, and prised the fork from her fingers. 'You said you wouldn't make any big decisions until whatever happens has had a chance to sink in, for all of this to calm down.'

'I want to sell, Paise. Please. I need you to tell the agent to go ahead and contact next door. Accept their current offer. She has all the information. I can't run this place from prison. Not that there's much left to run.' The winery had shut down. Grapes that had grown fat on the vines were destined to rot on the ground and wine to sit in barrels indefinitely. The bed and breakfast was just as impossible to run. The media presence had seen to that.

'And if you walk free, you'll want a new start.'

Callie stared, eyes glazed, into the fireplace, and instead of the sleek, polished mantelpiece and neat stack of logs Paisley had arranged once forensics had finished messing it up, she saw a raging fire, a burning, melting laptop. She saw photographs, a body, destroyed. And when she turned back around to Paisley, saw Dale, damaged and broken in the space on the floor where Paisley's feet, adorned in red heels, crossed one over the over. Callie hadn't been comfortable in this house since it happened.

'I'd need a new start. I can't live here. Not after what's happened.'

Paisley's expression was sympathetic. 'Okay. No problem. I'll sort it.'

'Thanks. What are you going to do?'

'I need to get back to New Norfolk, keep an eye on Dad and finally start cleaning the place up. There's a cottage on the property. Plenty of quiet. Plenty of privacy. When you're acquitted, you should come with me.'

'*When* I'm acquitted?' Callie laughed humourlessly. There wasn't much chance of that. But she let herself fantasise for a moment. 'Away from the reporters, where no one knows me. Sounds nice. Almost too nice. I don't dare hope.'

'Don't give up hope, Cal,' Paisley begged. 'It's all you've got.'

Callie stood, all too aware of that. 'I think I might take one of those pills. Goodnight.'

'Night.'

She went into her room and closed the door. She'd never sleep but sitting downstairs surrounded by Paisley's well-meaning sympathy was just making her nerves worse. She swallowed one of the sedatives and sat by the window, staring into the darkness. A light snapped to life as someone at the front gate got out of their car. A reporter getting prime spot at her gate? It was late, even for them. They'd plagued her from the day she'd been released on bail, through the preliminary hearing, through finding out she'd have to stand trial, then all through the hellish year of waiting for it. They just didn't give up. It wasn't as though no one had ever been murdered before, but something about this case had caught the public's interest. They were fascinated by the ritualistic murder.

And there were questions — so many questions. Had Dale been part of a secret cult? Could Callie really have been married to a sadistic killer and not known? Was she involved

46

in some way? Was killing Dale an act of self-defence or an attempt to cover up her own involvement? The list went on, with someone coming up with a new angle every week.

The car's interior light dimmed as whoever was at the gate climbed back in. Were they intending on staying there indefinitely? Hoping she might make a last-ditch dash for freedom and skip bail? She'd been lucky to get it. The idea she could already have been a year and a half in lock-up wasn't pleasant. Perhaps this person was just hoping for a quick word they could put on a TV morning show. One of the news stations had done an internet poll on how many people thought she was guilty. It was almost fifty — fifty. Callie supposed she should feel relieved that at least half the population were on her side. It didn't stop the nerves clawing away at her. When her eyelids drooped, she lay down and closed her eyes. Maybe tomorrow would be the day the jury made up their minds.

5

Central Highlands, Tasmania

'Connor — got a minute?' Kaicey slipped out from reception to catch him at the doors.

'Not exactly, but I got your message, if that's what you're about to tell me. I'm heading down to the stables to meet Cole's new rehab group now.'

'That's not it.'

'Okay, you want to walk with me, meet them?'

'Sure. I just wanted to query my last pay. There's too much money in there.'

'It's a raise.'

'A raise? Really?'

'You've earned it. You've been working above your paygrade for months. I'd like to talk to you about an official personal assistant role.'

Kaicey's eyes bulged. 'Yes! That would be great.'

He nodded. 'We'll discuss the details this afternoon then.'

They reached the petting farm. Kaicey gave one of the hand-raised steers a pat on her way past its yard. 'Do you think this is something you'll continue to do every year?'

'Give you a raise?' he asked.

She laughed. 'I meant the program.'

'Yeah. Logan's keen. And he scored Harvey from the first lot, so that worked out well.'

'He's a nice guy. I like him.'

'Let's hope this next group work out the same.' Connor couldn't have been happier with what they'd achieved from the first program: three teens employed and looking for all the world like they'd turned their lives around. 'There they are.'

The men were standing by the car, waiting with Cole. Two boys of no more than twenty, both tall and lanky and talking quietly. Off to the side was an older man, who was watching Connor and Kaicey's approach with interest. Tall and thin, with sharp, dark features, torn black jeans, black top and black hair long enough for a ponytail. No earrings, but the holes were there. And — really? — black nail polish. Connor knew the goth thing was popular with some of the young ones, but this guy had to be thirty. He tried not to be judgemental, even as he wondered just why the hell the guy had decided he wanted to be a stockman.

Connor realised Kaicey was no longer beside him, so he stopped and turned. She was a few strides back, staring past him at the group. Her face had lost almost all of its previous colour. Concerned, he went back to her.

'Kaicey, what is it?'

She turned eyes to him that were both upset and nervous. 'I think I might head back to the office.'

'Okay. Sure. But, ah . . . You want to tell me about it?'

'No. I — '

'Kristen.' The older guy in black approached

quickly, smiling, though he seemed nervous.

'It's Kaicey!' she snapped.

'Oh — right. Been so long I forgot. How are you?'

'Fine. Why are you here?'

He shuffled his feet, gave a small shrug. 'I . . . got caught up with some guys, ended up having to do a couple of years inside. I knew Dustin — for a while. He showed me a photo of all of you guys together on the last day. I thought . . . I thought I recognised you.' He stopped tripping over his words and took a breath, then lowered his voice. 'I got my envelope. I felt safe enough inside all this time but I'm getting out and . . . I didn't know what to do.'

'I don't know what you're talking about,' Kaicey bit out. 'I have work to do.' She spun around and, with a nervous glance back, walked away.

Connor didn't know what this guy was talking about either, but his presence had very obviously upset Kaicey. He studied him, waiting to see if he had anything else to say. But the guy was watching Kaicey's retreat.

'Everything okay here?' Cole asked, joining them.

'I need a word,' Connor said.

Cole nodded as though expecting it. 'Why don't you head back over to the others, Orson? I'll be with you in a moment.'

'What's he doing here, Cole? The program is supposed to be a training opportunity for young offenders. That guy doesn't fit the profile.'

Cole pressed two fingers to his forehead, gave

50

a small wince and nodded. 'The program parameters were extended so we'd get the numbers for funding. Not just young offenders now, but any prisoner undergoing the rehab program. Still only minimum-security inmates who're transitioning back into society. I sent you the email.'

'I didn't get it. What was he in for?'

'Drug supply charge. Got him twenty months inside. He's not a bad guy. Suffers bouts of depression and anxiety, takes meds. Model prisoner.'

'I don't know, Cole.'

'He needs this, Connor. I was hoping it wouldn't be a big deal. If we don't have the numbers, the funding will get pulled. Then kids like Jake and Matty over there don't get the opportunity. Just one chance. Please.'

Connor sighed heavily. The age issue really wasn't the problem, and he didn't want the other two to miss out. Besides, he'd been looking forward to running the program again. So he'd talk to Kaicey, and in the meantime told Cole, 'One chance.' And he'd have a word to Logan, let him know what had happened. 'Is Logan down here?'

'In the office, said he'd only be a sec.'

'Then let's go get introduced.'

⋆　⋆　⋆

By the end of it, Connor was deliberating between getting on a horse and taking off for a while or locking himself away in his office to get

51

some extra work done. Since the weather forecast wasn't pleasant and the wind was picking up, he decided on the latter. As he approached the upstairs office, he heard voices, so he stuck his head in Tess's door. She and Indy were looking at something on her laptop. The television was on in the background.

'Afternoon off?'

'I'm looking at a stallion for Flash,' Tess said. 'Indy was interested in seeing who I had in mind.'

'Don't want to use Rex?'

'Nope. I want patches.'

'Patches?'

'Of colour, yeah.' She spun the laptop around, showed him a picture of an impressive looking buckskin pinto. 'This boy's every bit as good as Rex, his conformation complements Flash's down to the ground, he has a great temperament and he's homozygous tobiano. I'll get patches.'

'You've already got patches.'

'No, I've got a sabino. This is different.'

'Good for you. I'll be in the office. Paying you money. So you can spend it on patches.'

Tess grinned cheekily. 'I earn every cent. Hey, the news is starting. Turn it up on your way out?'

He saw the remote on the coffee table and did as requested.

'*The jury has returned,*' the reporter said. '*We'll take you live for the results of the trial as soon as it breaks . . .* '

'What's that about?' he asked.

'That trial for Paisley Waldron's boss,' Tess said.

52

Paisley Waldron — Ned's little sister. Connor hadn't seen her since they were both small children. 'What trial?'

'The one where the wife killed the husband after he'd apparently slaughtered some poor woman to try and cover up an affair,' Indy told him, getting to her feet to follow Tess to the lounge.

At his blank stare, she shook her head. 'Connor, where have you been — under a rock? It's all photos and hearsay and the police can't find the woman's body. This has been in the headlines for months.'

'Yeah — I know the case. I just didn't realise it had anything to do with Paisley. Ned never said.'

Tess flopped down beside Indy and couldn't have looked less surprised. 'Paisley witnessed the husband's attack on her boss. She's a key witness.'

'That's quite a mob outside that courthouse,' he commented, watching the screen.

'It doesn't seem all that long since we went through the whole trial thing ourselves, does it?' Tess said.

'No. It was hell. And we weren't the ones on trial.' It wasn't as though Connor didn't already know he was an idiot. The girl he'd loved since primary school, been engaged to — almost had a baby with — was a drug-manufacturing criminal, and he'd point blank refused to believe it until she'd put a bullet in him and left him for dead. The consequences of her actions had culminated in a guilty verdict and finally, at sentencing, the judge passing down a couple of life sentences. Connor had sat in that courtroom through all of it. And now that it was done, he couldn't see any point in rehashing it. 'Still hard to believe, isn't it?'

'That Jules fell in love with a moron like Kyle Cartwright when she could have had you?' Tess asked.

'Actually, that she could have tied herself up with a family of criminals and made all that money off other people's suffering, but yeah, your answer will do.'

They grinned at each other, but there was regret on both faces. 'She made her choice. Now she'll live with it,' Tess said.

He watched as the female reporter fought with large gusts of wind to comment on the wife's possible sentence. 'So . . . wasn't there some debate about whether or not he actually killed the woman?'

'Not really,' Indy said. 'The police found the murder scene, and there were matching traces of female DNA from the site under his fingernails and a hair in the shower drain. But there was nothing in any of his vehicles, so they don't know how he moved her or where to. They'll know more when they find the body.'

'After all this time?' Tess asked sceptically. 'You think they will? They don't even know who she was.'

'That depends on a lot of things. The murder was particularly vicious, suggesting an emotionally driven, frenzied attack. A lot of times these murders aren't particularly well covered up, so it could just be a matter of turning over the right

54

leaf. And no one by the name of Lisa or anyone matching that description has been reported missing. But I know one of the detectives on the case up there, and Pat's pretty thorough. If it's possible to find the body or make an ID, she'll find a way.'

'He kept *photos*,' Tess continued, screwing up her nose in disgust. 'Who does that?'

Indy shrugged. 'That's a separate investigation. He's not on trial. She is.'

She's lovely, Connor thought as the wife appeared on screen being guided into the courtroom through a sea of reporters. Petite, with a flaming halo of auburn hair and a face as fragile as porcelain. Her skin was too pale, her features strained, exaggerating the big green eyes that looked . . . lost.

'He attacked her when he found out she'd seen the photos,' Tess said. 'She was trying to get away from him, not kill him.'

Connor found himself immediately on the wife's side. What real chance would a woman like that have in a physical fight against the man in the photo in the corner of the screen? He had trouble believing she'd take that man on on purpose with nothing more than a broken piece of crystal.

'So *she* said,' Indy reminded Tess, 'and Paisley Waldron backed that up. But the important question in this trial has been whether she actually killed him. If the jury decide she didn't cause the slip and fall that broke his neck, the worst she should get is manslaughter, or she could get off completely. But if they think she did cause the fall that killed him, it could be murder. Second, if the jury decide to pin her with his murder or manslaughter, what was the reason — self-defence or something else? It's possible to walk away from either charge if it's proven to be self-defence; anything else could see her in prison for decades.'

Connor cringed. 'What do you think?'

Indy shrugged. 'I can't call it. It looks like self-defence and sheer bad luck on the surface, but she'd also just discovered he was seeing the woman behind her back, possibly planning to leave her. And the report in the paper said he had a serious life insurance policy. All I know for sure is that I wouldn't want to be in her shoes — especially if she's innocent.'

'Well, if the reporter's right,' Tess said, getting to her feet, 'we'll soon find out. Want a beer?'

'Yeah, thanks.' Indy stretched, put her legs on the coffee table.

'Let me know how it turns out,' Connor said. 'I still have work to do.'

6

Sydney, New South Wales

The courtroom held its breath, a tense silence that filled Callie's already upset stomach with a sense of impending doom. She chewed on the stub of her little fingernail, then realised she was doing it and pulled her hand away from her mouth. Her hands were shaking so she linked them in her lap. Her legs were so tightly pressed together they threatened to cramp. Her back ached from tension, and if the proceedings didn't hurry up, she was going to be sick on the perfectly vacuumed carpet.

'All stand. This court is now in session,' the court official said.

There was a general shuffling of people. A trickle of nervous perspiration tickled Callie's shoulder blades. She barely kept her legs underneath her while the judge settled himself behind the bench, draped in robes that fit his imposing demeanour.

As everyone took their seats, the urge to get up and run screaming from the building was overwhelming. The room that smelled of wood polish and thrummed with too many people was closing in around her. She dragged in a ragged breath and glanced around her, caught the eye of her husband's parents. Cold hate seeped into her already frigid body.

Looking quickly away meant her eyes swept over hungry reporters. There were many more on the other side of the courtroom door, waiting like scavengers for their piece of her. Whatever was left.

At the request of the judge, the jury was brought in. Callie tried to gauge what they might be thinking by the looks on their faces, but they showed nothing but hints of tension and fatigue.

She was asked to stand, but it didn't register until her barrister nudged her from her seat.

'Ladies and gentlemen of the jury, have you reached your verdict?'

The jury foreperson, a tall man with thinning grey hair and a very ordinary brown suit, stood up. The paper in his hand trembled slightly; he was nervous. She supposed there were vastly different experiences of nervous. Why was he staring at the paper? Was he really likely to forget the verdict?

'We have, Your Honour.'

'Do you find the accused guilty or not guilty of murder?'

Callie's stomach turned inside out and she swallowed bile as time seemed to stand still. The juror flicked his gaze in her direction. 'We, the jury, find the accused not guilty.'

Her breath rushed out with a trembling sob and some of her rigidity eased. She held herself up, just, as the courtroom erupted into a frenzy of murmurs and hushed whispers. But it wasn't over yet, and they silenced quickly, expectantly.

'In the alternative, do you find the accused guilty or not guilty of manslaughter?'

This time the juror looked Callie in the eyes for two long beats, his expression softening. 'Not guilty, Your Honour.'

She dissolved into the chair. The judge demanded order over the sounds of general chaos in the courtroom, but the rest was lost as a hum like swarming bees filled Callie's ears, her vision swam and the tension turned to shaking.

'Congratulations, Callie,' her barrister said from beside her.

She looked into the face of the sharp-looking, middle-aged woman who'd defended her, unable to take it in. Was that it? Had the judge told her she was free to go? Was it over? She must have asked the questions out loud because her barrister nodded.

'We should get you out of here.'

Tears erupted from her eyes, unable to be held back. 'I don't know how to thank you. Thank the jury.' She looked at the men and women already leaving their seats. Some smiled, others were solemn and a couple more didn't look entirely happy. But she was free. They'd given their decision.

Callie stumbled out of the courtroom. Cameras flashed in her eyes and microphones were shoved under her nose. Everyone was talking, shouting — someone grabbed her arm. She tripped, righted herself, pushed through the throng of bodies. A security guard, then two, ploughed a way for her and her barrister. It reminded her of one of those crazy movies where celebrities dashed to waiting cars and zoomed away. Except this wasn't a movie, and there was no limo waiting at the bottom of the steps.

She heard support and condemnation in the questions and comments crashing around her. She spotted reporters who'd written facts and outright lies. The first few had cut deep, before she'd learnt to let them wash over her. And as she escaped, she wondered if she would ever really be completely free of all this. How long was it going to take for the hype to die down? How could she possibly get back to any semblance of a normal life, with this . . . chaos?

'You murdering bitch!'

She recognised Dale's mother's voice as it somehow drowned out all the others. Madeline Johnson had never been stable, but Dale's death had well and truly sent her over the edge.

'After everything we did for you!' Madeline hurled more abuse as the cameras turned and some of the congestion decreased as the reporters headed for her. Callie spared Dale's parents one short, apologetic glance, and noticed a man standing just to the right of them. Why he caught her eye she couldn't have said, except for maybe the intensity with which he was watching her. Had she seen him before? Dark hair — short and neatly cut, cold blue eyes, a well-worn suit that displayed rather than hid a tough physique. He stood absolutely still against the fluidity of the surroundings. Almost unnaturally so.

Something crashed into her and she turned away as the crowd closed in again. She had to keep her feet under her and keep moving.

'Caroline! This way.' Her barrister pointed to a car idling in front of them. Paisley's little red

Honda wasn't a limo, but it would do.

She made a grateful dash for it. 'Thank you!'

Her barrister leant over the open door. 'We'll talk soon,' she promised. Then the door was closed and they were inching away.

'There was a man.' Callie immediately craned her neck to look for him. 'Standing just next to Dale's parents. Did you see him?' she asked Paisley.

'No. Just reporters.'

As they crawled through the crowd, Callie briefly thought reporters were going to climb onto the car.

'It's almost as bad back at your place,' Paisley told her. 'I've hired security for your front gate.'

Callie let out a long, relieved breath, and felt the prick of grateful tears at the back of her eyes. 'Thank you. I hadn't thought of that. Without your help, I'm not sure I would have gotten this far.'

'Hey, of course you would have.'

'I don't know why you've done all this. You've been more like a mother or a big sister than a friend. You've gone above and beyond what most friends would do, over and over again.' She noticed Paisley's eyes sheen with tears, wondered at the stress she must also have been under recently, but then she was smiling.

'Big sister, sure, but seven years is not a mother — daughter gap,' she said indignantly, then sent Callie a soft look and a small shrug. 'I do think of you as family. From the day you gave me a job when I really needed one. I know when Dale first mentioned me you didn't think you wanted an assistant around the place, but you gave me a chance. That's important to me. And we just clicked, didn't we? How many days in the past four years haven't we seen each other? Our friendship is important to me. I saw what Dale did, I know what you've been through. I couldn't ever just walk away.'

'I'm so grateful. I don't how I can ever repay you.'

'You don't have to,' Paisley insisted.

But if Callie could ever come up with a way, she promised herself she was going to.

Exhausted, she dropped her head back onto the headrest and closed her eyes against the headache and nausea still battering her system. As the car finally made it above a crawl, she slept.

The reception at her home was as bad as Paisley had warned. The driveway was completely blocked and the thought of getting out to open the gate was frightening. But the crowd parted under a uniformed guard's instruction, though they tapped on the windows and did their best to get photographs. Paisley drove through the gates, which closed swiftly behind them, and a few moments later they were safely inside the house. She fell into a chair, propped her elbows on the table and rested her head in her hands. Callie's thoughts were foggy, her body stiff and fatigued. It occurred to her to wonder, *Now what?*

'Callie. Hey.'

She looked up to see Paisley grinning at her, eyes bright.

'You should smile. It's over. You're free.'

'I am,' she said and felt her lips curve up at the edges. 'I just can't quite make it sink in.' But it was, slowly. Home, with Paisley in a celebratory mood and a couple of hours sleep behind her, Callie could feel the relief creeping in. 'I want to thank the jury,' she decided. 'I just want to find and hug every single one of them.'

'I don't think you're supposed to do that. At some stage you'll end up making some statement or other, just throw in some general thanks there.'

'Good idea.'

Paisley's smile faded as she studied Callie's face. 'You're still wiped. You should go and have a proper sleep.'

'I don't think I can. I want to call the real estate agent, make sure we're good to go ahead.' She looked around and all she saw was the past and misery. 'I don't want to be here a day longer than I need to be.'

'She's already negotiating figures,' Paisley said as though that was what she'd been waiting for Callie to say all along. 'I think leaving is the right move.'

'My solicitor said the same thing. She suggested I lay low somewhere for a while. Just until the media hype settles down.'

'Agreed.' Paisley sat opposite and the smile returned. 'So come with me.'

'I thought a bit about that,' Callie admitted. 'About what I would do if I didn't go to prison . . . or when I got out. I need to work, to rebuild my life somewhere else. I think I'd like to go back to landscaping, kick off the business again. I want to change my name back to my maiden name, and officially make it Callie instead of Caroline. Tassie's as good a place as any to start over, but I'm worried the reporters will follow me, make your dad's place a prison like this one.'

'How will they find out? I'll somehow restrain myself from taking out advertising space in the newspaper.'

Callie got up and looked out the kitchen window down the long, winding drive to the front gates, watching the reporters. With her solicitor's help she'd prepare a statement to release to the media: she was relieved to have that chapter in her life over, was looking forward to putting it behind her — or something. That would have to do them. She'd already refused stupid amounts of money for interviews and decided to donate Dale's life insurance to charity. She could never take money from either source. It would feel dirty. Wrong.

It would be best for Paisley to get away from it all, too. She'd never missed a beat; dealt as best she could with the media, and the phone calls, the letters — those horrible, hateful phone calls and letters from Dale's family and friends that had threatened all kinds of retribution. No doubt that would get worse. They'd believe they'd been denied justice. She pressed her hand to her stomach and grimaced.

'It makes me feel so sick. You heard the reporters at the courthouse? They kept calling out, asking how could I not know? How could he keep that from me?'

Paisley put a hand on her shoulder. 'How could you end up being the one on trial for murder? Sometimes, there is no reasonable answer. Come on, just ignore them.' Paisley peeked out the window then closed the curtains with a snap. 'The sooner we get out of here, the better.'

As the curtains closed, a figure caught Callie's eye. 'Wait — open the drapes again.'

Paisley frowned but did so a touch. 'What?'

Callie stared at the man in the dark suit for the second time that day. Though he was quite a distance away, she could tell he was staring straight back with that same, still intensity. 'That guy in the suit, watching by the gate. He was the one I was talking about at the courthouse.'

Paisley stared. 'I don't know. He's a bit scary looking, I suppose.'

The phone rang. Callie stepped back from the window and answered automatically. 'No, I don't want to do an interview.' She put the handset down while the caller was still talking.

When it rang again almost immediately, Paisley pounced on it. 'Listen, you bloody bloodsuckers — oh, right.'

Callie frowned. Someone had Paisley's attention. She waited impatiently for the call to end.

'That was the real estate agent,' Paisley told her. 'They've reduced their offer.'

Callie laughed, and it came out harsh. 'Why wouldn't they? Of course they have, now I actually want to sell. I'd love to tell them to stick it, but honestly, I just want to get out of here as soon as possible.' She rubbed her fingers across her forehead. 'Are you sure you really want me coming with you?'

'Of course I do.'

'I'm going to need money.'

'I'll transfer some to my account — on paper it'll show as a redundancy package. Lucky me,' she added with a grin. 'I'll go down to the bank when we get home, draw it out so you have some cash to live off for a while. That way you won't have to flash around any cards until you've got your name change through.'

'You don't think anyone will recognise me?'

'I don't think it will be a big deal for long, and you're not going to be a social butterfly, so no, I don't think so. But if you like, we can do something about your hair, short term.'

'Okay.' Callie nodded slowly. 'How soon can we leave?'

7

Callie and Paisley crawled out of Hobart in a rented compact SUV that smelled of too much synthetic air freshener, but the air was so damn freezing she put up with it.

'It's beautiful down here, isn't it?' Paisley commented with a yawn.

Callie looked at the sky, where a sparkling blue horizon fought against a blanket of thick morning fog that rolled along the River Derwent on its way to the sea. The haze was taking its time to clear as she navigated the twists and turns of the unfamiliar roads. And yet, the drive had a feeling of coming home to it. Of sanctuary.

'Hmm. And cold.'

'Are you sure you don't mind driving? I can take over if you like.'

'You drove to the airport. It's not far, right?'

'Just follow Google. I might have a quick nap. It's been a long night.'

As Callie followed the two-lane highway out of town, her eyelids drooped. They'd been travelling since two that morning, using the darkness of the early morning to escape reporters on their dash to the airport. She dared take her eyes from the road long enough to find the right button and scanned for a radio station, hoping it wouldn't disturb Paisley. Noise, even quiet noise or chatter, would help to keep her awake while her friend hopefully continued to snore quietly.

The numbers flew through, stopped at 101.7 and a cheerful voice announced she was listening to 7HOFM. A recent hit song came on and she sat back, returning her full concentration to the road ahead.

She dropped the window a crack, shivering as the cold blast of air chilled her into alertness and added colour to her cheeks. A little further and she spotted the sign for New Norfolk, and another yawn had her considering pulling off the highway in search of coffee. She decided against it and kept driving, dragging her fingers over her eyes and through her straightened, dark brown hair. It was short now, barely long enough to get a band into. She missed the length, the curls, the colour.

How long was she going to have to hide down here? The money from the property sale would tide her over for a long time — properly invested, she might not even need to work. But that would drive her crazy. She really did like the idea of going back to landscaping. She could take a business like that anywhere. If she ever needed to move again, it would be much simpler than being tied to a place, like another bed and breakfast. Besides, hadn't all that really been Dale's dream?

She wondered if guilt would ever hit. It hadn't yet. Shock had come quickly, then fear, anguish, regret. But not guilt. Perhaps one day it would sneak up on her unexpectedly, someday when the pictures of Lisa's horrific death faded from the back of her eyelids. But she'd deal with that, like she'd dealt with everything else.

Eventually Callie turned onto the road that promised to lead to Paisley's childhood home. Again she caught her breath at the scenery.

As though sensing they were getting close, Paisley stirred and yawned. 'That didn't take long.'

'You were snoring.'

'Sorry.'

'Don't be. I really appreciate all this, Paise.'

'So you keep saying. If I print it out and stick it on the wall where we can see it every five minutes, will you stop feeling like you need to remind me?' Paisley turned her teasing eyes from Callie and pointed. 'See that sign for Waldron Park? Turn in there.'

'Oh — wow!' The cottage came into view first, a charming stone box tucked into the edge of a driveway laid with pretty pink gravel. An ancient climbing rose decorated the brickwork and framed the white cottage windows. The untidy gardens hugging the building were no less enchanting because of their neglect. Callie hoped she'd have a chance to care for them.

'Park at the side, there.'

She pulled the car up at the cottage and got out, stretched and looked around. She breathed in, releasing her breath slowly. This was the last place anyone would come looking or her. A bit further along the drive through the tall gums and liquidambars, she caught sight of a much larger building and found herself walking around the bend in the driveway to get a better look.

The driveway became wider and curved around a central garden. The house, constructed of the same stone as the cottage, towered above her to look over the river a short distance down the hill. It had two storeys and a tower, with decorative ironwork railings encompassing shady verandas.

'I've never seen anything so lovely.'

Paisley stood beside her to admire the house. 'Welcome home.'

'Thanks.' She couldn't quite read the expression on her friend's face, but there was an intensity to it that quickly evaporated.

'Only place to rival it around here is Tynwald, on the other side of the bend in the river. Similar appearance, slightly bigger, I think.'

'This place looks more like a hotel than a home.'

'Which is what I dreamt of turning it into. But never mind,' Paisley said briskly. 'Let's get settled in the cottage.' As they turned and walked back, she gestured to the smaller building. 'It's as small as the house is big, but it's cosy. At least it used to be. I gave it a fresh coat of paint last time I was down here, so we might need to open it all up, let it breathe.'

'You painted it?'

'We have a bit of trouble with water getting in. It stained the ceilings and the walls. Ned reckons he's got it under control, but I guess we'll find out.'

They unloaded their bags and stepped onto a small porch covered by a wooden pergola and set with a wrought iron table and chairs. Paisley unlocked the door and pushed it open, then stood back for Callie to enter.

The smell of fresh paint was overpowering, so Callie dropped her suitcase at the door and went across the lounge area to open one of the windows. The view onto the river was lovely, as was the fresh air that blew in. She stepped around a fireplace and opened another window, while Paisley went through a door on the other side of the room and Callie heard the slide of another window opening before Paisley reappeared.

'This is it. The spare bedroom is here.' Paisley approached a third door and opened it, swearing at an assortment of boxes littering the small space, covering the floor and bed. 'This is Ned's stuff. He said he'd have it out of here for us. Must have gotten caught up. We'll put it on the patio.'

Beyond the lounge room with its mismatch of simple furnishings and threadbare rugs was a small kitchen that looked basic but serviceable. A door next to the fridge on the back wall led to a shoebox laundry and tiny bathroom.

'I think the paint smell might take a bit of time to dissipate. Want a tour of the grounds?' Paisley offered. 'Or would you rather rest for a while?'

'Tour. Absolutely.'

A blue Corolla hatchback rolled in as they walked outside. The guy, who she guessed was probably around middle age, was tall, with a sinewy strength about him and a head of untidy, thinning black hair. He stared, then smiled as he climbed out of the car, his lined face suggesting years of hard work in the sun. 'Morning.'

'Hi. I'm — '

71

'You'd be Callie. I'm Paisley's brother, Ned.'

'Hi,' Paisley said. 'You're late.'

'Yeah, held up. So you brought her then,' Ned said with a glance back to Callie.

'Obviously.' Then, when he continued to stare with what Callie considered a little too much curiosity, Paisley sighed. 'What? Is everything okay?'

'Not sure Dad will think so.' Then to Callie he said, 'Sorry about all my stuff in the bedroom. I'll get it out of your way.'

'That'd be great,' Paisley said. 'I was just about to give Callie a tour.'

'Why does she need a tour?'

'So she knows where everything is, Ned,' Paisley said with unconcealed impatience.

'But — right,' Ned said, looking away. 'You go ahead. I can manage.'

Callie shot him a quick smile and followed Paisley out along the driveway. 'Ned seems nice.'

'You can see why he can't manage Dad,' Paisley replied. 'Sometimes I'm surprised he can manage himself.'

There were garden paths everywhere, begging to be explored. What once had been formal hedges were mostly overgrown, but the plantings gelled with the unkempt cottage garden look, so it was charming, even through the areas of chaos.

'I could play with this,' Callie offered, 'while I'm here. Bring it back to where it should be.'

Paisley's smile broadened. 'I knew you'd be itching to get your hands on it when you saw it. And honestly, I'd really appreciate it.' She stared up at the house with a wistful expression.

It wouldn't be hard to fall in love with, Callie thought. A big, gorgeous old home like this, on all these riverfront acres. They walked up a pretty path surrounded on both sides by pink and gold grevilleas. 'The house was built in the early 1800s, been in the family forever. There are seven bedrooms, five bathrooms and a huge cellar space. You'll go nuts when you see the furniture. It's almost all antique.'

Buxus lined a path that led to the drive and a pretty little bird-bath sat under an old elm that reached towards the house with long, twisted branches. 'This is so sweet, Paise. It's a shame it's not kept up.' She turned to smile at Paisley as she heard the step behind her, then yelped in surprise. She'd almost bumped into a man. He was short and slightly stooped. Deep lines marred his unfriendly face, and shrewd eyes stared out from beneath thick eyebrows. Overalls hung on his spindly frame. He needed a shave. In one hand was a thick wooden walking stick. In the other was a hammer.

'Who are you?'

'Dad,' Paisley said sharply from behind her. 'This is Callie.'

'Hmph.'

Callie stood uncomfortably and quietly while his eyes studied her in what seemed like minute detail. His lips thinned. 'Always bring trouble with ya.'

'Thanks for that. Callie's staying in the cottage for a while, remember?' Paisley said with an apologetic smile in her direction. 'We talked about this. Callie, this is my father, Cliff.'

'Pleased to meet you,' Callie said.

'Well, I'd be pleased if you went right back to where you came from.'

She flinched.

'Ned's at the cottage, Dad,' Paisley said calmly. 'He wants to talk to you.'

Cliff stared at Paisley, then back at Callie for a handful of unnerving seconds then, mumbling to himself, limped off.

'Um, if me being here is a problem . . .' Callie felt compelled to say.

'Nah.' Paisley smiled cheerfully. 'He just gets a bit edgy about having strangers on the place. I'm betting he thought I was sneaking in a real estate agent. Come and have a look around. I need to grab some sheets and towels.' Paisley put her hand on the front door, then paused. 'Do me a favour — try not to get lost in the mess.'

The door opened onto a large entryway with shabby green walls and scarred wooden floors. A long side table was equally well used and overflowing with what Callie decided had to be about a year's worth of unopened mail, newspapers and general rubbish. There were framed photographs, old and falling from their positions. She rubbed her arms in an attempt to stave off the sudden chill she felt and followed Paisley past a lovely staircase with a doorway leading somewhere underneath it, through to a living room beyond. Everywhere she looked, shoeboxes, cardboard boxes, piles of books and necessities sat in piles. There was an unmistakably musty smell, and the whole house seemed unnaturally dark. Heavy curtains lined the windows, and though the windows themselves were bright with light, it didn't filter well into the rooms. Odd, Callie thought. It was as though not even the sun wanted to be in this place.

'I see the packing's already begun,' she said to break the almost eerie silence. 'I thought you said he was only considering leaving?'

'He is. And this isn't preparing to move. This is just how he lives. I did warn you.'

The *thump, thump, thump* of a walking stick had Callie looking over her shoulder to see Cliff appear behind them. 'Nothing wrong with how I live!' he snapped. 'Or how I have my gardens,' he said for Callie's benefit. 'And I didn't invite you in, so scoot,' he told Paisley with another wave of his stick. 'And take your friend with ya!'

Callie was already three awkward strides towards the door when Paisley caught her eye and shook her head. 'All we're doing is getting some linen. Want me to freshen your room up while I'm in here?'

'Don't need anyone to change my sheets or — ' He stopped talking to catch his breath. Callie was concerned he was going to topple over. But he recovered and shot Paisley another scowl that was punctuated by a loud bang of his stick. 'And I don't need this one left here to spy on me! Isn't Adelaide enough?'

'I'm not — Dad, please.' Paisley pressed her fingers to her eyes and took a deep, steadying breath. 'We have to get past this.'

'Only thing you want to get past is me — to kick me out of my own house. And you won't. I'm not leaving.' He hefted himself back to his feet. 'It'll never be what it was. Not while I'm breathing!' He stomped out, huffing and puffing back the way he'd come.

Unsure what to do or say, Callie waited, watching Paisley compose herself.

'I'm sorry,' Paisley said and started up the stairs. 'He's being nastier than usual. It's the 'having to go into care' issue.'

'Who's Adelaide?'

'The community nurse.' Paisley walked along the landing to a linen cupboard and pulled out sheets and blankets, a few towels, then handed some of the load to Callie. 'She's lovely, and they've been friends for years. He doesn't mean to be difficult. He's just miserable.'

'I'm sure he didn't mean what he said,' Callie said as they returned downstairs. 'But I think having me here is only aggravating the situation. I should go somewhere else.'

'Absolutely not. He'll be nice as pie next time he sees you. It's me he's cross with.'

'Does he know the story behind me being here?'

'There was no way I could keep it from him. He knew I was working for you, knew a lot about all of it before the incident. The only other person down here who knows is Ned, because I want him to keep an eye out for the media or anyone else asking any inappropriate questions.'

They went back to the cottage and found Ned attempting to fit a box of DVDs into an already full boot. 'You send Dad looking for me?' he asked, somehow finding room between a radio and a doona.

76

'He's in a mood,' Paisley told him. 'I needed to get him out of my hair for a moment.'

Callie followed her inside and put her pile on the side table. Paisley ducked her head round the door to the second bedroom.

'Ned! There's still a heap here!'

'I know. I can't fit it all in,' he said, appearing in the doorway. 'I'll have to make another trip.'

Paisley swore under her breath. 'Can you do it today?'

'Doubt it,' he said. 'Gotta get back to work.'

'It can't stay here.'

Ned scratched his head and took a long look at Callie. 'I don't mind coming back after work, I suppose. Be late though. Want me to bring some dinner?'

'Not necessary,' Paisley said. 'Put it in the rental car and I'll run it out later on. I have to go shopping before I fly back anyway.'

He shrugged then nodded. 'Suit yourself.' He walked around to the driver's side of his car and leant on the open door to study Callie again. 'I can help you out, drop by if you need anything. Got a few long workdays coming up but you can give me a call, any time. Paisley can leave you my number. Or you can give me yours.'

'I appreciate that.'

'Guess I'll leave you to it then. If you come out with the rest of my stuff around twelve, I'll be back at the staff room in the guesthouse. Won't be able to find me otherwise till after dark at the bunkhouse.'

'I'll be there at lunchtime,' Paisley promised.

'Right. Nice to see you, Callie.'

'You too.'

'Right.' Paisley clapped her hands together. 'Let's get sorted.'

They cleaned, tidied, unpacked. 'We'll have to get some groceries, fill up the fridge and pantry, whatever other supplies you need so you don't have to go into town too often. And you're going to need a car. You can't be stuck out here without transport.'

Callie chewed on her lip. 'You're right. But until my name change comes through . . . '

'I know you're paranoid about flashing your name around town — or on paperwork — so I have a solution. Buy it under my name, and I'll sign the transfer paperwork straight back to you. You can stick it in a drawer until your name change is official, then swap it over.'

Callie thought about that, then nodded slowly. 'That'll work. Thanks, Paise.'

'Welcome. And I really am sorry about Dad.' Paisley's face reflected her disappointment and concern. 'I should have warned you about his moods, but the truth is you're really doing me an enormous favour staying. I said I'd go back to Highgrove and sort out the place for your buyers and I will. But I feel better knowing someone is here until I get back.' She chewed on her lip. 'I didn't realise he'd deteriorated this much. Ned's only here once a week and Adelaide just comes and goes as she can fit him in — I'm never sure if she'll show or not.'

Callie still wasn't completely certain this was a good idea, but if it made Paisley feel better she wasn't going to let her down, so she nodded

78

reluctantly. 'I'll keep an eye on him.'

'Thank you. So, how do you want to play this? If you need to rest, I can get the groceries, run Ned's stuff out and come back to take you into town later this afternoon. Otherwise we can go get a car, shop, then you can drive it back here with the groceries and I'll detour out to Calico Mountain.'

Callie really did want nothing more than to close her eyes for a few hours, and although Paisley had managed to nap for half an hour on the way out, she looked wiped out, too — it wasn't fair to have her doing all that extra running around. 'How about we just get everything knocked over,' she suggested, 'then we can come back and relax for the rest of the day?'

Paisley looked relieved. 'Perfect. Let's get Ned's stuff in and get going.'

8

'It's all going to have to go,' Bob Turley told Connor. A wave of the groundsman's arm encompassed the tangle of fallen pines and broken undergrowth that had stood between the guesthouse and the petting farm. 'It's a wonder no one and nothing was hurt. You're probably lucky that big storm knocked 'em flat while no one was out and about and the wind blew 'em away from the road, not over it. They've toppled like dominos.'

Connor had to agree. 'It's a shame. They were ancient. What about the broken ones, are they salvageable?'

Bob scratched at a spot behind his ear. 'They're as rotten as the rest and there's no windbreak left. They'll just come down next time. Maybe on someone's head. They need to go.'

'That's going to leave a big hole.'

'Yep. We'll need to extend the guesthouse gardens. Tie the area in with the rest of the place.'

Connor looked a long way back towards the guesthouse gardens. 'That's a big space to fill.'

'We'll do islands with winding avenues of grass — just like round the front and other side of the guesthouse. Put in the same sorts of trees and plants. Give it a few years, and it'll blend in real good.'

'Okay,' Connor agreed after a moment. 'Work out some costs and get back to me.'

'Will do.'

He left Bob to his planning and went back to the guesthouse where he met Ned coming up the guesthouse steps.

'Boss,' Ned said.

'Morning,' Connor replied, a bit surprised to see him there at that time of day. 'Late start?'

'Sorry, had to be out at Dad's early. I'll make it up.' The doors slid open and they went inside. 'Just gotta see Kaicey and I'll get back on with slashing.'

'Bob might be looking for help at some stage today,' Connor said. 'He's got to cut up and clear those fallen pines down near the petting farm.'

'Can do.'

'Did I hear my name?' Kaicey asked from behind the reception desk as they approached.

Ned nodded and leant on the desk. 'Paisley's going to turn up here at some stage round lunchtime. Just thought you'd like to know.'

Kaicey's eyes rounded. 'Paisley's coming here?'

'Your sister, Paisley?' Connor asked, wondering why it seemed to bother Kaicey.

'Yeah,' Ned said, watching Kaicey. 'Come to help with Dad. Didn't get all my stuff moved out in time for her to use the cottage and she doesn't want it at Dad's — she wants to tidy up, so she's bringing some stuff here for me. I'm stacking it in one of the unused bunkhouse rooms until I can sort something else out.'

'That's no problem,' Connor said.

'Uh . . . how is she?' Kaicey asked in a small voice.

'Good. She's good,' Ned said. 'Done well for herself.'

Kaicey smiled. Sort of. 'That's nice to hear.'

'Right. I'm off then. Boss.' Ned nodded at Connor and ambled away.

'You know Ned's sister?' Connor asked Kaicey after Ned had left.

'Used to. I haven't seen her since we were in high school.' She shook her head as though to clear it. 'Do you want this ad for the new cleaner placed today?'

'Huh? Oh, that'd be great,' he said. 'I'm getting some breakfast then heading back out; got the program this morning.'

'How are the new guys doing?'

'Not sure yet. I'll know more after today.' And because it was still bothering him, he said, 'You want to tell me anything about Orson?'

She dropped her gaze. 'He's someone else I haven't seen since school. The thing is, he was always in trouble back in those days. It's disappointing to see he's still in trouble, but not really all that surprising. I just don't want much to do with him.'

'Two old school friends back in your life within days of each other. What are the chances?'

'Yeah,' she muttered. 'It's quite the coincidence.'

By the time he made it down to the stables, Logan was saddling up horses with Harvey and the group. Everything seemed to be going smoothly, and he was drawn to the far end of the breezeway by Harvey's voice.

'You do it up slowly, not too tight right off, or the girth will pinch the horse. Then it won't want it done.'

'Okay,' Orson said and tried again.

There was a burst of laughter from Harvey. 'Not that slow! We'll be here all day.'

'Right! Show me then.'

Logan wandered over. 'Morning.'

'Morning. How's Orson going?'

'Getting on like a house on fire with Harvey, polite and friendly towards me and the other guys. Doesn't have much of a clue but he tries hard enough.' Logan frowned. 'Want to tell me why you almost look disappointed?'

'Kaicey knows him. She didn't seem particularly happy to see him.'

'Did you ask her why?'

'She said he has a habit of finding trouble.'

'I guess that's what got him here,' Logan said, and paused to watch Orson put the bridle on under Harvey's instruction. 'Right now he's fitting in just fine.'

'Logan, can we take them out?' Matty called.

'Yeah, as soon as you're ready.'

The group filed out, leading their horses, and lined up in the mounting yard. Logan talked them through the do's and don'ts then, between them, Connor and Logan got them on and walking the horses around. They practised stopping, starting and steering.

They were just beginning to get the hang of it when a car pulled up outside the stables.

'Who's the hottie?' Travis called.

Connor looked back over his shoulder to see Indy getting out of her car.

'Man, she could be your mum,' Matty said.

'She's my wife,' Logan growled good-naturedly.

'Damn,' Travis said with admiration, then his eyes lit up again. 'Is *that* one married?'

'That one's our sister,' Connor said as Tess climbed out of the passenger side. He stood, arms folded, daring Travis to continue.

'Ah, teenage hormones,' Logan sighed.

The women approached and Logan snagged Indy, giving her a dramatic kiss. She elbowed him playfully and stepped back.

'What's that for?'

'Showing off. Apparently, you're a mummy-aged hottie.'

Indy narrowed her eyes at the boys trying to watch inconspicuously. 'Hmm. I'll choose not to be offended by the inclusion of my age. How's it going out here?'

'Great. They're getting better with the horses. How'd you manage to get away?'

'From the case? Even I get a break.'

'Case?' Connor asked.

'Father of two murdered in his backyard,' Indy told him. 'It's pretty gruesome. I was called up there to help. Can't wait to wrap it up.'

'Saw that on the news,' he said. 'So we've got some sicko on the loose?'

'Sick all right,' Orson muttered as he rode past.

Indy's brow shot up as she put on what Connor called her 'cop face'.

'What?' Tess asked her.

84

'That didn't sound like a random comment to me.' She walked into the middle of the yard. 'Hold up.' Indy waited for Orson to pull up his horse. 'You know something, mate?'

'What? Nah — don't know nothing.' He stared down at his horse, uncomfortable. 'Just saying.'

She waited a few beats, letting him squirm. 'You sure?' she asked eventually. 'Because the thing is, ten years as a detective tells me otherwise. So you want to try again?'

'No! Man!' he whined.

'Just prison talk, that's all,' Matty said, pulling his horse up behind Orson's. 'Rumours coming over from max about some bad-ass dude out for revenge.'

'We hear shit like that all the time,' Travis said, joining in. 'Everyone's always trying to outdo everyone else, make out they know someone or something. Just survival in there.'

'But you weren't in max,' Indy said to Orson. 'How do you find this out?'

'Word filters down. It's just bullshit.' Matty moved his horse past Orson's. 'Come on, keep going.'

Indy returned to Connor and Logan. 'Interesting.'

'You really think it's bullshit?' Connor asked.

'I've got a few contacts in Risdon Prison. I'll see what I can find out.'

'Good luck.'

Connor was still helping out when they dismounted and cooled down the horses. He hadn't meant to spend so much time down there, but this was another keen group, a bit rough around the edges, though that was to be expected. And he couldn't fault Orson. The guy had done as instructed and thrown in a couple of jokes about his riding prowess that had the group joking back, laughing.

'Not bad,' Connor said to him when the man caught him watching as he put away his gear. 'Are you enjoying yourself?'

'A lot,' Orson replied. 'I wanted to thank you for the opportunity to do this.' He placed his saddle on its rack. 'And . . . I was wondering if Kaicey was around? It'd be nice to catch up with her.'

'Kaicey isn't interested in talking to you.' Then, when the guy looked gutted, Connor added, 'I'm sorry, Orson. She'd rather not become reacquainted.'

'No — it's all right. I get that. I wouldn't mind just one opportunity to speak to her though. After that, I'll leave her alone if that's what she wants.'

'That would be entirely up to her.' He turned to leave, but Orson kept pushing.

'It's really important.'

Connor turned back. 'Doesn't change my answer. But if you want to tell me what it's about, I'll pass it on.'

'Just a . . . um . . . ' Orson pulled at his earlobe, dragged his hand away and scratched at his arm, then shuffled his feet. 'I just wondered if she got a message, that's all. An envelope in the mail. It was a while back but it's important that she got it.'

It had been a long time since Connor had first

86

seen that envelope, but he knew Kaicey kept it around. 'You mean the black one?'

Orson's features fell into a frown. 'You're not . . . one of us, are you?'

One of us? 'Absolutely not,' he said, though he didn't have a clue what Orson meant. 'I just saw the envelope.'

Orson stood staring at him for several seconds, then nodded. 'Right. I see. You know what? It's not important. Thanks.'

Connor thought about that as Orson walked quickly away. He had a gut feeling something was brewing — something he wasn't going to like.

★ ★ ★

Because the conversation with Orson was still niggling at him when he went to get lunch, Connor almost walked straight past her — a woman in the doorway, hovering as though looking for someone. Tall and blonde, slim, pretty. And something about that face . . . 'Can I help you?'

She smiled. 'Hi, I'm Paisley. Paisley Waldron. I'm looking for Ned.'

It had been a long time since he'd seen her and back then she'd still worn her hair in pigtails and sported missing teeth. 'Connor Atherton. How are you?'

Her face lit with recognition. 'Great, actually. I remember you a bit. From when Dad came out here shearing. I think I was only six or seven.'

'Sounds about right. You stopped coming around after that.'

She shrugged. 'Hanging around smelly sheep wasn't really my thing. And Mum and I left when I was twelve.'

'That's right. How is she?'

'She's okay.'

'Good. Ned said he might be a bit held up, but he shouldn't be too far away.'

'Not surprised,' she said and looked around her. 'This place has certainly changed. It's incredible.'

'Thanks. We've had a few rough spots recently but it's on the up and up.'

'I heard there was some trouble. Ned said it got nasty.'

'It did.'

'So . . . wife, kids?' Paisley prompted.

'No.' And Connor was pretty proud of the fact his polite smile didn't waver despite the sharp shot of hurt that answer still caused. 'You?'

'Still looking.' The flick of hair and the accompanying obvious look should have piqued his interest. Paisley had turned out all right. More than all right. Wherever her life had taken her, it had been in the right direction.

'Ned said you've come down to help out with Cliff?'

'Yeah.' Her smile fell. 'He needs to go into some level of care.'

Connor grimaced. 'I hope it turns out okay. Do you want to join me while you wait? Grab a tea or coffee?'

The smile came back. 'Love to.'

He led her over to the coffee machine and waited while she helped herself.

'Paisley Waldron?' Tess's voice carried from where she and Kaicey were sitting.

Paisley turned, eyes narrowing thoughtfully on Tess, before she walked over. 'Tess, right?'

'Right. How are you?'

'Not too bad.'

'Hi, Paisley,' Kaicey said.

Whatever Kaicey was worried about wasn't reflected in the bright greeting Paisley sent her. 'Kaicey — right! How lovely to see you. It's been a while.'

'Sit,' Tess said. 'Tell us what you've been up to.'

'I'm dropping some things off for Ned.' She sat at an empty seat and placed her cup carefully on the table. 'It's been a hectic morning. We flew in early.'

'We've been following what happened to your boss,' Tess told her. 'Crazy stuff.'

Paisley leant her elbows on the table and sipped her coffee. 'The whole trial was a joke. She shouldn't have had to go through it.'

'No points for guessing whose side you were on,' Connor said.

Paisley shrugged. 'I lived it with her. I know exactly how it happened. A lot of people didn't think she'd walk away free, but it would have been an injustice if she hadn't.'

'We're happy for her. We watched the verdict come through on the telly,' Tess told her. 'And . . . you said you've brought a friend down with you?'

'I did?'

'You said 'we' flew down.'

89

There was a slight hesitation. 'Oh, right. Yeah. I needed some help to get Dad's place ready for sale. It's going to be a massive job.'

'So Waldron Park is really going up for sale?' Kaicey asked.

'Not much choice, I'm afraid. How's everything been with you?'

'All good.' And then with less enthusiasm, Kaicey said, 'I, um, ran into Orson.'

Connor couldn't help but notice the way Paisley's gaze sharpened. 'Here? Why?'

'He's involved in a rural skills program being run for parolees.'

'Parolees?' Paisley repeated. 'I wish I could say I was surprised.'

'You know him, too?' Connor asked.

Paisley dragged her eyes from Kaicey's. 'Sure. Kaicey used to live just down the road from us and Orson was out on . . . Dixon Street?'

Kaicey nodded once. 'Yeah, that was it.'

'Before Orson's father died, my mum worked with him at the nuthouse.'

Tess coughed. 'Nuthouse?'

Paisley shook her head in self-admonishment. 'Sorry — pet term for the old asylum. Mum used to complain that if you weren't completely nuts before you went in, the place tended to make you that way. Because of the conditions there she felt really sorry for a lot of the patients — and the staff. Which is the only reason she tolerated it.'

'I remember that place.' Connor sent his sister a teasing look. 'Tess tried to talk me into doing a ghost tour there once.'

90

Tess shrugged. 'Willow Court was the oldest running mental hospital in the country until it closed in 2000,' she said defensively. 'It goes right back to convict times. All sorts of strange things happened out there.'

Paisley frowned. 'I believe those tours are run in wards that contained patients that were genuinely violent and dangerous. Criminally insane monsters that would tear you apart given the slightest opportunity. Would you have gone to visit them while they were alive?'

Tess shuddered. 'No, of course not.'

'Then why would you go looking for them when they're dead?'

Tess's expression went blank. Then her brow creased thoughtfully. 'I never thought of it like that.'

Ned appeared at the table. 'Paisley. You ready to unload?'

'Hi. Yep. Sure.' She finished her coffee and got to her feet. 'Nice seeing you all.' She smiled once more, but it wasn't as bright as earlier.

As Paisley and Ned walked away, Connor scratched his head. 'That was an interesting outburst.'

'I wouldn't bring that place up in front of Paisley if I were you,' Kaicey said. 'Eileen worked there, Cliff was an outpatient of one of her colleagues there — that's how they met. That place was a big part of Paisley's life, and not always in a good way.' Then she said with a sigh, 'She seemed happy enough to see me though, didn't she?'

'Sure, why?' Tess asked.

'We had a falling out before she left. I was worried she might have held a grudge.'

'Must have been a good one if you were worried she was still pissed,' Connor said.

Kaicey shrugged. 'Everyone does stupid stuff when they're kids, right?'

He thought it was a bit strange the way she looked at them all in turn, waiting for their affirmation.

'Looks like she's gotten over it anyway. I have to get back to work.' Kaicey slid from her seat and, with a quick smile, walked back to reception.

'So,' Tess said, 'do you think Paisley's mystery friend is Caroline Johnson?'

'I wouldn't have a clue.' Though the way Paisley had been hedging, he wouldn't be surprised. He thought again about the image from the television, fleetingly wondered if she'd look as fragile in real life as she had on the screen.

'I reckon it's got to be,' Tess said. 'She's out there. I'm going to go say hi.'

'Tess . . .'

'Oh, come on! If she's escaped down here I bet she doesn't have a friend in the world other than Paisley.'

'And probably wants it to stay that way,' he said.

Tess just shrugged. 'She can kick me out if she wants. Can't hurt to say hello.'

9

Scratching. The sound was irritating, and dragged Callie from sleep. She reluctantly opened her eyes and didn't immediately remember where she was. She sat up, blinked a few times. What on earth had she been dreaming about? She felt like she'd run a marathon. Blearily, she focused on her bedroom window and noticed a grevillea branch with large apricot flowers scraping the window. With dawn the wind had picked up, and light rain was falling. Tasmania, she remembered. The pretty little cottage.

She'd driven herself back here yesterday in her new car. She had been thinking something small and economical but Paisley had shaken her head at the smaller cars and told her she needed something big, safe, gutsy and practical. She'd bought a Land Rover Discovery Sport in gunmetal grey. An ex-demo vehicle, it had few kilometres to its name and looked brand new. It had cost a large chunk of her savings but she wasn't worrying about that — she loved it already. But then what? She'd unpacked the groceries and taken another wander around the garden then, tired, she'd decided to lie down until Paisley came back. That had been mid-afternoon yesterday. She checked the clock beside the bed. Almost seven. She'd slept that long?

Not surprised to feel a bit hung over from the lengthy sleep, she dragged herself off the bed and stretched. She walked into Paisley's room. Her friend was tidying up, placing a china doll the size of a small baby on a shelf — a pretty young girl dressed in a floral summer dress.

'Oh, Paisley, that's gorgeous!'

'Thanks. Mum used to make them as a hobby. This is supposed to be me and this one — ' she pulled out another, ' — is Mum.'

Callie gently touched a delicate miniature hand. 'They're beautifully made. The detail in the faces is extraordinary.'

'I had them stuffed in a cupboard down here, thought it might be nice to bring them out. Guess I'm lucky they never broke.' She rearranged a couple of nearby books on the shelf around the dolls. 'How'd you sleep?'

'Like the dead.'

'I did come in once or twice to make sure you were breathing.' Paisley grinned. 'You'll feel better for it. You haven't slept in months.'

'And now I need coffee.'

'Already made.'

'You're amazing.' Callie went back out to the kitchen and made herself some toast to go with her coffee. After a few mind-clearing sips, something occurred to her. 'Who were you talking to last night? I think I remember waking up just enough to hear you.'

'Mum. Just letting her know we're here, that everything's going to plan.' She glanced at her phone and got to her feet. 'I'm going to have to get moving if I'm going to make the plane.'

Callie felt a stab of guilt. 'Are you sure you want to go back again already?'

'The faster I'm back and there's movement at the house, the less likely it will be that anyone will cotton on you've left. At least in the short term. Besides, I need to be ready for Monday. The new buyers are relying on me getting the place back up to scratch while they hire the staff they need to take over. You know this.'

'And I really appreciate it.'

Paisley's eyes danced with amusement. 'Again? Really?'

'Leave that.' She gestured to Paisley's cup and plate. 'I'll get those later. Have you got everything you need?'

'Almost.'

At the rental car, Paisley dumped her bag and turned back before getting in. 'So you're fine? No last-minute questions, concerns? The plane lands at two so call me after that if you need to. If you get desperate, call Ned. Thank you for watching Dad for me.' Paisley gave Callie a quick squeeze. 'So . . . six weeks. I'll get the business back on its feet and the new manager up to speed, pack up my stuff and drive down.'

'I'll be fine,' Callie promised. 'I have my car, know basically where everything in town is and you've left every possibly necessary phone number on the fridge.'

'And I'll try and get down here a few times in between.'

Paisley was so protective she sometimes felt more like a mother than a friend, Callie thought as she waved her off down the driveway. Then she closed her eyes and sighed deeply. The sun struggled to warm her against the cold of the winter's morning. She could hear a boat out on the river, birds — everywhere — and nothing else. It was wonderful. And all she needed to do was whatever she wanted.

She opened her eyes and turned in a slow circle. What should she do first? Her eyes settled on the grevillea outside the cottage, reminded her of the scraping of its branches on her window. She'd start by pruning it back and ensure there were no more nasty sounds to keep her awake at night. She went in search of the tools Paisley said she'd find in the garage of the main house. The tools were there, not as new and sharp as Callie would have liked, but she took them back to the cottage and got to work.

At one stage she stopped to stretch her back and survey her work, glancing up to see Cliff in the window of a second-storey corner room. She smiled and waved. He turned away and disappeared.

★   ★   ★

By the end of the day, Callie had worked longer and harder than she'd intended, and her muscles were well and truly complaining. Tired, but not feeling like sitting around inside, she decided to go for a walk to find the river. As she made her way down the hill, she found what should have been park-like gardens overgrown with clusters of trees and shrubs in a tangled mess of long grass and weeds. She'd have to invest in a decent sprayer if she was going to tackle this area. It really wouldn't take that much to at least give the gardens a façade of order, if not a full makeover. Paisley had done so much for her since all this began. And tidying the grounds was the only way Callie could think of to give something back.

A worn track that led into thick undergrowth veered away from the main gardens. Unusual symbols were carved into gum trees marking the path. Hiking marks? Did this lead to some sort of public trail? She took a few steps in, treading carefully. The trail got darker as trees towered overhead and shrubs stretched out to narrow her path. There was an interesting mix of native and introduced species. She recognised the tiny, fine leaves of tea trees, a few conifers, some tall and slim, others fat and squat, the spears of ancient poplars and silver-blue acacias. It was quiet, cool, pretty. She spotted more carvings on tree trunks, looked around, and around again. There was no sign of where she'd come from, or where she was going.

Enchanted, she pressed on until the path widened and the sun began to filter through the canopy. A narrow strip of grass bordered the river, where swamp gums entangled their roots in the wet ground and the branches of graceful willows touched the river. In the shallows, reeds and spike rush knitted together in competition for space. And everything rustled gently, dancing as the breeze slid off the sparkling water and brought movement and sound — the only movement, the only sound. She was on the outskirts of a bustling town, but right then she could have been anywhere, at any time. And the feeling of being lost in that timeless, happy space had her eyes closing and the first genuine smile in months gracing her face. She breathed deeper than she had in as long as she could remember.

She looked back, saw the top of the house's tower over the trees. It was impressive, old and thoroughly charming. So what was it about the place that had a slight chill racing over her skin, giving her the creeps? Her mind wandered for a few minutes, thinking about the way the light didn't penetrate the windows, the cold that had sliced through her by the stairs as she'd inspected the lounge room. Callie didn't believe in ghosts or monsters or any of that stuff designed purely, she believed, to scare children. But if she did, she wasn't sure she'd be able to set foot in that place.

Something crashed suddenly in the under-growth, sounding like it was moving towards her at speed. Heart in her throat, Callie spun. Waited.

The little brown dog with a happy smile and a shaggy coat might have had some Jack Russell in it, but beyond that was anyone's guess. Its damp muddy paws found her jeans as it leapt, leaving twin smears.

'Molly! Molly!' A young boy in linen shorts and a striped shirt crashed through the trees after the dog, looking equally as ragged. Chest heaving, his bare legs scratched — probably from his mad dash after Molly — his frantic gaze fell on the dog and turned to relief. Then his big

98

hazel eyes widened back into distress when he saw Callie and the marks on her jeans.

'Uh — I'm so sorry! She slipped out of her collar,' he explained, holding up a lead with a buckled leather collar attached. 'I guess I didn't make it tight enough. I'm so sorry. You're not gonna tell, are you?'

The words tumbled into each other and it took Callie a moment to catch up. Then she grinned. 'No harm done.' To prove it, she picked up the puppy, ignoring its state, to give it a quick cuddle. 'She's very sweet.'

The stricken look left the boy's face and turned to a smile. 'She was my birthday present. I promised Nan I'd take good care of her. I tried but . . . ' He held up the collar and lead again with a helpless shrug.

The gesture only made her grin more. 'Could happen to anyone. She looks happy and healthy. You must be getting most of it right.'

His chest puffed out a little. 'She's real quick,' he said proudly. 'And real smart. And she loves to run.'

'I can see that.'

'Sorry about your jeans.'

'It's no problem. I was doing some gardening. They're not exactly clean.'

'Are you new around here?' he asked, voice full of curiosity. 'I haven't seen you before. You're not really supposed to be here. It's private property. You don't want to mess with old Weirdo Waldron.'

She would not laugh. She. Would. Not. 'Weirdo Waldron?'

'Uh — I mean Mr Waldon,' he said sheepishly.

'That's okay, I'm a friend of his daughter. I'm staying in his cottage.'

'Oh,' the boy said as though that made everything better. He gently took the pup from her arms. 'You're one of us, then. I'm Jonah.'

'I'm Callie.'

'Nice to meet you, Callie. Sorry again.' He bent and struggled with the exuberant pup to get the collar back on. 'I'll do it up one hole tighter. See if that works.' He straightened as Molly tugged at the lead before jumping all over him. 'No, Molly. Don't jump. No.'

Cuteness overload, she thought. 'It was nice to meet you too, Jonah. This is a lovely trail; does it continue along the river?'

'Yep, just around that bend there. This one is Devil's Den. The other one that goes right around the point is called the Wallaby Trail.'

'Devil's Den?'

'Sure. The devils used to nest around here.'

And then it clicked. 'You mean Tasmanian devils?' she asked enthusiastically. 'I hope I get to see one while I'm here.'

'They still come 'round. For the dead stuff . . . you know. I better get back before I get in trouble. Bye, Callie!'

'Bye, Jonah.'

As boy and dog disappeared along the trail through the trees, Callie frowned. Dead stuff? She laughed a little, shook it off. She wanted to enjoy this place. Best not to focus on dead stuff and creepy houses, she told herself as she headed back up the track to the cottage. Jonah had

100

called her 'one of us'. That was a generous attitude. Did staying with the Waldrons automatically qualify you? She had it in her mind that you were never a local in a small town like this until your family was several generations in.

She rounded the last bend in the overgrown garden just as Ned's car appeared.

'Brought over some firewood for you,' he said as she approached. 'Case you get cold. I'll put it round the side on the patio.'

'Oh, thanks. I appreciate that,' she said. 'I've been gardening in four layers of clothing. I was wondering if it was just me who thought it was freezing.'

'You'll get used to it,' he said, lugging a crate from the back of his car.

'Let me take a load.' She lifted another crate of wood and followed Ned. It was heavier than she bargained for and she dropped it with relief next to Ned's, cracking her head on the fuse box when she straightened too fast. 'Ouch!' she grumbled, sore and a little embarrassed, but Ned had already walked away to get another load. She went after him, grateful he had the last container taken care of.

'Sleep okay last night?' he asked.

'Yes, it's very quiet.'

He nodded. 'You've got any problems while Paisley's away, don't forget to call. It's a bit hard to get away from work — copped a bit of flack about yesterday — but you just let me know. I'll get myself out here.'

'I appreciate that,' she said.

'Did Paisley give you my number?'

'Yes, thanks.' Her phone shrilled, and she pulled it from her pocket. 'In fact, this is her now. Hi, Paise, just a sec.' She smiled at Ned. 'Thanks again.'

Ned paused at the car door, smiling back across the roof. 'I'll see you soon.'

She nodded, then returned her attention to Paisley. 'Hi.'

'Settling in?'

'I've been gardening.'

'No!' Paisley said with exaggerated disbelief. 'I would never have guessed. And thank you. The house is going to be difficult and time consuming enough to clean up without even thinking about the grounds.'

'I met a little boy down by the river today. He had a puppy with him. He was curious that I was staying here.'

'Living in Weirdo Waldron's cottage?' Paisley guessed. 'It's fine. The house has an interesting history and a bit of a reputation. I'd keep quiet about where you're staying though if I were you. Just say the caravan park or something. A new face around town is one thing, a new face staying with me right after the trial in the same week Caroline Johnson disappears is another. There's already speculation up here among your loyal gatekeepers, and I dodged about a million questions from Tess yesterday.'

'Who's Tess?'

'Connor Atherton's sister.'

'And here I was convincing myself it wouldn't be big news down here.'

'All you need is one decent story to break

elsewhere and it'll blow over quick enough. In the meantime, don't give too much away. You look different, but not that different.'

'Yep. Got it.'

'And while I've got you, I just want to run through a few bits and pieces . . . '

By the time they were finished talking, night had closed in and a cold damp seemed to permeate everything. Callie kindled the fire, glad of the wood Ned had brought over, and made herself a simple dinner. She fought back a wave of sadness as the isolation of eating alone swept over her. Thoughts of sharing meals with Dale: simple barbecued lunches on the patio; candlelight dinners at their favourite restaurant; hastily thrown together breakfasts in bed after — she shoved the memories back, locked them away along with the sudden, almost crippling, sense of loneliness. She'd never been a loner by nature, had always enjoyed the company of other people. This was an adjustment. But this was what she'd wanted. What she needed. She'd get used to being on her own. She'd have to.

As she washed up her plate, Callie caught a glimpse of the river shining through the trees below. On a whim, she gathered a blanket around her and went out onto the patio to sit. It was cold but peaceful, listening to the sounds of the night, watching the stars in a sky clearer than she'd ever seen. A boat puttered along the river. Night birds sang to each other.

With a wisp of breeze came the low hum of song, rhythmical, repetitive. She strained to hear but lost the sound, imagined it floated back for another moment before being lost again. More lights had appeared on the river, but the song or whatever it had been was gone. Perhaps she'd imagined it, but something about the elemental sound stayed with her, and it was unsettling.

A quick look up at the house showed her the light in Cliff's upstairs window was still on. It was reassuring to know someone else was up, awake. *I'll become accustomed to this place*, she told herself again. Then she swished back inside, because she really wasn't sure she would, and locked the door.

10

For the next few days, blustery winds and the odd bit of sleet made conditions genuinely freezing and uncomfortable. Callie couldn't garden, so she'd tried to keep busy inside, reading, watching television and tidying the cottage. Because of its size, it hadn't taken very long. And now everything was shining and immaculate, except for the bags of rubbish she'd left at the door, reluctant to venture out. But she couldn't ignore it forever.

Layering up, she bundled the bags together and raced across the drive. Lifting the lid of the bin, she noticed empty boxes from microwave meals — at least a dozen. Cliff was living off these? They might be okay nutritionally, but he must get sick of them. She'd spotted him hobbling along the little garden path each day on his walks. He'd mostly ignored her, but had nodded politely yesterday afternoon and she'd smiled, waved, though she hadn't gotten either back. But she hadn't spoken to him either, hadn't been sure what to say. Perhaps Cliff was just feeling awkward. He hadn't asked for her to be here, invading his space.

She convinced all the bags to fit inside the bin — just — and was about to dash back to the warmth of the cottage when the sound of tyres on gravel had her turning to see an unfamiliar car drive past her on the way to the house. The small white hatchback pulled up right outside Cliff's door, a large sign attached to the car announcing the community nurse had arrived. A tall, slender woman with a severe silver bun emerged and fought the wind to close the car door. 'Hello, dear!' she said cheerily.

Callie made her way across the drive. 'Hi.'

'My name's Adelaide. You must be Callie. Paisley told me to expect to see you.' Adelaide opened the rear door of the car and ducked her head, emerging with groceries.

'Let me get some of those.' Callie took two bags and followed Adelaide up the steps. The nurse didn't knock, just let herself in, calling out, 'Cliff!'

'Upstairs,' he snapped.

Callie went ahead and put the bags on the kitchen bench. Because they were frozen microwave meals, she began loading them into the freezer.

'Thank you, Callie,' Adelaide said, unpacking bread, milk and a couple of tins of Sustagen. 'This isn't strictly in the job description, but Paisley appreciates it — even if the lord of the manor up there doesn't.' She chuckled. 'How are you settling in?'

'Well, thanks.' And she was pretty keen to get going in case the lord of the manor came down. 'I might leave you to it.'

Adelaide paused in her unpacking and nodded. 'I heard he wasn't very nice to you when you arrived.'

'It's not an issue. He has a lot to deal with.'

'We all do. That's life, I'm afraid. Our actions

106

always catch up with us in the end.'

Callie had no idea what Adelaide meant, but she smiled politely.

'You have a lovely afternoon,' Adelaide continued. 'Stay warm. I'll deal with Cliff.'

'Thank you.'

'It really is good that you're here, Callie,' Adelaide added as she was almost at the door. 'About time things got moving. Sing out if you need anything.'

Got moving? If Adelaide was referring to getting Cliff out of the house and into care, Callie was leaving that right alone. Nothing was going to happen until Paisley got back. But she smiled anyway and went outside, dragging her coat more tightly around her as she dashed back to the cottage.

She read for a while, but was restless enough after an hour to wander around finding things to do that didn't need to be done. Why couldn't she settle? She went to the fridge, though she wasn't hungry. Perhaps she could make something nice for dinner. So far she'd been existing on tinned soup and toasted sandwiches, but the fridge and freezer were full of good food, and Paisley had said the slow cooker in the cupboard worked. She should make a casserole, something rich and nutritious. She might even drop some over later to give Cliff a break from the packaged stuff. Assuming he'd want some.

A glimpse of someone in the garden outside the window caught her attention. Was that Cliff now? It was about the time he took his daily walk. But in this weather? She grimaced. Perhaps she should catch up with him, suggest her idea for dinner. It was silly to worry about approaching an old man, so she rugged up again, put a smile on her face and went out. She marched down the garden path, skirting the overgrown trees and shrubs and fighting to keep her hair away from her face, while expecting at any moment to run into him. But she couldn't find him.

'Cliff?' she called.

Had she been mistaken? She could have sworn she'd seen him — someone. She went a bit further, just in case, but saw and heard nothing. 'Cliff?'

Shivering, she blew into her hands to warm them, caught sight of something else out of the corner of her eye. A low branch in a nearby garden bed was swinging much more violently than those around it, as though someone had just let it go. Damn it, she wasn't imagining that! If it wasn't Cliff, who was it? Had a reporter found her? A photographer?

She ran in the direction of the branch with that one thought, angry that whoever they were, they were trespassing, about to make her life hell again. She was most of the way down to the river before it occurred to her how unlikely that scenario was. She pushed on anyway. The small clearing she found felt eerie and uninviting in the bad weather.

'Hello?' She took a cautious step around an old pine tree, but pulled up when her jacket snagged on the undergrowth surrounding it. She turned to untangle her sleeve from what seemed to be a wild rosebush, well overgrown and woven into the more innocent branches of an acacia. The movement of the clinging branches as she attempted to free herself revealed a small stone block with a badly tarnished plaque. It was difficult to read from where she stood, but she couldn't go any further to make it clearer. How sad that someone had cared enough to place a memorial and no one had bothered to look after it.

The wind picked up, howling through the trees. For a moment the sun broke through the cloud, only to be lost again as she released her sleeve from the last thorn and stepped away. The river rippled madly with the gusty wind, and the trees bent and swayed noisily. What had felt so peaceful on her last visit was desolate and uninviting today. And the niggle of not quite being alone teased the hairs on the back of her neck. It was time to return.

She hurried up the trail to see a car parked outside the cottage. Wary, she kept her distance as a woman slipped out with a friendly grin and a 'Hi!'

Late twenties, early thirties; Callie couldn't be sure. Long dark hair, curious green eyes, jeans, boots, jacket. She didn't dress like a reporter. But what would a reporter wear in this weather? Probably the same thing this woman was.

'Can I help you?'

'I'm Tess. I live out at Calico Mountain. I was talking to Paisley about you last weekend, thought I should come and say hello.'

'Why?' Paisley had said she'd dodged the

questions, not answered them.

'Because I wanted to. Paisley was choosing her words so carefully, I knew she had to have Caroline Johnson down here.'

'Were you just out here on foot, sneaking around in the garden?'

What appeared to be genuine surprise lit Tess's features. 'No, of course not. Is someone bothering you?'

You, Callie thought bad-temperedly.

'Look, Caroline — '

'Callie.'

'Huh?'

'My name is Callie. I don't go by Caroline.'

'Callie?' Tess studied her for a moment, nodded. 'I think that suits you better. I just came out to say hi.'

Now what? Callie couldn't stand there all day on the driveway and Tess wasn't taking enough notice of the *get lost* vibe she was sending out. Perhaps if she was nice, Tess would consider not telling everyone in creation where she was. She sighed.

'Would you like to come in for a drink?'

The smile widened again. 'That'd be great.'

Callie led Tess inside, her nerves on edge. If this didn't work she'd have to leave. 'Tea? Coffee?'

'Coffee would be perfect. I've only had one today. I'm a bit of a caffeine addict.'

'I only have instant.'

'Not a problem.' Instead of sitting at the table, Tess wandered over to the window that overlooked the river. 'It's lovely out here. I guess

110

as far as hideaways go, you couldn't pick much prettier. Of course, the weather could be better. It's supposed to clear up tomorrow.'

'I hope so.' Callie set the kettle to boil, retrieved some mugs from the cupboard and took out the milk, considering her words carefully. 'It is pretty. And quiet. Secluded. And I'd like to hang around for a while.' She paused until Tess had turned back around, then aimed a hard look in her direction. 'But pretty and quiet and secluded are no good to me if everyone knows I'm here.'

Tess's expression turned sympathetic. 'Understood. And I'm not going to say anything. But you should prepare yourself for people to find out. This isn't like a big city. And you can't stay cooped up in the cottage forever.'

'Not forever. Just until it all blows over a bit.'

'And you should know for the most part, people around here are nice, friendly. They'll give you a fair go. It was a good place to come for that reason, too.'

Callie nodded slowly. 'It's more the idea of the mob that was after me back home finding out where I am that bothers me.' The kettle clicked off so she poured in the water. 'I was advised to lay low for a few months.'

'Fair enough. Thanks.' Tess took the coffee and sat at the table. 'I can't imagine it's been easy.'

'No. It hasn't. But it's done,' Callie said, shutting the conversation down. 'So, tell me more about you.'

'I live out at Calico Mountain, which is a

tourist retreat and working cattle property about half an hour from here. It borders Mt Field National Park. You know it?'

'Paisley mentioned it. So you work there?'

'With my brothers, Connor and Logan.'

'Paisley said she spoke to Connor. She didn't mention Logan.'

'I only found out a little while ago he was my half-brother. Long story. If you ever want to hear about someone else's newsworthy dramas, ask about what happened out there a couple of years back.'

Tess seemed genuine enough about that to stir Callie's curiosity. 'It would be nice to have a conversation with someone that didn't revolve around me for a change,' she admitted.

Tess's gaze dropped to study her coffee. 'I'm sorry if you feel like I've barged in. I'll admit natural curiosity, but I also thought about you being alone out here, perhaps liking the idea of having someone you can call if you need anything.'

It was difficult to remain annoyed with Tess — she was too damn nice. 'It could be. I'm not exactly used to spending so much time on my own.'

Tess's smile brightened. 'Come out and visit one day when you've got nothing to do. I'll show you around and tell you all about it.'

'That's a kind offer.'

'Is that code for no?' Tess's head tilted to the side as her smile became assessing. 'You do look quite different with your hair short and brown. Stick on a hat and sunnies and I'm betting a lot of people won't even recognise you out of context.'

Callie wasn't sure she agreed but she smiled gratefully. 'Regardless, I'm pretty sure heading out to a tourist retreat is asking for trouble. I'll think about it.'

'Good. Before long I reckon I'll be desperate for an excuse to show you around, take a break. I have about a hundred plants to start putting in the ground in the next few days.'

'Yourself?'

'Oh, sure. Probably. We have a groundsman who was going to do it, but he did his back in yesterday, and if the plants sit around in their pots for too long where they've been unloaded I can't imagine it will do them much good.' Tess chewed on her lip. 'I've just got to figure out where to put them.'

Callie couldn't help sending Tess a quizzical look. 'You have a hundred plants and you don't know where they're going?'

Tess looked at the ceiling. 'We lost most of a stand of really old pines in a bad storm we had and pretty much everything that had been living under them died too. There was a big excavation to remove the trees at which time our brilliant groundsman — Bob — decided to reshape three acres of ground to continue the existing gardens right along the main drive to the stables to open everything up. Bob ordered all the plants, carved out all the garden beds and dropped in what he termed a few 'decorative boulders', then fell over one of them and completely wrecked himself. He's out of action for the foreseeable future.

Mum used to organise all the plantings, but she's taken off with a friend to do some travelling, so I stupidly put my hand up and was told to place the plants however I thought fit. Like I was being given the good job.' She pulled a face. 'Like it would be *fun*.'

'And it's not?' Callie guessed, trying not to laugh at Tess's horrified expression.

'It sounds like it should be, but I really don't have the first idea. I want it to look like a masterpiece and I have a feeling it's going to look more like a dog's breakfast.'

Suspicion crept in. Had Paisley said something to the Athertons about Callie's ideas to build a landscaping business? She really should stay out of it. It wasn't her place to come up with a solution.

Hell. 'If you consider the specific needs of each plant — direction, shade, light and water requirements — add in that you'll want to layer them in terms of size and texture and pick your colours so that each plant complements the other, then consider balance and uniformity with the existing gardens, you're halfway set up before you even have to think too much about it.'

At Tess's blank stare, she added, 'Aren't you?'

'How do you know all this?'

'I thought Paisley must have told you. I owned a landscaping business before I got married. I was thinking about starting it back up down here.'

'You — really?' Tess asked with enough surprise to suggest she really hadn't known.

Callie sipped her coffee, smiled. 'Once I feel

comfortable showing my face in public again.'

'So that hat and sunnies I mentioned. I'll provide them. And whatever rate you want to charge — within reason,' Tess said with a smile. 'Help me. Please.'

She sounded so desperately sincere, Callie felt a gurgle of laughter rise in her throat. 'It's not that difficult. We can sketch it out, I'll give you an idea.'

★　★　★

It wasn't as crazy as it seemed, Callie told herself as she tasted the casserole, decided it was as good as it was going to get, and turned off the slow cooker. Perhaps she shouldn't have allowed Tess to convince her to take a look. Perhaps she'd been a bit rash, but the desperate plea for help had caught her off guard and she'd ended up enjoying Tess's company. They'd sketched out a rough plan and that should have been enough. But Tess hadn't been completely sure what all the plants were, which didn't help, and so she'd agreed to drive out to have a look. Just a look. Anything further was only a maybe. If anything went wrong, if anyone so much as looked at her twice, Callie would bail. Just get in her car and leave.

As the sun faded outside, she noticed Cliff's kitchen light come on in the main house. She stared down at the casserole, then back at the house. She sighed. Damn it, it wouldn't hurt to try. She ladled half the casserole into a dish and set out across the drive.

She almost took it back again when, after several knocks on the front door, no one appeared. Then the *thump, thump, thump* of his walking stick as she walked away had her turning back around. The door opened. Cliff was wrapped tightly in a blue dressing gown, a necklace with a grey stone decorated with strange symbols hanging around his neck. 'What do you want?'

Her smile slipped at the edges, but she forced it back into place. 'Hi, Mr Waldron. I made a casserole. I thought you might like some.'

His eyes narrowed, adding more creases to his heavily lined face. 'Did you? Why would I? I can cook for myself.'

She thought about the microwave meal packaging in the bin and fought back a frown. 'Of course, but I hate cooking for one and as you're being kind enough to let me stay in the cottage, I'd like to share.'

'Had nothing to do with that.'

'Regardless, I appreciate it.' She kept her smile plastered on, determined to win.

He looked the dish over. 'Not poisoned, is it?'

'What? No. Of course not.' She stumbled over the words, genuinely shocked. 'No.'

He studied the covered casserole for another full minute while she stood there, feeling awkward, holding it in front of her. 'S'pose I may as well then.'

'Would you like me to carry it in — put it on the bench?'

'I got it.' He took it, juggling the pot and his stick with difficulty.

116

The door closed in her face.

'You're welcome,' she muttered. Then, pulling a face at the closed door, she went back to the solitude of the cottage.

11

Callie awoke the next morning with a tune in her head she didn't recognise and a vague recollection of pink. A pink what she couldn't say, but she was pretty sure Paisley's doll had been in there somewhere. And the memorial stone she'd found on her race down to the river yesterday. Just her mind jumbling together the events of the past week, no doubt. But she'd slept well and was looking forward, with a few nerves, to this morning. She got up with the intention of putting on coffee, was happy to see the weather had cleared. There was still a bit of wind, but the sky was blue, the clouds gone.

A humming sound caught her attention. She went to the lounge room window and saw Ned riding around on a large green mower, tidying the lawns that formed the paths between the areas of garden. The scent of freshly mown grass drifted into the house. He glanced up and caught her eye, waved. She lifted a hand in return, then when he cut the engine and climbed off, realised he was coming to see her.

'Shit . . . ' She made a mad dash into the bedroom and pulled on some jeans and a jumper, dragged her fingers through her hair to tidy it and by the time she was done he was knocking on her door.

'Ned. Good morning. How are you?'

'Good. Just getting Dad's lawns done early.

Need to get back to work.' His eyes roamed her face. 'Hope I didn't wake you.'

'No, it's fine. I was just about to make coffee. Would you like one?'

'Love one. If Paisley's left one of those travel cups around, I'll take it with me.'

'I'm pretty sure she has a collection of them. Come in.'

He stepped past her and she closed the door against the wind. 'Warmer in here,' he commented. 'It's clearer this morning and a few degrees colder with it.'

'Colder again?' She got the coffee started then added some logs to the fireplace and stirred it back to life.

'I've got this,' Ned said, taking over. 'You worry about the coffee.'

'How do you like it?'

'White and two, thanks. Thought you might have called, with Paisley away and no one to talk to.'

'Actually, Tess Atherton came around yesterday,' she replied brightly. 'She's lovely.'

'Yeah, she's nice enough all right, for one of the bosses. Good horse rider. You like riding?'

'I do. I had a sweet old grey pony as a kid. Haven't been on a horse for a long time though.'

'A pony? Guess you had a good childhood then?'

Ponies equalled good childhoods? They certainly didn't hurt. But nor did they make up for . . . other things. 'Sure. Not bad. It was just me and Dad.'

'No mum, then. Guess that was difficult.'

'We were all in a car accident when I was very young,' she said with a shrug. 'I don't remember much, but Mum didn't make it.'

'I see. Well, we'll have to organise a ride. Pick a day and I'll take you out on the trails.'

She smiled and handed him his coffee. 'One day, perhaps.'

'Thanks for this.' He took it in one hand, then reached out with the other and touched her hair.

She jerked back. 'What are you doing?'

'Huh? Oh.' He dropped his hand. 'Just wanted to know if it was a wig. You used to have lots of red hair.'

'Not anymore,' she said, slightly rattled.

'Shame. Want me to come back tonight? Break up the boredom of being alone?' he asked with a look that had warning lights flashing behind Callie's eyes. Hell, surely he couldn't think she was interested in him? *Shit.* 'I'm, ah . . . actually heading out to help Tess with some gardening today, so I'll probably be up for an early night.'

'Just a thought.' He opened the door and a cold blast of air swirled into the cottage. 'Got some more firewood for ya. I'll stick it round with the rest when I'm done.'

'I appreciate it,' she said a little brusquely. 'Thanks, Ned.'

'No problem.' He closed the door behind him and she went to the window, watching him walk back over to the mower.

What was *that*? It was going to be awkward if Ned was harbouring those kinds of ideas. She braided her hair and tucked the short plait up under the same dark green cap she'd pulled over

120

her head when escaping her home the night she'd fled with Paisley. She added some light makeup and sunglasses and took a deep breath. No, no one was going to recognise her. More eager than ever to get away for a while, Callie dashed to the car and instructed the GPS to take her to Calico Mountain.

★　★　★

'Fence maintenance is one of the biggest and most important jobs you'll have as a farm hand,' Connor told the group while Logan watched. The men were standing close by, holding their horses while three cattle dogs raced around them in playful circles, occasionally crashing into each other or dropping to roll madly in the long grass. The horses were too busy tearing at the ryegrass and chewing greedily to worry about the dogs' antics. Logan and Connor had agreed the men should ride the horses out, get as much time in the saddle as possible. A lot of horse work was being replaced by machines these days, but they still needed to be able to ride.

'Fences get old, worn out, and livestock love to test them. They'll use them as scratching posts, push their heads through to find feed and if they get a good enough fright, they'll just run right through them. You need to be handy at building them, spotting weaknesses and keeping them in good order. Ned, our stockman, was out here yesterday, patched up this hole a couple of cows had made. He noticed the posts were getting rotten, so we're going to replace this stretch right back to the corner posts.'

'Can't even see the corner post,' Travis commented.

'You will by the time we get to the end of this,' Connor promised. 'Over the years we've been replacing wooden posts with steel. That's what we're using today. Makes the process a bit more involved and costly, but they'll last indefinitely, saving time and money down the track. Logan's going to use the bobcat to pull out the old fence posts. It also has an attachment for digging the holes for the new posts. You're all going to end up with certification to operate a range of farm machinery, but for now, all you're going to need is a decent pair of gloves and some wire cutters. First, you need to untack your horses and let them graze for the day.'

'Won't they run off?' Orson asked.

'Where to?' Logan asked. 'They've got grass, shade, water and each other right here. They're not heading off into thick scrub where we're fencing unless you give them a good reason to. They might run down the hill a bit, that's about as bad as it'll get. And they're used to the sound of a rattling bucket of oats. Brings them back — most times,' he added with a grin.

'So, untack and get your gloves on, gentlemen. We've got a good kilometre of fencing to get done.'

Connor assisted with the horses, showing the men what to do. They'd work through the day, make as much progress as they could. Then he'd leave it as it was — let the group work on the fence for a few hours each week and see it through to completion. Fencing could be a bitch of a job, but it was one of the few jobs they'd do with a tangible outcome in the time they were here. He didn't need the paddock until summer and it would give the men a sense of satisfaction — hopefully — to see the finished product, knowing they'd done it.

'You coming?' he called to Orson. 'Or planning on standing there dreaming all day?'

'Yeah.' Orson stopped staring at his surroundings and pulled on his gloves.

'We need to cut this wire away from the fence posts.'

'No worries. Where's it going?'

'We'll bundle it into piles for Logan to push together when he's got the posts out. Like Ned is doing with the other boys further along.'

'Got it.'

They worked quietly for a while, with Orson shooting the occasional glance into the thick tangle of gum trees and scrub beyond the fence line.

'Something bothering you?' Connor asked eventually.

'What's on the other side of all this bushland?' Orson asked.

'More of the same. It's national park. Why?'

Orson shrugged. 'Just wondering. Any trails?'

'Plenty.'

'Any reason anyone would be out there?'

Connor stopped working when he sensed concern in Orson's tone. 'We have some access gates for hikers staying at the guesthouse, so it's possible we get tourists out on the trails back here. That's about it. Why?'

The stomping of boots coming quickly through the bush had Orson bolting from the fence line to pick up a large branch and wield it like a weapon. He waited, tense.

Matty pushed through the low branches of an acacia, got snagged, untangled himself then stopped dead at the sight of Orson. 'What the fuck's wrong with you?'

'What were you doing?' Orson demanded.

'A piss, mate.'

Orson dropped the branch, his body sagging. 'Shit, man.'

Connor relaxed, hadn't realised how tense he'd also become in those few seconds. 'You okay?' he asked Orson.

'Yep.'

'Serious reaction.'

'Just can't be too careful.'

'You're going to have to settle down,' Connor said, getting back on task. 'You'll hear lots of noises in the bush. Ninety-nine times out of a hundred it's going to be animals.'

'It's an animal I'm worried about.' Without further explanation, Orson moved ahead to work further up the fence line.

★ ★ ★

Callie's first glimpse of Calico Mountain had her gasping in appreciation. She'd driven out of pretty bushland and over a pebble creek via a low wooden bridge. Beyond the creek, long stretches of green paddocks led to a sprawling timber guesthouse, all red wood and glass and wide verandas against a backdrop of mountains still littered with bright splashes of colour that could only be from maples. She wondered just how much more spectacular they would have been in early autumn. She continued along the drive between dark post-and-rail fences, past the large circular drop-off area in front of the main building and followed a sign to guest parking. From what she could see, the sprawling beds of winding gardens already established had been moulded many years past by an expert hand.

With her fingers on the car door her nerves once again invaded her excitement. She checked her appearance in the rear-vision mirror. She looked different. Very different, she reminded herself. She looked around again, twisting in her seat to get a better idea of her surroundings. In front and to the right of the guesthouse were those cleverly planted gardens. To the left, where the drive continued to who knew where, there was a scattering of trees and bare organically shaped garden beds curved through an area still partially shaded in places by huge pine trees and gorgeous red and orange maples and golden elms. Set further off the roadside were pallets of plants and trees and large piles of mulch and manure. A couple of wheelbarrows sat loaded with tools. An impressive worksite and . . . yes, perhaps a little overwhelming, at least for someone who might not enjoy it quite as much as Callie knew she would.

Then she spotted Tess. Renewed enthusiasm had Callie getting out of the car and walking briskly in her direction. 'Morning!' she called.

Tess straightened from where she was bent over a potted conifer almost as tall as her. 'Callie! Thank God. You see what I'm dealing with?' She reached her arms out to encompass the project.

'Oh, wow, look at these plants!' Callie ran her gaze over dozens of advanced maples and elms, liquidambars, dogwoods and conifers. Further back were azaleas — masses of them — flaxes, rhododendrons, grevilleas. Pots and pots of colourful advanced trees, shrubs and groundcovers.

'Yes, look at them. *All* of them.'

'They're lovely.'

'I'm glad you're impressed,' Tess said. 'What the hell do I do with them?'

Callie laughed at Tess's dry tone. 'Why did you volunteer for this?'

'Because it's what I do: a bit of everything that needs doing. And the activities. I organise all of those, run PR and special offers for the lodge, a few dozen other things . . . and garden. Apparently. I took a photo of each of the established garden islands, thought perhaps this one . . . ' She scrolled through the photos on her phone. 'Looked a lot like the shape of this one, so we could just recreate that here.'

Callie took a look, shook her head. 'No.'

'No?' Tess asked in disbelief. 'Why not?'

'Because that garden bed faces north. This bed faces south. All those plants that look out so happily over in that garden will all want to face the other way in this one and the ground in this bed is bordering on soggy, with heavy shade.

126

These particular plants don't like having wet feet. They'll sulk and die. If you want to replicate that bed in your photo, you should do it over there.' She pointed to a sunnier position on the other side of the drive. 'You have other plants that will suit this spot better.'

'Right. Well, what about those?' Tess said, pointing to a group of pots. 'Can we plant them around that big rock there?' She pointed to another spot nearby. 'They'd look good out on the edge.'

'They're azaleas.'

'I know they're azaleas, they're planted all over the grounds here.'

'Yeah, but you're planting those ones in full sun on the western side. They prefer dappled sunlight or morning sun and light afternoon shade.'

Tess looked around the garden, considering that. 'You sure?'

'I'd be sure in my part of the world. Though I've never tried growing them in Tassie.'

'Then what am I going to put there?'

'I'd be inclined to use the liriope in front, maybe the grevillea behind. Or a weeping maple. We should place them out, make sure we find the right positions for everything before planting. Grab that cherry. I've got the perfect spot for it.'

It really didn't take Tess any time at all to get the hang of what to put where once she had the basics straight in her mind. Callie found herself enjoying Tess's chatter, laughing at her stories. The conversation went a long way towards taking the edge off her earlier conversation with Ned.

When they just about had the plants all placed out, she straightened to see the layout of the first garden bed. 'What do you think?' she asked Tess, who stood beside her to admire it.

'Gorgeous. I think it's going to look gorgeous.'

'Then I'll start putting these in.' Callie picked up a shovel and dropped it into the damp soil. A few tourists passed them, said hi and moved on. There hadn't been so much as a flicker of recognition for Callie. Perhaps the reporters hanging around at home, the phone calls and letters and interview requests were a thing of the past. Perhaps there was a chance she could put everything behind her. Get on with her life.

She scooped out the earth, picked up the robinia and tapped the edge of the pot to remove it before setting it in place.

'Hey, perhaps before we go any further, we should grab some lunch?' Tess said.

Callie's stomach was growling but . . . 'I'm not sure I want to go up there.'

'Oh — right. I tell you what, we'll go in the side entrance — straight to the staff room.'

Callie stretched her back, thinking about it. 'Okay. I suppose.'

She followed Tess up to the guesthouse, through the side entrance and down a short corridor to a relaxed area with tables and chairs, a kitchenette and a pool table. There was a fireplace teasing a few red coals and not much else; it was already bordering on too warm. Or was that just her nerves? There were only two other people using the room, and neither gave Callie more than a casual friendly glance.

'See? You're fine,' Tess whispered. 'You can come and get some food from the buffet in the dining room, or you can wait here and I'll grab you some pasta — that's what I'm having. It's chicken boscaiola today, I think.'

'Sounds great, ta,' Callie said with relief.

'Help yourself to a can of drink from the fridge, or tea or coffee from the machine. Won't be long.'

The two other people left, leaving her to herself. Callie found the fridge, grabbed a Diet Coke and chose a table by the window in the corner. What a beautiful spot. She would have killed for a job like this when she'd been landscaping. Just about any garden would look good with a backdrop like this, and the size and scale favoured big, beautiful plantings. This place was going to look amazing on the website she was already planning for her business. It was a promotional dream.

Movement in the doorway made her glance up. She almost dropped her can, fumbling it to the table instead. The guy was . . . big. Tall and built, with thick dark hair and a tough-guy expression softened marginally by a lift at one corner of his mouth. He was untidy and dusty in denims and a cotton shirt with the sleeves rolled up. His dishevelled state didn't detract from the way his presence seemed to shrink the room as he entered it.

'Hi,' he said in a deep — of course it was — voice.

Callie swallowed a trickle of nerves before answering. 'Hello.'

He came right over, leant on the chair opposite and studied her with direct, dark eyes. 'How is it that I don't know you?'

Luck? she thought, as she sat back as far as possible in her chair. *Or maybe you don't watch the news.* 'Is there a reason you should?'

'Yeah. You're in my staff room.'

'*Your* staff room?' So was this Connor Atherton, she guessed. Or Logan? She relaxed a little. Not just some random stockman. The thought was reassuring. Sort of.

'Yeah. And you're not staff.'

'Correct.' Where was Tess?

'Hmm.' His eyes narrowed thoughtfully and she was pretty sure he could see right into her mind and pluck whatever he wanted to know right out of it. 'You're not a guest who's lost her way?'

'Two for two.'

He laughed appreciatively. 'I'm Connor.'

'I figured.'

'And you are?'

'Callie,' Tess said, coming in with two steaming plates of pasta. 'I wasn't sure if you'd want a side salad. I can go back — oh, you've met Connor.'

'Not exactly,' Connor said, his dark eyes still framed with amusement.

'Oh.' Tess looked from Connor to Callie, caught on. 'Callie's a friend of mine who happens to be a landscaper.' She put a plate down in front of Callie, put the other down next

130

to it and sat. 'We wanted to avoid the chaos of the dining room, so we decided to eat in here.'

Why hadn't Tess told Connor who she was? It didn't escape Callie's attention that his eyes remained on hers the whole time Tess was talking. Maybe he did recognise her. *Shit.*

'A landscaper?' he repeated with interest. 'Then I'm guessing you've roped her into helping with the garden.'

'It's not a garden, it's a mass reforestation. And yes, Callie's helping.'

Amusement returned to Connor's face. 'Then the poor things have got a chance.'

'Hey! You were the one who wanted me to do it.'

'I didn't realise Bob was going to dump you with the entire project. I thought there would be some degree of . . . '

When he trailed off, Tess's eyebrows lifted. 'Supervision?' she asked, her tone somehow innocent and dangerous at the same time.

'Input,' Connor replied with a lightning quick grin, lifting his hands in self-defence. 'Just input. Which you yourself admitted would have been helpful.'

Callie relaxed. They were obviously close and easy with each other.

'And now I have it. We've laid out all the plants in the first garden bed, just need to put them in.'

He looked surprised. 'That's some serious digging. Are you tackling that today?'

When Tess sent her a questioning glance, Callie nodded and found her voice. 'We won't

131

get them all done, but we'll do as much as we can. We don't want them all falling over and rolling out of place if you get some wind come up.'

'What she said,' Tess told Connor. 'Come and take a look later, if you have time.'

'I'd love to.'

Callie wasn't sure what was with the smile that spread thoughtfully across Tess's face, so she dropped her eyes to her plate. 'Are you eating?' Tess asked Connor.

'I came back to pick up lunches for everyone out fencing, so I'll be eating in the south paddock. I'll see you later.' He stopped in the doorway. 'Nice to meet you, Callie.'

'You too.' Callie's breath rolled out long and slow as a coil released in her stomach. 'You didn't tell him who I was,' she said.

'I'll get around to it,' Tess said casually. 'And once he sees what you've done with the first garden bed, I'll get around to telling him we're hiring you to do the rest. Have you worked out your fees yet?'

Still feeling a little out of sorts, Callie was fast reconsidering agreeing to help. Maybe she was rushing into things. She'd been stupidly nervous during Connor's simple questioning and she'd give herself away if she couldn't get it together.

'Tess, I'm not sure this was really such a great idea.'

Tess swallowed a mouthful of pasta and smiled. 'Don't worry about Connor; he has that effect. It makes him good at business. People tend to fall in line.'

132

'Oh — no, he seems very nice. I'm just edgy about being recognised and having the whole media thing erupt down here, and I'm not technically ready to start. I haven't had a chance to register a business yet. I'm waiting on my name change to come through . . . I've only been down here a week.'

'We can work around that.' Tess picked up her lemonade. 'New business, new name. Here's to starting over.'

Still not completely convinced, Callie tapped can against can. 'Cheers to that.'

⋆ ⋆ ⋆

Connor returned with the lunches and watched the food vaporise from the containers. Hard work equalled hungry men, but there was plenty, and Logan's dogs, currently sitting on the ute salivating, would get a slice of meat or two before the remains were packed up.

As he sat eating with the men, Connor spent a bit of time wondering how it was possible that Tess had attempted to set him up with almost everyone in the phone book and hadn't introduced him to Callie. Had she finally given up assuming it was her mission in life to see him with someone? Was Callie already taken? Not that it made any difference. He wasn't sure why it was even crossing his mind. Sure, she had a snug little body and a lovely face and her eyes were an unusual dark green . . . he decided it was probably more the attitude that had sucked him in. He'd only spoken to the woman for all of

133

five minutes, but he'd enjoyed their exchange, would have liked to spend more time talking to her.

And for the briefest moment there'd been a quick flash of what might have been recognition, but he couldn't place her. Perhaps she reminded him of someone. It'd no doubt come to him.

As the men finally ate their fill and lay back as though dreaming of afternoon naps, Logan stood and got them on their feet and on the fence while Connor packed up. As he put lids on containers and rubbish in bags, he heard a whimper behind him, turning to see three dogs in a line straighter than the men could have made with bums on the ground and tails wagging, identically pathetic pleading expressions on their faces.

'Yeah, you poor things,' he said. 'You must be starving to have gotten off the lounge this morning and given up the fireplace.' Never in his life had he come across three more spoiled dogs. One, he supposed, deserved the lifestyle — Logan had rescued her from the bush — but her pups had been young, and they just didn't know any different. 'If I die, I'm coming back as one of you.' He tossed them each a generous helping of scraps before finishing up to continue on the fence.

They worked until late in the afternoon, and Connor had to call Cole to let him know they were running behind. It didn't take long to catch the horses and saddle up. He was about to lead them down on the ute when he noticed Orson heading off in the wrong direction. Had he missed something?

'Logan!' he called. 'Why's Orson heading over there?'

'No idea. Looks like he's spotted something.'

'I'll go round him up.'

Connor drove the ute along the new fence line. He stopped and got out when he noticed Orson looking into the scrub.

'Hey, Orson, what's up?'

'Nothing. Thought I saw one of the guys still out here, wanted to tell them we were leaving.'

Connor scanned the edge of the scrub, but couldn't see or hear anything. 'Must have been hikers or your imagination. We're all over there.'

'Hikers then,' Orson muttered and turned Bailey around. The horse suddenly stumbled, kicking out, and spun a half circle. Then it stopped, rigid.

'Don't move him,' Connor warned. 'He's caught his leg in the wire lying on the ground here. Just slide off.'

Connor held the horse while Orson dismounted, then carefully freed the horse's leg.

'Is he all right?'

'Yeah, no damage as far as I can see. It gave him a fright.' Connor stroked the horse's neck and walked him around to make sure he wasn't sore. 'A lot of horses would have panicked, run off and dragged the fence a long way before falling over it. Or got you off a lot of different ways. You've got to pay attention.'

'Sorry, mate,' Orson told the horse with genuine affection. 'My fault.' Then to Connor he said, 'Bailey's a good horse. A real good horse.'

'One of the best,' Connor agreed. 'You were lucky to have him assigned to you. He's good at looking after his riders. You'll do well with him.'

'Bailey the wonder horse!' Orson announced to the world when they both caught sight of the rest of the group watching and waiting. 'Is it okay to get back on?'

'Yeah, ride him back. I'll watch him move off, double check he isn't lame.'

Orson got back on and moved off, talking to the horse and shooting looks back into the scrub as he went.

Connor waited until he had some space between them before starting the ute. It was hard not to like a guy who could take responsibility for his actions, show real concern and affection for his mount. Perhaps Orson wouldn't turn out to be a mistake after all.

12

Callie was pleasantly tired when she pulled up at the cottage, and could easily have sat down on the patio and relaxed with a warm drink, maybe read for a while. But because she'd spent so long out at Calico Mountain, she was going to be late getting Cliff some dinner. Somewhere between planting the last of the groundcovers and heading home this afternoon, she'd decided to continue to feed him each evening. It made her feel better about being here, and perhaps might ease some of the awkwardness.

She unlocked the cottage door and went in, going straight to the fireplace to get some warmth underway before continuing to the kitchen and digging through the freezer, finding the spaghetti bolognese Paisley had frozen the night Callie had slept through dinner.

She pulled it out and heated some up then, leaving hers in the oven to stay warm, she headed over to Cliff's. She cast an unhappy gaze over the state of the buxus hedge that lined the driveway. Perhaps she could barter a meal for a chance to tidy it up.

She reached the door and knocked, but he didn't answer. She knocked again, waited, tried again. 'Cliff?' she called. She knew he was home because he never went anywhere. And she'd seen him walk back from the river as she'd driven in. She cupped her hands around her eyes and tried to see through a clear segment of the door's stained-glass panel. The lounge and hallway were skewed from the shape of the glass. The only light inside glowed from the top of the stairs.

Perhaps he was taking a nap. Should she check? But he was going to be livid if she interrupted his shower or something. She tried the door and when it opened she ignored the instant creepy sensation that washed over her and went into the kitchen to put down the bowl.

'Mr Waldron? Cliff?' Her voice echoed through the silent house. She moved to the staircase, tried again. As she stood at the bottom of the stairs she turned her head slowly towards the open door to the cellar. The darkness from within seemed to reach out and wrap around her. The feeling was so strong she stepped back.

'Callie?'

It was faint, but the call had her bounding up the stairs.

'Mr Waldron?' At the top she found herself in another lobby. The place was enormous, she thought as she looked at the hallway running left and right. She chose left, because it was the direction she thought the light she could see from the cottage came from. She passed two doors, kept going. Then she saw the light under the last door. 'Mr Waldron?'

'In here.'

She opened the door, peeked around it. He was on the floor, sitting up against the side of his bed. Blood was trickling from his temple. 'What happened?'

'Tripped over. Bumped my head.'

She crouched down beside him and examined the wound. It didn't look like much more than a shallow tear of frail skin, but she couldn't be sure. 'I think I'd better call for someone to take a look. Do you have a first-aid kit?'

She stayed with Cliff until the paramedics arrived. Two men, one young, one middle-aged, both friendly and reassuringly competent. They'd cleaned and dressed the small cut, checked his vitals, got him up and moving around.

'As far as the cut goes, he's fine,' the older one — Nathan — reassured her. 'Is he prone to dizziness?'

'I don't think so. But he seems a bit groggy to me. He's not, usually.'

'He has a tablet he needs to take now. Do you know where they are?'

'Bathroom,' Cliff said from the bed. 'And I'm not groggy,' he snapped, shooting Callie a glare. 'Mind's clear as a bell.'

She exchanged disbelieving glances with Nathan. 'I'll take a look.' She went to the cupboard, found a small pharmacy. 'There's . . . Risperdal, Abilify, Seroquel — '

'That's the one,' Cliff called in a raspy voice. 'Need the Seroquel.'

She brought the packet out with a glass of water and handed it to the other paramedic, Chris, who read the label before handing Cliff one. 'This is all you need?'

'Taken the other stuff I have to take. Thanks.'

'Hold up.' Chris took another, closer look. 'These are Risperdal.' He got up and went back to the bathroom. 'Here's the Seroquel,' he called. 'Looks like your pills are in the wrong bottles.'

'Darn chemist must have mixed them up,' Cliff complained. 'Adelaide only just got the prescriptions filled the other day. Said there was some new hotshot chemist in town.'

'This is quite the collection,' Chris said. 'You're not taking all of these?'

'Doctor had me experimenting with different drugs at one point or other to see what worked best, that's all.'

Both paramedics checked the other containers. Nathan shook his head. 'I've put these in the right bottles. How about we throw away the ones you don't need, in case you get confused again? Then we'd be more than happy to take you to the hospital for the night, just to make sure you're feeling better.'

'Been taking my own meds most of my life, thanks very much! And I'm already feeling better. Lotta fuss over a bit of a trip.'

Nathan gestured for Callie to follow him out into the hall while Chris packed up. 'Under the circumstances I can't force him to come to hospital, and I'm pretty sure he's fine. Being a head wound though, if you're worried at all, you call us right back.'

'Thank you,' she said, and when Chris had come out, she led them to the door.

'Is that your father?' Nathan continued.

'No. Just an acquaintance really. I'm staying in the cottage you passed on your way in.'

'He's on some serious drugs. All those antipsychotics, mood stabilisers, antidepressants and tranquillisers have to be carefully dosed out and taken at the right intervals. If there's any chance he's not able to self-medicate correctly anymore, he's going to need ongoing assistance.'

'I'll talk to his daughter. Thanks for coming.' She showed them out, heated up Cliff's dinner and, finding a tray, took it up to him in bed.

His eyes were closed but he opened them when he heard her. 'Dinner. Thanks for this. And that.'

'You're welcome,' she replied, slightly surprised by his mild tone. 'I'll wait while you eat, take the tray for you. Would you like a fresh ice pack for your head?'

'No, it's good. Don't need it.'

She looked around the large room and, ignoring the mess, admired the high ceilings and decorative cornice. The old glass lightshade that hung from it was beautiful. 'Your house is lovely.'

'Got a history about it. All up in the tower if you're interested.'

'I'd love to see it sometime.'

'Would you mind locking the house up for me? Haven't had a chance tonight.'

She really didn't want to stay in the house any longer than necessary, but — 'Sure.'

'In the drawer here . . . next to me.'

She opened it, saw a large padlock with a key inserted.

'That's for the cellar. The door that goes under the stairs. Haven't been careful enough. Not for a long time. With you here, better it's locked tight.'

As if the house didn't freak her out enough.

Callie considered the comment as she took out the large padlock, and questioned how much more her nerves could take. 'No problem.'

She went into the hallway and peeked inside the two doors she'd passed on her way to finding him. Bedrooms, large and furnished in the nineteenth-century style of the house. She enjoyed the elegance of the old furniture, the layout of the rooms. Despite the creepy feeling the house exuded, she could see why Paisley had dreamt of turning the place into a bed and breakfast.

She reached the staircase, looked along the hall beyond. From what she could see, that end of the house would likely be a mirror image of this side. She took a step down, then looked up the staircase to her right and hesitated. Cliff had said she was welcome to check out the tower. Perhaps another time.

She went downstairs and at the back of the house past the dining room and kitchen she found two more large, unused rooms plus a laundry and downstairs bathroom. She quickly checked the windows and two back doors were locked and kept moving. Coming in from the other end of the lounge room, she switched on the light. The furnishings were as lovely as she remembered from her quick glance in when she'd been here with Paisley. Antique, and in remarkably good condition. Dusty, but nothing a polish wouldn't fix. She kept going, coming to the front entrance.

Telling herself it was silly to be scared of an empty room, Callie walked over to the cellar door. What was so dangerous about the cellar that it needed a padlock? She wondered why the original lock was arranged so it could be secured from inside, rather than the other way around, and reached out.

Bang!

Callie leapt backwards as the handle ripped from her light touch and slammed closed. She waited, heart thundering, ready for anything, but the silence had taken over again.

What the hell was that? Just what the *hell*? Unnerved, she turned and took the stairs two at a time to the first floor.

Cliff had finished his meal and again had his eyes closed. 'Was that you banging?'

'The cellar door just slammed shut in my hand!' she said in an almost accusatory tone.

His eyes opened. 'Draughts under the house. Damn door doesn't shut properly, then slams at the first whiff of wind.'

'Right,' she said, her whole body sagging at the perfectly reasonable explanation. 'Can I take that for you?'

'Oh, yes. Thanks,' he said sleepily. 'You know how to cook a lovely meal. Appreciate it.'

'That was Paisley's cooking, but it was a pleasure to bring it over.' Noticing he'd finished his water, she went into the bathroom and filled his. In order to ensure there was space for the glass on the bedside table, she picked up a chunk of what looked like charcoal but was surprised at its weight. It felt like stone.

'Don't move that!'

She almost dropped it as she jumped, then

resettled it in its place. 'Sorry. What is it?'

'You don't know a piece of black tourmaline when you see it?'

'Ah . . . it's not something I've ever encountered.'

He sent her a long look and shook his head. 'Just has to stay where it is, that's all. They all do.'

All? She took another look around the room, noticed more rocks on each end of the window ledge, a small one above the doorframe. As she looked closely, she saw a strange circle drawn on the frame below the stone. Uneasy again, Callie put on the best smile she could manage.

'Okay. I just want to make sure you can reach your water and the phone. I'll check on you in the morning. Will you be all right up here alone tonight?'

'Not ever alone in this house. Go home, lock up. Goodnight, Callie.'

'Goodnight.' She took the tray to the kitchen, then, back at the entrance, eyed the cellar door suspiciously. She slipped her hand into her jacket pocket and smoothed her fingers over the padlock still hidden in there.

'Oh, for heaven's sake,' she muttered. She pulled it out, slipped it through the metal clip and locked it in place. 'No monsters,' she berated herself, 'no ghosts.' But with Cliff's *Not ever alone in this house* reverberating in her head, she wasted no time getting back to the cottage. And she did lock up, taking one extra look over her shoulder as she went in.

Safely inside, she called Paisley to fill her in.

144

'He's fine, don't worry. I just thought you should know. But he was saying some weird things and the paramedic is worried about him managing his medication.'

'I'm going to have to move faster on finding him somewhere to live,' Paisley said. 'This just isn't safe anymore. Did you say Adelaide got the prescriptions filled for him?'

'Yeah. And apparently there's some new chemist in town she wasn't fond of or something.'

'Okay. Leave it with me, Callie . . . thanks.'

Callie hung up and made herself a cup of tea while she wondered again why it could be so important to lock the cellar. Why her being there made any difference. What did Cliff think he was locking out — or in? Unnerved, she got on the internet and looked up black tourmaline.

13

Connor stood in the frost-crisped paddock and stared down at the dead horse while a sick, churning horror rolled in his stomach.

'Was that Bailey?'

'Yep,' Logan said. Connor hadn't seen that look on his face too many times in the past. But when they found out who was responsible for this . . . perversity, there wasn't a doubt in his mind that the deranged mongrel was going to need protection.

'Indy?'

'On her way. She said to keep it quiet for the time being. Just until she's had a chance to see what she's dealing with.'

'Right.' He didn't want to look at what was stretched out in front of him, but it was beyond him to look away. His mind just couldn't process the image. The horse's throat had been slashed and symbols had been painted in blood on its neck and flanks. 'There's just nothing I can say.'

'He was a good horse. A sweet one. He didn't deserve this.'

Nothing Connor could think of deserved this. 'Of course he didn't. Here's Indy,' he said with relief, as her four-wheel drive bumped its way through the paddock towards them.

'Larissa and Harvey are due soon. Can you keep them busy while I deal with this?'

'Sure.' He sent Indy a token wave and trudged

back to the stables, his jeans soaked to mid-calf by the wet grass. He was gutted for Logan; Bailey had been one of his best school horses. Mounts like that were treasured and impossible to replace. More troubling was that some sicko had been on their place.

Harvey had already arrived and smiled when he saw Connor coming into the stables. 'Hi, Mr A.'

'Morning, Harvey.'

'Where's Logan?'

'Just taking care of something. He said you should get started as normal.'

'No worries.'

'Morning,' Larissa said, appearing behind Harvey. 'What's going on in the paddock?'

'Ah . . . ' *Shit*. He was going to have to tell them something. 'Look, Bailey died last night.'

'Bailey?' Larissa's eyes teared up.

There was a loud bang as Harvey dropped the wheelbarrow and stormed into one of the stables.

'Yeah, Logan's with him now. Do you know what to do until he gets back?'

'Yeah. Yeah, sure. I'll help get these horses out while Harvey cleans, then start feeding up.'

'Just, um . . . just put them in the yards. Don't head out into the paddock yet, okay?'

'Sure.'

Satisfied Larissa was under control, he walked to the next stable to find Harvey. 'Hey, you okay, mate?'

'Yeah.'

'He was a good horse.'

147

'The best.' When his voice broke, Harvey bit down hard on his lip.

'It's okay to be upset. I know Logan is. If you want to take a minute, a walk — '

Harvey shook his head. 'Rather work.'

'Okay.'

Just as Connor headed out again, Harvey asked, 'Did you find that guy yesterday?'

'What guy?'

'Dunno. Turned up asking if Orson was around. I said he was out with the rest of Cole's group. He asked if they'd be back today, told him no, just Fridays. He left.'

'He never showed — probably couldn't find us. Did he leave a name?'

'Nup.'

No one should be visiting the guys out here. And after finding Bailey like that any stranger turning up on the place had to be treated with suspicion. He'd mention it to Indy. 'What'd he look like?'

'Ugly son of a bitch. Black hair in, like, a military cut. Had a Tasmanian devil tatt on the inside of his arm here.' He pointed just above the inside of his wrist. 'It was pretty cool.'

Connor committed the description to memory. 'If he comes back, let Logan or I know straight away.'

'Okay.' He sniffed, turned his back to keep working.

'Harvey?'

'Yeah?'

'You're a good man. I'm glad we've got you.'

Connor went back to the office, and asked

148

Kaicey if the mystery visitor had turned up at reception. He hadn't. Then he let her know Bailey had died.

'When?'

'Overnight.'

'Oh.' As expected she looked sad, then the sadness abruptly turned to worry. 'Was Bailey Orson's horse?'

'Yeah, actually. Why?'

'And you said some guy had been down at the stables — looking for Orson.'

'Kaicey, jeez — you look like you've seen a ghost. Sit down.' He guided her to a chair. 'What's going on?'

'How did the horse die?'

'Can't say,' he replied, and if it sounded as though that meant there was no obvious cause, then so be it. Logan had said Indy wanted it kept quiet.

'Okay.' She breathed out a long sigh. 'Okay, then. Could have been natural causes, right? Most likely.'

'Why would you jump to any other conclusion?'

'Oh . . . just, you know . . . Orson tends to have a habit of bringing trouble with him.'

Orson had been worried about someone in the bush, had been asking strange questions. A lump of lead landed in Connor's stomach. 'Trouble you thought would kill a horse?' he asked, almost speechless.

'Oh — no. I haven't ever heard of anything like that,' she said. 'Really. Besides, you'd know, right? If someone had done something to the horse it would be obvious.'

'Yeah. Yeah, it would.' He wanted to tell her the truth to see if she had anything to say when she heard the details. But Logan had said Indy wanted it kept quiet. So he'd tell Indy, let her talk to Kaicey.

Disgusted, angry, upset, he went back outside, nearly barrelling into Tess.

'There you are!' she said happily. 'What happened to coming out to check on the garden last night? Callie's come back this morning to try and get that first garden done. Would you have time to check it out? Because I was thinking — '

'Sorry, Tess. I'll do what I can, but something's come up.'

Her easy smile fell. 'What's happened?'

'Come with me and I'll tell you.'

★ ★ ★

Connor finally made time to find Tess and Callie around mid-morning. It wasn't that the garden hadn't been on his mind, but other things had taken priority. Guests had had to be steered clear of police, the horse had needed to be put carefully onto a transport after arrangements had been sorted for an autopsy. All in all, it had been a pretty damn terrible start to the day.

In the hope of settling his stomach, he swallowed a mouthful of ham and cheese sandwich and headed for the gardens, wondering why he shouldn't just sit down and put his feet up for two seconds. He didn't even particularly enjoy gardening. But Tess had mentioned the

150

bigger trees would take a bit of manoeuvring, so he should help with those. Besides, he needed something to take the image of that poor animal out of his head. The more difficult the better.

So gardening. Callie. Who was she, anyway? Where had she come from? Tess had never mentioned her before. He sure as hell had never seen her around here. He'd been left with the impression he'd annoyed her by interrupting them yesterday. Those moss-green eyes had been cautious and cool, just like the conversation. He had to wonder why. No doubt when he spent some more time with her he'd figure it out and the fascination would wear off, but maybe by then the image of Bailey might have dulled a bit, too.

Tess and Callie were hard at work when he found them. Trees and plants stood in position in pots or already in the ground. Connor studied the arrangement, deciding he liked the mix of plants and colours. He tried to picture the garden in a year's time — in ten. It would be right in keeping with the established gardens, he decided.

Callie dropped the shovel into the soil with enough force that it stood up, then swung down to pick up a plant. With one tap the pot fell away and the plant was dropped into the hole and backfilled.

'There you are!' Tess said, and Callie glanced at him.

'Here I am.'

'Everything sorted out?' Tess asked with concern.

'As much as can be for now. Morning, Callie.'

This time when she looked up, she smiled briefly. 'Hi.'

'Sorry I didn't make it back yesterday. Got held up. This looks great.'

'It does,' Tess agreed with forced brightness. She hadn't looked at Bailey when she'd followed him back to the stables earlier. Hadn't wanted to. He was glad of it. 'Grab a shovel.'

'All right. Anything I need to know?' he asked Callie.

Another glance. 'You just move the pots to the side of where they're placed, put the hole under where they were sitting and fill them in.' *It's not rocket science*, her tone said.

He smiled for the first time all morning. 'Got it.' He headed straight for the larger trees and started digging while Callie grabbed another shovel. Tess chatted away, and though not quite her usual self, she did a good job of puncturing the silence while he admired Callie's easy competence and speed. There was a different vibe about her out here. She wasn't the cornered mouse he'd met in the staff room. She was out-planting him with practised skill and while he wouldn't have said there was anything graceful about gardening, watching the deftness of those hands, the smooth movement of her toned body, changed his mind. When Tess queried the watering, a thoughtful crease appeared on Callie's forehead as she mentioned sprinklers, drip lines and trenches for pipes.

When the plants were in they shovelled mulch into wheelbarrows then spread it thickly,

152

avoiding the areas where irrigation lines would need to be laid. Callie was taking notes, he realised, as every now and then she pulled out her phone.

'I know a fair bit of time and energy has already been put into shaping these beds,' Callie said at one point, 'but the next one along really needs to be extended by around two metres to accommodate a tree that can be underplanted, or it will lean out over the path. The grass will only ever be patchy underneath and look messy. And the bed behind that one shouldn't curve in on itself — it looks like it will make a nice little knoll, but it'll be a nightmare to get the mower around.'

'That'll mean more digging, reshaping with the machinery,' Connor said.

'I can operate earth-moving equipment. I have the certification.'

'Do you?' he said, impressed.

'Anyone want a drink?' Tess asked.

'I could use one,' Callie said.

'Be right back,' Tess said, and dropped her gloves on a nearby rock. 'Connor?'

'Wouldn't hurt, thanks.' Once Tess was on her way silence descended, so he decided to test the bounds of the big 'keep out' sign Callie may as well have had tattooed on her forehead. 'So, how do you know Tess?'

Callie hesitated briefly before dropping another load of mulch onto the edge of the garden. It took her another moment to answer. 'We ran into each other one day and got talking. She mentioned this, and I offered to help.' She chewed her lip. 'We're going to need more mulch.'

'We have a tonne of it around the back behind the machinery shed. I'll show you where everything is.'

'Okay.' She dusted off her hands. 'Lead the way.'

'So you have a landscaping business?' he asked as they walked.

'Used to.'

'What stopped you?'

'I got married.'

There it is, he told himself, and acknowledged his disappointment. Whatever thoughts had cautiously entered his mind would have to stay there. Perhaps she just didn't wear her ring when gardening. Made sense. 'Being married meant you couldn't own a business anymore?'

'My husband already had a business he needed help with.'

'Right. So from landscaper to . . . ?'

An annoyed frown marked her brow as she considered her answer. 'Business manager.'

'Sounds like past tense?'

'Yeah.' She smiled at him with her mouth, but not her eyes. 'It didn't work out.'

'The business or the marriage?'

'The marriage.' There was an impatience in her tone he knew he probably should have heeded.

'How come?'

She stopped walking and faced him, hands on hips. 'He died.'

And then he felt like a heel. 'I'm sorry.'

'I'm not.' Her tone left no room for misinterpretation.

'You're not?'

'At all,' she said. There was no thoughtful sidestepping or wall building here. She stared back, defiance lighting her features. 'Anything else?'

'I wouldn't dare,' Connor muttered. Fascination now shadowed by caution, he wondered who this woman was. He studied Callie covertly as she turned to continue their trek to the machinery shed, noticed the haunted look that slid across her face when she thought he wasn't watching. It had that niggle of recognition teasing him again. She really was lovely. But she was just a bit too thin, and though the full mouth and bright green eyes looked made for laughter, her cheeks were hollow, her eyes lightly shadowed. And was her skin naturally that pale? He wondered how long ago her husband had died, and what had happened to put the defensive tone in her voice and the miserable expression on her face.

It shouldn't matter. He should mind his own business and leave Callie and her obvious dislike of him alone. At least until he knew more about her. And he wanted to know more about her.

Wanted to know more than he had about any woman in a long time.

*   *   *

'Happy?' Callie asked Tess and Connor a couple of hours later. They hadn't finished, but they'd planted all the plants, got the mulching mostly completed.

155

'Very,' Tess agreed, 'because one, it's going to look like it's supposed to, and two, it's getting done quickly. Thanks.' Then to Connor she said, 'I think Callie should officially be responsible for the gardens.'

'I thought she already was,' he said.

'*All* the new gardens.'

Callie noticed Connor's slight hesitation, no doubt brought on by her earlier outburst.

But he nodded and asked her, 'Are you looking for more work?'

She could see the value in finishing the job, in taking the promotional photos she'd thought about. It would be a great start. She'd been here two days and no one had looked at her twice, so it didn't seem like being recognised would be an issue. 'I suppose I could be,' she said. 'I only offered initially because I enjoy it and Tess needed some help. But . . . '

'But you will?' Tess finished for her.

'You'll want to see my rates,' she decided.

'Hearing them would do,' Connor said. 'What are we looking at?'

Callie scrambled to work it out — she hadn't completely settled on her rates yet, so she quoted on the high side of what she was hoping for.

Connor nodded. 'Sounds fair.'

'Excellent!' Tess said.

'And tell me what supplies you need for the irrigation,' Connor continued. 'I'll get them ordered for you asap.'

'I'll have to get back to you on that. I would usually quote you on costs, do the ordering myself.'

156

'Even better.' He held out a hand. 'Good to have you on board.'

'Thanks.' Callie wondered what it was about the man that made her feel so damn insecure, and why, after her earlier comments, he'd want anything to do with her. But she shook. His large, callused hand completely engulfed hers for a moment, then released her. 'It won't take long.'

'Would you like to come back up to the guesthouse for a drink to celebrate?' Tess asked.

'Not today,' she said. She'd be more comfortable going back to the cottage and starting a fire. Especially considering the state of her clothes. 'But thanks. Another time.'

'Sure,' Tess said. 'See you Monday?'

'I'll be here.' Callie dusted herself off and smiled a goodbye, then went back to her car. She was already thinking about what she'd need to order for the project. She'd taken enough notes to pull together a pretty good estimate and wondered if there was a local stockist Connor would prefer to use so she could contact them over pricing. This was exciting. Progress. Getting her life back on track looked like it would happen quicker than she'd planned. No doubt all the weird little things that had been worrying her about Waldron Park would fade away with some routine and structure to her days. With a job to do.

She wasn't entirely happy to see Ned waiting for her when she pulled in at the cottage.

'Callie,' he said, getting up from one of the patio chairs and giving her a brilliant smile. 'I was wondering when you were going to get back.'

'Hi, Ned,' she said with as much enthusiasm as she could muster. 'What's up?'

'Dad said you took care of him after his fall last night.'

She walked to the door, key in hand, and smiled briefly. 'It was no trouble.'

'I appreciate it. A lot. You could have called me.'

'I called Paisley,' she told him. 'I thought you wanted her to monitor that sort of thing.'

'Yeah, but I can help.'

She opened the door and walked in. 'Okay, well in that case . . . the paramedics said you should get rid of the meds your dad doesn't need.'

He looked blank, then shook his head. 'Paisley'll take care of that. Can I take you out to dinner to thank you?'

Okay, she needed to nip this in the bud. 'Oh, Ned. That's very nice of you. But it's not necessary.'

'I don't mind. I'd enjoy it.'

'Ned, I really don't — '

'Think about what night suits,' he said over her protest. 'Let me know. Oh, and I brought your dish back from Dad's and the travel cup. I washed them. Here.' He picked them up from the table behind him and handed them to her.

'Thanks.' Arms full, she hooked a foot behind the door on her way to closing it. 'Bye.'

'So you like my dad then?'

Was he kidding? With a sigh, she slid the dish

158

and cup onto the side table, and realised he was following her in. 'Huh? Oh, I don't really know Cliff yet. But I think he's warming to me. A bit.' She stood her ground, hoping he'd take the hint.

Instead, Ned leant against the door frame as though settling in for a chat. 'He wasn't always so mad at the world. He was good to all of us. Better than . . . well, Mum had other interests.'

'I'm sorry to hear that.'

'You like the house?' He nodded towards it.

'It's beautiful.'

'It was going to be mine, one day. Paisley would have gotten her share, of course, but it's a big house. Plenty big enough for a couple of families. Guess now we'll get to share a spot in a retirement home instead,' he joked. 'Doesn't matter much. Never got around to getting married. Not yet, anyway.' When his eyes met hers again they were warm. 'Open to it though.'

Ugh. She fought back the shudder. How was she going to be kind *and* get rid of him? She trod carefully. 'Once was enough for me. I don't even see any casual relationships in my near future to be honest.'

He nodded thoughtfully. 'Sometimes you don't see what's right in front of you. Doesn't mean there's nothing there.'

What an odd statement. 'Okay, well . . . I'll see you later.'

'Yeah. No worries. Let me know when you want to do that dinner,' he said.

She didn't bother to answer, just kept her polite smile on long enough to get the door closed.

The shudder she finally allowed herself wasn't quite a convulsion. The long looks, that suggestive pushiness, made her skin crawl. But she didn't want to embarrass Ned nor hurt his feelings. The guy had issues, she reminded herself. But he wasn't threatening in any way.

Threatening. There was something about Connor Atherton that had felt threatening, but only to her equilibrium. She'd wanted to close a door on him too. It had been challenging to hold her own under that steady, penetrating stare of his — and all that questioning. To keep her cool under the relentless interest. She'd felt attracted and — damn it — *vulnerable.*

Callie flopped on the lounge and scowled. What a stupid, crappy thought. Never again. That's what she'd promised herself. And yet she'd been down here five minutes and one frustratingly nosey, though admittedly rather hot, male had her all restless and worked up.

'Idiot,' she muttered and got up to retrieve her laptop. As she was — for some reason — thinking about him, she may as well figure out what she was going to need for his garden.

She worked for a long while, and by the time she finished it was getting on the late side for dinner, so she threw together a couple of ham and cheese omelettes, added salad to the plates, then rugged herself up and took one over to Cliff.

'Thought you'd forgotten me,' Cliff complained when he opened the door. 'Thanks.'

'No problem. How's the head?'

'All better. Was good of you. Not surprising, I

160

suppose.' He took the meal. 'See you tomorrow then.'

And Callie was presented with the door. She couldn't help but laugh. Progress was progress.

14

Working at Calico Mountain, Callie decided as she looked over her latest garden bed, was turning out to be exactly what she'd needed. She saw Tess a lot, but barely a hint of Connor. He'd stopped to say hi when he'd caught Callie and Tess eating in the staff room on Tuesday, and he'd sent her a wave yesterday as he'd driven past where she was working, but he never hung around, always seemed to be busy. And that was a good thing, as the little leap he encouraged in her pulse whenever he appeared hadn't worn off. And while it wasn't as though she particularly wanted that leap, she couldn't deny it was good to know she could still experience one. She was feeling generally better in lots of ways now she was working again and had people to talk to. Getting away from Waldron Park.

Though Callie had arrived early this morning, Tess had already been outside with a small gathering of people near the guesthouse. A tour group, Callie guessed. Tess had mentioned some of the places they took the guests, and she'd made them sound worth a visit. Perhaps when Callie had some time she'd venture out. She was already in love with the natural beauty of Tasmania, and she'd barely seen any of it. She pressed a groundcover plant into the earth among some low rocks. The cool blue of the prostrate conifer would spill out into the space perfectly.

'Callie!' Tess called as she jogged over. 'Early start.'

'It's a nice day. I wanted to make the most of it. What are you up to?'

'I have to do a run out to Cradle Mountain this morning. That's what all those people out the front are waiting for. I'll be gone until mid-afternoon. Is everything okay here?'

'Yes, of course.'

'Great. There's something I want to discuss with you but we're already pushing it for time. So can we speak when I get back this afternoon?'

'No problem,' Callie said. A man in a hoodie was standing at the back of the group bound for Cradle Mountain, and didn't quite seem to fit in. He was staring right at them. Her nerves jumped. *Who is that?* Between the sun rising at his back, the way people were milling around and that hoodie he was wearing, she just couldn't make out his face. The way he stood, watching, reminded her of the man who had done the same thing back in the Hunter, at the courthouse, at her gates. But it couldn't possibly be, could it?

'Oh, damn!' Tess said, sliding her hands into her jacket and dragging Callie back to the conversation. She pulled out a portable hard drive in a plastic case, looked around. Grimaced.

'What's wrong?' Callie felt compelled to ask, reluctantly taking her eyes off the man. She thought he looked a little on the thin side to be the same man. Probably a bit too rangy.

163

'Could you possibly do me a favour?'

'Um . . . sure?'

'I was supposed to give this to Indy at breakfast, but I didn't see her. Can you run it down to the stables? If you give it to Logan, he'll pass it on,' Tess said, handing the hard drive to Callie. 'Tell him Indy will know what it is.'

Indy? Logan? Callie didn't know who they were. 'Sure, I guess. But where are the stables?'

'Just around the bend through the trees on the other side of the last garden bed,' Tess said, pointing further down the drive. 'Can't miss it. Thanks!'

'No worries.' Tess left and Callie's attention went back to the stranger. She walked around the trees, keeping an eye on him, almost expecting at any moment that he'd stop pretending to be part of the group and make a break for her. She was so damn sure of it she changed her grip on the shovel, her only weapon.

The man swiftly turned as Tess arrived back at the bus and headed for the guesthouse.

Okay, Callie thought, relieved. *I'm fine.* He was probably just some random guy checking Tess out.

Connor came down the front steps talking to a group of hikers. The stranger turned again, back towards the parking area. Then he got into a car and sat, watching. *Weird*, Callie thought, her overactive imagination keeping her occupied as she decided whether it was safe or not to forget about him. Connor was over there. If there was any trouble she could just yell.

As though sensing her gaze, Connor looked up

164

and met her eyes. Damn it — now he was going to think she was spying on him. Did he really have to look up at that particular moment? She turned her back on him and started digging.

'Morning,' she heard a minute later.

This is what you get . . . She turned just enough to send him a small smile. 'Morning.'

'I paid the invoice for the garden materials. Some interesting stuff in there.'

She stopped digging and lifted her brow. 'Is there a problem?'

'Beats me. I didn't know what half that chemical-sounding stuff was.'

'Chemical-sounding stuff?' she asked, puzzled. 'You mean the soil additives, fertilisers? They're not — ' No, she wasn't about to get into a discussion about it. Instead she went for simple. 'They'll give your plants a good start. The soil is okay here but it could do with a boost. And I need to break up the clay base in garden five.'

'Who knew?' he said with wonder. 'I've always thought it was just a matter of digging a hole and putting a plant in it, maybe giving it a bit of water, letting mother nature take care of the rest. You really know your stuff.'

Horrified for whatever trees he may ever have planted, she restrained her reaction to a shrug. 'It's my job,' she said.

'Did Tess tell you she wouldn't be around today?'

'It's not a problem. I like working on my own.'

'I should take the hint?' he guessed with a grin. 'What are you up to now?'

As he clearly had no intention of leaving,

Callie leant on the shovel and pointed to the plants nearby. 'I'm going to plant out a lot of those azaleas on this long bank. Do you want mixed colours, or a couple of big blocks of single colour? I only ask because more than half of what you have in stock is pink. I need to use them up. Are you okay with that?'

'That's completely your call.'

'Okay. Helpful. What if I run the pink around the corner, mix the colours in front?'

His grin flashed. He was cute when he smiled like that, and was that a dimple? How could such a strongly constructed face hide a dimple? *God, Callie.*

'Seriously, you're the landscaper, so either way,' Connor said.

Her hands went to her hips and, though frustrated with him, she laughed. 'Do you have *any* opinion on what you like?'

'Not when it comes to gardens,' he said. She wasn't sure if she imagined the innuendo or not. 'Though . . . I went to Cairns once,' he continued. 'They had this Balinese setup. Lots of palms and tropical stuff. I liked that.'

'Then you'd better move a lot further north. In the meantime, I'll assume it's fine to do whatever I like.' She stacked some empty pots and tossed them in the wheelbarrow. 'You think you might take that hint now?'

She heard his chuckle, felt an answering smile creep back onto her face.

'Tess thought you might need some help getting those advanced trees you brought over yesterday into the ground.'

166

'They're for the next part of the garden. I'm not up to that yet.'

'Will you be up to it today?'

'Possibly. Later.'

'Okay. Let me see you move them by yourself and I'll leave you in peace.'

There was no way she could lift them, damn it. 'We brought them over with the bobcat.'

'And Logan's got that out in the paddock. So pass me a shovel and tell me where to dig the hole.'

'Okay. I guess we could get it done — '

The stranger was out of the car again. Staring again.

'Callie?'

'What?'

'Is everything okay?'

She watched as the stranger turned and walked up the guesthouse steps. After a quick internal debate she decided she should say something. 'Look ... I'm prone to being paranoid ... '

'So what are we dealing with, like, tin foil on the head in case the aliens read your mind? Or are you just really worried about too much pink on the corner? We can buy more plants. Different colours. Whatever you need.'

'Ha. No,' she said, one eye on the stranger, who was now at the top of the guesthouse steps. 'Do you want to hear what I was going to say?'

'Of course,' he said removing any sign of amusement from his face. 'Go ahead.'

'There's a guy.'

'Does he have a name?'

'I'm sure he does — I don't know it. Listen!' she added when he laughed. 'The guy was hanging around before with the Cradle Mountain group. He seemed to be watching Tess, then when she went back over he turned away and kind of faded into the background. He looked like he was heading for the guesthouse, but when you walked out, he quickly turned around and walked back to his car. He sat there while Tess and the group left, while you hung around on the steps talking to those hikers, then since you got here he's been fussing around, keeping an eye on us. Now he's practically bolted into the guesthouse.'

'Okay . . . that doesn't particularly sound like paranoia,' he said much more seriously. 'What did he look like?'

'Tall, all in black. I couldn't see his face. He had a hoodie on.'

'I think I'd better go check it out. You're okay here?'

'Of course.'

Connor strode away, his face grim. Callie was pretty sure he had an idea of who the man might have been and wondered what was going on. She nervously played with the drive Tess had given her. Something to do with that? She supposed she should find the stables and hand it over.

She headed in the direction Tess had indicated and stopped briefly at the busy farmyard of assorted animals to pet a cute black steer that greeted her with a snort and a stretch of his neck over the fence. He'd been watching the goings on in the garden since she'd arrived and she'd planned on coming down to see him and the other animals at some stage. There was a plaque on the gate suggesting this was Monte, so she greeted him by name and scratched him behind one ear.

'He loves that. It's his favourite spot for a scratch.'

She spun around, startled, to see an impressive cowboy-type carrying feed buckets across the yard towards her.

'Sorry. Didn't mean to scare you,' he said with an easy smile.

'He's very cute.'

'My wife's favourite. She raised him from a baby.' He stopped next to her and gave Monte a rub on the neck before dropping feed into a container in his yard. Monte stayed put a few more seconds, enjoying the scratch, before dropping his head to eat.

'Spoilt steer. There's plenty of grass, isn't there?'

The man smiled and nodded. 'Spoilt steer. I'm Logan. I run the stables and the cattle business. And this little menagerie.'

'Little?' There were multiple yards with chickens, ducks, geese, sheep, a goat, a couple of steers other than Monte, a jersey cow, two black and white pigs, a tiny spotted pony and — 'Is that a llama?'

'Yeah, it is. We were thinking alpaca but that guy needed rehoming so — llama.'

'It's quite the collection.'

'Don't get me started,' he said without heat. 'Are you staying here?'

'No, but I was looking for you — sort of. Tess gave me something to pass on to Indy.'

'Indy? Yeah, of course. And you are?'

'Oh, sorry — I'm Callie.'

Logan's gaze flickered. 'Indy mentioned you. You're staying in Cliff Waldron's cottage.'

'That's me,' she admitted. 'But I don't know Indy.'

'She and Tess are close. Tess must have mentioned it. Indy's at the stables. Let me run you down there.'

'Oh, I can just give these to you, Tess said — '

'You've already walked all the way over here and I'm sure Indy would like to say hi. It's no problem.'

She wondered why, but agreed. 'Okay then.'

He gestured to a white ute. 'Jump in.'

She supposed it was safe enough.

'So you're the new gardener?' Logan asked as he started the ute and rolled down the drive.

'I needed something to do and Tess needed help so . . . ' She shrugged.

'What you've done so far looks great.'

'Thanks.'

They reached a large stable building and a young woman in a polo, jeans and work boots came out. 'Logan, are you still doing that lesson at nine?'

'Yeah. We'll use Gypsy.'

'I'll have her ready.'

'Thanks.' Then to Callie he said, 'This way.' He opened a gate and she followed him into a paddock. 'Are you enjoying being out at Waldron Park?'

'Sure. I needed somewhere to stay for a while and Paisley's coming back soon.'

'When?'

'A few weeks.'

'How are you finding old Cliff?'

'Okay. Why?'

'Just wondering. It's been a long time since I've seen him.' He was leading her towards a tractor standing in the middle of a paddock that was partly slashed. She didn't see the woman up to her elbows in the engine until they had almost reached it. Music — loud rock — was coming from inside the cabin. 'She's fixing my tractor.'

Logan flicked off the noise and the woman in the snug jeans with the short brown ponytail looked up, eyebrows raised.

'You want me to fix this scrap metal, I need music.'

He walked around, snatched her to him and pressed a firm kiss on her lips. 'Callie needs to talk to you.'

'Callie?' Indy looked around Logan and smiled. 'Hi.' She wiped her hands, dropping the rag on the side of the machine. 'Good to meet you.'

'Hi,' Callie said. 'Tess asked me to give you this. She said you'd know what it was about.'

Indy took the hard drive. 'Right. More security footage.' She put it in her pocket. 'Looks like Bessie's going to have to wait.' She gave the tractor a pat and closed it up. 'Thanks.'

'No problem.'

Sharp blue eyes considered Callie in a way

171

that had her wondering if Tess had told Indy who she was. 'You've had a pretty rough time of it. How are you holding up down here?'

'Okay, so far.' That answered that question. Did that mean Logan knew too? Connor? How many other people already knew who she was? 'Everyone's being very nice.'

Indy took a sip from her water bottle and nodded, before walking back to the gate. 'We have it on good authority the trial came out the right way.'

Callie followed. 'Whose authority?'

'Pat Langdon.'

Had she missed something? 'You know the detective who ran my case?'

'I've worked with her in the past.' Indy put down the water bottle and leant against the gate, folded her arms. 'She's a good cop.'

'I don't understand. How — '

'Indy's a detective,' Logan said. 'Used to work in Sydney before she came down here.'

'Aren't you a mechanic?'

'Sometimes,' Indy said with a grin.

'She multitasks,' Logan explained, then let them through the gate. 'I need breakfast. You want a lift back?'

'Oh — no, it's fine, thanks. I like to walk.'

'If you need anything, let me know,' Indy said.

'Thanks.' Callie watched them disappear in the ute. Nice people who knew who she was and what she'd done and were still prepared to give her a go. Potential new friends. But were too many people finding out about her too fast? Could this get out of hand?

172

★ ★ ★

Connor didn't waste any time getting back to the guesthouse. It sounded for all the world like Callie had been describing Orson, and if it was, he was probably sneaking in to see Kaicey. But there was also a chance their mystery visitor had come back. Either way, he needed to find out what was going on.

He heard the commotion as soon as he hit reception.

'You shouldn't be here!' Ned was telling Orson while Kaicey stood behind the desk, chewing her fingernail, a worried expression on her face.

'You are! What's the difference?'

'That's enough!' Connor hissed, approaching them. 'There are guests walking around. Can we keep it down?'

'We need to talk,' Orson said to Kaicey and Ned more quietly — desperately.

'You don't get to tell us what to do!' Kaicey whispered forcefully.

'Orson, you need to leave,' Connor said. 'I told you it was up to Kaicey if she wanted to talk to you. You shouldn't have come in here.'

'I really just need to talk to her for five minutes. Or Ned. Can I talk to Ned?'

'No,' Kaicey said.

'Do you want to die?' Orson asked urgently. 'Because if you don't come with me — '

Stunned, Connor grabbed him and dragged him around the corner, out of sight of the entry. 'Did you just threaten her?'

Kaicey came out of the reception door. 'Stop!' she said. 'Please. He's not threatening me. He's just having one of his episodes. Probably hasn't taken his meds.'

Connor carefully released him. 'Episodes?'

'I wouldn't hurt Kaicey,' Orson said as though stunned at the idea. 'I wouldn't hurt anyone. I'm sorry. I didn't mean to cause trouble.'

'But you snuck in here when I wasn't looking because you knew I wouldn't approve,' Connor said.

'I'm sorry,' he said again. 'I just wanted to talk to her. To them. I *have* to.'

'I'll talk to you,' Ned said. 'On the way back to your car. Let's go.'

'But — ' Connor began.

'It's all right, boss. I've got this.'

Orson sent Kaicey one last look and gave Connor another apology before walking out with Ned.

Connor watched them go, saw Orson talking desperately with Ned as they went down the steps. He was angry and over it. And worried.

'You ready to tell me what all that's about yet?' he snapped at Kaicey.

'I — I told you. Having him here is risky.'

'You said 'episode'.'

'Orson suffers from a delusional disorder. It can make him overly suspicious and nervy. He used to have to take medication. I guess he still would.'

Cole had said something about anxiety, but a delusional disorder? 'I'll talk to Cole. This wasn't mentioned.'

174

'His parents used to have to spend a heap of dollars on therapy and meds. I know it cost them a fortune even with Medicare rebates and stuff. Maybe you should ask Cole if he still has access to all that.'

'Will do.' Connor spotted Indy and Logan coming into the guesthouse. 'Thanks, Kaicey.'

She nodded and went back behind the reception desk.

'Morning,' Indy said.

'Hi, got a minute?' he asked.

'As long as I can eat and talk, sure,' she said. 'Let's get breakfast.'

15

'Last one.' Tess put the lavender in the ground and Callie filled in the soil around it. The shuttle had gotten back about an hour before and Tess had come straight over to help. 'I think mass planting them in this corner was a good idea. They'll fill the gaps in this space in no time.'

They stepped back to study the work on the second garden bed before Tess looked at Callie. 'You're good.'

'You did a lot of that yourself, and you have a good groundsman. He was pretty spot on with plant varieties and numbers.'

'Actually, we don't. Bob's got months more rehab to go and he's nearly seventy. He's decided to retire. We're shouting him and his wife dinner in the restaurant on Friday week as a thank you and goodbye. You should come.'

The Friday Tess was talking about would have been Callie and Dale's anniversary. They'd done something lavish and special every year, usually something Dale had thoughtfully planned. He'd known her so well, had never disappointed her. And he'd always looked more pleased than she was when he saw how much she enjoyed his thoughtfulness. How could he have turned out to be a violent murderer? That Dale and her Dale still didn't gel in her mind. Perhaps they never would.

'Thanks,' she said, with every intention of

skipping the dinner. She wouldn't be good company. 'We should keep at this.'

'I asked Connor to help you get those big trees in. He didn't make it?'

'He was here and was going to but something came up. Besides, it's not necessary. You don't hire someone to do a job then do it yourself.'

'Callie, those trees weigh a tonne. If you were ordering plants yourself you'd order manageable ones, or at least organise for help to get them in, right?'

'True.'

'Well, all that didn't happen. So Connor will help. It won't hurt him, he's strong as an ox.'

As if Callie needed reminding of how built the guy was.

'The ox is back,' Connor said, arriving behind them. To Callie he said, 'Sorry I just disappeared.'

'It's fine,' she said. 'We don't need you.'

He picked up a shovel anyway. 'I haven't been put in my place since this morning I suppose,' he muttered.

She smiled an apology. 'I'm sorry. That wasn't meant to be rude.'

'I can handle it,' Connor said. 'You want to get those trees in now?'

'Okay, sure.'

Callie admired the muscles that moved and strained under his shirt as he lifted and placed the heavy trees. Acknowledged the little tug in her stomach. Dale had been handsome, perhaps more so than Connor, but in a refined, softer way. Connor's raw masculinity and sharp good

177

looks were sexier. And difficult to ignore, even in the place her mind was at. She knew it was crazy to think she'd enjoy another serious relationship. She didn't think she had it in her to blindly trust again, besides, who'd want to be with a murderer? But she could look, maybe even dream a little, and still keep Connor — and anyone else who came along — at a safe enough distance. Hopefully in time, everything else about her life could return to normal. It would be nice if she could have her natural hair colour back, stop hiding behind caps and sunglasses. That would be enough for her. And it would come. In time she'd put the props away. This was just the beginning.

'This is looking good.'

Callie groaned inwardly at the sound of Ned's voice behind her. 'Hi, Ned.'

'Boss, Tess,' Ned said to the others. 'You want to hang around tonight, have that meal?' he asked Callie. 'The restaurant here is very good. Not too busy on a Monday.'

'I can't,' she said. 'I have to get back to the cottage. Your dad relies on me to get his dinner for him each night.'

Ned's mouth turned downwards. 'Coped well enough before you got here.'

'On microwave meals.' She heard the judgemental tone leach into her voice and pulled it back. 'I don't mind. But thanks for the offer.'

'How about a quick drink then?'

'I have to drive.'

'Just one?'

Oh, hell, he looked so damn devastated. And

Connor was watching intently. Did he think Callie was being mean? Maybe if she just had a drink with Ned he'd leave her alone. Maybe that was a way out — the lesser of the two evils?

'Sure,' she conceded. 'Just a quick one at five, okay? I really do need to get back.'

Ned's whole face radiated with his smile. 'I'll see you up there.'

When he walked away Callie sighed and dropped her head back to stare at the sky. Connor's chuckle had her head spinning in his direction. 'What?'

'You look like you just agreed to host your own funeral.'

Her mouth opened and closed several times before she opted for the nicest comment that came to mind. 'He's lovely. He's helpful. He's Paisley's brother. But he's also . . . It's awkward. He won't leave me alone.'

Connor nodded. 'You're the latest crush.'

'Latest?'

'Ned is as sweet as they come,' Tess reassured her, 'but . . . you don't want to encourage him.'

'I wasn't!' she said, mortified.

'I know,' Tess said, 'but Ned's idea of encouragement compared to yours and mine is a little different. He has a habit of forming attachments to people.'

Callie had pretty much figured that out, but waited silently for Tess to elaborate.

Tess let out a laugh. 'Now I've worried you. He's completely harmless, but he can get a bit . . . inappropriately pushy if he decides he likes you. Best way to keep it simple if he asks you out

179

is to be very clear you're not interested.'

'I thought I had. His dad had a fall the other night and Ned wanted to take me out to dinner as a thank you for helping out. I told him it wasn't necessary, but he's insistent. I was kind of hoping if I just had a quick drink with him he'd stop pestering me. What are my chances?'

'Slim to none,' Tess said.

Connor dropped his shovel into the earth and checked his watch. 'It's almost four. If I shoot off now and do a couple of things, I can meet you for that drink, add a third person to the equation.'

'Why would you do that?' Callie blurted.

'Oh, so paranoid,' he teased, wiping his brow. 'Call it a small thanks for the work you did before we made this official. You know where the bar is?'

'I'll take her up,' Tess said. She was watching her brother with interest.

'Right, I'll see you there.'

'Why were you looking at him like that?' Callie had to ask.

Tess's eyes danced with amusement. 'He's just acting a little out of character. Let's get stuck into this part, head in a bit early and wash up before drinks.'

They worked fast, and by the time they went up to the guesthouse to wash, Callie wasn't really sure her appearance was satisfactory to be sitting in the bar. Even after she'd washed her face and hands and tidied her hair, she still looked like she'd been gardening all day. The bar area was just too lovely: quietly classy with

180

floor-to-ceiling views of the mountains.

Logan was already there and waved them over. 'Heard we were having drinks,' he told them. 'Connor's on his way. What will you have, Callie?'

'I'll stick to Diet Coke, thanks.'

While Logan was at the bar, Connor came in, freshly showered. There was that tug again. She felt it amp up several notches.

'Where's Logan?' Connor asked, taking a seat beside her.

He smelled of something slightly woodsy. His thick hair was damp and curling slightly at the edges and she wondered what it would feel like to run her fingers through it. *Damn it, Callie, what is wrong with you?*

'Getting me a Diet Coke.'

'Everything okay?'

'Should I be in here dressed like this?' she asked, as it was the first thing that came to mind.

He looked her over, and damn if it didn't send a shimmer of electricity through her.

'The management will make an exception,' he reassured her. 'On this occasion.'

There was nothing she could do — she just hoped she didn't smell the way she looked. Just in case, she shifted as far away from Connor as she could. 'I hope Ned isn't late. I really need to get back for Cliff.'

'It was kind of you to agree to this,' Tess said. 'Maybe not wise, but kind.'

'I already told him I wasn't interested,' Callie objected. 'When he talked to me about his inheritance and all but proposed. Other than carving it in stone and hitting him over the head with it, I'm not sure how else to get through. And I hate hurting people's feelings.'

Connor coughed and eyed her sceptically. She narrowed her eyes and the cough became a grin.

'There is another way,' Tess teased. 'Ned had a thing for Indy when she arrived. When Logan showed an interest in her, he backed off.'

'Showed an interest?' Callie repeated in a small voice. She glanced at Connor, who was watching her thoughtfully. 'Are you suggesting . . . '

Connor's warm, amused eyes met hers. 'Want to play pretend?'

'Uh . . . no!' And because it came out so definitively, she added, 'Thanks, but — '

Over the top of Connor's head, she saw Ned come in and give her a once-over.

'Callie,' Ned said. 'You ready to get that drink?'

'Here we go,' Logan said, returning with a tray of drinks and placing hers in front of her, before handing out the others. 'What are you after, Ned?'

'I was planning on a drink with Callie.'

'Pull up a chair,' Connor suggested. 'We all had the same idea at the same time.'

Ned's lips pressed together in a thin line. 'Suppose so.' He sat down.

'I'll get you a beer,' Logan offered and went back to the bar.

Tess told an anecdote about a few tree-climbing kids in her tour group earlier that day.

Connor followed it up with a report on the rehab program and Ned's sour mood slowly levelled. Logan got him another beer, and the conversation continued, easy and flowing.

Callie excused herself as the sun started to lower outside. 'I really have to get going. This was fun. See you, Ned.'

'Right. I'll walk you . . . ' he began but Connor was already on his feet.

'I just need to pinch you for two more minutes before you leave,' he told Callie.

'Okay, sure.'

When they were out of sight, she said, 'Thanks for that.'

'It's okay,' Connor said. 'I appreciate you don't want to hurt his feelings. It says a lot about who you are.'

A little embarrassed, she stepped back, looked around. 'Why did you bring me this way anyway?'

'I'll show you.' He led her into the kitchen, found a stack of takeaway containers and handed her some. 'Go fill these up from the buffet. Make up a few different meals for Cliff, give him one tonight and stick some more in his freezer for any night you can't get out there. Beats microwave meals.'

Hell. He'd just layered gratitude on top of attraction. 'Okay. Thanks.'

'Any time.' He led the way out. 'And if you need anything else, just let me know.'

'Why?'

He nearly ran into her when she stopped and spun.

'Why?' he asked slowly. 'Because ... I'm trying to be helpful?'

'As long as you don't think — I mean — I ... ' Now what? It was going to sound pretty obnoxious if she blurted out she wouldn't sleep with him despite his offer of a couple of takeaway containers. Shit. 'I just don't want to give anyone the wrong idea,' she finally said.

His brow shot up. 'If I made you uncomfortable with that offer to get Ned off your back, I apologise.'

'No, of course not,' she said, embarrassed. 'Sorry, I think Ned just got to me.' She laughed self-consciously. 'I'm going to go home. See you. And thanks again.'

* * *

Connor walked back towards the bar, a small smile on his face at the thought he might have flustered Callie — in a good way — at least a little bit, because she sure as hell had managed to get under his skin.

'Hey.'

He turned to see Indy approaching.

'Is Logan with you?'

'Yeah, just having a drink. We needed to play interference. What are you up to?'

'I've been looking at the footage Tess gave me, trying to pick up anything from the night Bailey died, and I got your message about Orson, and wanted to let you know I'd requested a history. What do you mean 'interference'?'

'Ned's developed a bit of a thing for Callie. He

was pestering her for a dinner, which whittled down to a drink, so we crashed the party.'

'You did? Smooth. Which reminds me. Did I see you gardening earlier?'

He had a pretty good idea where this was going and bit back the groan, then tried for casual. 'Yeah. So?'

Indy's expression was pure innocence. 'Just asking. Callie's doing a good job.'

'You've met her?'

'This morning.' Then she smiled again as though enjoying some private thought. 'You surprise me sometimes. I get a good vibe from her, but, you know. Just be careful. Until we get to know her a bit better.'

He frowned at that. 'I'm helping plant a few trees. I think my chances of survival are pretty good.'

'That's the spirit.' Her phone rang, so she pulled it out. 'I'll see you in there.'

Damn it, he was missing something — something Indy thought he must already know. Which meant Tess knew. He'd have to tackle her about it.

Kaicey had joined the others in the bar. He sat back down, ignoring the scowl Ned sent him.

'All these irregular days off haven't been properly logged,' Kaicey was saying to Ned. 'We'll have to get it straightened out.'

'Going out to help Dad until tomorrow arvo. We could discuss it tomorrow night — I'll be back for dinner. Catch me then if you want.'

'If that'll get it done. Does seven-thirty suit?'

'It does. Right then,' Ned said with another

unfriendly look for Connor. 'Got things to do. Evening, all.'

'Is Ned giving you a hard time over the roster?' Connor asked Kaicey.

Kaicey rolled her eyes. 'I only want him to tell me when he's taken time off. Anyone would think I was asking him to cut off a limb.'

'It's just that he probably can't remember,' Connor said. 'Don't stress too much. He's never baulked at putting in the overtime when needed.'

'You're the boss.'

'Indy's here,' Connor told Logan. 'She's on the phone outside.'

Logan drained his beer. 'Better go find her. Before I do . . . ah . . . you got anything to tell me?'

'Us,' Tess said.

Was he going to cop this from all sides? Really? 'What do you mean?'

'You seem to be spending a lot of time in the garden,' Logan said.

For the first time since Bailey's discovery, Connor saw humour in his brother's expression, so he kept the annoyance out of his own. 'It's not so bad. Gardening I mean.'

'Great. About time you . . . developed a new interest. I'll say this for you, you know how to pick 'em. I'll see you later.' Logan grinned again and wandered away.

Connor sighed. He wasn't worried about the unwarranted hassling over Callie — he wouldn't have expected anything less and denying it would undoubtedly make it worse. But what the heck was going on?

'Indy and Logan seem to know something about Callie that I don't,' he said to Tess.

Tess looked genuinely surprised as she put her drink down. 'Really?'

'Yeah, they both made strange comments.'

She shook her head. 'No, I mean — I thought you'd figured it out.'

'Figured what out?'

There was a thoughtful pause that had his stomach in knots.

'Callie. She's Caroline Johnson. Remember? Paisley said she'd brought a friend down to help with her father's garden and I said I was going to go and say hi . . . '

'Callie is Caroline Johnson?' Surprise came first, then he felt like an idiot. 'Yes. Damn it. I wasn't paying enough attention. You told Indy.'

'Thought I should mention it. I guess she said something to Logan if he knows too.'

'But you didn't feel the need to tell me?'

'The way you've been eyeing her off, I thought you knew, were wondering about her, possibly even questioning my decision to bring her here.'

'I wasn't eyeing her off,' he objected.

'Oh, please. You've been existing like something out of *The Walking Dead* since Jules put a hole in you. Then Callie turns up and you're a different person. You suddenly like gardening? At times I was surprised you didn't chop your toes off with the shovel, the amount of attention you were paying.'

'I'm going to leave that alone because you're being ridiculous.'

187

'You offered to play boyfriend. I can't even get you to *talk* to my friends generally.'

'Because you're always trying to set me up. You're hopeless.'

'Hope*ful*,' Tess corrected unapologetically. 'And on that note, you don't have a problem with Callie now, do you?'

He really wasn't sure. It was a bit of a shock but now he knew, a lot more of the conversation she'd had with him made sense. Especially the part about the dead husband. 'I don't think I have a problem with it. I haven't had a chance to get my head around it yet. She doesn't look like what I remember, but then I only saw her for a couple of seconds on the television.'

'She's going to get her landscape business up and running again properly. I wanted to talk to her about doing the rest of the gardens.'

'The rest of the gardens are already lovely.'

'But they could do with a tidy here, a prune there, maybe some new underplanting, mulching — the sprinkler systems on the new gardens are going to be great. We could get her to put more of those in.'

'That could take weeks.'

'Yeah. And?'

And he decided he liked the idea of Callie being around for a while. 'Sure, if she likes.'

Tess's grin was huge. 'Good. I'll bring it up with her.'

He sat finishing his drink long after Tess had left. So they had it in their heads that he had a thing for Callie. Did he? Maybe. But he certainly hadn't made any sort of decision to do

188

something about it. She was undeniably attractive, and now that he knew who she was, he had a moment thinking about all that gorgeous hair she'd hacked off. Shame. He could admit he enjoyed the challenge of trying to pry smiles out of her, and those eyes that could spit fire as easily as they could serenely damn you to hell still held that initial captivation factor, but it didn't mean he was going to jump into asking her out. He wondered if maybe he could test out the idea of doing something about it . . .

He shook his head. Callie was playing it cautious and cool, uncomfortable with the smallest amount of male interest. After what she'd been through, he completely understood. He finished his beer and got to his feet. Logan was right — he sure knew how to pick them.

★ ★ ★

Callie winced. She'd stiffened up a bit, was tired and a little sore. She hadn't done much of anything for more than a year, then between Cliff's garden and the Calico Mountain job, her muscles were complaining about the sudden onset of hard labour. A hot shower would go a long way to fixing that. She grabbed a clean towel and headed for the bathroom, flicking on the light switch. The fluorescent flickered, then sprang to life. She was halfway through her shower when the light went off.

'Shit,' she murmured. She dragged her towel around her and could see just enough from the

189

firelight in the lounge room to find her way back to the bedroom and locate her phone. She switched on the torch app, got dressed then, because lights were blazing from the main house, went outside to check the cottage's fuse box. It was freezing, and the wind had snuck in after dark, biting at her exposed face and arms. The main power switch had shut off, so she flicked it back on. The lights kicked to life. With a breath of relief, she went back in.

The power didn't go off again until she'd heated up Cliff's dinner. She ignored the dip in her stomach, ignored the little image she had in her mind of someone out there turning it off on purpose to lure her back outside. It took a bit of courage to retrace her steps into the darkness to the fuse box and flick the switch.

She plated up dinner as fast as she could, praying for the power to stay on. Then she took it over to Cliff's, shivering on the doorstep while she mentioned the power situation. He wasn't keen on her calling an electrician; Ned could do it.

Reluctant to ask Ned, Callie pushed — she was happy to pay for a professional. Playing around with electricity was dangerous.

But Cliff was adamant.

Giving in, she made the freezing dash back to the cottage and because it was there, she took more firewood inside with her. If the lights were going to stuff around, keeping the fire going would warm and light the room. She loaded up the dying fire and once it was roaring, spent several more seconds swearing in her head, then picked up the phone.

'Change your mind about dinner?' Ned asked in greeting.

'Ah, no. Actually, I'm having a few problems with the lights.'

'Raining out there?'

'I'm not sure if it's rain or ice to be honest but something's coming down.'

'It's the wires getting wet then. It happens,' Ned said. 'Didn't Paisley tell you?'

'She mentioned water was getting in, that you'd been working on it, but not that the electricity was playing up. She must have forgotten.'

'I can't get in the roof tonight, but I'll come over if you like — keep you company.'

'No. Thanks. I'd be happy to call an electrician. Cliff said I should talk to you first.'

'Nah, I'll do it. Just have to wait a bit.'

She didn't want to wait. She didn't want Ned to fix it. 'I don't expect you to,' she said. 'I'll pay someone to come out.'

'Whole place needs rewiring. No pro is going to do a fix-up job,' he told her. 'I'll get up there just as soon as it's safe.'

Because she could see the conversation going around in circles forever, she gave in and got off the phone and decided she really wouldn't mind an early night. After reading for a while she lay in bed, listening to the night. A wail that sounded like wind joined the rain, a long, pitiful cry that became more guttural as it progressed. Just another unusual noise. Nothing to worry about. An owl or something. It was followed by an

191

unearthly screech that just about catapulted her from the bed. She caught herself, and snuggled deeper into the blankets, burrowing her head into the pillow. Whatever it was, she was safe. Nothing could get into the cottage.

But she lay awake, watching and listening for a long time before finally dropping off to sleep.

16

'Nothing,' Logan said over the phone. 'Not one bit of evidence Indy could use to track down the bastard that did that to Bailey. Apparently looking for a hair or traces of blood or skin on a horse isn't easy.'

'I can't imagine it would be,' Connor said.

'I honestly don't have the first idea who would do something like that. Indy's already run checks on the guests, checked the stables' security footage — there's nothing there. The guy that asked after the group approached Harvey in the yards, so we didn't get anything on him. She even got more footage from Tess from around the rest of the guesthouse but there's nothing there either.'

'Don't forget how good your wife is. Indy will turn up something.' Connor believed it.

'She won't give up, I know that. And she did say she was looking into a similar case to see if there were any ties. But without any evidence . . . I hate this. I hate that someone might get away with it. I'm going to up security, keep the horses in the closest paddocks for a while so I can keep a better eye on them. Poor old Bailey would have walked up for a pat. I can't risk anything like that happening again.'

'I'm sorry, Logan.' The idea that the program Connor had been so keen to run might have brought this on them completely gutted him.

'Not your fault.'

Maybe not, but it sure as hell felt like it. Connor hung up and got up from his desk to look out the window. Indy would figure this out. She'd figured out the truth about Jules before anyone who supposedly knew her had been able to, even though he hadn't been able to believe it. He wasn't ready to give up yet. Logan saying that Indy was looking for ties to another case made him think of what Callie went through. Her husband had performed some sort of sick ritual on his victim, hadn't he? There didn't seem to be any shortage of fucked-up bastards in the world.

He watched Callie arriving. She'd run into Tess, and they were having a conversation that was ending in laughter. Tess waved and continued out, while Callie came in. It was lunchtime, he realised. He was due for a break himself.

He hit the dining room about the same time as Callie did. He loaded his plate and found a seat, intending on letting her get food and walk past to the staff room. Then he noticed shadows under her eyes and that some of the spring had disappeared from her step. He felt a sliver of worry creep in. Was she ill, or maybe tired? Without really meaning to, he caught her eye, so he gestured her over.

'Want to be uncool and eat with the management?'

She stopped and smirked. 'Sure, Connor, I'll pretend to like you for a pay cheque.'

He found himself smiling. 'Keep up the

flattery, you'll get a raise.'

'I'm not really a bat-my-eyelashes type,' she replied. But she sat opposite him.

'You're tired though. What's up?'

She played with her food, obviously debating whether or not to share. 'You're going to think this is nuts,' she said.

'But?'

'But I heard noises last night . . . one was like a woman moaning.'

He couldn't help but chuckle. 'You think some kids are sneaking out there to — you know.'

'No,' she said with a laugh. 'It was a sad, painful sound. Kind of. Then there was another one. It was like . . . a growl from hell.'

'Could've been devils.'

Her fork clanged on her plate as she dropped her hand. 'Oh, thanks, that's what I need to hear.'

A stray wisp of hair slipped across her face. He almost reached out to tuck it back. Annoyed with himself, he dropped his hand to the table.

'Tassie devils. I wouldn't think you'd get them out there very often but they can sound downright terrifying when they carry on.'

Her face cleared. 'Oh, right. Jonah said something about them.'

'Jonah?' He felt an unexpected jolt of jealousy, berated himself.

'Local boy. He walks his dog along the river.'

'Admirer?'

She pulled a face. 'He'd be lucky to be pushing ten.'

'He's probably still got eyes in his head.'

She fumbled over that a bit, then shrugged. 'Why, thank you. Anyway, I'm just not used to being out there, I guess.'

'You're locking up at night?'

'Of course.'

'You know Indy's with the police? If you're genuinely worried, you should talk to her.'

'I'm not. Besides, Cliff doesn't seem bothered by anything.'

'How's he going?'

She took a sip of water before answering. 'He seems okay.'

'It's nice of you to take care of his meals. He must be grateful.'

The frown fell away as her eyes lit with amusement. 'I'm sure he is — in his own way. He's not very chatty.'

'Did you know he used to come out here shearing with a mob of other men? Mum and Dad had merino sheep for a while.'

'Paisley mentioned something about that.'

'I was only young, but I remember he was a nice guy — wasn't above talking to the kids. He could turn his hand to anything, got on well with Dad. That's how Ned came to work for us. Ned wasn't ever much good at school, so he was following Cliff around from job to job from pretty early on. When Cliff and his wife broke up and Cliff was struggling to get Ned into some sort of regular work, he asked Dad. Ned's been here ever since.'

'Worked out well then.'

'I know Cliff was grateful for that.'

Callie stopped eating. 'Cliff doesn't seem to

have any friends — no one visits except the community nurse, and he doesn't go out. It's sad.'

'Happens too easily to older people. Ned goes out there a lot, keeps an eye on things. Speaking of . . . Ned,' he said when Ned turned up at their table.

'Boss,' Ned said. He turned his attention to Callie, smiled. 'I was just wondering if you need more firewood?'

'Um — I was thinking I should buy some, get a large stack of it delivered.'

He frowned. 'Don't need to do that. I don't mind chopping you up the odd bit. Plenty around. Gotta do it for Dad anyway.'

'I appreciate that,' she said kindly, 'but I know how busy you are.'

'Not too busy,' Ned said with a glance at Connor. 'Gotta keep warm out there. I'll do some tomorrow. The lights behaving?'

'They were fine this morning.'

He nodded at his boots. 'Only happens occasionally. Got a bit of a date organised tonight, but I'll try and check in more often, make sure you're okay. Oh, and Adelaide should be back tomorrow,' he continued when Callie opened her mouth — to object, Connor guessed. 'If you see anyone up at the house, it'll just be her.'

'Thanks for letting me know. I met her last week. She's lovely.'

'You're welcome, Callie,' he said warmly. 'Leave you to it then.' His eyes went stony. 'Boss.'

'I think he's staking a claim,' Connor said when Ned walked off.

'He did say he had a date though,' she said with relief. 'That's good, right?'

'Yeah.' Connor wasn't so sure. He knew Ned was sitting down with Kaicey over dinner to sort out the roster. It wasn't quite a lie, but it wasn't truthful either. And on that note, he reminded himself Callie hadn't admitted to him who she was, what had happened. That wasn't a lie, but it wasn't truthful either. She was working for him, so he could argue she should have disclosed the information, but more than that, he wanted her to trust him. 'Tess said she asked you to the dinner for Bob's send-off next week. Should be a good night. The restaurant is something special.'

'So I hear. She said you've been trying to get reviewers out to lift its profile.'

'Trying. We're a bit out in the sticks. I do have one possible lined up. A good one, from Melbourne.' When he thought about it, Callie's secrecy played into his confused feelings about her. He hated secrets and wondered how much he'd have to push to get her to tell him. How to broach it.

'If he comes out and the food is as good as Tess says it is, you should get a great result.'

'Hope so.' Perhaps if he . . . 'You know, if you don't feel like the big send-off thing, I could show you the restaurant another night.'

'You and me?'

'Unless you prefer to eat by yourself. Sure.'

She wasn't quite looking him in the eye. 'Like a date.'

'She says as though I'd just asked her to join me at the gallows,' he muttered, grinning into his coffee.

She smiled, but it dropped quickly. 'You don't want to date me, Connor.'

'Any reason why not?'

If he'd thought she looked anxious before, it was nothing on now. She almost looked sick. 'I thought Tess would have told you,' she said, shifting uncomfortably in her seat.

So that was it. He made sure her eyes were on his as he said, 'I know who you are.'

Relief overtook the discomfort but there was added disbelief. 'Then why would you want — '

He decided to go with honest. 'To tell you the truth, I've been trying to talk myself out of it. That's no reflection on you. It's just where I'm at and I don't have the prettiest history myself.'

'It couldn't possibly be anything as bad as mine.'

'I stuffed up a relationship,' he said. 'And rather than go down the more traditional counsellor route, my ex decided to shoot me.' The shock that came over Callie's face was about what he'd expected. 'So I've been less than keen over the past couple of years to consider giving the whole dating thing another serious go. Then you walked in and even with my past and your past and a few . . . current issues, that's changed,' he said. 'It just changed. Does it have to be more complicated than that?'

As she stared at him he pictured her lovely face as it should have been framed: in a tumble of long, luxurious hair the colour of a sunset.

The shorter, straight, brown style might have added something to the fine bones of her face, but it was a poor substitute. Nothing detracted from those eyes, though. Those eyes were what pulled at him. They made him want to discover her secrets. And as he looked into them he saw the uncertainty creep over her usual bravado.

Because he wasn't sure she wasn't going to bolt, he covered her hand with his. 'If you run for the hills it's going to make things really awkward. Just tell me what you're thinking.'

'I'm thinking I'm not there yet,' Callie said quietly. 'Where you are. Ready to try again.'

'Fair enough,' he said, and removed his hand.

'If I were,' she continued, surprising him when a hint of appreciation came over her features, 'I'd say yes. In a heartbeat.'

He felt the answering smile creep across his face. 'Nice going, Red, you somehow managed to let me down gently while boosting my ego.' He pressed a hand dramatically to his heart. 'That takes skill.'

'Enough with the 'Red',' she murmured with a tug at her hair. 'It's brown.'

'It shouldn't be. That there — ' he pointed, ' — is a crime.'

'Is a necessity,' she corrected, then the worry was back on her face. 'I thought you might not have wanted me working for you once Tess told you.'

He leant forward again, speaking quietly. 'I think it's screwed up that you had to do what you did, but if you hadn't, we wouldn't be having this conversation. You'd be dead, and that bastard might have gotten away with it. So no, I don't mind.'

He was pretty sure from the look on her face that he'd said the right thing, then had a moment of panic when her eyes glassed over. If she cried, he was toast.

Instead, she took one very careful breath and the smile came back. 'Thank you.'

'I mean it. Are we good?'

'Yeah,' she said, her voice full of relief. 'We're good.'

★ ★ ★

Callie took her tools down the track to the rosebush. She'd finished up early at Calico Mountain, hadn't wanted to risk bumping into Connor again until she had what he'd said straight in her head. So he was interested. And he didn't seem to mind who she was and what she'd done. She wasn't sure if that was an incredibly generous attitude or suggested an innate lack of self-preservation, but he'd hit her right in the heart with his understanding. Had known just what to say and, God, she'd *wanted* to say yes. Wanted to say, *Sure, no big deal, let's do dinner*. But she knew, she damn well knew it wasn't a good idea. She needed to recreate herself, discover who she was all over again. Now wasn't the time for getting wrapped up in someone else.

And even if she could convince herself she was ready to start dating casually, was it ever a good idea to date the person you were working for? If she started something with Connor and it turned bad, it could jeopardise her first real contract. A great contract. And at some stage it was bound to cross his mind to wonder. Could he really sit across from her at dinner and watch her play with her wineglass without thinking about it? She couldn't hold a glass and not picture it lodged in Dale's face. She was still so washed out emotionally. No matter how tempting it had been to say yes, she'd made the right decision saying no. She needed more time to heal before taking new risks.

She reached the tangle of shrubs that hid the memorial stone and studied them carefully. Was the rosebush salvageable? She'd somehow convinced herself it wasn't too bad but looking at it now, her confidence plummeted. Still, she was here with her tools so it was worth a shot.

The rose had been completely overtaken by rootstock, so she cut it back carefully, did the best she could to bring it back to life. The sad little stick she was left with looked pathetic next to the pile of cuttings she'd hacked from it, so she got to work clearing some extra space around and above it to help it survive.

She was so absorbed in her task it took her a while to examine the plaque. She rubbed it with a rag, trying to make out the engraving.

My little rose amongst the thorns.

An immense sadness filled her. What had happened? Who had that been? How long had this been here? 'Well, whoever you are, I hope your rose grows back for you.'

She smiled at the plaque as she would a child

202

in need of sympathy then shook her head at her own silliness. This thing with Connor had left her feeling particularly fragile. She cleaned up the plaque as best she could, fed the ground, gave the rosebush light by pruning back the trees around it and using her drink bottle and water from the river, she watered it. She'd polish the plaque better next time — bring some cleaner down.

'Why did you do that?'

She spun. 'Hi, Jonah. What are you doing down here so close to dark?'

'Just giving Molly her walk. I had homework this arvo, so we're late.' He came closer, Molly out in front, panting.

She greeted the pup, then straightened. 'You know about this?'

He started to shake his head. It turned into a hesitant nod, finished on a shrug. 'Kinda, not really.'

'The plaque was buried in the bushes.'

'Yeah.'

'What happened?'

He leant in, his eyes darting back to the big house nervously as he whispered loudly, 'It's not to be talked about.'

Confused, Callie pushed. 'Why not?'

'Nan says, 'You start messing with that stuff, it'll come back to bite you.''

'I'm not following.'

'Sometimes strange stuff happens,' Jonah said in a very mature way. 'Has strange stuff been happening up at the cottage, Callie?'

'What?'

'Whenever strange stuff happens that I don't like, my gran always sings, 'Back to bed, back to bed, pull the covers over my head. Monsters, monsters, go away, I am not allowed to play.'' He sang it like a nursery rhyme. Grinned.

'Does it work?'

'Oh, yes. The monsters have to do what you say. That's the key. If you forget you're in control, that's when they take over.'

The absolute conviction in his tone had some of her smile slipping. 'You seem to know a lot about monsters, Jonah.'

He shrugged, but there was pride in his stance. 'Lots of people don't believe in monsters.' And then the sing-song tone was back. 'But just because you don't believe in them doesn't mean they can't hurt you! Bye, Callie!'

What the hell was that? Jeez, the boy had goose bumps spreading over her skin. *Has strange stuff been happening in the cottage, Callie?* What on earth would possess him to say that?

She scattered some fertiliser around the base of the rose and mulched it thickly with the leaf litter already around on the ground. No, nothing strange had been happening. Particularly. Sure, there was the weird chanting she'd thought she'd heard when she'd first arrived, and the incident with the lights, and the screaming, the moaning. But nothing she wasn't pretty sure couldn't be explained. She tried to forget it. The silly suggestion wouldn't have been so difficult to shrug off, but Jonah's tone and delivery had left a mark.

204

She kept working, and was almost finished when she heard the shout.

'What do you think you're doing!'

At the speed Cliff was approaching, she was just glad he made it without toppling over.

'What have you done to it? You have no right!'

He seemed genuinely distressed, so she kept her voice calm. 'The longer a rose lives, the more care it needs. A neglected old rose like this one needs special treatment if it's going to survive and flower.'

'I didn't say you could touch it!'

'I'm just helping it along, bringing it back. I've removed the suckers and some of the old canes, thinned out the weak ones and pruned the younger ones back. You know that older rose varieties can live to fifty or more years when taken care of? This needed taking care of.'

'It never flowered,' he said in a much quieter tone.

'I'm not surprised. It's in heavy shade, the soil's compacted — I bet it hasn't ever been fertilised. With this little bit of help, you never know. It just might get a new lease on life.'

'It's not a bad rose,' he muttered, and the intensity with which he stared at Callie had her tripping over her words.

'What? No. It just needs some TLC.'

He nodded and there was regret in it. 'Often that's all that's required. A lack of it can be . . . devastating.'

He was halfway back up the path when he turned around. 'I'm sorry, Callie.'

She wasn't sure there weren't tears in his eyes.

'No, I'm sorry,' she said, relieved he'd calmed down. 'I was just trying to help.' He obviously had a sentimental attachment to the rosebush. 'Can I ask — who it's for?'

'Paisley never told you about — ' he watched her closely, ' — Ava?'

'Ava? No.'

'Guess I'm not surprised.'

He started back up the track slowly while she stared at the plaque. What had happened here? Must have been incredibly tragic. Some of that chill — and that sadness — returned. It would be better when Paisley was back for good. The place would feel warmer with company.

Not sure whether Cliff would need a dinner made up because Ned was at the house, she ended up frying sausages, just in case. It was an easy meal, and when it was done, she took some over. Cliff could always eat them the next night. She went straight in and saw Ned sorting through the piles of stuff on the dining table. One end of the room was already stacked with more garbage bags and a separate smaller pile was amassing at the other.

'Sorry to interrupt, just brought over Cliff's dinner.'

'You're not interrupting. Thanks, Callie.'

'This is a lot of boxes,' she said conversationally. 'I thought Paisley already had most of them out the other day.'

'Not even close. Not sure what to do with some of this stuff.' He waved his hand at the smaller pile he'd made.

She picked up a very old children's book from

a larger stack of leather bound and hardcover novels. The edges were slightly damaged but otherwise it was in great condition.

'You could have a look online. You might discover a site or two that'll tell you what's valuable and what's not.'

'Got the agent coming round to take a look in the next couple of weeks. Have to get through it. Paisley said she's coming down to help for the weekend.'

'Friday.'

'Reckons she can get the place all spick and span. I dropped some more wood over. It's on the patio.'

'Thank you.'

'Callie.' Cliff limped down the stairs with his stick. 'What have we got tonight?'

'Just some sausages,' she told him, 'but they're gourmet butcher ones.'

'Sounds good to me. Have you got a minute?'

'Of course.' She took the dish and followed Cliff into the kitchen.

'I want to ask you something, Callie,' he said, easing himself onto a chair.

Fascinated and concerned, she sat beside him. 'What is it?'

'What do you really think about this house? Do you feel comfortable here?'

She wondered why it mattered, and thought about her answer carefully. 'I think that once we open this place up, give it a good clean, let the light in, the air, it'll feel much better.' She believed it. At least, she wanted to, because for all the chills it gave her and the strange weight that seemed to hang around the place, she fell a little bit more in love with the house's charm every day. She could see possibilities.

Her answer seemed to appease him and with a nod, he lifted the lid on dinner. 'Will you eat with us tonight?'

'Great idea,' Ned said, coming inside. 'Been hoping to share a meal with you, Callie.'

'That's a lovely offer, thank you both, but I had a late lunch, so I couldn't eat yet. I'll see you tomorrow.' She hoped Ned hadn't assumed she'd made dinner for him too.

She'd just stepped outside when he caught up with her.

'How about dinner tomorrow night, after I fix your lights?'

'I'll make enough for you as well as Cliff, it's no problem.' She supposed it wasn't. Then she stepped back from the hand he placed on her arm.

'No, I mean, just us.'

'Ah, Ned, look. I appreciate how kind and thoughtful you've been. But — '

'It's no trouble, told you that. I could pick you up at eight, take you into town.'

'Ned, I'm not going to go out with you. I'm sorry. I don't want to hurt your feelings, but I'm not interested.'

'I see,' he said after an age of simply staring at her. 'You're still getting over your husband. It's a long process. We can start out slow, no problem. I don't mind.'

'Would you stop?' she snapped in frustration. 'You're not listening. I'm not interested in having

208

any sort of relationship with you. Not now, or ever! Is that clear?'

'No need to be rude,' he said, obviously hurt.

She pressed her fingers to the bridge of her nose and squeezed her eyes closed. Was there any right way to handle this guy? 'I didn't mean to be. I'm sorry. I just want to make sure you understand.'

He nodded stiffly. 'I get it.' She was halfway through a breath of relief when he added, 'I'll just have to work harder on changing your mind.'

'No! You w — '

'See you soon, Callie.'

The frustration made her want to scream at his back, but she let him go, stormed to the cottage and locked herself in. She'd been worried about hurting his feelings? Ha. Nothing she'd said had dampened his optimism in any way. He'd no doubt gone back to the house to plan their next date.

She realised she was chewing her nails and dropped her hand to her side. It had been an emotional day — and maybe that's all there was to it — but for the first time she started to worry about Ned and his refusal to take no for an answer.

17

The tools hit the crates in a series of loud clangs and crashes. It was almost time to go. Cole would be back for the men soon and Connor needed to catch up with Tess about some of the activities booked over the next couple of days. And finding Tess would probably mean running into Callie. They'd been talking about working together this afternoon when he'd seen them in the garden earlier.

He'd spent a few lunches with Callie this week. Conversation had been stilted for a couple of days, despite them parting well enough after the conversation about dating. Yesterday had been easier, at least to the point where her smiles more regularly made it to her eyes and the dialogue was relaxed enough that he didn't cross-examine every word before it left his mouth. He shouldn't have pushed. But as easy as it was to see the sense in leaving things be when he was alone, the second he spent any time with Callie, his logic evaporated. She'd surprised him by admitting the attraction wasn't one-sided and it had stuck in his mind. He still couldn't say whether he wanted her to reconsider or not.

He got his mind back on packing up, watched the men finish up on the fence. Orson was somewhere further down the line. He hadn't been sure he'd really wanted Orson back, but

Cole had convinced him to give him another chance on the condition he didn't go near the guesthouse again. So Connor had said yes, and Orson had apologised three times and, devastated over Bailey's death, had worked harder all day than the other two put together.

'What are you daydreaming about this time?' Logan asked, dropping his tools in the ute.

'I was thinking about something Orson said during one of his many apologies today.'

'And what was that?'

'He said thank you, because we'd given him a chance, that it's one of the few he's ever had. That no matter what happens next, he'll always be grateful for this.'

Logan leant on the side of the ute beside Connor. 'That's what this was all about. You wanted to intervene and turn their lives around before they were beyond help.'

'Guess I'd just like to think it's working.'

'Worked for Harvey, Blake and Dustin. Travis and Matty are working out and well, then there's Orson. I'd say that's a pretty good batting average. Might not always run that way, but I reckon you can give yourself a pat on the back.'

'I think we both can. A big part of this has been you. But if it's got Bailey killed, I'm not really sure how I feel about it all anymore.'

'I'm pretty sure I still feel good about Harvey and Blake and Dustin, about Travis and Matty, maybe even Orson. Not so much whoever did that. That guy can rot in hell.'

Ned shouted an instruction down the line to Matty, who answered with a 'Yep!'

Connor checked his watch. 'I think it's knock-off time.'

'Agreed. Let's call them back.'

The men were scattered along the fence line checking for stray bits of wire and rubbish they might have left behind.

'Right, guys! Let's go!' Logan bellowed.

Travis came back with Ned, then Matty appeared.

'Where's Orson?' Connor asked when he didn't show.

'No idea,' Ned said with a frown. 'He was up past me at one point. Then I lost him, thought he must have gotten round me to come back here.'

'Guys, have you seen him?' Connor asked Travis and Matty. Both shook their heads. He exchanged glances with Logan.

'Probably just nature calling,' Logan said, but he began walking down the fence line to look.

'Jump in the ute,' Connor said. 'We'll drive. He could be a lot further along. He's been working at full speed all day.'

But there was no sign of Orson. They drove back and forth repeatedly, calling, then traipsed into the scrub surrounding the paddock, while the knot in Connor's stomach got tighter and tighter.

'He can't have just vanished,' he said.

'He could if he took off in there,' Logan said of the heavy bushland.

'But why would he? There's no reason for him to take off.' Connor's imagination kicked in. Snake bite? Hole in the ground? Concussion? Was Orson lying somewhere, hidden and hurt?

212

The thoughts had him crashing further into the scrub, knowing that in conditions like these he'd almost need to fall over someone before spotting them. Then all the questions Orson had asked the first day they'd come out here resonated in his head.

'I'm going to call Cole.'

Logan nodded. 'And I'll call Indy.'

★   ★   ★

Callie wasn't sure what woke her, but it could have been the cold. She'd been dreaming she was in a pretty pink bedroom, playing with toys and chatting happily to a friend. Only it wasn't a friend sitting beside her, it was Ava's memorial stone. 'Weird,' she muttered with a shake of her head and a little laugh as she sat up. She'd kicked the covers off and the fire had all but died, only the faintest glow suggested it hadn't entirely given up.

She shivered and rubbed her hands over her arms in an attempt to generate some warmth, then frowned as she realised the bedside table clock was off. Then she noted the fridge wasn't generating its usual quiet hum. The power must've gone out again.

She dragged the blankets back up and located her phone, switching on the torch then padding out to put another log on the fire. She tossed one in and stood by it, allowed the warmth to seep into her. When she could feel her fingers and toes, she headed back to bed.

And couldn't quite stop the scream as the

torch beam swept around and lit up a set of eyes on the lounge chair.

'Oh my God.' She swore, then laughed at herself as the face of one of Paisley's dolls shone back at her. 'No monsters,' she told herself out loud, holding her hand over her heart in a desperate attempt to steady it.

It took a couple of seconds for a more insidious chill to wash over the desperate relief. It ran down her spine, settled in the pit of her stomach. How had the doll gotten onto the chair? In the darkness, with only the mad, flickering dance of the firelight and the harsh, direct beam of the torch, Callie could have sworn that white, glowing face was watching her, laughing at her.

She spun around, and around again. Dolls didn't move by themselves. They *didn't*. How did it get there? She pointed the torch into all the corners of the room. She went through the same procedure with the wardrobe, Paisley's room, the rest of the house. Everything was locked. Everything was as it should be. Except the doll. She picked it up. It was dusty, covered in a film of dirt that left a trail when she slid a finger across its face. How had that happened? She looked closer. Wait . . . this wasn't the same doll. She took it into Paisley's room, saw the other ones still in place on the shelf.

'What — are you multiplying?' she muttered. She tucked the doll in next to them with a trembling hand and noticed this doll had *AW* sewn into the bottom corner of the dress. She checked the other ones. Sure enough there was a

PW and a *EW*. She thought of the memorial, the plaque. Ava? Paisley had never mentioned a sister. But who else would have one of her mother's dolls? A cousin perhaps? Regardless, whoever Ava was wasn't really the point right now. It wasn't right that the doll had just turned up on the chair like that. She took another long look at the doll before hurrying out, firmly closing the door to Paisley's room.

She sat staring into the fire for a long time trying to rationalise what had happened. But she had no answers as she finally crawled back into bed. After an age, as she eventually drifted off to sleep, Jonah's words came to mind.

Have strange things been happening in the cottage, Callie?

★　★　★

Orson's legs were screaming, his breath was a wheeze, but he kept going. He had to get as far from Calico Mountain as possible. The cops had swarmed in and he'd ducked them all evening, but they'd disappeared with the last of the light. He hadn't seen anything but the faint gleam of moonlight on the dirt track for hours, but he was pretty sure he was headed in the right direction. A cop car had driven out this way as they'd wrapped up the search. Round every bend, over every rise, he'd hoped to find a road, a way out, but all he'd come across so far was more track, more bushland.

The chill invaded the extremities of his otherwise overheated system and his gut churned, empty. At the edge of the chill and the hunger lay what felt suspiciously like guilt for bolting on Connor and Logan, maybe getting them into some trouble. But hanging around was only going to get him killed. They all thought he was nuts. Kaicey wouldn't even talk to him. Ned had told him to leave. Hypocrites. They were as guilty as he was. Especially Kaicey. She'd cop it. He'd be long gone. He knew where he was headed, knew someone who would help him get there.

He almost fell out onto the road as a truck flew past. He was ready for the next one and thumbed it down.

It took him right through to New Norfolk. He jumped out, waved and made his way down the little street, found the house he was looking for and, stumbling with exhaustion to the door, knocked.

Lights came on and the scuffle of slippers got closer. The door opened. Surprised eyes looked him up and down. 'Well, whatever's happened to you?'

'I was working out at Calico Mountain, jumped the fence. I've been running all night, Had to get going. He's been there. He got to one of the horses.'

'Come in, come in. Let me get you warm, get you a drink.'

'Thanks. I'm sorry about the time. I didn't know where else to go.' He sat on a stool at the kitchen bench, accepted a juice while the kettle boiled.

'I bet everyone's searching for you out that

way then,' the woman said, putting bread and butter and homemade marmalade on the bench.

'The national park, yeah. They were. But I got away. Hard terrain to find anyone.'

'No way they could know you've come out here?'

'Nah. I was careful.'

'Good.'

He was handed a sandwich. It barely touched the sides as he took one mighty mouthful after another. 'Shoulda come here ages ago. Heard about Mike, tried to warn Kaicey and Ned. They wouldn't listen.' He kept talking between mouthfuls of food. He was starving, could have gone another sandwich.

'Done?'

'Yeah,' he decided, because he was more tired than hungry. Was she going to make that coffee?

'We'd better get you back then.'

He stopped sculling the juice and lowered the glass. 'What?'

'We can't have anyone knowing you came here,' she said, patting his hand. 'You're not one of us anymore.'

It took a moment to sink in. This wasn't how it was supposed to go. 'Why not?'

'You told tales, Orson. Nasty tales. That can't be tolerated. So, are you ready?'

'But — '

'It's no trouble.'

The voice behind Orson locked up the breath in his lungs and choked him with terror.

'I'll even give you a ride.'

He started to shake. The sandwich heaved in

217

his stomach, then his bladder loosened, soaking his jeans. He couldn't think, even to run. The mind-numbing terror was just too much. He turned, slowly, willing himself to be mistaken. He wasn't.

'Never mind, dear,' said the woman he thought would shelter him from the monster stalking slowly towards him. 'Our actions always catch up with us in the end.'

18

Connor didn't sleep well. They'd searched for Orson until nightfall and found nothing. He picked at breakfast, called Indy as soon as he thought polite to see if anything had happened overnight.

'Official conclusion is he's done a runner,' she told him. 'He's taken off before — they call them episodes, where he thinks he's being stalked by someone who wants him dead and he runs, then calms down and comes back.'

Connor cursed. 'But he'd just got through telling me how much he was enjoying the program.'

'Yeah and the day before that he was trying to convince Kaicey she needed to run away with him or die. We've got people out looking for him again this morning, checking all his known haunts, talking to everyone who knows him. He'll turn up.'

'All right. Thanks.' He hung up and walked to the window. He would have sworn from Orson's behaviour that he'd had something genuine to worry about. But what did he really know about mental illness? Not enough. He'd just have to hope Indy was right and he'd turn up safe and sound.

He buried himself in his office, got a couple of hours' work out of the way. But he was restless, unable to settle to anything more, so he decided to walk it off. He headed in the direction of the stables, had almost decided to grab a horse to take another look for Orson — just in case — when movement in the garden caught his eye. Callie. And she was attacking the mulch like it was the enemy. He guessed he wasn't the only one having a difficult morning, so he crossed onto the grass.

'Hi,' he said.

She glanced up, smiled. Sort of. 'Hey.'

'What are you doing here? It's Saturday.'

'That's okay, isn't it?' The rake she was wielding came down hard beside his foot.

He moved away, then changed his mind and put a hand on the rake at its next sweep. 'What's up?'

'I needed to get out of the cottage.'

The tension emanating from her had knots forming in his own stomach. 'Why? What happened?'

'Nothing. It's not important.'

Because she looked like she wanted to tell him, Connor waited her out. She took another swing with the rake, then another before huffing and glaring as though she was aware of his tactic.

'I woke up in the middle of the night and there was this doll sitting in the chair staring at me like something out of a bad horror movie.'

'A doll?'

'I'm possibly losing my mind, but I would have sworn absolutely blind it wasn't there before I fell asleep. The cottage was all locked up. No sign anyone could have gotten in — and

220

why would anyone break in to leave a kid's toy on a chair? The damn thing just . . . materialised.'

'There has to be an explanation,' he said.

'And all I keep thinking about is Jonah. I was down at the river tidying up Ava's memorial stone and he turned up and asked me if strange stuff had been happening in the cottage. That's odd, right? But I can't see a kid that age running around in the middle of the night to play tricks on me.'

'I'm a bit surprised a kid that age is running around all the way out there by himself ever. Who's Ava?'

'I don't actually know. And I'm sounding crazier by the second,' she admitted, 'because I tidied up a memorial for someone I've never met. But it was so sad to see it unkempt. It just pulled at me.' She laughed at herself. 'You're going to think you've employed a lunatic.'

'Then you'll fit in well around here. But if anything else happens out there that you can't explain, please tell me. Or Indy. If someone is messing with you, harmless or not, it needs to be sorted.'

'Okay. I already feel a bit better, actually, just for sharing. So thanks. Do you want a turn?'

'A turn?'

'I shared. And you looked about as cheerful as me when you stalked over here. So now it's your turn.' The smile she sent him nearly knocked him over. 'That's how it works. Come on, it'll take my mind off my own dramas.'

'You don't need to hear it.'

She surprised him by sitting on one of the large rocks in the garden. 'Well?'

Connor rubbed his forehead to forestall a brewing headache and sat beside her. 'Just a problem with one of the rehab group. Looks like he's taken off.'

'What happened?'

'He was up the back of the property where we were fencing the boundary line. He'd been asking the week before about what was on the other side of that fence, where it went, were there trails, that sort of thing. But I didn't think he'd bolt. I just didn't see it. I've since discovered he has a history of it.'

'Then he shouldn't have been here.'

'Probably not.' He stared into space. 'And I probably should have kept a better eye on him. I thought the program could be a way of making something good come out of something bad. But I think I've just brought more trouble here.'

'What was the something bad you were trying to turn around?'

'A situation with an ex-fiancée.' He laughed a little. 'I kind of summed it up the other day.'

'She shot you. Why?'

He sighed. He didn't even know where to begin. 'She got tied up with the wrong people, with drugs. When I found out, I wanted to help her get clean. She wasn't interested and I couldn't handle that so I broke it off. She shot back that she was pregnant.'

'Oh, ouch. Tough one.'

'I was worried about her, about the baby. I

found a treatment program that could help her manage drug withdrawal safely during pregnancy. She wasn't interested and we got into an argument. I went after her, and she stopped at the top of the stairs to tell me what she thought of me. But as she spun back around she stepped into thin air. I lunged to try and grab her but she went right down. She turned up the next day, told me she'd lost the baby. Then she went to stay with the guy who'd given her the drugs in the first place.'

He couldn't believe he'd just blurted that out. 'That's awful, I'm sorry.'

'So many people were put in serious danger because of the drugs that guy and his family were manufacturing. Indy, Logan, the family, the business — everything suffered. And I still thought I could get through to her, turn her around. I couldn't.' Connor smiled weakly. 'So I took on this program for young drug offenders, aimed at helping them get back on their feet so they don't reoffend. I thought that even though I couldn't change what happened with Jules, perhaps I could help other young people. Turn their lives around.' He rubbed his hand over his face. 'But now this. It was a mistake to take the program on.'

After several moments of silence, he heard her take a deep breath.

'So if we're talking second chances, is having me here a mistake?' she asked.

He knew there was probably too much warmth in his stare, but he couldn't pull it all the way back. 'Not from where I'm sitting.' He allowed that to sink in, then laughed self-consciously. 'I don't generally blurt out that story. Sorry. It's just been a hell of a couple of days.'

'I don't think there's any way to get through this whole life thing without stuffing up,' she finally said. 'So you may as well stuff up trying to do the right thing as the wrong thing.'

'When you put it like that . . . '

'You've done this before — I know because Harvey was telling me his story. He told me that three kids have jobs and a new start. This time you've got more looking like going the same way. The other guy — I'm guessing Orson, right? It sucks. It's not fair. But it's not on you. And you'll get this sorted, and in years to come it will be a distant bad memory. But this place will always be a good memory to those boys who succeeded here, who got their start. You haven't failed, Connor. If you shut this down tomorrow, five people's lives have changed for the better because of it. Isn't that why you began in the first place?'

Now she'd done it. She hadn't been staring, not sure of what to say. She'd been formulating the perfect answer. It took every ounce of willpower he had not to lean across the space between them and kiss her. If she hadn't already said no, he would have.

'Thanks,' he said instead, clearing his throat when it came out a little rough.

She gave him a solid pat on the leg as she got up. 'Anytime,' she said, her voice returning to its regular, brisk friendliness. 'I'd better get back to work.'

'Me too,' he said. 'If I don't see you at lunch, have a good weekend. You can call me, you know that, right? If there's any more trouble out there. I'll be around.'

★ ★ ★

Callie didn't have any more trouble over the rest of the weekend, and as Monday morning shone bright and clear, she got herself out to Calico Mountain early to take advantage of the cold but calm weather. She planned on starting by reshaping the garden beds she'd discussed with Tess and Connor.

She manoeuvred the bobcat around and scooped up the edge of the first garden bed, then drove around and dumped the earth into the already cut extension. She shaped, filled, smoothed until both garden beds were the form she saw in her mind — a better choice for the trees and for maintenance. Having the machine on hand made everything so much easier. She wondered if she should talk to Paisley about hiring one to tackle some of the more difficult areas of Waldron Park. She'd spent a long time in its gardens yesterday pulling weeds and breaking earth up by hand. It hadn't been fun.

A large tourist coach crunched into the drive and unloaded thirty or so people. Tess had warned her a couple of local garden clubs had joined forces and hired a coach for an outing. This had to be them. She hoped they stuck to the established gardens and didn't decide to watch her work.

Thankfully, they mostly left her alone. A few made small talk as they wandered by, others stopped momentarily to watch. She smiled briefly at each, but kept working; friendly enough, without encouraging conversation. It would only take one person to make the connection and she was screwed.

She glanced over her work and, happy, decided it was time to swap machines — she'd need the trencher for laying the larger pipes that would run water from the mains to the beds. It was her least favourite part of the job, but it needed to be done.

She noticed two more women had turned up. They were talking quietly, looking in her direction. Though they were too far away for her to hear what they were saying, something about their stance, their faces, triggered alarms. In her mind she could almost hear them.

'It's that woman who murdered her husband and got away with it.'

'A murderer works here? We're leaving.'

'Yes, and calling the paper. Everyone needs to know they're in danger.'

As they continued to stare and whisper, Callie's thoughts spiralled from suspicion to paranoia. She blocked the internal tirade. Told herself she was being stupid. But she was happy to be able to get back in the machine and turn it around, head away from their eyes and their whispers on the way back to the machinery shed.

★ ★ ★

Orson still hadn't turned up. Connor worried about this as he filled in on reception for Kaicey, while Indy had a quiet chat with her, at his request. He really hoped she'd talk, because he knew she wasn't telling them everything, and he felt a sense of responsibility to locate Orson whether anyone else thought he should or not. The moment things calmed down for two seconds, he intended getting an update.

'Hey,' one of two teens said, leaning over the desk. 'We want to book in a quad ride.'

'Right.' He put down the phone on his last call. 'I can do that for you. Just one second . . . '

He got them booked in, dealt with the general ins and outs of a few more bookings and queries, the last of the morning checkouts and the odd problem as it arose in between. And that's it, he thought, waving off another guest. He was going to lunch.

'Mr Atherton!' an older lady said, charging up out of nowhere.

He didn't groan, but it sat at the back of his throat. 'Good morning.'

'Lois McPhee.'

'Mrs McPhee, how is your holiday going?' he asked politely.

'Not so good, I'm afraid. I mean, this place is wonderful. In fact, we decided to extend our stay and had our daughter all booked in to come down and meet us — spend a couple of nights with us here with her little ones. But we've made a terrible mistake. We were sure we could cancel our reservation at our next stop without having to pay any fees, but the manager was so awful and told us the booking was non-refundable. And it was just so much money.'

He really wasn't sure what the woman expected him to do about it. 'I guess that really depends on the motel policy.'

'Yes, but . . . he was just so rude about it. I'm sure he could have done something for us.'

The phone rang. He felt his mood deteriorating again. 'Just a moment, please.' He went behind the desk to answer the call. While he dealt with a woman wanting information on a hen's weekend, he heard Callie's voice. She must have come up for lunch, but when he looked, he saw she had a sympathetic hand on Mrs McPhee's arm; the woman was clearly more upset than he'd first noticed. Callie glanced over. He could only imagine what she read in his face.

'We can take a look at that for you, Mrs McPhee, but as Connor said, it just depends on the motel's terms and conditions.' Callie's eyes hit his again, uncertain this time as she made a little gesture to ask if she could come around the other side of the desk.

Surprised and grateful, he nodded and got up to unlock the door as he continued his phone call. Callie slipped into the chair beside his.

'Did you say your daughter was meeting you here?' She got the woman chatting again — then she was smiling. Callie was obviously good with people. He reminded himself she'd run a small motel — or was it a bed and breakfast?

'Let's take a quick look . . . ' Callie pulled up the motel webpage and scrolled through the terms and conditions.

Then Connor got wrapped up in his phone call and the next time he looked, Callie was frowning.

'Are you a loyalty club member with the hotel chain?' she asked.

'Oh yes, we are.' Mrs McPhee pulled the card from her purse and placed it on the desk.

Callie picked up the phone. Connor finished his call while she began hers.

'Hi. I'm calling on behalf of Mr and Mrs McPhee who are staying with us at Calico Mountain. They've just attempted to cancel a booking at your establishment and were told the booking was non-refundable.'

Callie's friendliness evaporated as she became brusque. 'What's your name again? Blake? Listen, Blake, I'm going to give you a break because you sound pretty young and inexperienced. Are you young and inexperienced, Blake?'

Connor's lips twitched as Callie's eyes darkened with determination. He liked seeing the spark as she fired up. He'd take that over the sadness and nerves he too often read in her face, any day.

'I thought so. The thing is, Blake, you're either incompetent, or you're not being straight with me. Why don't you bring up their booking up on your computer and take a look? Yes, they certainly are members . . . Yes, of course I'll share that information with you. The number is . . . ' She rattled off the membership number. 'Now, as one of the motel chain perks clearly entitles members to cancel any booking up to twenty-four hours before the commencement of their stay, you should tell me what system you're using so I can talk you through the refund process. Really? Because I'm ready to hang up. Once I do, I'm contacting the hotel chain and, possibly, because I'm in the mood, having a very special rant on social media. Because there's nothing in your fine print about any of that rubbish you're spouting off to me. Do you know the penalties for false advertising, Blake?' She drummed her fingers on the desk. 'Yes, I'm sure it was just a misunderstanding. No problems. Wonderful. Thank you, Blake. Have a lovely day. Bye now.'

She hung up and smiled politely at Mrs McPhee. 'All sorted for you. You'll receive a refund in full in the next three working days.'

'Oh! You were wonderful, dear,' Mrs McPhee said.

'It was my pleasure,' Callie said. 'Enjoy the rest of your stay. I hope your daughter enjoys her visit.'

'Oh, she will! You've got a gem here, Mr Atherton. Don't let this one go!'

'I have no intention of it,' Connor said, smiling as Callie's eyes narrowed suspiciously at him. He waited until Mrs McPhee had thanked her several times and wandered off happily to lunch. Then he allowed the smile lurking at the corners of his mouth to spread. 'She looked like she'd just won the lotto.'

'Getting a refund probably amounted to the same thing. You should have seen the price of that place!'

'You're good at that. With people. I prefer to

manage behind the scenes but people are your thing, right?'

'Well, I would have been much nicer to Blake if he hadn't been such a twat. 'Oh, I'm afraid our motel is in very high demand. We couldn't possibly offer a full refund simply because they misguidedly chose to stay elsewhere,'' she recounted in what might have been a perfect twat accent. 'I'm not surprised he couldn't check his terms and conditions with his nose so far up in the air.'

It was a glimpse of the person she must have been before everything that had happened. It was fun and sexy. 'Okay,' he said, 'now I'm having lunch. You free?'

'Yeah. And starving.'

★   ★   ★

Callie walked into the dining room with Connor and a smile of her own. She had enjoyed helping out, hadn't realised she'd missed her old position at Highgrove until she'd had a taste of it just then. She considered that as she filled her plate. That didn't mean landscaping wasn't still her best option, but it was something to think about.

'Tess and Logan are over there,' Connor said from behind her. 'When you're done, come say hi?'

'Okay.' She grabbed a coffee and took it and her meal to their table. 'Afternoon.'

'Connor was just telling us you saved the day,' Tess said.

'I wouldn't go that far. It's just that when I

walked in, Connor looked more likely to drop a heavy object on the woman than play host.'

'Rough morning,' Logan said. 'He hates reception.'

'I can take over now until Kaicey gets back,' Tess offered, and looked over their heads. 'Hi, Ned.'

Again? Callie's eyes closed as she whispered a curse. When she opened them, Connor was watching her. He didn't look as laid back about Ned's interruption as he had in the past.

'Tess, everyone,' Ned said, eyes on Callie. He put his plate down on the table next to theirs. 'How are you, Callie? Haven't seen you all weekend.'

'Fine, thanks.'

'Wanted to apologise for our little tiff the other night. Bought you some flowers. They're on the patio table waiting for you when you finish work.'

Tiff? Flowers? She felt her blood pressure rise and fought for calm. 'It wasn't a *tiff*, Ned,' she objected. 'You didn't want to hear what I was trying to tell you.'

'Just a misunderstanding,' he said amicably. 'We'll talk about it this evening when you get home.'

The way he made them sound like a couple was more than wrong — it was creepy. Instinctively and without really meaning to, she leant just an inch or two towards Connor. He immediately moved his arm to rest it along the back of her chair, his fingers lightly brushing the nape of her neck as they settled. That sent another shiver through her, this one much more pleasant. Connor shot her a look of interest that suggested he'd felt it, before returning his attention to Ned.

'Did you get that new water system up and running in paddock three?' he asked.

Ned briefly turned his gaze from Callie to stare at Connor's arm. His frown was stern as he answered, 'Got a bit more work to do. Be finished this arvo.'

'Good,' Connor replied, and continued discussing odd jobs that were lined up, drawing Logan into the conversation. Ned's gaze kept returning to Connor's arm, and she didn't realise how tense she was until Connor's fingers began casually kneading the back of her neck. Liquid warmth spread through her system. She could have purred under the gentle pressure. She stopped worrying about Ned and had to focus on dragging her concentration back to the conversation to answer a question from Tess.

When Connor sent her a look so full of desire that it blew her away, she decided it was for Ned's benefit. But it curled in her gut and spread little lightning bolts of awareness to every point in her body. She had to think he was acting but — holy hell — if that look was pretend, what would the real thing be like?

She was pretty damn sure that fighting this attraction was impossible. Part of her wanted nothing more than to melt into a puddle where she was, the other part warned her to run for the hills. The latter part eventually won.

'Right, well. Better get back to it.' She slipped out of her seat. 'Lots to do.'

'Bye,' Connor said, snagging her hand and squeezing her fingers. 'See you after.'

'Thank you,' she mouthed, back turned to Ned.

Amusement briefly dominated the warmth in his eyes, then it was gone.

★ ★ ★

Connor very slowly released a long breath. That had been an interesting line to walk. He wasn't entirely convinced she'd deliberately sent him an 'I've changed my mind, let's play pretend' signal, but some protective streak he hadn't known he possessed had had him playing the part when she'd all but shrunk towards him. The way Ned was carrying on, he wasn't surprised, and he didn't like it.

'Something going on with you and Callie, boss?' Ned snapped.

'Something,' Connor answered smoothly. 'Why?'

Ned didn't answer for several seconds, just stared, hard. Finally, he shrugged. 'Just wondering.'

'So, man to man, Ned, I'd appreciate it if you'd back off Callie for me, okay?'

Ned pushed to his feet. 'Reckon Callie can decide for herself.'

'I *reckon* she already has,' Connor countered with equal force. Who was this man? He didn't even recognise him. 'So you're going to keep a friendly distance, understand? Anything else is harassment and I won't have that in my work-place.'

234

'She might work here but she doesn't live here.' He said it like a threat. 'Maybe it's you that should back off.'

'Oh, dear,' Tess taunted as Ned stalked away. 'I'd be sleeping with one eye open.' Then, her expression sharp and curious, 'Is it true? Are you and Callie seeing each other?'

'No,' he said with a dismissive gesture. 'I was just trying to get the message across to Ned.'

'Then can I say wow? That was a convincing few minutes.'

'Yeah. I'd be pretty pissed at you,' Logan said. 'You really know how to act.'

Connor didn't laugh. Maybe he was defensive of Callie because of the feelings that were niggling at him, but he hadn't liked the look in Ned's eyes just then. 'She's told him and told him to stop but he just thinks he needs to try harder to win her over. It's try it this way or he's heading for a knock on his arse. Ned's no rocket scientist but he's not so stupid that he doesn't know right from wrong. I don't like this obsessiveness. I haven't seen him as focused as this on anyone before.'

'That's true,' Tess said. 'There's been so many little crushes and they've all just dissolved. I've never known him to become the least bit aggressive over anyone.'

'Okay,' Logan said. 'We'll all keep a closer eye on him. Hope it blows over.'

'Yeah,' Connor said. 'Thanks. I'm going to go make sure he hasn't followed her out, and check if Kaicey's back.'

No one was on reception and he was pretty

sure by now Kaicey should have been, so he decided he may as well start the afternoon by finding her. He walked past Callie heading back to the garden with the trencher, but there was no sign of Ned, so he continued to the bunkhouse.

Kaicey answered after the first knock with red-rimmed eyes and a face devoid of any colour.

'What's wrong?' he asked.

'I'm sorry, I know I should be working. I'm just — I can't.'

'Is this because of Bailey?'

But she looked too upset, even for that. 'Sort of. And I'm worried about Orson. He's a pain but . . . '

He tried to feel sympathetic, but as he was pretty sure she wasn't telling him everything, he found it difficult. 'Okay, I get that, but the guesthouse has to run. If you're too upset to come in you need to let someone know. I don't expect you to work, I do expect you to tell me if you can't . . . ' He looked past her to the disaster of her room. A suitcase was open and clothes, personal belongings littered the bed. 'Are you leaving?'

'I'm sorry. I have to go.' She wiped her fingers across her face and sniffed, then went back to her bed and quickly threw what she could inside the suitcase.

She wasn't just upset, Connor decided, she was scared. And it had to come back to knowing more than she was saying.

'You're just walking out? No explanation, no notice?'

236

She turned on him. 'You should have told me how Bailey died!'

'Why?'

She zipped up all that would fit and lugged the suitcase to the floor. 'It doesn't matter. I'll come back as soon as I can.' She looked around as she walked out, eyes everywhere, her steps hesitant.

Not good enough, he thought, and followed her out. 'Hey. Wait! What's going on?'

Again and again her gaze swung around. 'I can't be out there.'

'Why not?'

She got to her car, hefted her case in.

'Why not?' he demanded. 'Kaicey, a man's missing and a horse is dead and you know what's going on. You can't just drive away!'

'I didn't want to believe he'd found us. I don't know if he's found me. If he had, I think I'd be dead, too. I'm the only one left, I have to go.'

'Who's *he*? What do you mean 'the only one left'?'

'Tell Indy I'm sorry, but half the town was one of us. I don't know whose side anyone is on. I — you wouldn't understand. Please. I *have to go*.' She got in the car and started the engine.

He had his phone out calling Indy before she'd disappeared down the driveway.

'What happened with Kaicey?' he asked when she picked up.

'I questioned her about the comments she made to you regarding Orson and Bailey and bringing trouble with him. She really didn't want to talk but when I hinted at the circumstances surrounding Bailey's death, she lost it. Left. I thought I'd let her calm down before tackling the subject again.'

'You might have just missed your chance. She's packed a bag and taken off. She was saying things that didn't make a lot of sense.'

Connor heard Indy's sound of frustration. 'I didn't want to let her go but I couldn't hold her. You'd better tell me what she said.'

19

'They're all in,' Callie told Connor as they looked over the irrigation pipes she'd just finished laying. 'I'll hook the lines up to each garden as I get them completed and these trenches can get on with grassing over. I won't have to dig up any more of your lawn.'

'I can't believe you did all this yourself. It's a massive job.'

'This isn't your average garden. It would have been faster if I could have dug all the lines at once, but I had to go bit by bit so none of your guests fell into any holes.'

'My insurance premium appreciates that.'

She chuckled, dipped her eyes when they landed on his warm ones. Callie had received a few looks that had curled her toes this week. She'd reminded herself it wasn't smart to go there, but damn, he had her wondering. Had her wanting. 'Anyway,' she continued as she felt the heat creep into her face, 'I can concentrate on planting out again, which will be good for those plants still in pots.' She stretched, thought about calling it a day. It was early, but there was no point beginning something else at this stage.

'How about I go and get the ute?' Connor said. 'We can pack the rest of this stuff onto it. It'll save a lot of trips with the wheelbarrow.'

'Yes, it will — thanks.' She started gathering everything together while he was gone, but straightened quickly when she caught movement in front of her. A woman had appeared seemingly from nowhere. She recognised the face but it took her a moment to place it: this was one of the women from the bus tour at the beginning of the week.

'Can I help you?'

'I need to speak to you, Caroline.'

The reality of hearing the name out loud was as much of a shock as a punch in the stomach. She knew the blood had rushed from her face, wondered if there was any way to disguise the panic the woman had set off. 'Sorry?'

A couple of guests strolled past. 'The gardens look lovely here,' the woman said brightly. 'You're doing a wonderful job.' Then the jovial tone and accompanying grin both dropped when the guests had passed. 'They're watching you.'

'What?' Callie asked. The woman's tone had her trembling. 'Who?'

'You need to leave. Get away. Fast.'

'What? Wait!'

But the woman wasn't waiting. She swept around the next garden bed and vanished from view.

What the hell? Just what the hell? *They* were watching her? Who? The media? That strange woman's friends? And why had she been whispering? Callie looked around her, walked in slow circles, expecting reporters with their cameras and their microphones to burst into view at any moment. Nausea rolled in her stomach. *Calm down. Think.*

★   ★   ★

Connor steered the ute across the lawn to where Callie had everything ready to load on. She was there, but staring into the trees. She seemed tense. She pulled her cap further down and walked — though quickly — towards him. Her eyes darted left and right, forward and back. She was in the ute before he could get out.

She was pale, shaky, her features drawn. She'd been fine a moment ago. What could have happened?

'Callie, what's wrong? What happened?'

'Can we go?' she asked. 'I'll explain when we get inside.'

'Sure, of course.' He drove back to the guesthouse, parked around the side and took her straight up to his office, then, taking another look at her face, decided they didn't need interruptions and steered her through the door to his adjoining apartment. 'What happened?'

As though it was beyond her to keep still, Callie walked in small circles. 'There were women, the other day. With the garden group, I think. They were watching me work and whispering and I know they recognised me. They went away but one just came back. She told me I was being watched, that I needed to go.'

He bit down on his lip, kept a vicious curse in his head. 'Okay.'

'And I don't know — I don't even know if I can stay in Tasmania because if the media come sniffing around, Cliff's place will be inundated. You don't know what it's like, being a prisoner in your own home. They camp out day and night, bang on the door, leave notes, the phone doesn't stop ringing — '

'Hey, calm down.' He got her a glass of water and put it on the table in front of her.

'And the woman said to get away. Fast. I mean — *what?* What are you doing?' she asked, startled, when he took her arms and tried to guide her to a seat.

'You need to sit, calm down, drink some water.'

'No. No, I'm fine. I just need to go. I'm sorry. I can't work here anymore.'

First Kaicey and now Callie? 'Hold on,' Connor said with as much authority as he could muster under a decent hit of his own panic. 'Just wait a minute. Please.'

When she nodded, he perched on the chair opposite. 'You didn't actually admit to anything, did you?'

'No, but she *knew*, Connor.' And what she'd gone through must have been hell, because the look, the tone, was devastated.

'Yeah. Okay,' he said much more calmly than he felt. Until that moment he hadn't realised exactly how much he wanted her to stay. He struggled for the right thing to say. 'It's going to happen, Callie. Sometime, somewhere. No matter where you go. How long do you think people are going to chase you? How long are you going to keep running, wondering if the world's moved on?'

'I don't know. But longer than this.'

'Would you at least take a few days to think

about it? You told me Paisley's due down for the weekend, right? Talk to her. See what she thinks. Nothing might come of this. At least, nothing we can't handle.'

'We?' She shook her head and got back to her feet. 'There is no *we*. I won't drag you into this!'

He reminded himself this was exactly what he'd told himself he didn't want: no more drama, don't get involved. But right at that moment he realised he already was. And the thought that this mysterious woman could jeopardise these new feelings before he had a chance to get his head around them enraged him.

He pulled Callie to him, hoping to hell he hadn't misread her feelings, and covered her mouth with his. He lost all sense of the purpose of the kiss the moment his lips met hers. It was no longer about proving a point or showing her something he couldn't explain. It was just about her: the feel of her, the taste of her, the sensations she set off in him as her rigid body trembled in response. Then that initial shock dissolved and her arms came around him while her body sank against his. By the time she stepped back, they were both breathless.

Eyes wide and face flushed, she stared at him, swallowing hard. 'This is a mistake.'

'It doesn't feel much like one.' He pressed a finger to her lips as she opened her mouth to object again. 'And assuming it's okay with you, now there is a *we* and you didn't drag me into it — I dragged you.'

Her eyes softened but she was shaking her

head again. 'It's not okay! You don't know what you're doing. What you could be getting into.'

'I'm already in. Let me help.'

But she stepped away. 'I said no! I need to go back to the cottage. I need to think.'

'Can I at least drive you?'

Callie sucked in a breath and closed her eyes in a visible attempt to calm herself down. 'No — honestly, I'm fine to drive. I'll, um . . . talk to you later,' she said, voice steadier. 'Let you know . . .'

'Callie, it'll be okay,' Connor promised as she turned for the door. Somehow, he was going to make sure of it.

★ ★ ★

Her brain had sunk to her feet when Connor had kissed her. It had been too long since she'd been held like that, *kissed* like that. And on top of the drama of the few minutes before, of course she was going to be out of sorts. But with time and distance, she was starting to process. If she stayed away from Calico Mountain — at least in the short term — anyone poking around looking for her wouldn't be able to find her. They had no way of connecting her to Waldron Park.

But she had to wonder who that woman was. It hadn't just been the recognition, but the urgency in the woman's tone that had sent Callie into such a panic. But no one else had bailed her up, so unless the woman knew of some impending invasion — unless they were waiting for her at the cottage . . .

The thought had her ready to make a quick exit as she turned cautiously into the driveway. But where would she go? She had nothing with her, no escape plan. *Stupid*, she told herself. She should have been better organised.

She was relieved to find the driveway empty. She could still be okay if she kept her head down for a few days. If that didn't work she'd go somewhere else. Callie really didn't want to let Paisley down by leaving before she could get back to sort out Cliff, so she'd play it moment by moment.

She got out of the car on legs that weren't quite steady to let herself inside and was surprised to see Paisley's bag in the middle of the room. She wasn't supposed to arrive until tomorrow.

'Paisley?' A quick look around the cottage showed her friend wasn't there, so she must have gone to the house. Callie cleaned herself up, and because she didn't feel like cooking, heated up a meal she had in the freezer courtesy of Connor and went to deliver it to Cliff.

Paisley met her at the front door. 'Surprise!' she said warmly. 'I wrangled an extra day off so I came down early.'

'Hi. And great.'

Paisley sent her a speculative look. 'What happened?'

'Bit of a drama at Calico Mountain.'

'Drama?' Paisley asked as she stepped back to let her in.

'I'll, um . . . tell you in a minute. Just let me put this down. Your dad's dinner.'

'Do me a favour and stick it in the oven? I need another ten minutes. Dad's upstairs sorting out his record collection so I'm sneaking out as much rubbish in the bin as will fit.'

Callie stepped past the rubbish bags and sorting piles and did so. Not sure she was quite ready to talk, she looked around. 'Can I help?'

'While I finish here, could you take those couple of tied-up rubbish bags out, put them by the bin?'

'Sure.'

'The skip is coming tomorrow. I'll load it all in then.'

Callie took the bags, then came back in and noticed Paisley had made her a cup of tea and was sitting, waiting.

'So?' Paisley asked.

'I was bailed up by a woman out at Calico Mountain today. She recognised me, told me I should go. It sounded almost more like a threat than a friendly warning.' Callie peered into another box, this one full of touristy tea towels.

Paisley stared, frowned. 'What?'

Callie took her through what had happened and afterwards Paisley was quiet, digesting it.

'You didn't actually admit to being Caroline, did you? Because I have to think if this woman is as strange as she sounds, who's going to believe her?'

'I don't know. I don't know who she is, what she knows. I'm not sure I shouldn't leave, go somewhere else for a while.'

'Again? You've just done that. I agree with Connor. Lay low for a few days.'

246

'You know what the media were like at home, Paise. We don't need that here.'

'You said the woman was from the garden club. Which one?'

'I don't know. There were a couple there. They shared a coach. Why?'

'Because if we can figure out who she and her friends are, we might get a better idea of if there's anything to worry about. I believe Adelaide's involved with one of the clubs around here. She might be able to help. What did the woman look like?'

'Short, maybe sixty, hair was brown and curly but the roots were grey. Round face, nice clothes. And if you do ask Adelaide, you'll have to tell her who I am. Then someone else will know.'

'I'll figure that part out, trust me.'

'Okay. But it's not just that.' Callie wanted to be careful about how this next bit came out. 'I've been having a bit of trouble making Ned understand I'm not interested in seeing him. Romantically.'

Paisley smiled in understanding. 'It's nothing to worry about. If he's being a bit full on I'll talk to him again. I already told him to leave you alone. I guess he didn't take enough notice.'

'That's just it,' she blurted out. 'Everyone said he's harmless, that he just gets a bit fixated from time to time, but I think this is more than that. I'm not comfortable around him.'

'I'll talk to him,' Paisley promised again.

'Thanks,' Callie said, and could only hope Paisley would get through. 'Let's get more of this done.'

They got twenty minutes in, then Cliff came down looking for dinner and as he ate it, he kept a close eye on Paisley, complaining about nearly everything she tried to toss out. 'I might need that!' he said of a chipped vase, and 'That's too good to go in the bin,' when she tried to throw out an old tin money box showing signs of rust. Callie supposed each held a memory and it was difficult to see your life sorted into important and unimportant piles. It was never that simple, she knew that only too well. Too many of her own things, of Dale's things, still sat in boxes in storage. She hadn't been able to throw anything away.

She quickly discovered there was no rhyme or reason to the variety of items in each pile of stuff. A cutting board, several old fishing books, an unopened box of Bic pens, some underwear — thankfully still in their plastic — and a packet of rice were in the box Paisley had pushed at her, as well as an Easter egg that had whitened with the years and several birthday cards yellowed with age which had been nibbled on, along with most everything else in the box.

Callie screwed up her nose and, even though she was feeling sympathetic, wondered if the whole thing could just go out as it was. She opened her mouth to ask and noticed Paisley flicking through pages of a book, a wistful smile on her face.

'What is it?' she asked.

'One of my old yearbooks.'

'Can I see?'

'Sure. I might take it back to the cottage, hold

on to it.' Paisley handed it to her then went into the lounge room, so Callie sat and flicked through it. She found Dale in his year seven class photo. It would have been the year before he'd moved up to the Hunter with his family. Another photo in among a collage showed him dressed up at a school function. Paisley was there, too, some other kids who looked a couple of years older and a pretty brunette with her arm thrown casually over Dale's shoulder. *Cute*, she thought, and put it aside, because when had that sweet-looking boy turned into a monster?

Paisley came back in with another box and placed it in front of her, then went back and retrieved yet another. 'You want to try sorting some, Dad?' she asked Cliff.

'Not finished on the records. Lotsa good ones I'd forgotten about.'

'But are you ever going to listen to them? I can download them for you, show you how to — '

'Don't sound the same!'

'But you haven't listened to them for how long?'

They argued it out, and in an attempt to smooth over the tense silence that followed, Callie asked, 'What are those markings on the wall? The flowerlike ones?'

'They're hexafoils,' Cliff told her with a disappointed look at Paisley. 'You bring her here and you don't explain? Don't tell her anything?'

'You're right, Dad,' Paisley said patiently, 'I'll make sure I explain it to her.'

'Don't agree with any of this,' he mumbled. 'I'm going back to my records.'

'So?' Callie prompted.

'Look . . . this house . . . ' Paisley looked around reflectively. 'A lot of bad things have happened here. You know Dad's a diagnosed schizophrenic. He goes through highs and lows with his illness. When it gets the better of him, he ties the stories into his psychosis.'

'What stories?'

Paisley drained her tea. 'I only know the basics. The house was built by convicts for one of the early overseers of the town, a man named Phillip Waldron. It was pretty harsh out here in the beginning. Most of Phillip's children and his wife all died, his one remaining son Clarence became a soldier and spent time stationed at Norfolk Island prison. He got tied up with a particularly nasty warden out there and when he came back, he'd changed.'

'Changed how?' Callie asked, curious.

'He was into . . . stuff. Really dark, nasty stuff. Norfolk Island prison was barbaric. Being sent there was considered to be a fate worse than death. It was said Clarence carried out a lot of the torture. It must have screwed with his head, because when he came back he wasn't the same. Ex-convicts who worked at the house started dying or going missing, there was talk of rituals and sacrifices held here. Clarence became progressively more insane and eventually hung himself. But one of his surviving sons was said to have carried on with the whole black magic thing and then the next after him, and so on.'

'Nice story,' Callie said with a shudder.

'This house has loads of them. There's an old

tunnel that runs from the river beside the house right under the town to the asylum. It was used to transport patients who weren't deemed fit to be on the streets.'

'A tunnel? Really?'

'There's loads of them under New Norfolk. But keep that to yourself. Dad's convinced if the local academics get wind of it he'll lose the house to some historical heritage bill or something. Anyway, it's said some patients never made it. That Clarence Junior used to pinch them off the boats and use them in his rituals.'

'Ew. Good grief.' An uncomfortable chill washed over her because what Dale had done was never far from her mind. She wondered what motivated people to do such terrible things.

'People have whispered about seeing figures with burning torches down by the river, hearing chanting in the early hours of the morning, even finding the odd mutilated animal corpse. There's a record of all the truths and legends in the local library, and Dad's got a heap of stuff upstairs.'

'It's taken seriously? Even now?'

'That's why we're the Weirdo Waldrons,' Paisley said with a smirk.

'And these symbols on the walls?'

'Hexafoils are supposed to trap bad spirits by confusing them. They're drawn to following the lines and the lines are continual, so they just go around and around forever and get trapped in there.' At Callie's sceptical look, Paisley shrugged. 'They've been here forever. I don't know who put them up.'

Callie picked up another box and hefted it onto the table. 'So if I told you I think I heard chanting one night?'

Paisley smiled reassuringly. 'I'd tell you it was music from boats echoing off the river. It comes up the hill distorted. Trust me, I grew up here.'

'Right,' she said, feeling better. She had enough to worry about without century-old singing ghosts. However . . . 'Paisley, speaking of . . . strange things. There's something else. Can we go over to the cottage?'

'Of course,' she said. 'Let me say goodbye to Dad.'

They walked back to the cottage and Callie took Paisley into her room to show her the doll. 'That,' she said. 'It just turned up.'

Paisley's face lit up. 'You found her! Where was she?'

'She found me, and honestly, I'm not comfortable about it. She was sitting on the lounge chair one night after the power went off.'

'Really? She's been missing forever. Did you ask Ned or Dad if they'd found her and dropped her over? Callie, are you all right?'

'Yeah, sure. Except if they did, they snuck in through a locked door while I was sleeping.'

'Oh, they'd both have keys,' Paisley said dismissively as though it was no big deal.

But it was. The idea Ned might have been in the cottage watching her sleep straight out gave Callie the creeps. And she intended on ramming that point home just as soon as Paisley got over her initial distraction of finding the doll. That reminded her. 'Who was Ava?'

Paisley slowly lowered the doll. 'What did you say?'

'Ava. I was wondering who she was.'

Paisley put the doll back on the shelf and walked out to the kitchen to pour herself a generous glass of wine. She threw back most of it before speaking. 'Ava was my little sister. She died.'

'Oh, I'm sorry. You never mentioned her.'

Paisley poured another large glass, took another deep drink. 'Because it was my fault. It ruined our whole family.'

Callie hoped Paisley would share, but her friend put a forced smile on her face and walked to the fireplace.

'Let's not worry about Ava or strange women or over-the-top brothers and let me tell you what I have planned for the next couple of days. I was hoping you might come with me.'

20

Callie woke up to the sun shining brightly through her window. She'd slept later than usual, which probably had something to do with the wine she'd had, mostly to stop Paisley demolishing it all herself. She supposed that could also be responsible for why she still felt tired. If there was anything reliable about Paisley, it was that she'd deal with stress by drinking herself into the ground. She yawned, blinked and caught an image in her mind of pretty china dolls twirling to music. Ava's stone. A giant wind that roared and blew them all away, replaced them with darkness. *Okay . . . too much wine. Too much talk of dead children and mysterious dolls.*

Paisley's hushed voice floated in but Callie couldn't make out the murmuring so she got up, draped her dressing gown around herself and walked out. Paisley was sitting at the table sipping coffee, phone to her ear and a scowl on her face. On the table in front of her was a music box.

She must have made a noise, because Paisley looked around and smiled. After muttering something into the phone she ended the call.

'Morning!'

'Morning. What's this?' Callie moved to the table and picked up the music box. It was ornately designed, circular, decorated in purple and gold carousel images. A little gold plaque on the lid read *Ava*. When she opened it a familiar yet unnameable melody flowed as a ballerina twirled. 'I've heard this before.'

'It's Mozart's Lullaby. You haven't seen this?'

Callie studied it carefully. 'I don't think so . . . I know the tune, I just didn't know what it was called. Why?'

'I thought you must have left it here.'

'Me?' Then another thought had her heart skipping a beat. 'Did it turn up during the night? Because that's what happened with the doll.'

Paisley raked her fingers through her hair. 'I'll ask Dad and Ned. But I don't know how they would have found them.'

'There is a big clean-up going on.'

'Yeah but . . . Mum used to run a support group here for mentally ill outpatients and their families. While the meetings were on, the kids would play around — we'd just be left to entertain ourselves. One of the teenage boys used to enjoy teasing Ava. He was horrible, would break all her toys, used to think it was funny. So she took to hiding her most treasured possessions whenever there was a meeting coming up. She called them her secret spots. When she died, we couldn't find them. We searched everywhere.' She took the music box and set it carefully back on the table. 'The doll and the music box were two of them.'

'How old was she?'

'Not quite five. God . . . ' Paisley drew in a deep breath and it trembled back out. 'It's like someone's trying to punish me, to remind me.'

'Paisley.' Callie sat and smiled with sympathy. 'What happened?'

'She drowned. I was supposed to be watching her on one of those meeting nights and I fell asleep. She went down to find the other kids and ended up in the river.'

'How old were you?'

'Twelve.'

'You were only a child yourself.'

'I stopped being a child when I dragged her out of the river.'

'*You* found her? Oh, Paisley, that's horrible. I'm so sorry.'

Paisley shrugged. 'It was a long time ago. It's just seeing her things has brought it all back.' She got up and walked into the kitchen. 'Anyway, why don't you have some breakfast? Then we'll get moving.'

They went into Hobart to look at a retirement community for Cliff, then Paisley shouted Callie lunch at a cute little café called Ginger Browns, just down the road from the facility. They ate focaccias and drank coffee, and with the normality of it all, some of the tension of the morning faded.

'How's the coffee?' Paisley asked.

'Good,' Callie said. 'So's the food.'

'You're off in Callie land though. Why?'

'I don't want to bring it back up, but we haven't actually figured out who's leaving Ava's things in the cottage.'

'I haven't asked Dad yet. If it wasn't him, it might be possible there's another key or two floating around. Dad used to lease the cottage out for extra income after Mum and I left. I can't figure out why any of them would have Ava's toys, or feel the need to return them, but just to cover all the bases and make you feel better, maybe we should change the deadlock on the front and back doors.'

'Sounds good to me,' Callie said with relief.

Paisley studied her over the rim of her mug. 'If you're really worried, why don't you consider staying in Hobart — at least until I get back? Have a bit of a holiday. You can café and restaurant it all you want. Be around people.'

'And do what? The only time I actually feel normal is when I'm working at Calico Mountain.'

'And you want to keep that up?'

'Of course. But is it safe? I promised Connor I'd call, but I don't know what to tell him. He probably thinks I've already bolted.'

'There's been no sign of any media at the cottage and Connor would have let you know if anyone had turned up out there, right? Callie, you were proven innocent. You need to be able to live your life. I really think you should stay. I've got Adelaide chasing down your mystery woman. Give it a few more days.'

Callie took a sip of her coffee and nodded. 'Okay.'

'Oh, and I talked to Ned.' Paisley put down her cup and folded her hands together. 'He said he'd initially only spoken to you to check how you were going when he was bringing firewood or doing the lawns — both of which I asked him to do. But calling him when you're frightened

257

because the power is off, having drinks with him after work, offering to make him dinner . . . that's kind of encouraging him, don't you think? It's difficult for me to tell him to leave you alone when it sounds as though you've instigated as much of the contact as he has.'

'None of that's anything like he made it sound!' Callie replied, her temper immediately skyrocketing. 'I spoke to Ned because your dad told me to talk to him about the electricity. I wanted to ask if I could call out an electrician. I told him I'd have a drink because he kept at me and at me over a dinner I'd said no to and he didn't want to take no for an answer. Connor and Tess and Logan all joined in so I wouldn't have to sit with him alone. Connor even pretended at one point to be interested in me as a clear signal to back off and *still* Ned came back acting as though we were just having some little lovers' tiff because I'd told him loud and clear to back the hell off!'

'Connor Atherton?' Paisley asked, curious.

'Yes. My point is I'm not making this up or leading Ned on!'

'Okay, okay, calm down,' Paisley said. 'I've told him to steer clear. Back to Connor — what did he do?'

Still bristling a little, Callie told her, and Paisley laughed. It unwound some of the tension in Callie's chest.

'So you and Connor . . . no wonder you want to keep working out there.'

'On that occasion he was simply trying to dissuade Ned.'

Paisley nodded but her eyes were sparkling. 'On that occasion? Why do I suspect there's another occasion you're not telling me about?'

'Because there was,' Callie admitted. 'And on *that* occasion . . . ' Her smile broke free. 'He most definitely was not pretending.'

Paisley's eyes were wide and interested. 'Tell me all.'

'There's not much to tell.' But when Callie finished her story, Paisley was grinning like a Cheshire cat.

'He's gorgeous and loaded and available. And so are you. So?'

'I — well, okay. Yes, he is. But look how that turned out for me last time.'

'Oh, don't you dare use that excuse to back away. Honestly, from what you've told me, he has just as many reasons to be distrustful of relationships as you do, and he's willing.'

'And I didn't say I wasn't. I'm just not really . . . prepared.'

'When is anyone, ever? This is good. Great. I thought you were sworn off men forever.'

'So did I,' Callie admitted with a heavy sigh. 'Apparently one *might* have gotten under my skin a little bit.'

'A little bit? With a kiss like you just described?'

Callie grinned and pressed a hand to her stomach. 'I didn't think I could feel those kinds of sensations again. He only has to look at me a certain way and I — it's almost embarrassing.'

Paisley laughed. 'It's fantastic.'

'It could be,' Callie agreed, then changed the

subject. 'So what are we doing this afternoon?'

'Packing boxes?' Paisley asked hopefully.

Callie groaned good-naturedly. 'Right. Let's get started.'

21

Callie flopped on the bed and rubbed her eyes. Following yesterday's efforts, she'd again spent the morning with Paisley checking out the last couple of retirement options for Cliff, before having lunch and spending the time leading up to Paisley's flight wandering the Salamanca Markets.

It should have been a good day — was a good day — except her mind kept wandering back to her contract and what to do about her feelings for Connor. Was she going back? What if she went back, started something with Connor, and then had to leave after all? She groaned even as she smirked. Who was she kidding about *starting* something? It was already well underway. She was at least half in love with him and a lot of this current feeling of restless anxiousness was, if she was honest, because she hadn't seen Connor for two days.

Feeling a little bit pathetic, she got up, took some soup over for Cliff, then rekindled the fire and poured herself a glass of merlot. She should call Connor. And tell him what? She was going back tomorrow, or she wasn't? She became at least partially engrossed in the end of a movie while she contemplated that. And then the power shut off.

'Again?' She dragged herself to her feet. She didn't like her chances of Ned bothering to fix the power any time soon so she headed out into the cold and flicked it back on. It wasn't raining, which left her wondering why it had shut off. Was it about to pack up altogether? The television had sprung back to life and she flicked through the channels, sitting through part of a game show, then caught the start of the local news. A story about a local woman feared drowned after a boating accident on the River Derwent appeared. A search was underway. The glass slipped from Callie's fingers as she stared at the screen in shock. It was that woman! The one who had turned up in the garden and warned her to leave.

She nearly jumped out of her skin when her phone rang. 'Hello?'

'Hey, Callie, it's Tess. How are you?'

Tess? Why was Tess calling? 'Good question, actually,' she answered, still watching the screen.

'What's up? You sound strange.'

'I'm pretty sure I know who the woman that bailed me up out at your place was.'

'Oh? Who?'

'The same woman who was just on the news. They think she's drowned.'

'Really? Give me a sec.' True to her word, she was back on the line fast. 'We're coming over.'

'Who?'

'Indy and I.'

'Now? Really? Why?'

'Because Indy said we are,' Tess replied.

'Then I'll sec you soon,' Callie said, curious but grateful. She went to her laptop to pull up the story so she could show Indy when they arrived. She studied the picture of the woman on her screen. It was just coincidence. What else could it be?

She yelped when the electricity clicked off again. Twice in one night. Maybe the wires really were caving in. She walked into the bedroom and saw Cliff's light on. It was definitely just the cottage power supply playing up again.

The window went dark as a silhouette blacked out most of it.

Callie fell back from the window.

Then the silhouette was gone.

Her breath trembled out and she sucked another back in. Listened. A step in the leaf litter on the patio outside had her spinning. Then the door handle rattled. Her eyes went to the fireplace, to the poker.

The lights sprang to life just as three sharp bangs on the door shook her.

'You there, Callie?'

Ned! Her breath came out in a rush. 'Yeah, coming.'

She opened the door halfway. 'What are you doing here?'

'Just wanted to tell you I'd been up in your roof earlier. Think I know how to fix the power, just need a few bits and pieces.'

'I appreciate that,' she said coolly. 'It's been off twice tonight and it's not raining.'

He dragged a hand along the back of his neck. 'Guess I might have stirred things up a bit playing around. Sorry about that.'

'No worries,' she said. 'Goodnight, Ned.'

'And I also need to apologise for my behaviour

last time we spoke. Didn't mean to upset you.'

It surprised her that he actually looked as though he meant it. Paisley must have gotten through.

'I just think you're a special person. Was hoping to spend time with you. But I realise I shouldn't have gotten cross because you prefer Connor to me. I'd like it if we could get back to just being friendly.'

Oh, hell. The guy was grovelling. And this version of Ned was just pathetic enough to have her feeling silly and guilty at the same time. 'That's okay. Sure.'

'Something smells good. Dad said you made him some soup. I haven't had a chance to eat anything tonight.'

She wrestled with her manners. This might smooth over the awkwardness . . . and give her a chance to get some answers. Besides, Tess and Indy would be here soon. 'I can heat you some up to take back?'

'That's really nice of you. Wouldn't say no.'

She walked into the kitchen, pulled the leftovers from the fridge and put a bowl in the microwave. The heating time amounted to a couple of minutes of uncomfortable silence — for her. Ned seemed right at home.

'Paisley said you looked at some places for Dad.'

'Yes. One in particular was very nice.'

'So Paisley said. Gardens look good out at Calico Mountain.' He paused. 'Made quite the impression on Connor, haven't you? He's not right for you though.'

264

'I'm enjoying the gardens,' she said. 'It's a lovely place to work.' She took out the bowl and got some foil to cover it.

'Don't worry about that,' Ned said, taking the bowl from her hands. 'Only take me a minute to eat. Got a spoon?'

She gritted her teeth and retrieved one from the drawer.

He swallowed a mouthful, made a happy noise. 'This is good. You know what would go well with it? A nice glass of red wine. You want me to top up the fire for you?'

'Ah . . . no. Thanks. I'm afraid I don't have any wine.'

'Dad's got a few bottles lying around. I could — '

'No, really. I don't drink much.'

He frowned. 'Paisley says you own a vineyard.'

'Yes, at least I did. But it was more my husband's side of the business. I ran the bed and breakfast.'

'Right.' Ned ate more soup. 'You want to know why Connor's no good for you?'

When would she learn? Had she really thought Ned would just give up? 'No. Actually, I wanted to talk to you about Ava's things. About you bringing them over to the cottage for Paisley.'

'Already told Paisley it wasn't me,' he said, scraping the last of the soup from his bowl. 'Not about to come in uninvited, leaving stuff around.'

'I wouldn't be upset,' she lied. 'I'd just feel better knowing who it was.'

His eyes met hers and she thought maybe she

265

saw something calculating behind the innocence. 'You sure you didn't find them yourself?'

'Why would I find them myself, then accuse you of doing it?'

'Just saying, you don't need a reason to get me over here, that's all. You don't need to make stuff up to get my attention.'

Oh my God. 'Do you really believe that?' she snapped. 'Is it really possible you don't understand that hearing you say those things makes me feel ill?'

Ned got up slowly and, bowl in hand, approached her, his gaze unreadably blank.

She stepped back.

He continued to the sink, let go of the bowl. It crashed, making her jump.

'Appreciate the soup,' he said.

'Tess and Indy are on their way over,' she said, heart in her throat. 'You should go.'

'I'm going,' he said and walked to the front door. 'But don't forget I'm at the house for the time being. Not far at all.'

Something about his stare made her genuinely frightened.

The sweep of headlights signalled an arriving car and his face brightened into a smile as his tone lightened. 'He's not right for you — Connor. Here's your friends. Goodnight, Callie.'

She waited for Tess and Indy to get out of the car. Smiled as best she could. 'Hi. Thanks for coming.'

'Hi,' Tess said.

Indy was busy watching Ned's retreat with

interest. When her eyes swung back to Callie's they were friendly, assessing. But there was something about the look. And her stance had authority written all over it.

'What was Ned doing here?'

'He's spending a lot of time here keeping an eye on Cliff and tidying up. And my power went out. Ned came over and turned it back on, asked for some soup.' She led them inside. 'I've been cooking for Cliff and Ned's gotten a bit used to getting some too.' Not sure what to do with herself, she got a glass of water, noticed her hand wasn't steady as she sipped it.

Indy's expression was thoughtful. 'So you called Ned then, after you'd spoken to us?'

'Ah . . . no. Why?'

'Then how did he know your power was off?'

She had no answer. 'I don't know . . . I guess he saw all the lights off perhaps. I saw someone outside my window, which must have been him. Gave me a heart attack. He was probably looking in to see why all the lights were off.'

'He shouldn't be creeping around outside in the dark. Is that what's upset you?'

'Huh? Oh.' She supposed she wasn't hiding it very well. 'He was a bit intense. Then he wasn't. I can't explain it. He's — '

'Scaring you,' Indy decided. 'Want to file a complaint against him?'

'File a complaint against Paisley's brother? For what? He hasn't done anything. Exactly.'

'Isn't that a bit harsh?' Tess asked.

'At least keep a journal,' Indy said. 'Put everything in you can think of up to this point in

267

time specifically outlining anything he's said or done that's bothered you and anything you've said or done about it. Keep it up to date. Then if it does come to you feeling like you need to take it further, we have it all down.'

'You're the first person who's taken this seriously,' Callie told Indy. 'No offence, Tess, but everyone else says, 'Oh, it's just Ned, don't worry.''

'I'm a cop,' Indy said. 'I've seen the results of not worrying about it a few too many times.'

'And I'm not offended,' Tess said. 'He was really possessive the other day at lunch. Connor wasn't happy about it either. Told him well and truly to back off.'

He had? 'I guess I'll do the journal then. Just in case,' Callie said.

Indy looked around. 'This is a nice little cottage.'

'Yeah. I'm enjoying it. Mostly. It just seems to be that so many people are finding out I'm down here. And now that woman's probably dead and I'm sure it had nothing to do with me but what are the chances, right?'

'Marcie Williams.' Indy pinned Callie with what she could only think of as a very cop-like stare. 'You're sure it was her?'

'Yes. Positive. And she was so nervous and on edge the entire time she was talking to me. She kept looking around like she was expecting to be caught out. And the way she spoke . . . '

'Can you tell me exactly?'

'Of course. She said, 'They're watching you', and 'You need to leave. Get away. Fast.' I

268

thought — think — she meant the media, because who else would care that I was here? It's got me spooked that she's missing. Maybe dead.'

'Marcie had a few issues. I'd be surprised if Paisley didn't know her. She was part of a group her mother ran for families coping with mental illness.'

'Paisley mentioned that group,' Callie said. 'Apparently the kids entertained themselves on the grounds while the adults held their meetings.'

Indy flicked a glance at Tess. 'Orson's family also attended.' Then to Callie: 'I wonder if Paisley would mind giving me a list of all the group members?'

'I'm sure she wouldn't. Paisley's dead sister's things have been turning up in here without explanation and all Paisley could think of is that someone from back then might be bringing them over.'

Indy's brow lifted. 'Someone's been in here?'

'Yeah. Marcie hasn't turned up?'

'No, no yet.'

'It must be hard on the family,' Tess said.

Indy shook her head again. 'The only relative ever recorded was a daughter who died giving birth.'

Tess winced. 'How sad!'

'Yeah, it is.' Indy went outside and looked around. 'Even worse — with Marcie's issues, the courts wouldn't let her raise the baby. The child went to the mother of the man who'd allegedly raped her daughter.'

'That's horrible!' Callie muttered.

269

'Yes. He'd only just gotten out of prison on drugs charges a few days prior. Two officers attempted to bring him in for questioning over the incident and he attacked them. Got another nine years for assaulting police. His mother, on the other hand, was some sort of pillar of the community. Go figure.' Indy looked around, frowning in thought. 'We should put a couple of security cameras up on the corners of the cottage. If anything else out of the ordinary happens, we can see what's going on. Wouldn't hurt to make the outside lights sensor lights, either. How are the locks on the doors and windows?'

'We changed the deadlock yesterday.' And suddenly, with Indy's input, all the little things that had been worrying Callie seemed far more serious. 'How concerned should I be, exactly?'

Indy's expression softened. 'Sorry, Callie, I didn't mean to scare you. This is for peace of mind. You'll feel safer if you put these precautions in place.'

Callie let herself relax. 'Okay. And you're right, I will.'

22

Connor usually enjoyed the stroll from the guest-house to the stables, especially on a morning still tinged with sunrise. But this morning he was pre-occupied. He found Logan saddling his stallion.

'Morning,' Logan said.

'Hey. I thought I might borrow a horse, head out to where we last saw Orson.'

Logan dropped the saddle flap back in place and reached for the bridle. 'Mate, he's long gone. And the cops have been all over it.'

He knew that, but, 'It doesn't seem right to do nothing.'

'You want some company then? I've got to give Rex some exercise.'

'Yeah, sounds good.' Connor turned and looked down the breezeway at the sound of a car. 'What's Indy doing here?'

Logan looked around him and waved at his wife. 'Come to see Ned I reckon. He's working this morning. She'll want to catch him before he goes back to Waldron Park.'

'Why?'

'She and Tess went out to Callie's last night. Someone's been poking around or something.'

Indy strolled down the breezeway and gave Rex's golden coat a pat. 'Morning.'

'Morning,' Connor said. 'Was there a problem last night? Is Callie okay?' Why hadn't she called him?

'She's fine.' Then to Logan she said, 'Is Ned around?'

'In the yards. Hold on.' He went out, whistled and gestured for Ned to join them.

Connor's temper flashed. 'Ned was creeping around?'

'I'll handle it,' Indy said under her breath as Ned ambled in and looked at them all suspiciously.

'What's up?'

'Morning, Ned,' Indy said. 'I heard you went over to Callie's last night and turned on the electricity to the cottage.'

He shrugged. 'Didn't want her sitting around in the dark.'

'Right. What was with the creeping around, looking in the windows?'

'I wasn't creeping around,' he said with a scowl. 'I walked onto the patio, knocked on the door.'

'That's not how Callie recalled it. You peeked in her bedroom window, didn't you?'

'Was wondering why she was sitting around in the dark. Someone's gotta look after her,' he said to Connor.

Connor's fists clenched at his sides as he took a quick step forward. 'I'll give you — '

Indy's hand against his arm pulled him up. 'We're upping the security on the cottage,' she told Ned.

'In what way?' Ned asked. 'Not sure Dad would appreciate — '

'Property improvements?' Indy said. 'I'm sure he won't mind. We all want Callie to be safe and

272

enjoy her privacy. Don't we?'

'Of course.'

'Good. Because next time we talk about this, it'll be at the station. Clear?' Her tone and accompanying glare didn't suggest she was making empty threats.

'That it?' Ned growled.

'Just one more thing. You wouldn't happen to know a Marcie Williams, would you?'

'Huh? Um. No.'

When she stood there silently doing what Connor had come to think of as the Indy stare, Ned shuffled uncomfortably.

'Well, could have, as a kid. Friend of Mum's. I think.'

'Any idea why she'd warn Callie to leave town?'

Ned's head snapped up. 'She shouldn't be doing that!'

'Why not?'

'Just shouldn't. Got no right. Always was screwy. One of Mum's nuts. Are we done? I need to keep working.'

'Sure. That's all for now. Thanks, Ned.'

Ned scowled again, but nodded and stalked out.

Connor rubbed his hands over his face. 'Ned's never hurt a flea. He's always been the least scary person I've ever met. But I don't know what to make of him at the moment. I could have knocked him flat just then. Is this crush of his dangerous?'

'I consider any unstable personality with a habit of developing inappropriate infatuations as

273

a potential time bomb. That said, threat or no threat, some security will make Callie feel better. If my husband of five years who I trusted just about more than anyone on the planet suddenly morphed into a cheating, murdering liar who tackled me over morning coffee with the intent to violently kill me, I'd be jumping at every shadow, every noise, every possible threat too.'

'Speaking of Callie, did she happen to mention if she's planning on coming in this morning?' he asked.

'Not immediately. Tess and I are taking her security shopping.'

'Great. Indy, thanks,' he said.

'You'll get your turn. You boys can do some installation.'

'We can?' Logan asked, then grinned at the looks they sent him. 'Sure we can. But first we're going for a ride.'

'Okay — make sure you take the dogs with you,' she said. 'They need a good run.'

'Will do,' Logan promised. 'Go grab a horse,' he said to Connor. 'We'll get moving.'

They rode quickly as far as the boundary, traced the fence line, though Connor knew any chance of finding a clue to where Orson had gone was all but hopeless. Then they got up onto the national park trails, followed them as far as horseback allowed.

'We knew it was a long shot,' Logan said when the horses dropped their heads to amble and the dogs, tongues out, began to fall back. 'The chances of him setting up camp out here were always slim. We should head back.'

'At least I got a pretty ride out of it,' Connor said. 'And your dogs got their exercise.'

'True.' Logan whistled. The dogs loped back to the horses. 'So what was that about someone trying to scare Callie off?'

'A woman — I'm gathering they've figured out it was that Marcie Indy asked Ned about — turned up while she was working, told her she should leave.'

'So she's taking off?'

'I hope not,' Connor said. 'But I don't want to call her and hassle her.'

'Ah . . . now I see.'

'What do you see?'

'If you love them, let them go?' Logan teased.

'Shut up,' Connor said and moved his horse around a fallen tree to cut through the scrub.

They picked their way through the easiest of the terrain, re-joined the trail in places where the scrub was too thick to ride through comfortably. The dogs were getting further and further behind so Logan stopped, whistled them up again. When they didn't show he had another go, and heard a bark somewhere off to their left.

'What've they got bailed up, I wonder?' Logan said.

'Let's go find out.' Connor turned his horse in the general direction of the sound and Logan came up beside him. 'There they are,' Connor said, spotting a dog sniffing around.

'Oh, shit! Damn it. Bloody hell. Get back!' Logan whistled again, gave a sharp, curt command for the dogs to return. They reluctantly left their find, moved around behind the horse.

Connor stared, unable to move as what he was seeing sank in. Orson was lying on a patch of roughly cleared ground, hands and feet staked inside a red circle. He was pretty sure the spray-painted lines partially obscured by his body formed a pentagram. Deep wounds had been carved into his body and his neck was almost severed by the slash under the jaw. A waxy substance had been poured over his head, hands and feet, and something oily had pooled in the crevices of the wounds. Flies and insects covered the body, and the smell threatened to turn his stomach.

A crow cawed from a low branch of a gum beside the body and Connor moved forward to scare it off. The insects were bad enough.

'Don't go any closer!' Logan warned. 'That's a crime scene. Indy'll skin you.'

'What kind of a sick son of a bitch does something like this?'

'I'm guessing the same sort that'd do it to a horse,' Logan replied in disgust. His phone was to his ear. 'I can't get a signal. We're going to have to go back a bit further before I can call.'

Connor eyed the bird again. 'How far? We can't just leave him.'

'It's still a few k's back but it won't take long. We'll mark the spot.'

'How did he get all the way out here?'

'We'll know more once the scene has been analysed. Let's go.'

Could they really just leave Orson? Connor didn't feel right about it. 'I think I should wait here.'

'Not a chance in hell,' Logan growled. 'Mate, whoever did this could still be around. Orson wasn't a small human. He was young and fit and strong, and still someone managed this. Recently — there's no way a police search team missed this last week. We stick together. Let's go.'

★ ★ ★

Because Indy had been called back to work in the middle of their security shopping, Tess suggested they head out to Calico Mountain for lunch, maybe do a bit of gardening together. It was a show of support, a chance to ease back in with company, and help if anything went wrong. Callie appreciated it. And seeing Connor would be better than calling him. So she agreed.

They'd just gotten to the point of placing plants in the third new garden bed when they noticed a trio of women standing on the side-lines, watching with interest. Callie exchanged wary glances with Tess but kept working, and after a couple more minutes, obviously over it, Tess straightened and approached them.

'Can I help you?'

'Hello,' the taller of them said, her eyes moving from Tess to study Callie.

Oh shit, here we go again. She almost ran. Wanted to drop her things and get out of there. But she needed to know what they were going to say. She needed to start standing up for herself, facing it.

'Yes?' Callie asked instead, moving over next to Tess.

'Did you do all these garden beds?'

'Yes, she did,' Tess answered for her.

'They look absolutely stunning. You should be proud of yourself.'

Relief was her overriding emotion, and Callie smiled. 'Thank you.'

'You're like that woman,' another one said and Callie's heart pounded again.

Callie pulled the cap a little lower over her face. 'Which woman?'

'The one on *Better Homes and Gardens*, who can do all those male jobs with the tools and things. Tara someone. You were managing all that plastic tubing by yourself.'

'Oh, well, it's not that difficult.'

'Do you have a card?' the first woman asked. 'Because we only live up at Devonport and I'd love something like that first garden over there in our backyard. We have a couple of acres . . . '

When they left, Callie let herself smile. She'd taken the woman's number and promised to call her as soon as she'd finished out here. It lifted her mood dramatically.

'And there you go,' Tess said, grinning back. 'Not all strangers are bad news.'

'Thanks for stepping in, just in case.'

'I had my trusty — ' She held it up. 'What's this?'

'Trowel,' Callie said with a laugh.

'That's a nice sound,' Connor said.

She turned around, her smile dropping a fraction as she searched his face, hoping to read what he was thinking.

He solved the problem by planting a light kiss

278

on her mouth. 'Hi.'

'Ah . . . hi,' she said, melting. He was watching her with so much warmth, any traces of concern that he might have been annoyed by her absence vanished.

'Yeah, hi,' Tess said loudly, 'and can I ask, when did this happen?'

'The definition of 'this' isn't quite sorted yet,' Callie mumbled.

'I'm glad you're back,' Connor said.

'So am I. I'm sorry I didn't call but — something's happened,' she said. Because his smile had dropped and he wore the expression he'd worn when Orson had gone missing.

'Yeah, it has,' he said and paused. 'We found Orson's body this morning.'

'What? Where?' Tess and Callie asked simultaneously.

'Up in the national park. About five kilometres from our back fence.'

'But the police searched there,' Tess said, confused.

'Yeah. Um . . . Indy thinks he was brought back there for the . . . murder. It looks like he's been there since the day following his disappearance.'

'Murdered,' Callie repeated quietly.

'Yeah.'

She guessed there was more he wasn't saying. She didn't mind, as she wasn't sure she needed to hear it anyway. This was no doubt the call Indy had raced off to.

'Do we know who killed him?' Tess asked.

'Not yet. And yeah, Indy and her team are up

there working on it.'

'So Indy's a homicide detective?' Callie asked.

'Among other things.'

'It doesn't really surprise me,' she said.

'Does this mean we have to shut down the guesthouse for an investigation?' Tess asked.

'No, it's not looking like it. None of us are suspects — we can all vouch for one another, and his body was left in the park. There's no evidence anything took place on the property. It's fine to keep running.'

'You look exhausted,' Callie said. 'You should go rest.'

'I don't think I'd get that image out of my head. But I'm going to head up, get something to eat. Maybe a drink. How are you ladies going?'

'I think we could just about call it a day,' Tess said. 'Callie?'

'Yeah,' she said, no longer in the mood for work. 'That'll do.'

★　★　★

An hour later Connor led Callie back to her car. 'Thanks for the drink,' she told him as she dug out her key.

'Yeah, no worries.' He wasn't sure why she was thanking him, he'd barely said a word. Tess, as usual, had done everything she could to brighten everyone up. People liked that about her, how she always bounced back. It was a trait he admired most of the time. No doubt tomorrow, or the next day, she'd draw a smile out of him. But he was dog tired and done with today.

Seeing Callie was the only thing that hadn't pushed him towards his apartment, a bottle of scotch and a probable hangover. 'How'd everything turn out with the woman that bailed you up?'

'Not so good for the woman. Her name's Marcie. She's missing.'

'That's no good.' He saw the smirk. 'Is it funny?'

'No,' she said with a burst of quickly contained laughter. 'It's about as horrible as your attempt at sympathy. You were thinking she won't be able to bother me anymore.'

'How the hell did you get that?'

'If you're going to pull back the words, you need to remember to pull back the face too.'

He pressed her back against the car and knocked the cap from her head, raking his fingers into her hair as he crushed his mouth to hers. She made a *hmm* sound in her throat as she accepted his hot, hungry demand and met it with her own.

By the time he managed to pull himself up, he was out of breath, his whole body throbbing. 'Thank God you came back,' he muttered, and dived in again.

When he lifted his head the next time, Callie's lips were swollen and her eyes dangerously dreamy.

'Exhibitionist,' she murmured.

Having no idea what she was on about, he looked around and noticed the tour bus had pulled up and people were milling around, pretending to mind their own business. 'If you'd prefer some privacy we can . . . '

The chuckle came from deep in her throat and went straight to his loins. 'I'm going home,' she told him, lifting on her toes to place one final kiss on his mouth. 'Bye.'

He watched her go, pulling himself back together as best he could before heading inside.

'Connor, office?' Logan said from the top of the stairs.

Curious, he hurried up the stairs. Indy was waiting with Tess. 'When did you get back?' he asked her.

'Just now. You were, ah . . . otherwise engaged,' Indy said with an attempt at amusement that didn't quite light up her tired eyes.

'How did you go out there?'

'I doubt I'm going to be able to keep this quiet so I'm telling you now,' Indy said as they sat around his dining table, 'Orson's not the only victim of whoever is responsible for this. There was another victim killed in the same way a few weeks back. During the initial investigation it was revealed the victim had been burying his dog at the time of the attack so no one thought too much about the animal's grave site. I sent a team out there an hour ago and had them dig it up. It looks as though the dog might have been killed in a similar fashion to Bailey.'

'And you're thinking you could be dealing with a serial killer?' Logan asked in disbelief.

'I'm not ready to put a label on this yet,' Indy said. 'But whoever this is, they're incredibly skilled at not leaving evidence.'

'Have you found Kaicey?' he asked, worried.

'She assumed Orson was dead before we even knew what was going on. She told me she was the only one left. She knows who this is.'

'We can't find her, but we're still looking.'

Connor swore. 'I brought this here.'

'Oh, come on, man, don't do that to yourself,' Logan said. 'You've got to learn that sometimes fucked-up things happen. You don't have a damn crystal ball. You're not responsible for this any more than you were responsible for Jules. And honestly, you're starting to piss me off. We've got enough to worry about without making everything your fault.'

'All right,' Connor said. 'What are we going to do?'

'Keep a close eye out for anything or anyone out of the ordinary,' Indy said. 'Whatever this is, it's not centred around or directed at this place. There's no reason to think the killer will come back here. I'll let you know when I can share anything else.'

23

Callie sprang awake, freezing and shaking, arms over her face protectively as she fought for breath. Little by little the dream cleared and her pulse resumed its regular, steady beat, and her hands dropped back to her sides. It was morning. After *that* nightmare, thank God it was morning. What had started as another dream of pink and pretty things had darkened and contorted into a terrifying black hole of menacing shadows and dangerous shapes clawing and pulling at her, robbing her of breath. The images continued to dance around the edges of her consciousness as she got up and calmed herself down. *Just a dream*, she told herself. *Just a very vivid dream.*

She pulled up the blankets and heard the thump of something hitting the floor. A book.

What was a book doing on her bed?

Frowning, she picked it up. It was heavy and old, its dark-red cloth cover marked, its spine faded and damaged. The gilt title read *The Fairy Tales of Brothers Grimm*. A first edition, she noted, flicking through the aged pages with their detailed illustrations. They certainly weren't pictures that would have helped her sleep as a child, she thought, looking at a little boy and girl being lured into the dwelling of an evil old woman. She went to the kitchen for coffee, wrinkling her nose at the remains of the tuna mornay she'd eaten right before sleeping last night. She was pretty sure indigestion could cause bad dreams. She'd refrain from eating late from now on. Perhaps would never eat it again. She took the book over to the shelf. Before she went into a meltdown panic she'd make sure Paisley didn't know anything about it. They had brought some books and other bits and pieces back while she was here; perhaps it had gotten caught up in her doona and she hadn't noticed. Callie wasn't sure she really believed it, but they'd changed the locks on the doors. She was now the only person in existence with the keys. No one could get in.

It was early, but Paisley would be up, so she called her.

'I have no idea,' Paisley said when Callie mentioned the book. 'I remember the edition, because the stories in there aren't the sweetness-and-light fairy tales of today, so I used to read it to freak myself out when I was little. Maybe I did bring it back with us to the cottage, but there's something else I need to tell you that's more important.'

Callie didn't like Paisley's tone, and the book was suddenly forgotten. 'What's wrong?'

'There's a good chance Dale's parents are going to sue for a share of the property money.'

'They *what?*' Callie put her hand on her head and swore in disbelief.

'I know, right? Pair of arseholes. I couldn't believe it either, but you know how reliable Tracy Marks is with that sort of gossip. She swears Francis just came right out and said it in the middle of her hair colour.'

'What kind of share?'

'They think they're entitled to Dale's half of everything. Apparently they have an appointment with their solicitor next Friday. Francis said because of the circumstances of Dale's death and the fact they threw money at the place to help get it up and running, they should be entitled to his share.'

'They can't!'

'That I don't know, but maybe think about talking to your solicitor to make sure? You know they're friends with Myra from the estate agent. I wouldn't be surprised if she let slip the offer on the place and that got them thinking about all this.'

'I will. See if there's anything we can do if they do decide to go ahead with it.'

'Sorry to drop that on you.'

'Better that I know in advance. I'll let you know what I find out.' Callie ended the call and found her solicitor's number. It wasn't difficult to dig out — it was stored in her phone and she almost knew it by heart. She left a message, hoped it wouldn't take long to hear back.

Anger sat on her chest and threatened to strangle her. She wanted to call Dale's parents, tell them what she thought of them and promise they wouldn't get away with it. To escape the temptation she grabbed her jacket and went out into the cold to breathe some fresh air.

The river sparkled as the sun broke through a rising blanket of fog. Callie turned the radio on to stop the chatter of her own thoughts and sipped her coffee as she watched the day wake up from her position on the patio. As a song faded, the radio host announced a beautiful clear day following an impressive Bridgewater Jerry. Was that what they called the fog around here?

She heard a car and peeked around the corner of the cottage to see Indy pull up.

Indy smiled when she spotted Callie, getting out of the car and taking a thick, wool-lined jacket and a plastic folder from the backseat. 'Morning. Aren't you cold?' she called.

'No. But I have six layers on. Coffee?'

'It would be appreciated. Is the fire on inside by any chance?'

Callie smiled, hoped it looked normal. 'Hey, you're the local, aren't you supposed to have thick blood or something?'

'It must take more years than I've been here.'

Callie got up and opened the door. 'Come in.' She headed straight for the kitchen. 'So what's up?' Though Indy's tone had been brisk and cheerful enough, something told her this was business.

Indy slid into a chair at the table and took the coffee-filled mug, wrapping her hands around it. 'I suppose Connor would have told you about Orson Lovett?'

'The one who was murdered up on the national park trails behind Calico Mountain.'

'Right.' Indy inhaled the steam from her mug, took a cautious sip. 'Did he happen to give you any details?'

'No. Why?'

'I'll get to that. Can I show you a couple of

287

photos? I want to see if you recognise anyone.'

Callie couldn't see why she would, but she didn't have any objection. 'Sure.'

She took the first photo. Studied it. Fair hair, nothing outstanding about the man that would make her remember him or even look twice. 'No.'

'Okay, what about this one?'

'That's Orson.'

'Yes.'

She took another look at the first photo. Perhaps . . . 'Wait — what's this one's name?'

'Michael Smythe. But he'd been going by the name Mitch Walker. Why?'

'Hold on.' Callie went to the bookshelf and scanned the titles, finding Paisley's yearbook. She flicked through to the page she was looking for and found the photo of the group of kids at the function, checking their names. 'Did you know they were friends at school?'

'Woods and Lovett? No. I didn't know about that connection.' She took the open book and studied it closely. 'That's Mike and Orson. Dale — your husband? And Paisley, Lisa Mathers, Kristen Callaghan — '

'Kaicey.'

Indy looked closer. 'You're right.'

'They're in different classes and year groups. But in the social photos it's clear they were friends. Dale moved up to the Hunter the year after this.'

'Dale never mentioned any of these people?'

'Paisley, of course. He might have mentioned the others, I can't remember.'

288

Indy nodded, put down the yearbook and pointed to the girl with her arm around Dale's shoulders. 'Callie, I'm sorry to go over this so graphically, but you know how badly mutilated the woman in the photos was, so I need you to tell me — because you saw her alive — could this be the same Lisa who turned up on your doorstep?'

Callie's stomach sank but she considered the image carefully. Could it? 'I suppose it's possible but she really didn't look anything like that. She looked . . . sick, thin, and her hair was dyed.'

'When all this started back in the Hunter, was Lisa the only stranger to turn up?'

'Initially, yes, though later there was one guy.'

'Who?'

'I don't know. He came to the house a couple of times during the trial. Then I saw him again, outside the courthouse afterwards. He wasn't media.'

'Have you seen him down here?'

'No.'

'Okay. If that changes, let me know.' Indy looked up from the notes she was taking and took another sip of coffee. 'Next, I want you to think back to just prior to the night of Lisa's death. Did you have any pets go missing or die?'

Callie shook her head slowly. 'We didn't own pets. Dale wanted a dog but we were so busy and with guests coming in and out all the time, we thought it might be a bit too much to juggle.'

'No neighbours out looking for pets, no stories of anything nasty?'

'The only thing even close to that was when Dale came home that next morning and said he'd hit a kangaroo with his car. He told me because he had scratches on his face he was trying to explain. Oh, and Lisa said her cat was dead. She just kind of blurted it out while saying she needed to tell, to end it. It was a weird statement. Didn't make any sense.'

Indy's eyes flared with interest. 'That wasn't in any of your transcripts.'

'I honestly forgot all about it.'

'Okay,' Indy said, noting that down.

'Indy, where are you going with all this? What has Lisa and a dead cat got to do with Orson's death?'

'I'm still working on that.'

'But you think it's all tied together. They all knew each other, but you didn't know that before you got here. So there's something else.'

'I'll let you know when I can.' She smiled. 'Did you mention that support group list to Paisley?'

'No — sorry. Something came up and I forgot.'

'No problem. I'll give her a call. Can I borrow the yearbook?'

'I guess. I don't think Paisley would mind.'

'And if you don't mind, I might get you to sit down with a sketch artist. Get something together on this man who was bothering you during the trial. Just to be on the safe side.'

'Sure. If you really think so. When?'

'How does today sound?'

* * *

290

Connor was looking forward to a ride. The sky was brightening over a clear horizon and the forecast was cold but sunny. He jogged downstairs and out into the guesthouse before anyone could catch him. He'd deliberately left his phone in his apartment. He'd be an hour — two, tops. Tess could deal with any dramas until he returned. He'd take Bracken and Gypsy, head over to where Callie would be working and surprise her with a ride out on the trails, see if they could get as far as the national park. He'd avoid the area Orson was found, of course, head up somewhere high where Callie could get a sense of the size of everything out here.

The animals in the petting farm were noisy — breakfast time, he realised. Sure enough, Logan was unloading feeds from the ute and dispensing them. Two enormous pigs guzzled theirs from a trough while innumerable other hand-raised, generally placid animals complained noisily about how hungry they were.

'Morning!' Connor called.

Logan waved, dumped some hay for three fat steers, and walked across. 'Where are you sneaking off to?'

'You lot are always hassling me for not getting out of the office. So I'm getting out of the office. Early. Before too many things can go wrong without me.'

'Well, I've got one problem I can tell you about,' Logan said. 'Missing goat.'

'Really?'

'Yeah, Peggy. She'll come back when she's hungry.'

'That'd be a pretty safe bet.'

'What are you up to?'

'I thought I might take Bracken and Gypsy out. That okay?'

Logan pulled another two feed buckets from the Gator tray. His eyes gleamed with laughter. 'Can barely get you to take one horse out usually, now you need two?'

'I'd like to show Callie around, let her see the place.'

'It's no problem. Enjoy.'

'Thanks. I'll go find her first, make sure she's — '

The scream was sharp, loud and bloodcurdling.

'Bunkhouse?' Logan guessed.

'Yeah, I reckon.'

The two feed buckets hit the ground as they took off. Connor was puffing hard by the time they rounded the bend in the garden, loped up the stairs and down the hallway.

'Ah, hell.'

The scream had come from Meghan and now she cowered from the pretty black and white pet goat swinging from the fan light in the room Kaicey had stayed in. A circle of blood had dripped from its neck onto the bed. Other staff stood behind Meghan, all equally as repulsed, eyes wide, voices hushed.

Logan switched off the fan and examined the goat. 'Throat's been cut,' he muttered unnecessarily. With an oath, he spun on his heel and walked out, fists clenched, head tipped back to the roof. Then he turned around. 'We can't touch anything. Everyone needs to get out.'

Connor already had his phone in his hand. 'I'll call Indy.' Guilt and anger made his words difficult as he relayed what had happened. What kind of fucked-up lunatic were they dealing with? Normal people didn't do this shit. Bailey, then Orson, now Peggy — in Kaicey's room. He took one steady breath, then another, fighting against the urge to lose his breakfast.

'No chance of keeping this quiet any longer,' Logan said.

'No,' Connor agreed. 'Prepare for panic.'

★　★　★

Callie was a good couple of hours behind by the time she reached Calico Mountain. She'd followed Indy to the police station and waited for the artist to come in. Working up an identity sketch wasn't a quick process and at some point during it, Indy had stuck her head in to say she had to rush off, and Callie had been left with the quiet, friendly Daniel to finish the sketch. She'd been pretty happy with the end result though. It wasn't perfect, but the stare that had met hers from the page was alike enough to send prickles of unease skidding over her skin.

She was looking forward to seeing Connor, though nerves danced in her stomach as she remembered yesterday's kiss. She hadn't wanted to complicate her life like this. But it didn't seem to matter what she told herself, as soon as he touched her she forgot all her own good advice.

She looked down the drive to the bunkhouse

and saw two police cars and a couple more unmarked vehicles outside. Her stomach dipped. What was going on? She thought about Orson. Someone came out of the bunkhouse wearing what looked like a surgical suit. She turned her car towards the parking area and called Connor.

'Should I be here?' she asked when he answered. 'What's happened?'

'Where are you?'

'Just pulling into the carpark.'

'I'll meet you out there.'

She wasn't sure where he came from, but he was already jogging across the gravel as she got out.

'Hey,' he said with a smile, but there was enough tension in it to tell her it had taken some effort.

'Did someone else die?'

'Hold on.' He pulled her in for a kiss. 'Good morning.'

He fried her brain when he did that. It took her a few seconds to remember her question. She cleared her throat. 'Morning. So?'

'It's an animal, not a person.'

That didn't make sense. 'Four carloads of police for a dead animal?'

'Yeah. I know how it sounds but — '

'But that horse was killed before Orson and you said Kaicey took off because she was worried about that. Was that animal in Kaicey's room?'

'Yeah.'

'So there's a pattern. Dead animal, dead person.'

'It seems so. You'd have to ask Indy.'

'I tried. She doesn't say much.'

'You tried? When?'

'She came to the cottage to ask me some questions this morning. It ended up with me going into the station to meet a sketch artist to describe some guy who was hanging around during the trial. She was asking if I knew of any animals that had been found dead just prior to Lisa's murder. She *must* think there's some kind of connection.'

He frowned, putting an arm around her and trying to guide her towards the guesthouse. 'Or she's simply ruling one out. Why don't you come inside? Have you eaten anything? Do you want a coffee?'

How could there be any connection between what Dale did and what's happening down here? Dale was dead. Could the media have been onto something with their theory about some sort of cult? Callie shook her head and ducked out from his hold. 'Don't fuss.'

'I'm not fussing,' Connor objected. 'Fussing's what little old ladies do.'

He sounded so insulted Callie laughed. 'I'm fine. I'd rather get stuck into it.'

Though they couldn't see the bunkhouse, Connor's gaze slid off in that direction. 'I might help for a while. Stick around out here.'

'Still fussing,' she said.

He gently grasped her chin and looked into her eyes. 'I was going to ask if you'd like to go for a ride this morning. I had the horses organised. I wanted to take you up into the mountains — it's beautiful out there and I could have had you to myself for a couple of hours to . . . fuss.'

She felt the colour work its way up to her face. 'That might have been . . . nice,' she said.

'I could do a lot better than nice,' he promised, then stepped back, dropping the pressure building between them before it erupted. 'I won't fuss, but I would like to help you in the garden. That all right with you?'

Could she speak? She cleared her throat, decided it was worth a shot. 'Sure. Gardening. Right.'

24

On Friday night the devils returned. Callie had woken up to screeching and the sound of what she thought might have been two of them fighting. Even telling herself she knew the source of the Armageddon being waged outside her window wasn't enough to stop the damn things completely freaking her out and keeping her awake, so when she arrived at Calico Mountain, bleary eyed and yawning, she went straight up to the guesthouse in search of coffee.

Connor was taking Meghan through something on the reception computer and spotted Callie as she walked in, his smile warming before he looked her over with a furrowed brow. 'Don't move,' he told her, and finished his conversation with Meghan before coming out from behind the reception desk. He put an arm across Callie's shoulders to pull her in for a kiss and steer her into the dining room.

'Where are you thinking we're going?' she asked.

'I haven't had a coffee yet and — don't take this the wrong way — you look like you need one.'

She looked at him, eyes narrowed. 'What's the right way to take that?'

He grinned. 'What if I said you looked . . . adorably sleepy?'

'I'd call you a liar. I was already headed for

coffee. And maybe some breakfast.'

She followed him over to the coffee machine then they found a table. She took one long, blissful mouthful of coffee and moaned. 'Last night I spent way too much time awake listening to the devil apocalypse.'

'The devil apocalypse?'

'It's not fair. I wasn't having that stupid nightmare for a change and, bang, they turn up, fighting over something or other. That sound they make is unnatural.'

'How do you think they got their name? What nightmares?' he asked.

She thought about it, shrugged. 'It's just one dream — it doesn't start out bad, but the further I get through it, the worse it gets. It's like every time I have it there's a little bit more tacked on, and that bit gets worse and worse. And I can't breathe. My whole chest just freezes and I have this feeling that someone's there — someone bad. I know they're bad because everything around me turns nasty. When I wake up, I almost expect to see that someone still there, standing over me.'

'That doesn't sound like much fun.'

'I actually looked it up on the internet this morning. Read an article about how unresolved issues can manifest as nightmares. Like how Dale and I started out so perfect, then everything went bad and I haven't fully faced up to it or something. I know — ' she laughed at herself, ' — Google diagnosis. But it was interesting.'

'Do you think you should talk to someone?'

'I am — you. Because I figured you, more than most, might understand unresolved issues.'

'I would?'

She could see she'd surprised him, but tested her theory anyway. 'Did you speak to your ex after she shot you?'

'Wasn't game,' he joked, but his smile fell. 'No. I'll admit I've thought about it once or twice but I don't know that she'd want to talk. I don't know that I do.'

'I wish I could.' At Connor's sceptical look she shrugged. 'We had some really good years together. Dale was warm, caring, a wonderful husband. It doesn't gel with what he ended up doing. I guess I'd just like to look him in the eye and know what he would say. Whether there was anything he could tell me that would explain it. Even if there wasn't, at least I'd have some sort of closure. But that's never going to happen for me.'

Connor's hand covered hers, warm as he squeezed. 'If you'd feel better out of the cottage, you can stay here.'

She knew her face reflected suspicion when he smiled in amusement.

'And though I'd be more than willing to share my apartment, you could have your own room, your own space.'

'I appreciate that, but I'm fine where I am.' Callie turned her hand over under his and linked fingers. 'Thank you.'

'At least tell me Ned's fixed the power out there?'

She pulled a face and shook her head. 'I don't

think he's talking to me. I'd get an electrician — I'm happy to pay for it — but he refuses to let me, and it's not my cottage, so I'm stuck. Anyway, Paisley's coming down to stay for another weekend.'

'We'll have to get the power sorted and those cameras up,' Connor said. 'I'll talk to Logan about — oh hell, here we go. She's still wearing that face.'

Tess stalked in with an unimpressed expression and headed right for them.

'Face?'

'All women have a face,' Connor assured Callie. 'That's Tess's.'

'What happened?'

'A hen's party trashed the spa suite last night. They broke one of the big mirrors and clogged up the spa. How is it?' he finished as Tess joined them.

'It looks like the remnants of a world war waged with champagne flutes and chocolate wrappers. I'm going to have to call someone to fix the spa. Don't get me started on the confetti. Then, of course, I have to reorganise a booking in order to clean it up. *Then* in the midst of all that, the father comes in to pay for the party — this is five minutes ago — and when I mentioned the damage, he comes on to me and offers to take me to dinner to make up for it!'

'What did you do?' Callie asked with interest.

'Smiled and gave him a bill that wiped the damn smirk off his face.'

'Do you need a hand to clean it up?' she offered.

'I'll ask one of the cleaners to help, but thanks. I need a serious breakfast before I tackle it.' Tess got up again and headed to the food.

Connor grimaced. 'It's my fault, because I booked them in. She'll remind me of that six times while she eats that big breakfast.'

'I could distract her with my story,' Callie said.

'I doubt a tornado would distract Tess at present, but by all means, try.'

Callie laughed and Connor's eyes went dark and dropped to her mouth. She realised he would have kissed her had he been closer, and was tempted to lean in.

'Thanks.'

'For what?' she asked, wrestling her senses back into order.

'Making a shitty morning better.'

Tess's plate hit the table and she sat down. 'So, as for hen's parties from now on . . . '

★　★　★

Callie spread mulch around a newly planted azalea, deciding she'd have to get another scoop of it from the pile.

'Looks good.'

'Paisley! Hi. I didn't expect to see you until tonight.'

'I needed to get off the property. Dad's in a mood. This is nice work,' Paisley said with a sweep of her hand. 'Are all these yours?'

'Yep. And now that you're here, you can help. I'll dump the mulch in piles, you spread it with the rake.'

'Okay.' She took a rake and did as Callie asked. 'So how are the Athertons?'

'A bit shaken up by this thing with Orson.'

'Orson? Kaicey had said he was here. What happened?'

'He was murdered on the mountain behind us.'

Paisley looked shocked. 'When?'

'Just after you left last time.'

Paisley stared at her, then her gaze moved beyond Callie, lost in thought. 'That's awful.'

'Indy was going to call to ask about the support group. I thought she would have told you.'

'Yeah she called . . . left a couple of messages. I haven't had a chance to call her back. Anyway, there was never an official list as such. People didn't want everyone outside the group knowing about their problems. Some of the issues were the 'don't show your face in public' kind. At least, back then.'

'But Orson and Marcie were involved.'

'Marcie? There's a name I haven't heard in forever. How do you know her?'

'She's the one who bailed me up in the garden.'

'Really?' Paisley asked with interest. 'Did Adelaide find out for you?'

'No. I saw her on the television and recognised her. She was involved in a boating accident. She's missing.'

Paisley's face fell. 'Hell.'

'Hey,' Connor said, appearing on the path from the guesthouse. 'Hi, Paisley.'

Paisley visibly pulled herself back together. 'Hi.'

'I just wanted to remind you about tonight,' Connor said to Callie, and turned to Paisley. 'We've got this thing on — a farewell do for our groundsman. You should come. We're taking over the restaurant. It's a send-off, but it won't be as boring as it sounds, and the chef is sensational.'

'Sounds good to me,' Paisley said easily enough.

'Great. Make sure you bring Callie,' he said with a teasing grin. 'I think she wants to bail.'

'You just leave Callie to me.'

'Are you two just about finished?' Callie asked, annoyed. 'Because I'm going home.' All day she'd been trying to forget it was her anniversary. She didn't want to dress up and eat in a restaurant, it would just remind her of every other damn anniversary, every other damn dinner in every other damn restaurant. She didn't want to think about how just a couple of years ago she and Dale had celebrated by driving down the coast, eaten seafood in a charming restaurant by the ocean and wandered hand in hand along a deserted beach at midnight. She didn't need to remember how he'd gently woken her at sunrise and made love to her with the waves crashing and the gulls calling just outside their window. Because how could he have been dead just a few short months later? How could any of what followed stay buried in the back of her mind when she thought about the rest of it?

She didn't expect Connor to know all of that,

but she expected Paisley to.

Yet Paisley just grinned at her before returning her attention to Connor. 'See you tonight!' she told him.

★ ★ ★

'We should go,' Paisley insisted when they were back at the cottage. 'It won't take long to throw something on and get back out there.'

Callie had been waiting for it — Paisley loved a party. 'I just don't really feel like a big social gathering tonight. You know what day it is, right?'

Paisley thought for a few seconds then understanding flooded her face. 'Your anniversary.'

Callie flopped into a lounge chair. 'Yep. I'd rather just stay home and mope.'

'Moping is no good for you.'

'I don't much care! I don't want to go. I want to make your dad some dinner and eat ice cream and have an early night.'

'Piker.' Paisley smiled sympathetically at Callie's grumbling. 'Ned's over there. He can make dinner for Dad.'

Callie frowned. 'I wasn't sure about that, actually. Your dad's staple has been microwave meals. And they're fine, I know, but week in week out, I imagine he must get bored. Besides, won't Ned be going to this thing tonight?'

'Didn't think of that. I'll talk to Dad. Let him know what's going on.'

'He's probably not there. He goes down the

track every evening about this time and stares at Ava's plaque.'

'Mum put it there.' Paisley went to the window and looked out.

'I thought perhaps that was it. I cleaned it up, gave the rose some attention. Cliff was grateful.'

'You — really?' Paisley looked around in surprise. 'That was nice of you.' When her eyes filled with tears, she pressed her fingers to them. 'Sorry. I should have known coming back here would bring up bad memories.'

'Paisley, *I'm* sorry. I shouldn't have mentioned it. Especially on top of telling you about Orson and Marcie.'

'It's fine.' She pulled a pitiful face. 'But can we not be morbid for a while and go and have a nice dinner?'

Damn it, she really didn't feel like it. 'Are you going to carry on about it all night if I don't?'

Paisley wiped her eyes and a smile took over. 'You know I will.'

'Fine.' Callie sighed heavily. 'After we get your dad some dinner.'

'Which will make us late. Which . . . is fine by you.' Paisley sniffed again and laughed. 'Okay. Let's make Dad dinner.'

They arrived at the restaurant just as everyone was sitting down to entrees. There had to be at least sixty people there, Callie estimated, yet spots had been left for them on Connor's table, with Indy and Logan and Tess.

'You made it,' Connor said when he saw them. 'I thought you might not show.'

Callie thought perhaps he might not kiss her,

since they were standing in the middle of a room full of everyone he knew. But Connor pulled her in gently, touched his mouth to hers and lingered for a moment before lifting his head. 'Let me introduce you to Bob and his wife Shelley.'

She ignored Paisley's smirk and turned to the next table to meet the older couple, chatting for a couple of minutes about the gardens. Then their table was served its entrees and Callie took her seat.

'We weren't sure you were coming,' Tess said.

'She didn't want to — wedding anniversary,' Paisley told them.

Tess grimaced. 'Ouch.'

Callie smiled at Tess, before Connor leant in. 'You okay?'

'Fine,' she said. 'Just wasn't sure I really felt like . . . all this.' She smiled a little sadly. 'I should have told you. We used to do something every year — go out and have an adventure of some kind and finish off with dinner at a lovely restaurant. It just feels a bit wrong, I guess.' She leant back as a fancy meat dish was placed in front of her, before a prawn salad was delivered to Connor. She eyed them both.

'Yours is garlic butter pork belly with butternut puree and apple crackling. It's good,' Connor said.

'I prefer prawns.' She looked at him hopefully.

He laughed and swapped them over. Callie saw Paisley and Tess eyeing them and talking quietly. They smiled spectacularly when they caught her watching them.

306

'How did you go getting the spa clean?' Indy asked Tess.

'It took all afternoon. But I still can't get the jets working, I've stuffed up the vacuum cleaner and I need a new broom.'

Logan choked on his wine. 'What happened to the last one — crash landing?'

Tess's eyes narrowed a second before she bounced her bread roll off his forehead. It landed in his prawns.

'Overkill!' he exclaimed.

'Overkill would have been my plate of pork belly launched at your head. Or, as I'm apparently a witch, turning you into a frog.'

'Careful,' Logan teased and glanced at his wife. 'You're threatening to assault me in front of a police officer.'

'Off-duty detective,' Indy clarified. 'And as you're my sister-in-law,' she continued, 'I feel I have to advise that although you could theoretically be charged with assault over a pork belly attack, there's no law I know of against turning someone into an amphibian.'

'You hear that, *Kermit*?'

'You think witchcraft is funny?' Paisley snapped.

There was a surprised silence as everyone looked at each other, immediately uncomfortable.

'No?' Tess said slowly.

The glare gradually left Paisley's face and she smiled in apology. 'Sorry. I didn't mean to snap. It's just hearing about Orson. He was always a bit of a pest as a kid but nice enough. I guess the news just got to me. Where's Kaicey tonight?'

'She took off,' Indy said. 'When Orson was murdered. She seemed to think she was next. I wasn't going to bring this up tonight, but as we have, you wouldn't happen to know Adam Mansfield, would you?'

Paisley's expression darkened. 'He was a local drug dealer.'

'Right, who ran a rather nasty gang in Risdon Prison. The one connection I can find to him and both my victims is that they testified against him in the court case that saw him end up inside for twelve years.'

'Both of them?' Paisley gasped. 'He got Mike?'

'Yeah. Why?'

'He was a friend in high school. He changed his name. Moved away. They all moved away. I remember Dale's mum saying how pleased she was they were going — that the guy was just sick enough to worry about.'

'Are you saying Dale testified too?' Callie asked with a churning feeling in her stomach. 'He never mentioned anything like that.'

'It was two minutes on the stand more than a decade earlier,' Paisley said. 'He probably didn't ever think about it again.'

Callie looked at Indy, wondered why she hadn't mentioned it. Indy was watching her as though expecting her to put something together. 'Was Dale friends with this Adam guy?'

When Indy's gaze moved back to Paisley, Callie's followed.

Paisley shook her head. 'They knew each other, but they weren't friends.'

308

'Were they involved in any way with your mother's support group?'

Paisley hesitated. Nodded. 'Dale's mum had anxiety issues, Mike's father had depression. Adam was . . . ' She chewed her lip, thought about it. 'You should check out Adam's psych assessment. There was something very wrong with him. I'm not sure what his diagnosis was. He was just . . . wrong.'

'There wasn't anything much in there.'

'I mean the one from childhood. He was one of Mum's many patients. It's probably locked in one of the old hospital files somewhere.'

'What would I find?'

'Like I said, I'm not sure what they called what his problem was, but I'd challenge anyone who doesn't believe in true evil to spend five minutes with Adam and walk away whole. If you so much as looked at him the wrong way, he'd cut the wings off your pet budgie or chop your dog into pieces. Mrs White accused him of stealing from her shop once, so next time her ninety-year-old mother walked down the main street to see her, he ran past and pushed her in front of a car.'

'Oh my God,' Callie said.

'He also used to do break and enters, steal stuff. Burn stuff down. Whatever he wanted.'

Indy nodded. 'So very possibly graduated to killing people.'

Paisley shook her head. 'It's just a thought. I could be completely wrong.'

'Thanks for telling me,' Indy said.

'Wish I could say the same,' Tess said with a

shudder. 'Let's talk about something else.'

The rest of the courses came and went, there was a speech for Bob, applause and some general rounds of humour.

'Are you enjoying yourself?' Connor asked.

'I am,' Callie said. 'Why?'

'You're frowning.'

She hadn't even realised. 'Paisley's drinking a lot,' she said, watching her friend move around the table. 'I think that conversation about Adam has upset her.'

'It upset all of us. Not the best table talk.'

'What are you two up to?' Paisley asked as she reached them and leant on Callie's shoulder.

'Just chatting,' Callie answered. 'Why?'

'Because you look too serious for a party. Who cares about an old wedding anniversary when you have a gorgeous man by your side?'

Callie lifted a brow and sighed. 'Right now, I have a drunk friend on my shoulder.'

'We should be drinking to making new memories!' Paisley said with a wicked look at Callie. 'And you know the best way to celebrate?'

'No,' Callie said, catching on. 'Absolutely not!'

Paisley took the wineglass from her hand. 'Tequila.'

'I'm in!' Tess said. 'Indy?'

Indy shook her head and lifted her palms in defence. 'I don't do spirits.'

'Me neither,' Callie said. She knew how this turned out. And she wasn't fooled. This wasn't about an anniversary. It was about Paisley writing herself off.

'I'll get a bottle. We've got salt and lemons . . . ' Tess headed for the bar, Paisley behind her.

'Don't want to play?' Connor asked.

'I don't want to embarrass her, ruin the night or play mum,' she told Connor. 'But if she starts to have too much, I might have to do something.'

'She's okay.'

'You say that now. When you have to pour her into a taxi later you'll regret it. Then I'll have to get her out of it again and I'll regret it more.'

'Here we go!' Tess said.

Callie had one shot with them, then opted out. Tess kept up with Paisley, while Indy watched with what Callie decided was a look of amused scepticism.

'This looks like fun.' Logan came back from wherever he'd been socialising.

'It's a non-anniversary,' Tess whispered loudly. 'We're celebrating.'

'Here you go, Cal.' Paisley sent her another one.

'Okay, listen, Miss Cast Iron Stomach and your secret country twin here, I'll pour, but I'm not playing.'

Connor's arm slipped over her shoulders and she snuggled back. She noticed the glances they received, but she was relaxed enough not to mind. She was more intent on slowing Paisley down without coming on too strong.

'Any chance Tess is about done?' she asked Connor.

'Doubt it. Tess will walk away and not have so much as a hangover in the morning. She's managed to drink a lot of people under the table over the years.'

'We've run out,' Paisley complained when they drained that half-full bottle Tess had started with.

'The day this place runs out of alcohol . . . ' Tess got up and Connor cleared his throat, sending her a look. She dropped back to her seat. 'Maybe later,' she said.

'How about I get you some water?' Callie offered.

'Can't think of why,' Paisley said, going back to the wine.

'Paise,' Callie began, grimacing as Paisley drained her glass.

'Okay, you win,' Paisley said. Then she said to her new best friend, 'Tess, sorry I was such a bitch earlier. When you grow up with the town witch, you get a bit touchy about it.'

'Town witch?' Tess asked. 'So that's true?'

'Oh, yes. The real deal. You must have heard about Winston. I copped a heap over him at school.'

'I have,' Logan said. 'That's the Willow Court ghost.'

'Mum worked there and she's a Waldron, so of course she must have run that little séance that caused all the trouble. Yep. You too can be one of us, just sign away your soul.'

Connor stiffened and Callie glanced up to see him exchange glances with Indy.

'One of us?' Indy repeated.

'They're everywhere,' Paisley whispered dramatically. 'And they'll do anything to get what they want. Don't mess with them.' She got out of her chair, stumbled, laughed. 'God, I feel like a teenager. I'll go see about a taxi to get us home.'

'Hold it,' Connor said. He got up. 'I'll be back,' he promised Callie, and led a stumbling, giggling Paisley away.

Callie watched them go, then turned her attention to Tess. 'You don't look anywhere near as drunk as she does.'

'I probably am,' Tess promised. 'I just hide it better. So, you and Connor have finally come clean about being a couple?'

A couple? 'We're not!' Callie said. 'We're just . . .'

'Oh, you're 'just'. Of course. Can I say, I'm very glad you're 'just'?'

'Remember, she's drunk,' Indy pleaded with Callie. 'Or she'd notice you were ready to deck her and she'd shut up.'

'Okay,' Callie said.

'But we are all very happy about the 'just',' Indy continued, sending Tess into a fit of laughter.

'Indy,' Callie said, changing the subject to settle the panic the conversation had lodged in her stomach. 'What do you think Paisley meant by 'one of us'?'

'Don't worry about that now.'

She almost argued, then decided it wasn't the time. 'Right. Then I'm going to go see if they've organised a taxi.' Was it really her imagination, or was everything a little strange around here? A stream of images flashed through Callie's mind as she said goodbye and wandered out. Black tourmaline, hexafoils, the strange charm Cliff wore around his neck. Paisley's talk of witches and ghosts. The chanting. The objects appearing in the cottage. Jonah's weird comments.

'Whoa!'

'Huh?' She looked up, nearly crashing into Connor coming the other way.

'Where's the fire?' he joked, reaching out to steady her. 'I sent Paisley off in the direction of room eleven. There are two single beds in there. I'll show you where it is.'

'I thought she was getting a taxi.'

'I wasn't sure she'd make it.' He took her hand and they walked down the hall towards the room.

'I guess it was borderline. Thanks for this.'

'Here.' He pushed a key into her hand as they reached the door then wrapped his arms around her. 'You know, I shouldn't have kissed you like that earlier.'

'You shouldn't? I did wonder if you might not want to — '

'I should have kissed you like this.' He took his time, his hands sliding into her hair to support her head as he lowered his slowly.

This was a deliberate, drawn-out and intoxicating battering of her senses. It rammed her heart into her throat and dissolved the strength in her legs. To stay upright, she slid her hands around his neck and held on, while his fingers moved up and down her rib-cage, smoothing and caressing.

Eventually he lifted his head, releasing her slowly. 'What's that look?' he asked gently.

'It would be very easy to fall for you.'

Shock and humour filled his face. 'You mean you haven't?'

'Maybe a tiny bit.'

The grin spread. 'That's just the tequila affecting your judgement.'

'All two of them?' she teased as she slipped the key in the lock. 'Perhaps it doesn't mix well with wine.'

He held the door open for her to step through. 'Goodnight, Callie.'

'Night.'

When the door closed she leant against it, released a breath. She might not have followed him up tonight, but she acknowledged the temptation to switch rooms had been there. It was beginning to feel inevitable.

25

Callie woke up the next morning with a headache and a growling, uncomfortable stomach. She tiptoed past Paisley and into the bathroom for a shower, and having no choice, put last night's dress back on to go out and get some breakfast.

When she entered the dining room she saw Connor right away, so she took a couple of pieces of toast, some butter and an apple and headed over. 'Not yet!' she said when he opened his mouth, then went back for coffee. To save time, she filled two of the small cups and took them both back. When she sat she took a deep breath of coffee steam.

'Okay, go ahead.'

'Unless you want me to take you upstairs and ravage you, you should be more specific with your invitations.'

She was halfway through her first sip and almost dropped the cup. 'What?'

'Ah, now you're awake. You had a bit of a post-apocalyptic zombie thing happening when you walked in. How did you sleep?'

'Well,' she lied. 'Despite Paisley's best impersonation of a dying steam train.'

'I didn't. Thanks to you.' His warm, teasing gaze swept down to the table. 'You got coffee. Twice.'

'Because I'd like more than one sip,' she said

and held a cup up for inspection. 'These don't even try to mean it. I've seen more generously sized egg cups. If I was a Barbie doll,' she added in disgust, 'I'd consider this a decent-sized cup of coffee.'

'If you were a Barbie doll it would be proportionately big enough to bathe in.'

'Now we're talking.'

He grinned. 'You didn't drink very much, but you look washed out. Headache?'

'Thanks and yeah, just a niggly one. Mixing wine and spirits — even in small amounts — never does me a lot of good.'

'It was nice to see you less cautious for a change.'

'Less cautious? Not enough to let you take me upstairs and ravage me though.'

He smiled and leant in to her to speak quietly. 'If I'd pushed, you would have.'

She considered denying it. 'You're probably right.'

His expression was appreciation with a touch of dare. 'I've got some time now.'

'Sorry, the tequila's worn off.'

'I could buy a case of the stuff,' he said, reaching across the table to skim a finger over her wrist. 'Or I could just prove you don't need it.'

The scattering of her pulse and that warm look of his was melting away her bad mood whether she liked it or not. 'It wouldn't be hard to prove,' she said honestly. 'But the whole idea of becoming involved with someone again so soon after getting my life back is a bit scary. I'd

317

decided I wouldn't go there again. And now there's you. And I don't know what to do with you.'

He watched her over a sip of coffee. 'How old are you?'

Her eyebrows shot up. 'I think there's a rule about not asking a woman that.'

'I just want to calculate how many years you think you might prefer to be alone for. How many years you have left for that bastard to ruin.'

The comment got her back up. 'Having a man in my life is not the be-all and end-all of my existence, believe it or not!' she snapped.

'No,' he agreed amicably enough, 'but you're a people person. You get lonely. Not everyone does, but you would. You could socialise, join clubs, do any number of things to keep from being lonely, but we're not talking hypotheticals. You're talking about giving up a chance at exploring something you think you might want because you've set yourself a rule on the basis of one — admittedly horrific — experience.'

Callie was having trouble deciding whether his even temper and quiet argument were soothing or as annoying as hell. 'I was being as honest as I could. I wasn't giving up on anything. It's just, Tess called us a couple last night and my stomach went into knots. Damn it, Connor. I'm not ready to fall in love with someone!'

'I don't think that's a choice.' He put down his cup. 'I'd like to see where this something might take us both . . . if you do. No expectations, no promises, I'm just asking you not to put limits on

318

something incredible before we've even really started.'

'No expectations, no promises. Okay.' And her stomach did a nervous little twist as she wondered exactly what she was getting herself into. If he really knew what a big step just that much was for her to take.

'Paisley just staggered in.' He finished his coffee, got to his feet. 'Morning,' he said over her head. Then he tipped up Callie's chin with his fingers and kissed her hard. 'I'm in love with you, too.'

Callie stared, stunned. She hadn't said she was in love with him. Had she? But he'd said it. Just like that. Like it was . . . no big deal? She swallowed panic mixed with excitement as Paisley dropped like a stone into the chair Connor had just vacated.

'Next time chain me to something out of reach of the alcohol. Callie?'

'Huh?' Callie was too busy watching Connor leave the dining room, her head spinning.

'Never mind. Is one of those coffees for me?' She snatched it before Callie could argue. 'Sorry if I carried on a bit too much last night.' Paisley put a hand over her forehead and leant on it. 'I hate making a fool of myself.'

'You didn't particularly stand out — lots of people drank too much, so don't worry about it.'

'Thank goodness.'

Callie made herself concentrate on the conversation. This was important, too. 'But I know you well enough to know something was wrong. I'm guessing that something was to do

319

with that Adam whoever-he-was.'

'He was a genuine monster,' Paisley said quietly. 'I'm sure I'm not the only one who wished he'd rotted in jail forever. He's the one who used to break Ava's toys.'

'He was at your house?'

'Mum ran the support group from home. His parents were part of it so, yeah, he was.'

Callie felt another moment of panic, this one all bad. 'You don't think he's bringing them back?'

'No! Hell, Callie, if Adam was bringing them back they'd be in pieces.'

'But he's not going to come after you, is he?'

Paisley shook her head. 'No, I didn't testify. I wasn't involved in all that, and Ned was off shearing with Dad, or on the fishing boats. He wasn't involved either.'

At least that was something. 'And there's nothing else? Nothing you need to tell me?'

'No. There's just been a lot of bad memories to deal with lately. I was feeling sorry for myself last night.'

Callie accepted that, decided to try and cheer Paisley up. 'So what are we doing today?'

'I need to talk to Dad about those places we found last weekend. I'm so glad you were here when he had that fall. I have to convince him of how lucky he's been that someone's been on hand both times. Even if I come back for good, he still has to navigate stairs, get in and out of showers and make food. It only takes a second to lose your balance and I can't hold his hand twenty-four hours a day.'

'I think the only thing you can do is take him

320

out to show him, let him feel like he has a say in where he goes. He might even like it. I'm sure he gets lonely, whether he admits it or not.'

'Then that's what we'll do. But not until I feel semi-human. I have a feeling this discussion could lead to war. I need bacon.'

★ ★ ★

'You're not dumping me in some bloody nursing home!'

Callie shifted in her seat and wished she was anywhere else. This was going exactly as Paisley had feared it would. Callie had thought having Ned there, talking about it casually around the table, might have been the best way to go. But from the second Paisley had brought it up, Cliff had gone into meltdown.

'No, we're not,' Paisley replied calmly. 'We just thought you might like to look at a villa. It has no stairs; all your cooking and cleaning are done. It's right by the water, Dad.'

'Don't need to see it to know I don't like it. You go into those places, next thing, you're dead! Treat you like a baby and feed you like one. No wonder people give up.'

'If that's true, we walk out again. Because this place isn't like that. You can be as independent as you like. If you don't like it, we'll leave. Please, will you just look?'

'I won't. I told you I'd help with a clean-up. Not move out.'

'Dad, you can't cope here anymore,' Ned finally said.

'What will you do if I sell? You'll be homeless. You're not a saver. Not good with money. But what you do get, you often put into this place, keeping it up, and looking after me. Should be yours.' Cliff turned to Paisley. 'Where were you while he was doing that all these years, putting all that in?'

Paisley's face went red, but her tone remained calm. 'Kicked out, remember? Forced to leave with my mother.'

Callie reluctantly took her eyes off the crushed look on her friend's face to stare hard at Cliff. 'She's trying to help you.'

For a second, Callie thought he might have been about to apologise. Then he got unsteadily to his feet, the chair sliding back noisily. 'Day I leave this place will be the day I die.' He picked up his walking stick and stomped up the stairs.

'Guess I knew how that was going to go,' Ned said. 'I've got to get back to work.' He headed out, pausing at the door. 'Worth a try, Paisley. I'll keep on him about it.'

Callie blew out a long breath and smiled in sympathy. 'Maybe when he calms down he'll think about it. He might change his mind.'

'You don't believe that any more than I do,' Paisley said sadly.

A loud crash from upstairs had Callie and Paisley on their feet. They ran. Cliff was on the floor at the bottom of the steps to the tower.

'Dad!' Paisley fell to her knees beside him.

'Go on, say it,' he told Paisley breathlessly. 'You told me so.'

'Don't be ridiculous. Where does it hurt?'

'Wanted to prove you wrong and get up there, find some stuff. I was angry, not being careful.' He paused for breath, pain etched deeply into his face. 'Got a bit dizzy. Side's a bit sore.'

Callie pulled out her phone and called an ambulance.

'Don't try to move, Dad,' Paisley said when he grimaced and tried to sit up.

'Said I'd die before leaving this place. Didn't mean today.' Cliff tried to laugh but sucked in a pained breath instead.

'The ambulance is on its way,' Callie reassured him.

'Always calling me ambulances,' he said faintly. 'Can't thank you enough, Callie.' It came out as a whisper as his eyes closed.

'Dad!' Paisley cried.

'He's breathing,' Callie reassured her. 'He's probably passed out from the pain.'

'I feel so horrible. He tried to get up there because he was mad.'

'Mad at you for trying to do the right thing? Mad because you had a point and he didn't like it? Paisley, don't go there. Everything you're doing is to avoid this exact situation. Maybe this time he'll figure that out.'

Cliff hadn't regained consciousness when the ambulance arrived, so the paramedics took him to the hospital. Callie and Paisley were shuffled into a waiting room and left wondering what was going on for over an hour.

When finally a doctor did appear, Callie didn't like the look on his face.

'He has a badly broken hip.'

'Will he need a new one?' Paisley asked.

'If it comes to that. But we can't do surgery while he's this weak. We'll have to see if he recovers enough over the next couple of days.'

'If it comes to that?' Paisley repeated. 'He's going to lie there with a broken hip for days?'

'He's heavily medicated. Ms Waldron, I think you need to prepare yourself for the possibility he might not make it.'

'What? It's just a broken hip. Old people get them all the time!'

'The fall has been a massive shock to his system. He's very weak and elderly. We'll do what we can.'

'We want to see him.'

'Of course.'

Inside the sterile room, Paisley held Cliff's frail hand. 'I should have come sooner. I shouldn't have hassled him about the home.'

'Not your fault,' Cliff wheezed, his eyes slowly blinking open. 'Couldn't stand the thought of seeing anyone going into that house. Not anyone who doesn't know what's what. You mind that, Paisley.'

She nodded rapidly, struggling to keep her emotions in check. 'You need to rest. Get better.'

'Not getting better, not this time.'

Tears escaped down Paisley's cheeks while Callie fought her own battle to keep hers in check. She put a supportive hand on Paisley's arm.

Cliff's eyes followed the move, then met Callie's. 'Paisley, would you go ask the doctor if I can have some more painkillers?'

'Sure. I can do that.'

When she was out of sight, Cliff said, 'They took my amulet off. It's on the table with my glasses.'

'I'll get it for you.'

'I want you to wear it. You put it on. Right now.'

Callie picked it up, studied the pale-coloured stone with the unusual markings and slipped it around her neck. 'Thank you.'

He nodded to himself. 'You're a lovely girl, Callie. Thanks for being kind to a cranky old fool. You deserved better.'

She squeezed his hand and smiled. 'Cranky? Who?'

He closed his eyes and took some breaths before opening them again. 'I'll miss your visits. Had me fooled there for a while. Thought the ghosts were coming to get me in the night.'

'What do you mean?'

'Mostly stayed in bed. Heard the footsteps up the hall. Always stopped short, turned around, went back.'

She almost told him it wasn't her, but she didn't want to stress him out. He was obviously confused. 'I enjoy our chats when I visit. When we get you home I'll cook you your favourite meal. Roast chicken, isn't it?'

'I've left you something. I want you to take care of it.'

She touched the amulet, but he shook his head.

'Something else.'

'Doctor's coming,' Paisley said, coming back

to the bed. Her brow rose as she spotted the amulet around Callie's neck but she said nothing, just sat down and took Cliff's hand in hers once more.

'I want my ashes buried at Ava's stone. Promise me.'

'Dad, you're not going to die. I — '

'Promise me.'

'When it's that time, then yes, I promise.'

Again he paused as though exhausted, but he gripped Paisley's fingers. 'I'm sorry. It was never your fault. Any of it. Wish you'd stayed.'

Paisley's face lost all colour and her tears fell freely, then she pressed her lips to his forehead. 'I love you.'

'Always loved you kids. Should've done better. You look after each other,' he said. Then he turned his gaze to Callie. 'Family don't need to be blood. You're family.'

She bent and kissed his cheek. 'Get better, okay?'

Ned appeared in the doorway. 'Dad. What's happened?'

★   ★   ★

When Paisley's phone rang early the following morning, Callie knew it wasn't going to be good news. She got up, started coffee, found a way to keep busy until Paisley appeared, face ashen.

'Dad passed away during the night. I don't know what to do. They're saying I need to make all sorts of arrangements.'

She wrapped her arms around her friend. 'I'll

326

help. One step at a time. I'll call the hospital back, see what needs to happen.'

'Thank you.' Paisley reached out and touched the necklace still around Callie's neck and smiled sadly.

'What is it?'

'It's a runic charm charged with protection against evil.'

'He asked me to wear it at all times.'

'It'll keep you safe.' Paisley surprised her by hugging her hard. 'Always.' Then she wiped her eyes and left the room. 'But it's pretty too, so wear it.'

'Sure.' *Safe from what?* she wondered. *Monsters,* whispered a voice somewhere in the back of her mind.

★　★　★

She called Connor first thing, let him know what had happened, then spent the day helping Paisley and Ned with the arrangements. Ned had been quiet, Paisley teary. She made them dinner, then Ned went back to the house and Paisley went to bed. Callie went early herself. It had been a long, emotionally draining day.

She woke up sometime through the night, surprised it was possible anything could have dragged her from her dead sleep. But something was scratching. A grating, repetitive *scratch, scratch, scratch, scratch.* Perhaps it was because there was someone else in the house, but as she lifted her head, she decided she didn't care and went back to sleep.

Paisley was up and dressed when Callie woke again. She found her out on the patio.

'Morning.'

'Morning.'

'You're up early,' Callie said. 'Did you sleep okay?'

'Not really.' She sipped her coffee, stared up at the house. 'It already looks and feels so empty, doesn't it? Dad more than owned that place. He was part of it.'

'It'll take some getting used to,' Callie admitted. 'I didn't know him for long but it won't be the same if I'm not ducking over with meals. Once he stopped shutting the door in my face, I think he enjoyed my visits.'

'He probably enjoyed them even when he kept shutting the door in your face.' Paisley smiled. 'Stubborn old bugger.'

'It's yours now. Yours and Ned's.'

'Nope.' Paisley got up and turned towards the door. 'Ned wants to sell it as soon as possible.'

Callie felt Paisley's disappointment and her heart ached for her. Two losses on top of each other: her father and her childhood home. 'Maybe he'll reconsider.'

'Yeah, right — he's already talking a retirement plan by the water. He'd get a nice nest egg for his half of what this place will be worth.'

When her voice wavered, Callie got up and gave her a hug. 'You'll get through this.'

'I know.' Paisley dabbed at her eyes, laughed a little. 'I know,' she said again, though it was no more convincing than her first attempt. 'Mum's been talking to me a lot more lately, giving me lots of advice and support. It's nice that she's back in my life. Between the two of you, I know everything will be okay. I can do what needs to be done. I should get my bag.'

'Are you sure you're okay to fly back? Maybe you should stay another day.'

Paisley shook her head and drained her coffee. 'I've already called a taxi.'

'Why? I said I'd take you.'

'All good. You've done enough.' Paisley went inside and collected her things, brought them to the door.

'I guess I'll see you — what are those doing there?' Callie hadn't noticed them heading out of the house but she saw them clearly now, going back in. They were the same hexafoils she'd seen in Cliff's house, and they were carved into the door frame of the cottage.

'Those?' Paisley asked, tracing one. 'They were always there.'

'No, they weren't.'

'What I mean is, they were already there but had faded. I cleaned them up.'

'Why?'

She shrugged. 'I couldn't sleep. Thinking about Dad, I guess. I know I'm rushing off again but I have a meeting tomorrow morning. I'll come back at the end of the week. The ashes should be ready for collection on Friday. We'll do a little . . . something for him.'

'Okay, sure.' So that's what she'd heard last night — symbols being scratched into the cottage. Callie was starting to feel odd again.

First Cliff gives her the amulet and tells Paisley to keep her safe. Now Paisley's scratching out devil traps. It felt like something was building, something dangerous. But she couldn't for the life of her figure out what it was.

★ ★ ★

He found Callie in the garden. He'd hoped she might have come to him first to talk out the stress of the last couple of days. It didn't matter that she and Cliff hadn't been particularly close, Connor knew the strain of dealing with death, of caring for people suffering from loss. But he wasn't entirely surprised to see her back at work, dealing with her feelings alone. The attraction, the physical pull between them, was off the scale but Callie kept a part of herself back — the part that was as scared as he'd been of trying again. Was he taking too big a chance, opening himself up to someone who was likely to close the door on him? Perhaps her reluctance was actually spurring his conviction?

She was sitting on the ground putting sprinklers together. The last of the new garden beds was planted out and close to completion.

'Hi,' he said. 'Thought I'd come find you, see how you were doing.'

'Hey,' she said and smiled at him. 'I'm fine. Paisley's pretty cut up, obviously.'

He nodded. 'Ned turned up. Logan told him to take the day off, but he said he'd only be sitting around thinking about it.'

'Paisley had to fly back for work, so I've taken

care of the arrangements. She and Ned decided to have Cliff cremated. No service as such — he wasn't religious, and Paisley said it's only her and Ned that need to say goodbye, so they'll do that themselves when they spread his ashes.'

Callie wasn't okay. She was forcing the sprinklers together, and her voice was flat and she was staying in her own space.

'You're shaken up about it. You've organised everything, been a rock for Paisley and kept it all in.'

'I thought I was fine. I *am* fine. But I've been sitting here thinking about it and it's just so sad.' She shoved another sprinkler into place. 'A person lives a whole life — all the ups and downs and good and bad, successes and failures — ' she dug into a plastic bag, shoved another sprinkler head in place, 'only to just — be blown away in the wind. To have less than a handful of people even care.'

'Okay,' Connor said quietly, and pulled her to her feet to wrap her in a strong hug.

'What are you doing?' she mumbled into his shirt. 'I said I'm fine.'

'Sure you are. It's just that I'm worried about the last of the sprinkler systems.'

She huffed out a laugh and when she lifted her head, her eyes were glassy. 'Your sprinklers will live to water another day.'

He kissed her, keeping it light. 'You're amazing. You've done a great job of helping Paisley and even Ned, but you're allowed to be sad too.'

When a tear spilled over she pressed her face

into his shoulder. 'He apologised for being cranky and told me I was family. Left me stuff. He didn't need to do that. It was nothing, what I did. I could have done more.'

'Don't do that. You added something good to the last few weeks of his life. Something he appreciated. Be happy about that. Be proud of it.'

She sniffed, nodded and pulled away. 'Thanks.'

'Let me help? I don't feel like being in the office on a morning like this.'

'You don't have to hang around.'

'And yet I still don't feel like being in the office.'

She stared at him suspiciously through wet eyes. 'You really want to put together sprinklers?'

'Absolutely,' he assured her. 'I'm all yours.'

★ ★ ★

Callie wasn't entirely sure that she wasn't all his. She worried over that as he worked with her, balancing her need for independence against the way Connor made her feel, what he made her want. But he had her smiling and laughing by the end of the day. And when he kissed her goodbye he had her toes curling and her pulse rocketing.

Conflicting emotions plagued her on her way home, so the last thing she needed was a call from her solicitor with bad news.

'They want half.'

'What?'

'They want Dale's half. They're arguing you

shouldn't be entitled to it because there was no will and you killed him.'

'Not according to the courts, I didn't.'

'I'm not saying they'll get it, but you know how they feel about you, Callie. They'll draw this out, push for every cent they can get. And they'll use the media, stir everything up again.'

She hated that the solicitor was right, and scrambled for a solution. 'Offer them the eighty they originally put in. Tell them that's all they're getting.'

'I will. Callie, if you were to invest the money straight into another home, another business, no court in creation is going to make you sell the place you live in and forfeit your income to give some back. Especially with the offer you've just put on the table.'

'Okay,' she said. 'Let me think about it.' When she hung up she called Paisley and filled her in.

'They suck,' Paisley said down the line. 'Bastards. But, hey, if you need to find something to invest in quickly, half of Waldron Park is available.'

Callie didn't miss the plea behind the joke. She walked outside and looked up at the house, thought of the possibilities. It was a beautiful old property. It had scope for development, could be the gorgeous bed and breakfast Paisley had dreamt of. Callie acknowledged the way Paisley had put her own life on hold to help her out since all this began. That she was pretty sure Cliff would have liked the idea of them taking it on. That if she didn't want to be dragged through the courts — and the media — again in a petty legal battle, she needed an investment fast.

'Callie?'

She thought out loud as she processed the idea. 'We'd need to get a valuer out to make an estimate on what the property is worth. No doubt a house like this will be valued at quite a lot, and due to its age, it's sure to have issues. To turn it into a bed and breakfast there'll be renovations, furniture to buy, redecorating to be done. It won't be cheap — but that's not necessarily a bad thing. It might not work, might not be financially viable . . . '

'But it's worth taking a look at the figures, right?' Paisley said, and the hope in her voice put a smile on Callie's face.

'Let's get things moving. Get some of those figures on the table.'

She hung up and, excitement already building, she wandered, ending up down at the river, wondering if a trim of a tree here or there might be possible to open up the trails. As her enthusiasm increased, she thought about adding some benches down here, somewhere for guests to sit and watch the river.

'Is he really dead?'

She spun, startled. 'Jonah. Hi. I haven't seen you for a while.' She bent down to pat Molly before the pup could jump on her.

He smiled sheepishly. 'Nan found out I was coming out here. I got in trouble.'

'And yet you're back? How far away do you live, anyway?'

'I live in the blue house a bit further back

towards the bridge.' He waved a hand in that general direction.

That didn't give her much of a clue, but she nodded. 'Perhaps you should head back then. Before you get in trouble again.'

He nodded and looked up the hill towards the house. 'Aren't you scared being all the way out here by yourself?'

'I'm not really by myself much. I did hear those devils you told me about though. They were a bit scary.'

'Yep. Aren't they?' he said with enthusiasm. 'Some people will tell you they never come around here. They don't know. They don't know how quiet demons can be to trick you into thinking they're not there.'

'Devils,' Callie corrected, her smile dropping. 'You mean devils.'

'Oh . . . yeah,' he said as though confused. 'You know they come from under the ground, right?'

'Under the ground?'

He looked at her strangely, as though he thought she was being vague. 'Yeah. I'd better go. Sorry about your friend.' He ran a few steps away with Molly before stopping to look over his shoulder. 'Be careful, Callie. Bye!'

Callie turned to Ava's plaque. 'Okay,' she told it. 'Either there's something not quite right about that kid or my nerves are shot.' The conversation had dulled her enjoyment of the river, so she made her way back to the cottage to think about nicer things.

An exciting possible future.

26

'No. No one's job was ever threatened, no one was gagged. Don't be ridiculous! Are you that desperate for a story?' Connor slapped his hand against his forehead and came up with a few creative curses in his head. He should have known the goat episode would get attention. If he was honest, he was surprised it had stayed quiet as long as it had. And he really didn't want it in the local paper. 'No, we don't believe it was a disgruntled employee. Yes, the police are looking into it.' Someone knocked on the door, and when he didn't immediately open it, the knock came again, more insistent. 'I'm afraid I can't comment on the nature of the incident . . . no, I'm not able to provide details.' The knocking continued. Between the prying of the reporter and the pounding on the door, his temper was simmering, threatening to boil over. 'Look, I'm afraid I'm out of time, I have a business to run. Goodbye.' He ended the call and ripped open the door. 'Yes?'

It was Tom, who stepped back from the door, startled. Wasn't he supposed to be doing a shuttle pick-up from the airport?

'What is it, Tom?' Connor asked, much more calmly.

'I've brought the guests back but we can't get into reception to check them in.'

'Where's my sister?'

'I don't know. I don't have any phone numbers.'

'Thanks, I've got this.' Connor grabbed his keys, thought perhaps it was Meghan, not Tess, who was supposed to open reception this morning. And sure enough, he spotted Meghan as he jogged down the stairs. She was making some sort of apology to a couple of big men while children darted around them, keeping themselves occupied. The rest of the new guests were impatiently hanging around, spilling into the guest lounge. Why was she apologising and not opening the office?

He excused his way through the jammed foyer. 'I'm sorry, ladies and gentlemen,' he raised his voice above the noise of unhappy guests. 'I'll have this sorted in just a moment.' He keyed the code into the door to open the office. Nothing happened. He tried it three times before he decided it wasn't him getting it wrong. He located the physical key on his key ring, but it wouldn't go into the lock. A closer look showed a key had already been broken off in it. What the hell was going on? He went back around the front to the roll-down security window and tried it out of desperation. It wouldn't budge.

'That's why I couldn't get in,' Meghan said.

'Someone's changed the code. Just . . . bear with me.'

Tess came through the doors. 'What's going on?'

'Where have you been?'

'Checking equipment for my abseilers this morning. What's happened?'

'You don't know anything about this? The code won't work.' He dragged his hand over his face. 'We need to call the security company to come and get reception unlocked.'

'The key won't do it?'

'There's already one stuck in there.'

'That makes no sense.'

'I don't even want to think about how it's possible until we get in there and clean this up.'

'On it,' Tess promised, already looking up the security company on her phone.

Connor waited while she spoke to them. She grimaced. Pushed harder. When she hung up she sighed.

'Two hours. Three, tops.'

'Seriously?'

She frowned, offended. 'It was going to be Monday!'

'Thank you,' he said more gratefully. 'Let's go explain to the guests.'

As they walked around the corner back to the guests, Callie arrived. She skirted the crowd, on her way to the coffee, he supposed. Then she saw him, smiled, and approached.

'Busy morning?'

'Hey, I wasn't expecting to see you today. There's a problem with the electronic door lock. The code's not working.'

'Has the power to it been disrupted?'

'No. The screen's displaying.'

'And you don't have a physical key as a backup?'

'Yep,' he said, dangling it. 'Another key's jammed in there.'

'What about the security screen over the desk, is there any way to get that open from the outside?'

She was trying to help, but she was just going over everything he'd already tried. 'No. It's as solidly reinforced as the door. We're going to have to wait for the security company to get in.'

'Which means we can't check the guests in,' Tess explained. 'Hence the chaos of a busload of people.'

'You can't access your system through another computer? Anyone with any sort of electrical device can no doubt access their booking online and you can manually check them in, update the computer once you access it.'

'We can't write the cards for the door keys until we get into reception. I can get them in with my master key, but they won't have any security until we sort this out. Any other ideas?' he asked.

Callie was chewing the inside of her cheek and studying the door thoughtfully. Then she swung her gaze up to him. 'Got a magnet and a pair of tweezers?'

'A magnet?' he asked. 'Would that work?'

'If it's a steel key it might.'

'I have fridge magnets,' Tess offered.

'Not strong enough,' she said.

'I wouldn't have a clue,' he said but a call to Logan revealed there was a decent magnet in his tool kit.

It took a bit of careful manipulation, but between Logan's magnet and Tess's tweezers, they wriggled the broken key out.

'Callie, I could — ' *Stuff it*, he thought. And kissed her full on the mouth, letting go with a 'Thank you.'

'You're welcome.'

He put his own key in and pushed open the door as he turned back to Tess. 'Can you help Meghan get this underway?'

'Of course. I'll let everyone know.'

'Connor,' Callie said.

He spun around. The way she was staring into the office had him stepping around her and pushing in.

⋆ ⋆ ⋆

Callie couldn't move, couldn't take her eyes off the sight of Kaicey, spread out on the floor, a macabre offering in a red circle. Kaicey's sightless eyes reflected the horror of the last moments of her life. The memory of how Lisa had looked blurred with the sight in front of Callie and her legs lost their strength. She slumped against Connor as he pulled her out of the office and closed the door.

'Tess!' he called before his sister could rally the guests. 'No.'

Callie stepped away, slid down the wall and sat, trying to breathe against the tension in her chest.

Tess stepped around Connor. 'Hey, are you okay?' she asked. 'What's wrong? Are you sick?'

Callie shook her head. 'We need to call the — ' She cleared her throat when her voice cracked. 'Call the police,' she finished. 'Call Indy.'

340

Tess reached for the door.

'No!' Connor said, but she pushed it open.

Much as he had Callie, Connor grabbed Tess and closed the door.

'Crime scene,' he said gently. 'Come away.'

Tears began to stream down Tess's face, but she brushed them away and visibly pulled herself together. *I have to do the same*, Callie thought. She couldn't fall apart in the hallway. She got back on her feet, fought the shock and the spots clouding her vision. What the hell was going on? How could this possibly be happening?

'Indy's not answering,' Connor said. 'I'll call — ' His phone lit up and the relief in his face said it was Indy calling back. 'You need to come to reception,' Callie heard him say with quiet urgency as a couple of curious guests glanced around the corner. 'You need to come now. We just found Kaicey. Same as Orson.' He hung up. 'She said to wait here, not say anything and keep out.'

Callie looked around the corner to the foyer. Something still needed to be done with the guests. They couldn't all be milling around like this when the police arrived.

A middle-aged man holding a little girl approached. 'Can someone please tell us when we'll be able to reach our rooms? This is getting ridiculous.'

Callie glanced back over her shoulder to Connor; he was talking to Tess. 'We're working on that now, sir.'

'What's wrong with her?' he said, meaning Tess.

'A private matter. Please, come back to the main entrance.' She walked with him, had absolutely no idea what to do or say, and found herself apologising to more people.

Then Indy was charging through the doors. 'Callie,' she said, pulling her aside. 'You're aware of what's going on?'

'Yes.'

'Great. I need you to move all these people out of the way for me, okay?'

'But . . . ' she said to Indy's retreating back. Now what? Why couldn't she *think*? How was she going to get these people out of here? When a young woman in a staff polo appeared, she waved her over. 'Who arc you?'

'Amy. Do you know what's going on?'

'There's been an incident. Amy, I've seen you on food service, haven't I?'

'I'm the apprentice chef. I was cleaning up from breakfast.'

'Great. Is anyone else in the kitchen?'

'Yeah.'

'I need any and all cakes, pastries, fruits, cheeses — anything you can lay a hand on that might pass as morning tea out on the buffet, as quickly as possible. Make sure there's lots of tea and coffee available, cold drinks for the kids. I'm sending everyone in.'

'Now?' The young girl's eyes widened dramatically. 'Everyone? Who are you anyway? I've seen you around a bit but — '

'I'm the one in charge . . . for now,' Callie said, mentally crossing her fingers and hoping she was doing the right thing. 'Please just get set

342

up. This is a situation where we need everyone working as fast as they can.'

'Why?'

'Because lots of police are about to arrive.'

Amy's eyes moved to reception and her face took on a concerned frown. 'Okay — I'm on it.'

'Callie?' Meghan asked tentatively. 'What's happening?'

'I don't want you to worry about that right now. I need you to check all this luggage in.'

'The bag tags will be in the office.'

'Hey,' Callie said when Meghan's gaze drifted to the hallway. 'There must be some elsewhere.'

'Um. Storage room.'

'Great. Let's go.'

Connor was talking to Indy. Tess had disappeared. Callie led Meghan right past them, helped her find what she needed. If she could keep working logically, automaton style, she'd get it done. Get through it.

Heart in her throat, she left Meghan waiting by the entry to the guest lounge and climbed the first couple of steps in the foyer to get some height.

'Ladies and gentlemen, may I have your attention!' She got them moving and had the last of the guests disappearing into the dining room as a dozen more police moved in. Then she followed the guests to the dining room to help out.

Because the police were still swarming in and out of the office when the guests had eaten their fill and she couldn't find Connor or Tess, she talked to the staff and organised a shuttle run to Mt Field. Tess came back and took some outdoor activities, and Logan got back from his morning trail ride and offered to do another one, while Larissa took a petting farm tour. Callie sat those who refused all those options in the guest lounges with free beverages and snacks, to rest or play pool or darts, or watch television.

Callie was so pumped full of adrenaline from running in all directions for so long that she jumped when Connor put a hand on her shoulder from behind as she raced back to check on the dining room for lunch service.

'How's it going?'

'Okay, I think. Everyone is fed and doing something — except these few in here. I won't say they're not feeling put out, but at least most of them are busy.'

'What did you tell everyone?'

'I said it was an electronic tampering incident. That they couldn't be checked in until their privacy and security could be ensured. That we appreciated their patience and cooperation and that all refreshments and activities would be complimentary while we sort this out.'

'And the staff?'

'The same excuse. I didn't think it was my place to tell them anything else.'

He sighed heavily and rested his forehead on hers. 'I don't know what we would have done without you this morning. Thank you. Are you holding up okay?'

She drew back, nodded. 'As long as I don't think about it. I've been busy so I'm fine. What was she doing back here, do we know? I thought she was gone.'

'It looks like she came back to the bunkhouse for some reason, because she went to her room first, then she's come in here. The killer must have gotten in behind her.'

'You're not going to be able to use reception for a while. Can you use your equipment out here?' she asked.

'Yeah, I'm thinking I'll set up in this corner of the guest lounge. Then it's not too far to secure everything in the storeroom tonight.'

'I'll give you a hand.'

They set up a fold-out table, used power-boards and extension cords and got the equipment working.

'Connor,' Indy said, appearing just as they finished setting up. 'I need you again. Oh, and Callie, I haven't spoken to you yet. Give me ten?'

'Sure.'

'Meghan!' Connor called. 'Can you get started please?'

Meghan appeared, nervously eyeing the equipment. 'I only just started on office. I'm not sure . . . '

Callie didn't really believe the excuse. Meghan was shaken up. She knew something far worse than a tampering incident had taken place and they couldn't have an upset employee manning the desk. 'I can do it,' she found herself saying.

'Really? I don't want to get in trouble.'

'You won't because you're going to help elsewhere. The kitchen could really do with a hand. Setting up, cleaning up . . . You okay with that?'

'Yes,' Meghan assured her with a trembling smile. 'Yes, I can do that.'

If it had been anything less than second nature, Callie would have realised what she was doing and collapsed in a mess in the middle of the foyer. She'd dealt with more people in the last few hours than she had in over a year. She spotted a couple of staff hovering and got them moving luggage and assisting guests into their rooms. It was almost lunchtime, and she had to hope that would be under control. If the guests out on activities kept coming back in staggered lots, the check-in and lunch processes should be smooth enough.

★ ★ ★

Connor took Indy into his office so they could talk in private, and closed the door.

'Any idea what she was doing here?' Indy asked him.

'None. But you said she'd been at the bunkhouse?'

'Her car's there.'

'Maybe she just needed to collect some more things. She wouldn't have known about the goat.'

'And she didn't confide anything else to you?'

'She wouldn't say much about any of it. She was never really herself from the moment she got that envelope in the mail.'

'Envelope?'

'Yeah. It was black. Had some strange message on the back. Arrived around the same time I overheard her on the phone with a friend. She sounded worried.'

'What was that message on the back?'

'I can't remember.' He thought. 'She said it was just something from an old friend. She never actually opened the envelope and it didn't feel like there was anything in it. The message sounded like a title for a play or a movie or something. I don't remember what it was. I'll have to think about it.'

'That would be great. How's Tess holding up?'

'She was being Tess last time I saw her: trying not to be devastated, already planning how to handle the guests. But then Callie stepped in and took over, thankfully, so she didn't have to. She went to do what she does — activities.'

'I got Callie moving,' Indy admitted. 'I saw the look on her face and gave her something to do.'

'It was a pretty big shock — she saw her first.'

'It would have been an even worse shock because last time she saw something almost identical was the day her husband attacked her.'

'Oh, hell.' Connor dropped to his chair. 'I didn't even think of that. I should have.'

'You've had a shock yourself. You're holding up. That's enough for now.'

'Are the guests safe?'

She nodded. 'I believe so. All the victims have been connected in a way no one else here is.'

'Indy, Callie said she thought you might be trying to connect what happened to her to what's happening down here. Is she right?'

'Maybe.' Her phone rang and she pulled it out, headed for the door. 'I'll keep you updated.'

★ ★ ★

Callie stretched her arms above her head and stifled a yawn as she sat behind the temporary desk. The police had been in and out. For the most part, Indy had dealt with the situation. Callie had been hoping for an update or two, but none had come. There was simply the endless procession of police in their various roles, collecting evidence, taking photographs, asking questions. She'd learnt nothing since hours earlier, when they'd zipped Kaicey up in a nondescript black bag and carted her away.

Tess came in, her eyes widening when she spotted Callie. 'You're still here?'

'I didn't want to leave the reception hardware unattended. I wasn't sure what else to do.'

'Where's Meghan?'

'Her shift finished half an hour ago.'

'Thank you,' Tess said.

'Actually, I kind of took over your guesthouse. I hope you still think I was helpful when you see what I've done. You know about the complimentary drinks and for the ones I could shove out the door, complimentary activities. Also Meghan ended up helping with food prep, because there was a greater volume of people than you normally deal with heading to the buffet at the same time. And two couples checked out earlier. I couldn't print them out receipts so I've promised to email them. You'll have to do that because I didn't think I should touch your email account. Also, there was a problem with room fifteen's heating so I moved the guests into twenty-one. It's an upgrade but there weren't any equivalents available. Lastly, there are rumours circulating about what happened this morning and many of the staff ended their shifts quite upset that they'd been kept in the dark. You're probably going to have to deal with that first thing.'

'That all sounds perfect. Are you okay?'

'Yeah. You?'

'As okay as you are,' Tess said with a small smile. 'Connor went to the police station. I don't think he's back yet. Do you want to have some dinner, or a drink or something?'

'No, but thanks. I think I'll just head home.'

'Okay. Callie . . . do you think you could help out again in here tomorrow — just until we get organised?'

'Of course,' she said. 'No problem.'

She got into her car and leant her head on the steering wheel to take some deep breaths. Had she really just done that? Taken over the guesthouse, organised activities, made executive decisions and dealt with dozens of people for most of the day? It beat the hell out of her little bed and breakfast.

She flopped back in her seat and started the car. She'd go home, cook an easy dinner and rest. Because it looked like she was doing it again tomorrow.

A bang on her window jolted her from her thoughts. Ned. She slid the window down.

'What's up?'

'Was gonna ask you that.'

'You'll have to talk to Connor. I can't — '

'It's Kaicey, isn't it?'

'Ned, please just talk to Connor.'

'I want to know!'

'Then talk to Connor!'

As soon as he straightened from her window, she took off.

She got home, showered, made a sandwich. But when she sat down to eat it, she couldn't. Had she thought she was hungry? Tired? She was both, yet she didn't think she'd sleep any more than she could eat.

When headlights swept onto the drive, and an engine stopped outside the cottage, she closed her eyes and prayed it wasn't Ned. She didn't have it in her to be polite tonight. She went to the door.

'Connor.' His face was devoid of colour, his eyes tired, but he smiled as she let him in.

'I thought you might like some company.'

'Company?'

'Today was bad enough, then Indy reminded me that last time you saw something like that was the day you lost your husband, and I'm guessing got arrested and had your whole life turned upside down.'

'That pretty much covers it. Except the 'and thought I was going to die' part. That was a pretty big part of the — '

He silenced her with a kiss. A long, desperate meeting of mouths that she needed more than oxygen. She wrapped her arms around his neck

350

and walked him inside.

'This is not why I came,' he said against her mouth. 'I just wanted to — '

'Shut up.' She didn't want to talk.

His hands, those big, rough hands, slid up and down her back, pressed her closer, slid into her hair. Wherever they touched they ignited sparks.

'Are you sure?' he asked.

'I want to feel. I want to forget.'

'God, so do I.'

She tugged at his jacket and drew him into the bedroom. Their mouths remained melded as clothes fell, scattering. She tripped over her jeans as she kicked them off, falling onto the bed. He came with her. Everything was heat and light and energy as he touched, tasted, teased. And then she exploded; a flash of intense pleasure before he plunged inside her, his own needs sending him quickly over the edge.

She felt his weight, enjoyed it as the aftershocks of their love-making reverberated through her system. She almost complained when he rolled off to lie beside her. But she could breathe again. And as she did, her heart rate slowed. She turned her head to see him watching her, his expression warm.

'Thanks for getting there quickly,' he murmured with a wicked grin.

'I have to say it was my pleasure.'

He chuckled, twisting onto his side to rest his head on his elbow. He gently stroked the hair from her face. 'I came over to make sure you weren't a mess.'

'I was working my way up to it, I think. I've been on autopilot all day.'

He pulled her onto him, so she was in the crook of his arm, resting her hand over his heart. When she finally pulled away to sit up, she glanced around the room for her clothes.

'Guess we made a mess.'

'Guess we did. I think most of your stuff ended up over in the corner.'

'I see it.' She got up to retrieve it and he snagged her wrist. He drew it to his mouth, grazing the sensitive skin with his teeth, kissed the same spot.

'You're beautiful.'

'Every woman likes to hear that.'

He put his hands on her cheeks and touched her lips lightly. 'And amazing, and strong and capable.'

'We all just did what we had to do.' She burst into tears.

He held her quietly and stroked her back as she pulled herself together.

'Sorry,' she said when she could speak.

'Had to happen,' he said, holding on. 'It's been a hell of a day.'

'And you want to get going.'

'You think I'd just leave?'

'I don't expect you to stay.'

'It's not about expectations.' He brushed his fingers lightly down her cheek.

'Okay.'

'Oh — I brought food. In case you'd decided you weren't going to eat. It's still in the car. I wasn't expecting . . . '

'To be ambushed?' she asked with a watery smile.

'Any time — seriously. But that was my fault. Traditionally I think I'm supposed to offer you dinner *first*.'

She laughed, which she assumed was his goal. 'Dinner wasn't what I needed.' But it surprised her that she was now hungry. 'What did you bring?'

'A bit of everything. I'll be back.'

She set the table, poured two glasses of wine. She had no idea what he liked in reds, hoped the merlot was okay.

He returned with six containers.

'You weren't kidding,' she said when she saw the amount of food.

'Wasn't sure what you'd feel like. Want me to heat up the meat and pasta?'

'I'll do that. I opened a merlot. I hope that's okay.'

He tasted it, nodded. 'It's good. Want me to start the fire?'

'Yeah, that'd be great.'

They ate by the fire, and through unspoken, mutual consent, talked around today's tragedy rather than about it.

'I thought Ned might have turned up. He came over to my car when I was trying to leave. He wanted to know if it was Kaicey.'

'Yeah, he found me. Has he been bothering you again?'

'Not at all,' she said quickly. 'Other than right after Cliff died, I haven't spoken to him. He's gone into his shell.'

'Logan said he can barely get a word out of him. It'll take time. He's grieving. His father was a really big part of his world.' His finger traced the line of her jaw, sliding up to play gently with her hair.

A sigh trembled out of her. 'I hope this is the end of it. If it is that Adam person, I hope he'll be satisfied with his revenge and stop killing. At least long enough for Indy to catch him.'

'She'll get him,' Connor said with absolute conviction. 'It's what she does.'

'Right, of course. It still doesn't explain — ' She stopped, tilted her head to listen as a sound outside caught her attention.

'What is it?'

'I'm not sure.' When it didn't return, she shrugged. 'Probably nothing. I think the atmosphere out here is getting to me. Do you know about the history of this place?'

'Bits and pieces. It's pretty bad.'

'Cliff had black tourmaline all around the house. He told me it had to stay exactly where it was.'

'What is that?'

'I didn't know either, so I looked it up. It's a grounding stone that channels healing so I suppose he believed in crystal healing. It's also believed to be a powerful protection against dark energy. So I wondered why it was on all the doors and windows. Was I imagining being freaked out in the house? And what's with the strange circle things? Every time I go in there I spot another one. They're there, but they're not all that obvious until you really look. Cliff said they're hexafoils and Paisley told me Cliff thought they trapped demons.'

A smile slid across Connor's face. 'Do you think the house is haunted?'

'You don't suppose it's possible, do you? These dreams I keep having, they're so weird. They started just after I found Ava's plaque down by the river and tidied it up. I don't even believe in all this stuff but it's almost like she's trying to tell me something, connect with me in some way. It makes no sense, I realise. Jeez!' She jumped from her chair as a loud scream rang out from not too far away.

'You're okay,' he said, and took her hand to gently tug her back into her seat. 'That's definitely a Tassie devil screech.'

Callie released the breath that had caught in her throat and allowed her fingers to remain linked in his. 'It's a seriously disturbing sound.'

'We get them out at our place occasionally, but I would have thought you were too close to town here.'

'Apparently they used to have burrows by the river. Jonah said his nan used to see them a lot.'

'That's great.'

'He also said they came out here for the dead stuff.'

'Interesting kid, this Jonah. Devils are carrion feeders, so I suppose they could be encouraged to come around if food was left out for them.'

'He is an interesting kid.' She smiled. 'He also tells me he knows all about monsters.'

Connor laughed. 'No wonder you're on edge out here. Maybe you need some of that tourmaline stuff. I could draw a circle for you — hey,' he objected when she punched him playfully.

She grinned and yawned, suddenly tired. Then she jumped. 'Jonah said, 'Sorry about your friend.''

'Okay . . . and?'

'I thought it was a strange way to refer to Cliff.' She shook her head. 'Nah, I'm being paranoid. He couldn't have meant Kaicey. No one knew until this morning.'

'Come on,' he said, and pulled her up. 'You need to sleep.'

27

'Where have you been?' Tess asked as soon as Connor arrived back at the guesthouse.

'Isn't there something you should be off doing?'

'I'm doing it — minding reception. So? You were at Callie's, weren't you?'

'And if I was?'

Her smile was brilliant. 'I think it's wonderful.'

He didn't know whether to be pissed off or amused. She just knew him too damn well. At least she was giving him the third degree and not crying in the corner somewhere. He could tell by her eyes she'd spent a decent amount of last night in tears. He felt a bit guilty, then shook it off. Kaicey had been an employee and a friend, and she didn't deserve to die the way she had. He'd grieved yesterday and he'd grieve for some time to come. But he wouldn't regret those few hours of reprieve with Callie.

'Thanks. How are you holding up?'

'Okay. Better because Meghan and two other staff have called in sick but Callie's going to be helping out again and she's really good at all this. She did a great job yesterday.'

He was certain the staff members weren't sick and silently thanked Callie. 'She won't be long — wasn't far behind me.' He did a quick walk-through of the building, spotted Indy in the dining room.

'How's it all going?'

'Hi. You should have your reception room back tomorrow. We're just about finished up. I've organised for someone to come in and give it a forensic clean before the end of the day.'

'Appreciate it. Have you got the bastard yet?'

'No.'

'When you do, can I have five minutes alone with him?'

'No,' she said again, this time with a definite tone to her voice.

'One?'

'You'd have to get in line. Connor, I firmly believe we're chasing Adam Mansfield, and no word of a lie, this guy is as dangerous as they come. If by some weird twist of fate you do get near him — and I don't say this lightly — get the hell out of there.' Her hand shook a little as she replaced her cup on the saucer and she laughed humourlessly. 'I've spent most of the night looking at the violently murdered victims of a satanic sociopath. The last thing I probably need is caffeine.'

'Can you prove it's him yet?'

'You know I can't discuss the details of the investigation with you.'

'He was in there with her, doing those things . . . ' He swallowed back the bile. 'She went through all that while I was sleeping peacefully upstairs.'

Indy sighed heavily and chewed her lip in a way he knew meant she was debating something with herself. 'Okay, look. She didn't suffer it out the way the other victims had. I'm gathering that even gagged, he must have been worried she'd make too much noise. It looks like he strangled her. The other injuries are post mortem.'

At least that was something. 'Thanks. So what's next?'

'He's not getting out of the state. We've got his picture everywhere and we're going public with a plea for information as to his whereabouts. The media are posting his image on the news tonight in the hopes someone might have seen something.'

'Indy. Sorry to disturb you.'

'No, it's fine. Hi, Jared.'

'Hi,' Connor echoed, recognising the policeman from Jules's case. 'How are you?'

'Good, you?'

'Not too bad. What are you doing here?'

'Actually,' Indy said, 'Callie spotted him keeping an eye on her case up in the Hunter. She wasn't sure who he was so I had her work up an image with a sketch artist. I was pretty sure it was Jared when I saw it. And sure enough . . . '

'You were up there? Why?'

Jared performed a one-shouldered shrug. 'My father ran the Waldron case down here years ago. He was never really happy with the outcome. When Paisley was involved in that case last year, I thought I'd keep a bit of an eye on the trial. See how it played out.'

Connor thought there must be a bit more to it than that. 'Why?'

'Let's just say he's not a big fan of the Waldrons,' Indy told him. 'But Jared's knowledge of the area and people is proving to be very useful to the current case.' She got to her feet. 'I'll see you later,' she told Connor, then gestured for Jared to walk with her.

'Was that Jared?' Tess said, appearing behind him. 'I wonder what he's doing here?'

'Hopefully making progress,' he said. 'What's up?'

'I have to take a group out to Mt Field.'

'Be careful.'

'I will. And the group I'm taking includes half-a-dozen built male hikers, so don't stress, okay?'

He nodded, deciding to take the remainder of his coffee up to his office. He was behind in more ways than he wanted to think about. He'd left Logan with Travis and Matty, and hoped his brother had that under control. He went up, let himself in and sat at his desk, dragged his hand over his face. A friend, an employee, had been murdered, but he still had a business to run. With everything that had been going on, there was more to do than usual.

He didn't leave the office for the rest of the day. When his eyes started playing tricks on him and exhaustion had his brain fogged to the point of uselessness, he finally got up and went in search of Callie. At least that part of the business had run smoothly.

She looked neat as a pin in black silk pants and a jade green shirt. Her dyed hair was straight and tidy around a face painstakingly made up — he knew now — to hide the light smattering of freckles that would give away her true colouring. For a moment he wondered if she was

360

real or if his mind was playing tricks. But she gave him a smile that turned sympathetic — he knew he must look like hell — and strode across the foyer to greet him.

'Rough day?'

'Just what you'd expect. You look like a dream.'

'What kind?' she said with an attempt at humour. 'Because I think if I don't eat soon I'm going to become a nightmare.'

'You didn't have lunch?'

'I somehow lost track of time.'

He wrapped his arms around her and pressed his forehead to hers. 'I realise you don't really want to do this. So thanks.'

'You know I don't mind,' she said, her arms linking around his waist. 'Have you heard anything else?'

'The police are going public on Adam, appealing for information.'

'When?'

'Evening news.'

Her arms dropped and she stepped back. 'Uh-oh.'

'What?'

'Connor, you haven't even told your staff yet. How are they going to feel when they find out about Kaicey on the television?'

He swore and shook his head. 'I hadn't thought that far.'

'You need to call an emergency staff meeting.' She checked the time. 'In half an hour.'

And here we go again, he thought, admiring the way she could morph into motel manager.

'What am I going to tell them?'

'The truth.'

★ ★ ★

Callie stayed on reception duty while the staff gathered in the staff room. She hoped the fallout would be manageable. Connor had asked Indy to come back and address them with him and she'd returned just in time, due to having to pre-record a news piece. Guests milled in and out of the guesthouse, but there wasn't enough to do to keep Callie occupied.

Time ticked over slowly until eventually the staff began filing down the hallway with red eyes and dull expressions, some quiet, others whispering, some sullen, others anxious. Connor came out last, with Indy and Logan. It was difficult to figure out who looked worse.

'How'd you go?' she asked.

'As expected,' Indy answered. 'I think I'm going home for a soak and a glass of wine. I need a break. Hey, you haven't managed to remember what was on that envelope by any chance?' she asked Connor.

'I thought you were taking a break. And no, just that it was black.'

Black envelope? Callie frowned, but even as she wondered what was going on, she murmured, ' "The longest night".'

'Yeah — that was it,' Connor said. 'How did you know?'

'Dale and Lisa had them.'

'Do you know what happened to them?' Indy

asked with interest.

'Um . . . I don't know what happened to Dale's. I gave it to him and he took it away somewhere. Lisa had hers in her bag. How do you know about them?'

'Because Kaicey got one too,' Connor told her.

'They all had them . . . ' Indy's gaze moved past her shoulder and was thoughtful. 'Where did you see Kaicey's?'

'She was playing with it in reception. You don't think she was after that, do you?'

'It wasn't anywhere obvious,' Indy said. 'But we didn't go through all your filing cabinets.' They went into the office. 'Does anything look out of place?'

'Everything is. There was — ' shit, he didn't want to say it, ' — blood spatter. Things were thrown out, wiped clean, reorganised.' But he looked around and after several moments spotted something on top of one of the shelves. 'That.'

Indy pulled on a glove and took the shoebox down. 'This isn't yours?'

'Never seen it before.'

She took off the lid, lifted a note from the top. ' 'In case anything happens to me',' she read and flicked through, finding the black envelope and some photos Callie couldn't get a good look at before Indy replaced the lid. 'Excuse me,' she said. 'I've got work to do. See you later.'

Stiffly, Callie moved her head to the side, grimacing as she tried to loosen the knot that had formed there.

'We should call it a day. No one's checking in

363

or out now and we'll be back in the office tomorrow.'

'Okay.' She massaged her neck again. 'The news was just on.'

'And?'

'And I'm not sure if Indy told you but she didn't mention Calico Mountain in the statement, she just referred to Kaicey as a 'local resident'.'

'Which would be why the phone isn't running off the hook.' He rubbed his hands up and down her arms. 'Will you stay?'

'Here?'

'Please. I'd feel better if you were close by, just for the time being.'

'Okay,' she said. She didn't really want to go.

'Thanks. I have a couple of things to finish off down here. Go on up, shower, and I'll be there soon.'

'Okay.'

She felt a bit strange about being in his apartment without him, but she found herself a towel, had that shower, then wrapped herself in his robe and had just decided to sit in front of the television to wait when he came through the door. He stopped, looking her over in a way that had her skin tingling.

'How is that sexier than the little black dress from the party?' he wondered out loud.

'I have no idea. What's that?' she asked of the small bottle in his hand.

'I'm going to fix that neck.'

'It's not that bad.'

He smiled in a way that said he didn't believe

her and put the bottle on the table. His warm palm slid up her neck, his fingers probing and kneading before delving into her hair to massage her scalp. Her eyes closed of their own volition.

'I take it back,' she groaned. 'Don't stop.'

He stepped behind her and continued to work on her neck and her shoulders. Large, warm hands, exerting just enough pressure to find and relax the aches and kinks. She was drifting, swayed. Then she squealed as her legs were swept out from underneath her. She hung on as he carried her over to the bed and gently put her down.

'Lie down. Let me do this properly.'

'You're as exhausted as I am.' She scrambled to get up, but a moment later she was somehow exactly where he wanted her, a firm hand on the base of her spine holding her in place. 'You'll undo all my good work. Stay still.'

When those hands went back to working on her they were slick with oil. There wasn't enough strength left in her to argue with the heat spreading through her veins. When the progress of his fingers was interrupted by her robe, she slipped out of it to give him full access to her back. He continued working right down to her toes. By the time he worked his way back up, his mouth trailing his fingers, she'd moved past relaxed and right up to out of her mind.

'Stop squirming,' he murmured against her skin. 'You're meant to be relaxing.'

'I think I've been as relaxed as I'm going to get. Unless . . . ' She sat up, twisted and pressed her mouth to his, then moaned in approval as those strong hands moved to her waist and pulled her hard against him. 'Unless that.'

'I aim to please. Let me get that sorted for you.' He went to work.

When she awoke the next morning the bed was empty and the shower was running, so she got up, scavenged in Connor's wardrobe and found a shirt to wear that fell below her knees. She'd just gotten into it when he came out of the bathroom.

He stopped, looked her up and down, grinned. 'You look like a child in that.'

'You're bigger than me. This was not the largest shirt you had in there.'

He pulled out a suit and draped it on the bed.

Her smile dropped. 'That's formal for you. I'll have to put on yesterday's clothes.'

'You're not.'

'Excuse me?'

'I've already sent your clothes down to the laundry. You're staying put.'

Her hands went to her hips. 'I'm not lying around up here all day like some kind of sloth. Don't be ridiculous.'

'You put that idea in my head, I won't get a thing done. But you'll be more comfortable up here for the next couple of hours than down there.'

'Why's that?'

'Media. And they're out for blood.'

'Oh.' She pressed a hand to her stomach.

'I'll try and give them enough to satisfy them this morning, and hopefully they'll leave before too long. Order up some breakfast, relax. Unless you want to add fuel to the fire by letting them know Caroline Johnson is here.'

'Absolutely not.'

But by the time she'd had breakfast she was already getting impatient. She opened the window and heard the chaos on the guesthouse steps, heard Connor directing the reporters into the staff room — most likely to stop the spread of panic to the guests. Then she called down to Tess, but couldn't get through for several minutes.

When she did, Tess sounded flustered. 'I'm dealing with everything from mass check-outs, to demands for refunds, to reporters, to people just being nosey. I'm supposed to be running activities this morning and I don't have time to breathe.'

'Can you divert any calls up to Connor's apartment?' Callie asked. 'I can't do anything else up here.'

She heard the sigh of relief over the phone line. 'Thank you! It might free me up enough to call in someone else to run activities.'

By lunchtime everything had calmed down to a manageable level and Callie had her clothes back. She got changed and noted just one media van still packing up in the carpark. She watched from the window as it drove away. Then she went downstairs to see what was going on. There was a tightness in her chest from the media presence, a feeling of claustrophobia from being pinned down in Connor's apartment. The lunch sign was on the reception desk, so she assumed that's where Tess had gone. There was no sign of

Connor. He'd be around, probably busy, so although she knew she'd only need to call for him to find time for her, she didn't want to bother him.

Instead she went outside and walked through the new gardens, checking on the plants. They looked good, healthy. So she walked around the established ones next, got an idea for tidying, pruning, replacing, adding. She couldn't garden in her current clothing — it was one of only two office appropriate outfits she had with her — she'd need to go back to the Hunter Valley at some stage, organise for everything in storage to be shipped down, sold off or thrown away. That had seemed like such a monumental task, something to dread whenever she'd thought about it. Now she couldn't wait to get on with it.

It was time to begin her new venture. Between Connor and Waldron Park, her life felt fuller than she would have thought possible six months ago. A new business, a new relationship. How could she have been lucky enough to have such an amazing second chance?

She was anxious to see what value the real estate — damn it! She'd promised to be at the house when the agents came through. She checked the time, relieved to see she still had enough to get back.

She raced up to Connor's apartment, grabbed her things and scrawled him a note. Then she went to Waldron Park, met the real estate agent and opened the place up for them to look around. The agent suspected there was rot in two of the bathrooms, and there was a smell that could be detected in some areas of the house, suggesting a problem with rodents. Light was a problem. But she was pleased when the gardens were mentioned as a plus. When they were finished, she went back to Calico Mountain and spent the rest of the afternoon in the office.

She had just decided to leave when Paisley called to give her the figure the estate agents had put on the house. It was a lot, but it was manageable.

'I'm going to get a loan from the bank,' Paisley said, 'so we can go halves in the renovations. I've ordered a structural report and a pest inspection for next week. And I've set up a meeting with the solicitors for when I come down next, so assuming you're still happy to go ahead, we can get it rolling officially. This is so exciting! I can't wait to get down there.'

Assuming she was still happy? She couldn't let Paisley down now. It had probably been premature to jump in so quickly, but she'd just have to hope the reports weren't disastrous.

By the time she got off the phone, Connor had appeared.

'Hey, you're still here.'

'I had to go home, but now I'm back. You didn't get my message?'

'If it's in the apartment, I haven't been in there. Anything I need to know?'

'Yep. Three staff members have called in sick. Said they can't possibly come in tomorrow.'

'It's been a big shock for everyone.' He sat, resting his elbows on his knees. 'I can understand they're grieving, but the place has to keep running.'

She rubbed his shoulders. 'And to you, the guesthouse is your life, but to your staff, it's a job. I would guess because they don't know very much about the circumstances of Kaicey's death, some of them might even feel scared it could happen to them.'

'Indy filled them in.'

'She didn't tell them more than she had to though, did she?'

'No. She can't risk the case by giving away too many details. We're just lucky we've got you.'

Callie smiled as he stood and pulled her into his arms. 'I have some news.'

He leant back to look at her. 'Is it good?'

She laughed a little. 'I'm going halves with Paisley in Waldron Park. We're going to turn it into a bed and breakfast.'

His face lit up. 'Hey, that's great — congratulations!'

He seemed genuinely excited for her. She gave a long internal sigh of relief.

'I'll bet Paisley's thrilled?'

'Understatement. I'm going to get moving soon. Get over there and keep playing around.'

'Which staff aren't coming in tomorrow?'

'Meghan, Amy and Gemma — the new cleaner. Why?'

'I've just placed an advertisement for a new assistant and a receptionist. I think two people is sensible considering neither will know the ins and outs of the place for a while.'

'I agree.'

'I contacted the temp agency for temporary staff to fill in in the meantime, but after all this, I don't like my chances. I was hoping I could convince you to help out a bit longer — just until I've filled at least one of the positions.'

'Of course I will.'

'Thank you.' He nuzzled her lips. 'Before you rush off, let me express my heartfelt appreciation?'

She wrapped her arms around him. 'I guess I can squeeze in a bit of time.'

28

Indy turned up early at Callie's place the next morning, just as she had on her first visit. 'I wanted to catch you before you went out to Calico Mountain,' she said in greeting. 'Have you got a minute?'

'Of course. Come in. Give me two seconds.' Callie went into her bedroom and got dressed, then put the kettle on. 'What's up?'

'I want to show you a picture of Adam.'

'Ew. Okay, sure.' She took the offered photo. It looked like a prison shot of a man with a shaved head, a long face with sharp deeply grooved cheeks and pale, poxed skin. His nose was crooked, his lips thin and downturned. But it was the eyes that drew a shiver from her. They were dark, blank and cold.

'Okay, thanks for that,' she said with a hollow laugh.

'You haven't seen him before?'

'No.'

'Are you certain?'

'Indy, that's not a face I'd forget.'

'I need you to be aware, I was able to confirm everything Paisley told us by accessing those records she suggested I look at. I compared them to his prison files. I had a psychologist reclassify him. His initial diagnosis as a young teen gels with what he's devolved into. To give you an idea, the guy is basically your classic evil sociopath with a lot of other problems thrown in. He has a loyal group of followers in prison that he's promised all sorts of rewards to for joining him when they're released. He's also been keeping in touch, writing seemingly innocent emails. However, when we took the first letter of the first word of each sentence and put them all together, we discovered he's spelling out the names of each of his victims, so his followers still in prison can keep up with who he's killed. It's like a game to them.'

'So you have proof it's Adam! Why are you telling me?'

Indy's face softened in a way that had Callie bracing herself. 'Because Adam is taking credit for Lisa's murder. And for Dale's.'

'He's lying.'

'Maybe about Dale's, but — Callie, we don't have any proof Dale actually killed Lisa.'

The legs that had been unable to keep still dissolved underneath Callie as the implications of that sank in. 'I don't know why he did it, but he did it. He hid the photos, burned his clothes, had scratch marks all over his face and he came at me — he came at me when I tried to run.'

'I'm sorry to dredge all this up, but can you be sure of his motives for attempting to prevent you leaving that morning? Did he actually say anything that was a direct threat to your safety?'

She didn't want to think about it but it wasn't difficult to bring back. '*You saw that and didn't tell me? What were you going to do? Dob me in?*' There had been anger, frustration. '*I didn't want it to turn out like this. I'm sorry.*' She'd run, he'd grabbed her. '*Let me explain!*' But she'd been so mad, so scared. '*There's no way to make that better!*'

She shook her head slowly, pushed the images from her mind. 'He didn't tell me why. He was so angry. I was terrified.'

'Angry or panicked? Could he simply have wanted to prevent you leaving, wanted to explain because there was another threat — to himself and, because of that, possibly to you?'

'No,' she said shakily. 'No. He hid the drive, showered, strolled out asking for coffee like he didn't have a care in the world. He said he'd hit a kangaroo. He went nuts over the photos . . . '

'There's a pattern to Adam's murders. He tortures his victims with the same methodology over and over. It's ritualistic, cruel and distinctive. And it's very much his own. I can't completely rule out that Dale somehow knew how to exactly copy that methodology, especially as we're working off photos of Lisa's body, but all the evidence points to Adam having committed the murder.'

Something inside Callie, something she'd been trying to repair since all of this began, crumbled. 'If he didn't do it that means I killed Dale and he was innocent.' It was barely a whisper. 'He was trying to protect me? Oh my God!' She dropped her head into her hands and began to shake.

'We don't know,' Indy said clearly and calmly. 'And I want to remind you that you didn't kill Dale. The fall did. Even if he didn't kill Lisa, he was there, Callie. He was involved in some way. And he chose to keep that from you. He wasn't innocent, and there are too many unanswered questions for you to start beating yourself up.'

'But he wasn't trying to kill me. And I . . . How do I live with that?'

'We don't know that!' Indy reiterated. 'And nothing changes the fact that he cornered you, grabbed you, knocked you to the floor, hurt you. He did all those things. I don't know why yet, but even Paisley was convinced he was going to kill you and she wasn't the one whose judgement might have been clouded by thinking she was about to be murdered. In no way, no matter what comes out of this, was Dale's death your fault.'

Indy's words, the kindness in them, didn't stop the guilt from flooding Callie. 'I think I want to be alone for a while.'

'Callie . . . '

'Please.'

'Of course.' Indy gathered her things together and stood. 'I'll get to the bottom of it. I just need you to hang in there.'

'Do I need to worry about Adam Mansfield?'

'I really can't see any reason why he'd come after you or Paisley, but just keep your eyes open, and if you're worried at all, call me straight away.'

She let Indy out then sat on one of the kitchen stools and stared into space. The sick, hollow feeling threatened to swallow her whole. Knowing she'd contributed — even accidentally — to her husband's death had been almost unbearable. But she'd justified it by telling herself he had intended to hurt and probably kill her.

Now what? What was she supposed to do with this *weight* in her chest? She picked up the phone and called Paisley, wasn't surprised when she got voicemail. She blurted out words, she wasn't sure if they made sense. When her voice cracked she ended the call.

★ ★ ★

'So we only have two for the trip out to Cradle Mountain, but if I move it to Thursday those two will still be able to make it and I'll pick up eight more. It means you'll have to take the quads if anyone wants to go out, or we cancel that timeslot, but it also means I can be in reception all day tomorrow.' Tess flopped back in the spare chair opposite and looked at him expectantly over his desk.

'That'd be great,' Connor said, checking his schedule. A knock at the door had them both glancing up. 'Indy, hi.'

Indy came in and dropped into a chair next to Tess. She sighed heavily. 'Where do you keep your scotch?'

'It's ten o'clock in the morning.'

'Is that all? Damn. Okay, I'll forgo the drink, but I want you to go out and get Callie's security in order. Today.'

She didn't look particularly on edge, and her tone didn't carry any real sense of urgency. She looked tired, maybe unhappy. But he needed to check anyway. 'Indy, if you're going to tell me that weird stuff going on in Callie's cottage has anything to do with Adam Mansfield, stuff the security, I'm going to convince her not to stay there.'

'And I'll add an extra push to that,' Tess said.

Indy shook her head. 'Adam has a pretty distinct MO so I'm sure we've got it covered — he hasn't murdered without motive. And he doesn't play games. He strikes and he kills. Why would he break methodology to taunt Callie? She's been alone out there for weeks. I believe he hasn't gone after her because she's not of any interest to him. He has no motive to kill her.'

'He's some kind of sick sociopath,' Tess argued. 'Isn't that motive enough?'

'Everything he's done so far he's managed to do without leaving any physical evidence tying him to the crimes. He's thought about this every step of the way and carried each murder out meticulously, so I don't believe he's about to start randomly killing people for the fun of it. He's achieved the goal of paying back the people who put him in prison, and he thinks he's gotten away with it. His next goal is setting up his gang of ex-cons for whatever sick purpose he has in mind.'

'But that doesn't have you in here demanding alcohol,' Connor said. 'What else?'

'I just had to tell Callie that her husband most likely didn't kill anyone. That he may not have had any intention of killing her.'

'Oh no.' A thousand thoughts raced through Connor's mind as he contemplated how Callie would be feeling, what she would be thinking. And none of them were good.

'Then what's the urgency with the security?' Tess asked.

'Two reasons. The first, we don't know what's going on out there and if there is a threat, we don't want to miss it because it's been overshadowed by the Mansfield case. And two.' She looked at Connor closely. 'I'm as worried about her state of mind as I am of any outside threat, so I think she could use some company this afternoon.'

He closed his eyes and shook his head. 'Hell, it's just one thing on top of the next. She's going to be destroyed.'

'That's a pretty good description of how she looked. I didn't enjoy it but I need questions answered and so does she. She deserves the truth, doesn't she?'

'Yeah, when you've got it all figured out. What if you're wrong? What if Dale had every intention of killing Callie? What if he and Adam were in this together?'

'Then I'll tell her that, too. As soon as I figure it out. In the meantime, some of what I said might trigger something, a thought, a memory, that could be vital to the case. We have to catch this guy.'

'I don't know what to say to her,' Tess said sadly.

'If she brings it up just keep reinforcing that her husband's *accidental* death was a result of his actions, not hers.'

'We'll all head out there,' Tess said. 'Bombard her with company so she can't stew on it.'

'Maybe for a short while,' Connor said,

though he was pretty sure Callie needed them all converging on her about as much as she needed a hole in the head. 'We'll try and take her mind off it, take some food, drinks, lots of casual conversation. Then you lot will take off,' he told Tess, 'and give me time to talk to her about it if she needs to.'

'I'll give her a heads-up that we're coming,' Tess said.

'Take Logan too,' Indy said. 'He can help with the set up. I'm sure he can wrangle a couple of hours. I'm going to go back to work. If it's going okay, I'll see you out there later. If not, just let me know.'

★ ★ ★

Even though Tess had promised to bring dinner to the cottage, Callie made up a platter of snacks, put out some chilled water, Diet Coke and a couple of bottles of wine. Everything — at least she hoped everything — she needed for the security upgrade was stacked on the small kitchen bench as she'd bought a new tablecloth and set the table. Because she hadn't asked if Connor and Logan would bring their own tools, she'd selected what she thought they'd need from the garage. Most of the installation instructions didn't look particularly difficult — she would have managed — but it didn't matter. It was all good. Because she couldn't think about Dale any more. Refused to.

She'd allowed herself to feel everything during the course of the day: guilt, pain, anger, regret.

She'd run through a thousand different 'what if's' in her mind. She'd cried, walked, slept and cried again. And after all of it, after hours of torturing herself, it all still came to the same end. Dale was dead. And no amount of grieving over what might have been if she'd handled things differently was going to change that.

In the end, it all went in a bit of a blur. The Athertons turned up and huddled around the security equipment, chatting and studying instructions, installing cameras and lights and dishing up endless amounts of food and drinks. When Indy turned up a bit later, they all ate together and if Callie was a little quiet, she still managed a smile or a comment here and there. As they filed out after, she accepted a friendly hug from Tess, then Indy. Logan stopped talking to Connor to say goodbye and followed the women out. Connor stayed put.

'You're not going with them?' she asked.

'I brought my own car,' he said, and she noticed it on the other side of Logan's as the others reversed out.

'I guess Indy told you what she told me.'

'The gist of it, anyway.'

'I don't really want to talk about it.'

'Then we won't.' He topped up her wine, handed it to her. 'Will we sit on the patio for a while?'

'Under the new sensor light.'

'It's a good one. Got a coat?'

They went outside. The night was clear, freezing and beautiful.

'The stars look so bright down here,' she

commented, looking for something to say.

'Cold air doesn't hold as much moisture as warm air, so you don't get as much haze in the sky, hence brighter, clearer skies.'

'No wonder they're brilliant.'

'If you're too cold we can head in.'

'I think I might like to call it a night,' she admitted.

He touched a finger to her forehead, skimmed it down to scoop a tendril of hair behind her ear. 'I'll get my things.'

'No. I — I think I'd like to be alone.'

'Are you sure?' he asked, and began raining kisses over her face.

The sensations were divine and for a moment she had trouble remembering the answer.

'Stop,' she said.

He did as requested to look her in the eye. 'What's wrong?'

'It's overwhelming. All of it. I shouldn't have started this. I went from not ever being interested in another relationship to jumping head first into one with you. And now every spare second — okay, that came out wrong,' she said in appeal to his sudden scowl. 'I love this. Us. But . . . I have to get my head around what I did to Dale. And I can't do that with you here. Besides, I need to know I'm making my own life, not just fitting into someone else's.'

He nodded slowly. 'Okay,' he said finally. 'So which is it, because it sounds as though there are a couple of things going on here. Is it that you don't want to be with me, or you don't think you're allowed to be happy because of Dale?'

She threw her arms out in frustration. 'I don't even know.'

He didn't say anything for several seconds. 'There's nothing I can do to erase what happened to you. I can't talk you into trusting me — or yourself. It has to be your choice. And you need to come to it on your own. Or not. But everyone — Indy, Paisley, a judge, a jury — the whole damn country has agreed you didn't kill your husband. If you can't let go of the past, you're going to be stuck in it forever.' He sighed. 'I expected more, Callie. I thought this was worth something.'

It may as well have been a physical blow, it had the same crippling effect. 'Hypocrite,' she muttered after giving an unhappy laugh.

He turned slowly and she saw real anger on his face. 'What?'

She pointed to the spot where she knew a small circular scar sat on his shoulder. 'You're not just carrying that one around on your shoulder, are you?'

'Don't make this about me.'

'Are you really that blinded by your own guilt that you can't see that woman for who she was?'

'Who she was? Callie, you never even met her.'

'I don't need to shake her hand to form a conclusion, Connor!' she snapped, wanting to turn the conversation around to make it about something else — anything else. 'Be sorry about the baby. Be sorry that his or her health and welfare were never her first concern. Be sorry that even before she fell down those stairs, that baby never had a chance. But don't be sorry you found out what a selfish, manipulative bitch that woman was before you spent the rest of your life being miserable.'

'You don't know what you're talking about! She was lost. It was the drugs. The baby.'

'Bullshit,' she scoffed. 'Plenty of people become addicted to drugs, but they don't do what she did. Plenty of people go through the trauma of miscarrying a child, but they don't do what she did. She was making bad decisions before she was addicted. She was running around dealing drugs before she was addicted. I'm betting she got herself pregnant in order to trap you into marriage, didn't she? *Before* she could blame the baby's loss for her behaviour.

'She wasn't made bad by anything you did or didn't do. She was always who she was and everything else was just an excuse. She wouldn't take responsibility for her own actions and she never will, because that's the sort of person she is. So you took on the responsibility for it, because that's the sort of person you are. But you need to stop. She didn't want to listen to what you had to say because it didn't matter to her. That's on her.'

'You weren't there, Callie.'

'Okay, then imagine you hadn't gone after her that night, that you'd let her walk out and let her have her way with her drug habit and still married her. Do you really think she would have gotten clean, become a happy wife and mother? Was that ever who she really was?'

'Callie — '

'I'm not finished. Or, more likely, when she

miscarried later due to the drugs, or gave birth to a stillborn child, or when the baby was born addicted to heroin and or suffered lifelong problems because of that woman's addiction, or when she simply got sick of you and walked out with the baby to raise it with a family of drug manufacturers, would you not have blamed yourself for those things, too? You're so desperate to make me believe I should move on, maybe first you need to go look in a mirror.'

When he turned and walked out, she closed the door. How had she managed to get herself into this? She'd started out not wanting to hurt him, but then had slammed him with a tirade. She'd be lucky if he ever forgave her.

29

'Morning,' Tess said, popping her head into reception. 'I'm off early with a group to Mt Field. Is everything under control?'

'Yeah, it's fine.'

'Are you sure?'

Connor ran his hand over his head. 'I just said so.'

'So why are you down here? Where's Callie?'

'I don't know. I'm not even sure she'll turn up.'

Tess slipped through the door and closed it. 'Did something happen?'

'Apparently I need to give her some space.'

Tess hesitated. 'You know, I realise you don't need your little sister giving you words of wisdom when it comes to your personal life, but as that's never stopped me before I'm going to say that given recent findings, I think it would be just about impossible to be able to focus on a new relationship.'

'I realise that. It doesn't make it any easier.' When the phone rang he sent Tess an apologetic smile. 'Thanks.'

'All right. I'll see you later.'

Connor answered the phone, and his sniffling head chef told him she really wasn't feeling well. He told her to soldier on and get herself in here or he was finding a replacement. Enough was enough.

'Morning.' Callie burst through the door like a lightning bolt and slid straight behind the desk.

'Where have you been? I've got every man and his dog home sick.'

She barely spared him a glance as she spoke at a million miles an hour. 'They're not *all* sick, some of them are just worried about what happened to Kaicey. You need to address this. Properly. The rumours currently circulating are worse than facts. You're putting out an email this afternoon, outlining changes to the rosters and strategies that will make your staff feel safe. The ones who don't have the flu will come back.'

'I'm what? You don't think you should have given me a heads-up?'

She looked him levelly in the eye. 'I'm giving you one now.'

'Any idea what I'm supposed to be telling them? Indy doesn't want any more details of the case getting out yet.'

'I spoke to Indy. This is *her* advice. I thought you must have known. They don't need details, they need to know why it's not going to happen to them.'

'And how am I going to convince them of that?'

'Indy suggested keeping two late staff on each area together at all times. No one person is on lock up. And increasing security surveillance, temporarily employing a security guard to be visible around the guesthouse from dusk until dawn.'

Connor was too pissed off generally to want to admit Callie had it under control, so he looked for the flaw. 'And how are we going to do that when I can't get anyone to come in?'

'I told you. They'll come back when they feel safe. We can cope with who we have for one day.'

'Great, especially if those who are on don't decide to come in late.'

Her eyes flashed at that and he had a moment to think, *Uh-oh*, before she snapped.

'I've been here since six cleaning rooms because Gemma didn't want to be here.'

He closed his eyes and took a breath. 'I'm sorry. That's not part of your job.'

'None of this is *part of my job*, is it? And yet here I am.' She stood up. 'I'll be back.'

'Where are you going?'

'To get a coffee.'

★ ★ ★

Callie almost collapsed on the other side of the door. She'd done it. She'd spoken to Connor without breaking down, had been efficient and businesslike and gotten out of there again before there was any chance of getting off topic. Now she just had to keep it up indefinitely.

Connor had looked pale and drawn, tired around the eyes. The staff shortage wouldn't be helping with that and neither, probably, was she. She didn't deliberately stay out of his way all day either, they just didn't happen to cross paths again. Whether that was by accident or intention, she wasn't sure, but by the time she had a good chance to think about it, it was almost time to go

387

back to the cottage. So she'd leave it today. She'd created the divide, and she'd have to suffer through it.

She locked reception. The foyer and first guest lounge were sparkling and warm, inviting. On the wall, the brochure display was full and tidy. The enormous windows that showed off the mountains were spotless and late afternoon colours tinted the sky. Beyond reception, the guest lounge, with its gleaming floors and raging fire, deep, soft lounges and sprawling floor rugs, promised comfort and relaxation. The firewood was neatly stacked, the lights dimmed just enough for atmosphere. A few patrons were scattered around, holding delicate glasses filled with good quality wine or nursing generous mugs of tea or coffee, perhaps hot chocolate.

Knowing she'd played a part in everything running so smoothly gave Callie a real sense of satisfaction, of peace. For everything that had gone wrong in the last few days, the guests were tucked in for the evening, warming themselves after the adventures of the day, relaxing before dinner. Everything was as it should be. She'd just check the kitchen was in order, then go home and maybe treat herself to a glass of something red, something mellow, like a nicely aged merlot. Or lighter, like the pinot she'd sampled with Paisley a few nights ago.

She smiled at several patrons as she crossed the lounge, spoke briefly to a couple who wanted to thank her for the complimentary bubbles for the fiftieth wedding anniversary. She found both dining areas immaculate, and was still smiling as she pushed through the double doors into the kitchen.

The chaos was palpable. Amy the kitchenhand and one of the temp agency fill-ins were frantically preparing food. Clarissa was in the corner. She looked like death, her voice alternating between a crackle and non-existent as she barked out orders.

'What's going on?'

Clarissa slipped from her perch and Callie threw up her hand in a stop signal. 'Not a step closer. Why are you even in this kitchen?'

'She tried to call in sick,' Amy said, 'but Leeza's got it worse and Connor said he'd replace her unless she made it in.'

Callie recited several very bad words in her head as she thought that through. 'Okay. Have you been anywhere near any of this food?'

Clarissa shook her head and pointed to the corner.

'Good. Go home.'

'We have twenty people booked for fine dining tonight! We're trying to prep for service. We can't do this,' Amy said.

'And we can't risk infecting this food with whatever apocalyptic germs Clarissa is carrying.'

'That's why I'm in the corner,' she croaked.

'I appreciate the loyalty, Clarissa, but hygiene comes first. Point me in the direction of the restaurant bookings and go home. You will not lose your job.'

'What are you going to do?'

'I'm going to reschedule as many of these

bookings as possible and the rest, Amy and I are going to handle.'

'I can't.'

'You've assisted, right? Watched Clarissa and Leeza work?'

'Yes, but I can only do three of the dishes. Maybe a couple more but not as well as they can.'

'Are the desserts already prepped?'

'Ready for plating as we need them.'

'Then we can do this.' Callie collected a clean apron from the supply cupboard and dropped it over her head, tying it around her waist before drowning her hands in sanitiser.

'People are starting to gather at the entrance,' Michelle, the temp, said.

'Go seat them.'

'You're not a chef!' Amy said.

'I'll have you know I'm a damn good cook! I've run a successful bed and breakfast.'

'That's not exactly fine — '

'It's exactly enough for tonight. We'll reduce the menu to suit what we can do. Michelle, get Amy to show you which dishes she can handle then explain the situation to the guests and reschedule anyone who doesn't mind.' Callie dried her hands and blew out a breath, scanned the benches. 'Let's get this done.'

★ ★ ★

Connor didn't see Callie again all day, and when he hadn't been able to find her at the time she normally would have left, he assumed she'd gone home, still pissed off. He certainly hadn't given her a reason not to be; he was feeling a bit that way himself. He hadn't needed the lecture about Jules. Even if Callie made a few good points, given him something to think about. And that had been the tone of the argument that had played through his head most of the night.

Then somehow yesterday had rolled into today and he still couldn't decide what to do about it. He answered two calls, one of which was another sick employee, and hung up with a curse. Where was Callie anyway? He wouldn't make the mistake of assuming she wasn't here. Not two days in a row. The phone rang yet again. He was tempted not to answer it.

'Connor, it's Mitchell Marks from the fine dining review.'

Hell — this was the last thing he needed. He'd been chasing this guy for months and he decides to get in touch now? 'Mitchell, how are you?'

'I brought in a reviewer last night.'

He held his breath on a curse. 'And?'

'And it wasn't what we were expecting. I don't think I'd be too keen to pick up the paper on Friday morning if I were you.'

'Damn it,' Connor said quietly.

'Look, don't get me wrong, what we ate was very well prepared and well cooked. But the menu we were promised wasn't offered. We were told that if we wanted to sample the complicated dishes we'd have to reschedule. Marcus doesn't do rescheduling.'

'Mitchell, look, a staff member was murdered here last week and half of the employees are

391

barely turning up for work. On top of that, the rest of our employees have come down with some horrible virus.'

'I see.' There was a long pause, a loud sigh. 'Maybe under the circumstances I can keep it out of the paper. But don't hold your breath for another chance.'

Callie came in, waited.

'Thanks, I appreciate it. Please apologise on our behalf.' He put down his phone. 'What's up?'

'I need to know if Amy is coming in today.'

'No, she just called. Swears she has the flu.'

'Okay.'

'A heads-up you were leaving last night might have been good,' he said when she would have left.

'I was tired. Who was that?'

'That was our chance at making a name for our restaurant far and wide. Which was blown because half the menu was missing.' He saw some of the colour leave her cheeks, wondered why that meant so much to her. 'I'm going to find Clarissa, ask her for answers.'

'She wasn't there. She went home.'

'What?'

'I sent her home.' Callie swept out of the room.

He couldn't believe what he was hearing. *Callie* had ruined everything? He found her in room five taking out her mood on the furniture. Apparently, the cleaner hadn't finished all the rooms.

'Listen, sweetheart, I'm still the boss here. I

392

told Clarissa she had to come in.'

'I don't really care, *sweetheart*! You told a sick employee that she had to work. In the kitchen! The *kitchen*! It's just lucky she had the sense to stay in the corner away from the food. I'm telling you, my life flashed before my eyes just looking at her from across the room. I literally had to force my hand not to dig into my purse for a tissue or cover my entire head with the nearest tea towel to avoid airborne contamination and you thought it would be okay to have her handle food and prepare meals?'

He took a minute to consider whether or not to accuse her of exaggerating. The look on her face had him deciding against it. 'I didn't realise she was that bad.'

'No, you didn't. But you should have checked. You should have known.'

Connor lifted his hands in defeat. 'Okay. You're right, I should have. I thought she just didn't want to come in because of Kaicey. But — '

'And instead of being a dick you should be thanking me.'

'What did you call me?'

'I called you a dick. And that's kind, comparatively, to what I'd like to call you.'

'I'm trying to apologise.'

'Is it as painful to do as it is to watch?'

He felt his own temper boiling back to the surface. 'Right now? Absolutely. Would you please stop fluffing pillows and talk to me?'

'Fine.' She tossed the pillow in her hand haphazardly onto the bed. 'It's your motel.'

'Guesthouse.'

Her fingers squeezed into a tight fist and back. Twice. Apparently needing something to do with them that didn't involve wrapping them around his neck, she began tidying up the table.

'Now what are you doing?'

'The stationery wasn't where it was supposed to be.'

'By what?' he asked, as she put it all back almost exactly where it was. 'Three millimetres? I didn't realise you were OCD as well.'

Callie turned around, the look on her face pure fury. 'As well as *what*?'

'Uh . . . ' For some reason the whole situation suddenly had a ridiculous edge to it that could have — but thankfully didn't — made him laugh. 'Forgiving?'

'You'd damn well want to hope I'm 'forgiving', because I don't need to be here! And if I wasn't, you wouldn't be getting a bad review, you'd be getting your kitchen closed! Oh my God, are you *smiling*?'

'No,' he said very absolutely. 'I wouldn't dare.'

'Damn it, Connor, you drive me — '

'You fixed it,' he cut in. 'You fixed it,' he said again when she'd stopped to take a breath. He approached — carefully — and put his hands on her shoulders. 'You fixed everything. Forget the review, you saved the evening for the guests, went above and beyond. And you're exhausted and pissed, because you started at six yesterday and didn't leave, I'm guessing, till nearly midnight last night. And here you are again. I get it. I was a dick.'

'We're finally on the same page. Can I fix the pillows now?'

His smirk just couldn't be contained. 'Whatever makes you happy. Just don't do that.'

'Do what?'

'That face. It kills me.'

'Well, if you'd go away, you wouldn't have to see it.'

'All right. I do have to go — take care of something. I'll get back as quickly as I can.'

'I'll be fine,' Callie mumbled, already engrossed in what she was doing.

Connor didn't doubt it.

30

So maybe this wasn't a good idea, Connor thought for the umpteenth time since he'd sat, waiting for Jules to be brought out to speak to him. He hadn't really had a clue what it was going to take just to get into the maximum-security prison: background security checks, biometric scans, more ID, a PIN . . . All done at the visitors' reception centre before he even got into the women's building. Then he'd walked past a sea of fences, cameras, razor wire, through two sets of gates with more security checks, then inside the next reception area with airport-style checks and the biometric scan again. He almost felt guilty just for being there.

There was a glass partition between them but it didn't do anything to diminish the shock of seeing Jules again. She looked thinner, meaner, as though prison life had hardened her even further.

'This was unexpected,' she said as she sat opposite him.

'Yeah. A bit on my side too.'

'Then why are you here, Connor?'

'Honestly, I don't know. I thought if I saw you again, had that conversation we should have had before you shot me, it might help . . . '

'Chase away the demons? Oh,' she sighed sweetly, 'are you still feeling guilty?'

He scowled at that. 'Did I ever really know

you? Did you even ever care about the baby?'

'Of course I cared! That child would have put your ring on my finger! And the best part?' She laughed. 'It wasn't even yours!'

'What?' Cold shock spiralled through him. 'You would have let me believe — '

'Oh, give me a break! You come in here like you're still all cut up about it while you're fucking someone else! You look down your nose at me and shack up with a murderer? What the hell do you want, Connor? A there, there?'

'How do you know about Callie?' he snapped.

The smile was cold and calculating. Her eyes dropped briefly to a badly drawn tatt on her wrist before returning to his. They were filled with hate. 'Enjoy it while it lasts.'

'Jules, do one decent thing in your life and tell me what you're talking about,' he demanded, but she put the phone down and got up. As she was let out she smiled nastily over her shoulder at him. Then she was gone.

Connor stood and ran his fingers through his hair. How could he ever have been fooled, ever have considered *marrying* that woman? He didn't recognise her at all anymore. He told himself he should never have come, but of course he should have. He'd never have known about the child or the threat to Callie. He tried to memorise the tattoo he'd seen on Jules's wrist. A rough prison job? She hadn't had it before. She'd looked at it in a way that made him think it was relevant. He had no idea how, but he intended on telling Indy about the visit as soon as he could get out of here.

He called Logan from the car, learnt Indy was working, so he drove to the police station and found her talking with Jared in her office.

'How'd it go?' she asked, inviting Connor in.

'It was . . . about what you'd expect.'

'You want me to leave you two alone?' Jared asked.

'No,' Connor said. 'You might want to hear this. First up, Jules knows about Callie.'

'Let's just clarify,' Indy said slowly. 'Knows you are seeing someone called Callie, or knows you're seeing Caroline, former wife of Dale Johnson.'

'Option two. She told me to enjoy it while I could, as though she knew that Callie was in danger.'

'Does anyone other than your close circle of friends and family know about Callie?' Jared asked.

'I would have said no. Except that woman who bailed her up in the garden — Marcie — knew. So who knows who else could?' He paused. 'There's something else. Jules had a — I'm not even sure if it was real — but a tattoo just above her wrist. It looked like maybe a snarling dog. She glanced at it when she was making those comments about Callie.'

Indy and Jared exchanged glances, then Indy was up and digging through some papers in a folder behind her. She pulled out a photograph. 'Like this?'

Connor took the photo and looked at it. This time the tattoo was on a man's forearm. It was a much better quality. It wasn't a dog, it was a devil, mouth open wide. 'I think hers was supposed to be that. Why?'

'Do you remember when the last group of rehab boys had just started at your place? They were riding and one of them mentioned he might have known something about a gang within the prison claiming responsibility for a murder I was working on.'

'Vaguely.'

'Well, this is their emblem. And the guy that was running the group — at least while he was on the inside — was Adam Mansfield.'

'How would Jules know Adam?'

'Jules could easily enough be communicating with her ex, Kyle, through a third party. He also sports one of these.' She tapped the photo. 'There are fifteen inmates all up who have it somewhere on their bodies. And they're spread through the various buildings. We're trying to figure out exactly what's going on but it's not easy.'

'And none of that explains how Jules knows about Callie.'

'The only way she could know is if someone on the outside — mostly likely a member of that group — has seen and recognised Callie.'

'And who could that possibly be,' Connor said, feeling sick, 'other than Adam, who's never met her?'

'That's what we need to figure out,' Indy said.

★   ★   ★

She was exhausted by the time she returned to the cottage. Almost ignored the knock on the door that followed only seconds after she'd fallen in a heap on the lounge.

'You there, Callie?'

Shit. Ned. What could he want?

'Coming!' She got to her feet again, opened the door. 'Hi.'

'Hi. Been waiting for you.'

'Why am I not surprised? What's up?'

'What's that mean?' he asked with a frown.

'Just that everyone's needed me for something or other all day,' she improvised.

'Oh, right. Paisley told me you're going to buy me out.'

'That's right.'

'Was just thinking, you know, if it means that much to you, it might not be necessary.'

Oh, hell, this is not going to be good. He was going to throw a spanner in the works, she just knew it. 'What do you mean?'

'Can I come in?'

'Ned, not right now, okay? I'm tired.'

'Tell you on the doorstep then. I've been doing lotsa thinking since Dad died. Was thinking maybe I might not mind holding on to the place after all. I won't be ready to retire for ages. I could put some time and effort into keeping this place up. We could make it real good.'

'We?'

'Could you just at least sit down out here?'

'I — fine.' She slipped through the doorway and closed the door, sat reluctantly on one of the patio chairs.

Ned sat down, taking his time. She chewed on the inside of her cheek to stop from snapping at him to hurry up.

'We get on okay, don't we?'

'Sure, Ned. Of course.' He didn't want in on the bed and breakfast, did he?

'I'm looking to settle down,' he told her, looking into her eyes. 'So an investment would be good.'

Damn it — he was. 'With who?'

'Wouldn't mind a son, so I need someone young enough for that. I'm pretty taken with you, Callie. I could give you all this.' He waved a hand at the house.

The jolt of realisation almost had her slipping from her chair. 'Wh — me? Are you suggesting I marry you for the house?'

'We could try a date, first.' He laughed as though she were the one being ridiculous. 'What do you say?'

She put her head in her hands and prayed for patience. 'Ned, I thought we'd sorted this out. I'm not interested in you.'

'I did think about that. But I figured you just don't know me well yet.'

'And I don't want to. I'm sorry but you need to *get that.*'

His face darkened and he pounded a fist on the table, shocking her again. 'It's Atherton, isn't it? I *knew* you were messing around with him.'

She got to her feet and backed towards the door, eyes never leaving Ned.

'I won't hold it against you!' he said as though impatient with her. 'I can handle that there's been others.' He got to his feet and when he stepped in close she twisted her arm behind her and opened the door. 'But if you want this place, a happy life, you might want to think about giving us a try.'

The conversation was wrong on so many levels that she couldn't immediately come up with a reply.

'If you're not one of us, you're not worth anything!' he exclaimed, and then, thankfully, stalked away.

Callie went into the cottage and locked the door, realising how much he'd frightened her when her hand shook on the lock. Ned had been annoying, pushy, even a little freaky at times, but he'd never, never had that look on his face, that tone in his voice. He'd never had the blood freezing in her veins. This was out of control.

She almost picked up the phone to call Connor. Not because she was scared or because she thought she might need help, but because she wanted to share what had happened. Such a simple realisation, but a powerful one. Connor wasn't just a lover, he was a friend. And she'd pushed him away because of her own insecurities, because he turned her inside out and had her feeling things she couldn't even remember feeling with Dale. Connor was kind and sweet and thoughtful . . . and overworked and stressed out and grieving for a friend. And he wanted to be there for her, even when he didn't have time to blink. Even when she pissed him off. And she was throwing it away.

She stewed over that for a while, until she began to feel like an idiot. Was there any chance of salvaging what they had? There was one step she needed to take before heading off to find

402

out. Perhaps she could get the restaurant another shot at a good review. She gathered her courage, not knowing for sure what kind of reception her call would receive.

'Mrs Bates. It's Callie. How are you?'

A few minutes later she got in the car and drove back to Calico Mountain.

★ ★ ★

Connor wasn't in his office but the adjoining door to his apartment was unlocked. She let herself in without knocking first — just in case he wasn't inclined to talk to her. The thought made her nervous, but she'd gotten herself here; she needed to get the words out. The shower was running. Last time she'd waited to have a serious conversation with a man she loved he was getting out of the shower. She shook off the stupid thought and because she couldn't keep still she paced around, waited impatiently.

'Callie?' Connor came out with a towel around his waist, his damp skin shining under the bright lights of the lounge room. His hair was ruffled from the towel. Damn it, he looked amazing. The sight of him helped dispel the memories of Dale.

'You were right.'

'About what?'

'Me and my stupid excuses.'

Connor stayed where he was and considered her for several nerve-racking seconds. 'What are you saying?'

She went across the room to stand in front of him. 'I'm saying I hope I haven't ruined it. Us.'

His sigh was long as the tension seeped out of his face. 'That's not something you need to worry about.' He wrapped his arms around her.

'I know I need to let go of it — I want to try,' she said into his chest. 'And I'm sorry about what I said. About Jules.'

It was several moments before he spoke. 'I hadn't really thought about the rest of it. I'd never really let myself get that far. I just keep seeing her go down those stairs.' His hands slid up and down her arms, then he pressed his lips to her forehead. 'I would have blamed myself for whatever happened. You're right. I cared about her, thought if we loved each other enough, things would turn out okay. But . . . that thing I had to take care of this afternoon? I went to see her.'

Callie looked up, stunned. 'You went to the prison? You talked to her?'

'I needed to see her one more time, close off that chapter of my life once and for all.'

'I think that's great,' she said. 'Did it help?'

'It did. It really did. I can let go of that, and I'll explain it all to you if you want to hear it.' He dropped his head to rest his forehead on hers. 'Everyone else has been telling me this for so long. Why did it take you telling me to make me hear it?'

'Maybe you were just finally ready to listen.'

'Maybe I needed a reason to.' He caught her fingers, lifted her hand and kissed her knuckles, turned it over to kiss the sensitive skin on the underside of her wrist, then drew her back to him. 'I'm glad you changed your mind.'

'I thought you might have made it a bit harder.'

'Finding out about Adam and that Dale might not have been trying to hurt you had to be hell. I'm not going to hold it against you,' he murmured against her lips. 'Callie?'

'Hmm?'

'I want you to have as much space as you need to be who you want to be, but all those times in between. I'm going to be taking up a lot of those. Is that okay with you?'

She smiled against his lips. 'I think I can work with that.' Some of that smile faded as she remembered the other part of her reason for coming. 'And I wanted to tell you, I just had a visit from Ned . . . '

31

During the next few days everything slowly returned to normal. After the office had been cleared for use the equipment had been moved back in. Callie had had a moment, stepping into the room where Kaicey had been murdered, but then so, it seemed, had everyone else. And then it had been the weekend, and just as busy.

Callie finished mopping and straightened her back. The floors were clean and, happy with that for now, she took the mop to the laundry. 'Paisley?'

'Yeah?' her friend said from the top of the stairs. Paisley had turned up yesterday, and a small gathering had been held by the river for Cliff, with his ashes buried in front of Ava's plaque and his name added to it, as he'd requested.

'Do you want to get started on the lounge room?'

Paisley wanted to move on the house, set up a business name, make plans. 'Are you ready for that?' Callie had asked, because Paisley had barely had time to grieve, but she'd said yes, because Ned wanted money in the bank. At least he'd given up on holding on to his share, so they'd made a morning meeting with her solicitor, got the ball rolling.

'I don't think we have enough furniture polish.'

'I bought four cans.'

Paisley grinned. 'I know. And yet . . . '

She hadn't mentioned Ned's behaviour because Paisley had been upset over Cliff, and Ned had left her alone. Completely alone. He'd stared at her with an empty expression at the service, hadn't looked at her at the small gathering back at the house afterwards. She put his earlier behaviour down to grief, knew it could affect people in different ways, and told herself to forget it. It wasn't as though he'd threatened her — exactly. He'd sulk and get over it. Or he wouldn't. And if he came on too strong again, she'd go to Indy. Besides, Callie told herself, pretty soon he'd be out of her hair for good.

She walked into the lounge room. It was already tidy, just needed a good dust and polish. The house would feel different once they'd cleaned it all up, made it theirs. Guests would fill it, there'd always be work to do. That would chase away the old energy, would make the house happy and full of light and sound.

'Want to take a break?' Paisley asked from behind her. 'With everything going on, I forgot to show you something I brought down with me.'

'Okay,' Callie said, curious, and put the kettle on while Paisley dug in her bag, pulling out some bank statements. 'What are these?' she asked, taking them.

'The highlighted numbers are loans Dale made to a company over a five-year period.'

Callie scrolled through them. 'Isn't that one of his investment companies?'

'That was what he loosely termed it. That

trading name is registered to his parents. I looked up the investments because they weren't in your portfolio and I thought you should look into cashing them in. Then I remembered once, ages ago, Dale told me his parents were going through a rough time, so he was loaning them money and filing it under investments. Sure enough, that's them.'

'What?'

'They lent him money to start up his business. He just saw that as a way of paying them back. But it went way past that. They ended up owing him more than you both ever owed them. He didn't tell anyone because apparently they were embarrassed.'

'Why are you only telling me now?'

'When they decided to sue, I thought they must have already paid the amounts back. But then I checked while I was finalising everything up there and I can't find any record that they ever did.'

'And now they're trying to sue for more? I can't believe this.'

'If they don't let it go, those figures might be handy.'

'Thank you, so much! I'm going to go put these somewhere safe.' Callie couldn't believe it — the nerve of those people! She'd take the paperwork back to the cottage, file it with her other important papers. She opened the front door and nearly barrelled into the figure on the other side.

'Sorry!' she said automatically. 'I didn't — You!' She scrambled back from the doorway,

408

heart thundering in her chest. It was the man from the court case, the one who had stood outside her gate and watched the house.

'It's okay,' he began.

'Like hell it is, get out!'

'Callie!' Indy said, puffing from her sprint up the steps. 'This is Jared Marshall. He's a cop.'

Callie studied him suspiciously. 'A cop?'

'Yeah. I apologise for scaring you,' he said with a friendly smile.

'When? Just now? Or for weeks up in the Hunter?'

'To be fair, I only called by your place twice.'

'What are you doing here?' Callie demanded. 'What do you want?'

'I recognised Jared from the sketch you provided,' Indy said. 'It turns out he knows a lot about the case. His father worked the Ava Waldron drowning, and a few . . . other things. We're here to see if we can talk to Paisley.'

'I guess,' she said. Just being a cop didn't eradicate the worry this man caused her. But she let them in, called out, 'Paisley?'

'I've just boiled the kettle, do you — what are you doing here?' Paisley demanded of Jared. 'Damn it, I thought it was you back at Highgrove — told myself it couldn't possibly be. But it was, right?'

'Hi, Paisley,' Jared greeted coolly. 'We've got some questions.'

'You mean your father didn't do enough damage with his?'

'If he had've, your mother and quite a few others would have gone to prison.'

'It might be better if we do this at the station,' Indy suggested with a warning glare at Jared.

'Am I under arrest for something?' Paisley snapped.

'No, of course not. I just thought if you found any of the details difficult, you might prefer to talk in private.'

'I'll talk to you here,' Paisley said. 'I'm not going anywhere.'

Indy blew out a breath and considered that, nodded. 'All right.'

'Would you like to sit down?' Callie asked, swallowing her trepidation and wondering, *What now?* At a nod from Indy, she took them into the lounge room.

'This is just an informal chat,' Indy said to Paisley. 'You don't have to answer any questions you're not comfortable answering, okay?'

'Just get on with it,' Paisley said, still scowling at Jared.

'Okay.' Indy cleared her throat. 'We've been working on the idea Adam has murdered everyone who testified against him during his drug case.'

'Yeah, we know. And?'

'Actually it's a but,' Jared said. '*But,* we were hoping you could tell us what happened on the nights of your mother's so-called support group meetings.'

Paisley rubbed her hands over her face. 'We went through it a million times back then. Why?'

'Because we think what was going on at those meetings could give us a better insight into Adam's state of mind and what his next move might be,' Indy said.

'I don't see how.'

Photos dropped onto the table. 'Your mother ran a cult, Paisley,' Jared said impatiently. 'A nasty one. Adam grew up with that — with the beliefs, the practices, the philosophies, the rules. He's also a sociopath with a very high IQ and a narcissistic personality disorder. He doesn't believe we'll catch him or if we do, that we'll be able to prove he was responsible for the murders. From what we can gather, he's collecting a new generation of followers around him, suggesting he's thinking of starting up again. So, Paisley, what's he likely to do next?'

Callie gasped as she stared at the photos. They were hazy — taken by an old camera without a flash. That just made the images more menacing. Dark-cloaked figures stood around an altar. Flaming torches, a goat, blood leaking from a wound at its neck. Symbols painted on the walls — some she recognised from around the house and grounds. Evil. Horrifying, stomach-turning evil. She looked up to see Paisley staring blankly at the table.

'Where did you get these?'

'Kaicey left a box of things for us to find.'

'We weren't part of that!' Paisley exploded and swiped the photos from the table. 'That was the adults. We knew they were doing it because we'd sometimes sneak looks through the cellar window — that's why Adam did it — but we weren't allowed in. We were too young. We weren't allowed to play with monsters. Adam wanted in more than anything, he did horrible

411

things thinking that would convince Mum to let him be part of the group. But she said no. She always said no. It pissed him off. No one said no to Adam. But even he wasn't brave enough to take on my mother. She had too much power.'

'Power?' Indy prompted.

'She was a control freak not a murderer,' Paisley muttered as she dragged her hands across her face.

'Can you explain that?'

Paisley shifted in her chair and picked at her fingernails. 'Mum never really believed in any of that shit. It was all smoke and mirrors. Séances, rituals, fortune telling, curses — they were all manipulations.'

'For what purpose?'

'Whatever she wanted. Right, Paisley?' Jared asked when Paisley didn't speak. 'Your mother's 'group' was a bunch of drug addicts she'd handpicked from her work at the hospital. She'd play on their illnesses, feed them their drugs and they'd do anything for her. You want your dose, you do as I say. You fail? The evil spirits will get you. She completely screwed with their heads.'

'Your father never proved any of that!'

'Mostly they just gave her money or things because she'd tell them the devil ordered them to do it, right? She wanted a new television, someone would steal it for her. Rough someone up? No problem. Torch a house? Too easy. And because if you crossed her something would inevitably happen to you, even the sane people in town started to wonder, started to get spooked. People were nice to her all right — people kept their mouths shut. Not because they didn't believe she was a witch, but because they did. This house has been used for evil for generations. Everyone in town knows that.'

'I thought this was supposed to be about Adam?' Paisley snapped.

'Adam wanted what she had. The power. The fear. The control. She was performing satanic rituals with a group of fragile personalities on mind-altering drugs. What could possibly have gone wrong? Adam, with no empathy for anyone or anything, who only cares about what he wants, is introduced to black magic through your mother. He believed it, didn't he? He thought it would bring him supernatural power; the guy was just as sick then as he is now. Only he got off on torturing animals back then. And now it's people.'

'Yeah, I told you — he was evil. But because he was one of us we had to tolerate him.'

'What's with that?' Indy asked. 'What's the 'one of us' thing you all say?'

Paisley was silent for so long, Callie didn't think she was going to answer, but eventually she dropped her head back and spoke.

'The coven wanted a name, but Mum thought an official title would draw too much attention to her little gathering. So it was always simply you were one of us, or you weren't. That's it. Look, it wasn't an easy way to grow up, but most of that stuff was kept from us.'

Indy folded her hands on the table in front of her and pinned Paisley solidly with her gaze as she asked, 'Where's your mum now?'

Paisley's head shot up. 'I'm not bringing her into this! She tried to end it, tried to make it right. Do you honestly think I'd tell you all this if I thought you'd find her? I told you because you need to understand Adam. What he wanted. That's it.'

Indy and Jarred exchanged glances. 'I'm sure she tried to make it right,' Jared said. 'It's her method I'm questioning. All those drugs found in Adam's house a week after the night of Ava's drowning were the same ones your mum had been doling out. It was a setup, wasn't it? For something he did. Only whatever it was, it would have drawn too much attention to the coven, so she improvised, made it about something else.'

'You don't honestly think I'm going to verify that?' Paisley said.

'Paisley,' Indy said kindly. 'We're not asking questions so we can persecute you or your mother or anyone else from back then. We just need everything we can get on Adam. When we get him, I want him locked up forever.'

'Can you do that? Can you put him in prison and know that he'll never be released this time? Ever?'

'Yeah. With enough evidence, I can.'

Paisley hugged her arms around herself and stood, walked across the room and stared out over the gardens. 'When I woke up that night and Ava was gone, Adam had drawn a gravestone with RIP on it on the door,' she said. 'The cellar door was always locked during rituals and I couldn't make the parents hear me. I ran down to the river. I heard whimpering and saw

414

our little dog Pixie tied up the way the group would tie one of the goats for sacrifice. The other kids were carrying on, stumbling around, laughing, but when they saw me they stopped, looked behind them. Adam was sitting on a fallen tree by the river. He had Ava on his lap, like she was asleep. He told me they were going to let me join their circle. All I had to do was sacrifice Pixie. I refused. She was my dog and I loved her. I didn't want to join his stupid circle. I went to untie her and he got up and dangled Ava by one leg over the river. She started to make this pathetic little noise and I realised she hadn't been sleeping, she was hurt. He'd already hurt her and he was going to drop her in the river if I didn't do what he said.

'I told him he wouldn't dare, but I knew he would. He didn't care about getting in trouble, not like a normal kid would. And he told me it was such a shame I was left in charge, that I let Ava wander down to the river to drown. And they did nothing. The others did *nothing*. They all just stood there, staring. They hadn't believed him up until then, they said later, but they still could have stopped it. They just didn't. So I picked up the athame and I told Pixie . . . ' Paisley's voice broke and she swallowed hard before continuing. 'I told my dog I was sorry. And I killed her.'

'Oh, God, Paise. That's horrible.' Callie put a hand on her friend's shoulder. Why had she never told her any of this? Why hadn't Dale?

'Adam laughed this triumphant laugh and said he couldn't believe I did it. And he let Ava go.

415

Like a piece of rubbish. He just dropped her straight into the water and raced over to see if Pixie was dead. And the others . . . they ran away. They didn't help. I screamed and screamed. It was so dark in the water. A storm had come across. It was raining. The current was moving . . . The adults finally heard and they came. They tried to help. Adam just kept laughing.'

A solemn silence filled the house while everyone processed that. After a deep sigh, Paisley turned, her face saturated with tears. 'The elders had a meeting, scenarios were hashed out. The truth of it was, Adam had them over a barrel. If they went to the authorities, the details of the coven, the rituals, the sacrifices would come out. Families would be torn apart, pulled through the courts. It wouldn't just be Adam who suffered for what he'd done. It would be all of us. So yeah, the adults planted drugs in his bedroom. Then they had the kids call the police, tell them he was dealing. There was a raid. Because he was only sixteen he went into juvenile detention. They did that to save the coven. To keep it straightforward.'

'But then he got out,' Jared said.

'Determined to pay back everyone who put him in there. Mum kept track of everyone when they left, when they changed their names.' She walked unsteadily back to a chair and sat. 'She sent them the black envelopes. They almost had to be sent out once before: the first time he got out. But Adam was only out a few days then he bashed up some cops. He was back in pretty

416

much straight away. In Risdon this time, charged as an adult. The envelopes were a warning, that's all. So everyone would know he was out. To be careful. And yeah, Mum supplied the group members the drugs they needed. So what? It's easy to sneer and call them drug addicts, but a lot of those drugs were for the patients themselves — drugs the families couldn't afford. And yeah, there were others — carers — who maybe needed something to keep them going. Everyone always says, oh, that poor person has all those problems, lucky they have a carer. But who worries about the carer? Worries about the impact it all has on *their* life? If the system were fairer for everyone, none of them would have been in that situation in the first place. They wouldn't have been desperate.

'So, there it all is. Will that do, will you stop chasing me now?' Paisley asked Jared bitterly.

'Thank you, Paisley,' Indy said. 'And you need to realise that none of that was your fault. You were just a little girl in a horrible and impossible situation. I think you should talk to someone about all this. I heard guilt in your voice that just shouldn't be there.'

Paisley got up again and shook her head. 'I think you should go now.'

'Just one more question,' Indy said. 'What do you think he's going to do next?'

'Anything he wants,' Paisley said. 'And because this time he knows you're out to get him, you won't. He's crazy as fuck but he's smart with it. Whatever you do, don't let him know it's you on his trail.'

'Of course.'

Callie saw them out, then went back into the lounge room. 'I didn't realise things were that bad for you growing up. I'm so sorry, Paisley. That night must have been horrific.'

'That night was the worst of my life. The rest of it . . . It wasn't as bad as it sounds. The meetings were only once a month and we didn't see much. And it got us some pull in town. Everyone was nice to us and we'd get free ice creams at the corner shop on Sundays,' she said with a grin that wasn't quite convincing.

Callie crossed the room and hugged her friend. Paisley held on. Burst into tears again.

32

'So how is she today?' Connor asked after Callie relayed the conversation between Paisley and Indy and Jared over lunch.

'A little quiet. She's flying home today, finishing up at Highgrove and driving back with all her stuff next week. I hope Indy finds Adam soon. I know there's no reason to think he'll bother us, but it's dredging up the past. It's hard to move forward with all that going on.'

'I feel pretty awful joking about her witch of a mother after hearing just how bad it was.'

'She never said. I can't even think about it without feeling sick. Paisley was trying to justify her mother's behaviour. Part of me is furious neither she nor Dale ever said anything. That's a whole chunk of their lives that was kept from me. Though I'm not surprised she doesn't want everyone to know.'

'Let's hope she can put it all behind her now, get on with seeing her dream come true for Waldron Park.'

'Hi,' Indy said as she came in. 'I was hoping to grab Callie for five minutes.'

'What's going on?' Callie couldn't help but be suspicious when Indy had her friendly-cop face on.

'Nothing serious. Just a couple of things I wanted to ask you yesterday but it got a bit

419

intense with Paisley. I think we outstayed our welcome.'

Callie nodded. 'She was a mess last night. Bringing all that up was difficult for her.'

'Bad enough she went through it, worse she never got a chance to get over it, heal, because it was all hushed up. She didn't feel she could talk about it.'

Indy dug out her phone and scrolled through her images, showed Callie one of a Tasmanian devil head, its mouth open in what might have been a growl. 'Have you seen this before?'

'No. Why?'

'It's a gang tattoo. Some of the members are in prison, Adam was the leader. The people wearing these tatts know who you are. They know Caroline is Callie. Have you got any idea why that might be the case?'

'No. Were they friends of Marcie?'

'I'd love an answer to that myself. Paisley had already told me there's no list, no record of members, and she can only remember a handful of them. I'm guessing because of the nature of what they were doing there, they wanted anonymity.'

'What about Adam's parents? Dale's?'

'Adam's mother walked out on him and his father five and a half years before Ava's death. His father disappeared shortly after the night of that meeting. We haven't been able to locate either of them. Dale's parents and a couple of others I've been able to locate refuse to talk until Adam's caught. They're scared.'

'Was Adam the one who raped Marcie's daughter? Paisley said he got out and hurt some

420

police. It sounded very much like what you'd told me.'

'Yeah. It was him.'

Something was niggling at the back of Callie's mind, something Paisley had said that Jonah had also mentioned. And then it hit her. 'They weren't allowed to play with monsters.'

'That's what Paisley said,' Indy replied. 'Why?'

What the hell was that rhyme Jonah was reciting? ' 'Back to bed, back to bed . . . pull the covers over my head. Monsters, monsters go away . . . I am not allowed to play'.' Callie lifted her gaze. 'Jonah told me that. He asked if strange things had been happening in the cottage, and he told me he knew a lot about monsters. That his nan had taught him.'

'Jonah's nan?'

'And there's something else. The day I met him and he found out I was staying in the cottage he said, 'You're one of us.' I didn't think anything of it at the time but . . . '

'Who's Jonah's nan?' Indy asked.

'I never asked. But he said they lived in the blue house back a bit closer to the bridge from Waldron Park.'

'I need to go and find it,' Indy said. 'Why don't you come with me? You know Jonah. It might make things easier.'

'Happy to.'

⋆ ⋆ ⋆

'Do you think this is it?' Indy asked as they sat outside a pretty old fibro with a wild garden.

421

'I think it's a strong possibility. It's the closest blue house to my place.'

'It's the only blue house we could find.'

'So I'm going to go with yes, but you're the detective.' She exchanged grins with Indy.

'Let's go.'

Indy stepped onto the veranda first.

After a couple of knocks, Adelaide answered the door. 'Yes? Oh, hello, Callie. What a nice surprise!'

'Adelaide,' she replied, pretty surprised herself. 'Adelaide is the community nurse who looked after Cliff,' she said to Indy. 'Adelaide, this is my friend, Indy.'

'Nice to meet you,' Indy said. 'We were wondering if you had a few minutes to have a chat about Jonah?'

Adelaide's face went blank, and for a moment Callie thought they must have the wrong house after all. 'Jonah? Why on earth would you bring up Jonah? Come in, please.'

The house was as neat as the woman. Nothing was flash, hadn't been updated for what she guessed could have been a good thirty years, but everything was spotlessly clean. Callie looked around, hoping to see Jonah, but there was no sign of him. In fact, there was no evidence whatsoever a child even lived in the home. It didn't seem right.

'Now, can I offer anyone refreshments?'

'We're fine, thank you,' Indy said as they were led past a frilly kitchen into a small sitting room.

'Then how can I help you?' Adelaide asked, sitting on a velvet lounge chair.

Indy sat opposite so Callie followed suit. 'I'm interested in talking to people who were involved in a support group run by Eileen Waldron many years ago.'

'Oh dear,' Adelaide said sadly. 'Why would you be digging back into all that?'

'We think that might be connected to something else going on today. You'd be familiar with Adam Mansfield?'

'I knew the Mansfields. Lovely people. The boy, Adam, was a troubled soul.'

'Well, now we're interested in talking to him in connection to several recent violent murders.'

Adelaide stared thoughtfully into space. 'I suppose that's not really surprising. But I'm afraid I haven't seen any of those people in a very long time. Now, why don't you tell me why you're asking about Jonah?'

'He mentioned something to Callie about monsters. It was very similar to something a surviving member of Eileen's family said.'

'He spoke to you?' she asked Callie, hand over her heart. 'Led you here?'

'Yes. I hope I won't get him in trouble. I enjoy his visits with Molly, though I know he's not supposed to be there.'

Adelaide's eyes welled and she took out a small white handkerchief and dabbed at them. 'He has Molly with him?' she asked. 'Oh.' She walked over to a dresser and dug around, pulling out a photo. 'I do miss him.'

Indy glanced at Callie, but she just shrugged. 'What do you mean?' Indy asked.

Adelaide put the photo down. It was old, black

and white. A young boy was cuddling a small dog. 'My brother Jonah died almost fifty years ago.'

The earth seemed to tilt while Callie's breath halted in her lungs. Dizziness filled her head and black spots appeared in front of her eyes, making it difficult to look at the photo. 'No,' she said, even as she saw the evidence in front of her. 'No, I *saw* him. I *talked* to him!'

'It's that place!' Adelaide said. 'It's wrong out there, it's just wrong.'

Callie wasn't quite ready to believe it. The chair scraped back noisily as she recoiled from the picture and got to her feet. 'He said you were his nan.'

Adelaide blew her nose and wiped her eyes. 'We were raised by our nan. Wonderful woman.'

Callie's head was shaking almost of its own accord. 'I *saw* him!' She felt herself caught from behind when her knees buckled.

'Let's go outside,' Indy ordered and all but pushed Callie out the door.

She couldn't breathe. It didn't make any sense. 'I'm telling you I *saw* him. Spoke to him. He was as real as you and me!'

'Get your head down before you pass out.'

Callie did as she was told.

Indy disappeared for a minute, came back out. 'Let's get you home.'

She stumbled to her feet. 'I've been speaking to a kid who's not there — patted a pup that's been dead fifty years. What the hell is wrong with me?'

'It's that place,' Indy said, mimicking Adelaide

and opening her door. 'There's nothing wrong with you. But maybe there's something wrong with Waldron Park.'

33

Connor watched Callie work, looked for signs of any of yesterday's distress. She hadn't talked much about it. She needed time to process, he understood that. Maybe he needed time for the same himself. He wasn't really comfortable with what had happened. He'd got his head around the fact the majority of the Waldrons had issues. He even understood that because Eileen surrounded herself with mentally ill followers, a lot of the people involved in the investigation were going to have issues too. But not Callie. It wasn't *catching*. So now he had a choice to make. Did he start believing in ghosts? Or did he send the woman he was in love with in search of professional help? It helped to see her running the place this morning with her customary competence while Tess was out with a tour group. But he was worried.

'If you have time to stand around in the doorway indefinitely, I'm revising my share of the workload.' Callie's sharp green eyes flicked over him before returning to the computer screen.

Amused, Connor pushed away from the door and sat in the seat opposite the desk. 'Place is running like clockwork. Thought you might be getting bored.'

The harried look she sent him said otherwise. 'I've just rearranged shifts to cover for a sick cleaner, argued with the plumber over when he can get back to fix the spa in room four, which he managed to leave in way too many pieces after he left for some emergency yesterday, paid the stack of invoices you've got your feet on,' she said, slapping at his shoes to make him lift them, 'organised times to interview the new reception staff you're after, answered a complaint about a possible spider sighting in room eleven and made about twenty calls. I just need time to take two or three life-saving breaths — that's if the phone stops ringing — then I'll work up a suitably scathing reply to your comment.'

'And knowing you, it'll be efficiently emailed to my desk by close this afternoon.'

'Do you really not have enough to — there! Answer that phone.'

He chuckled to himself and picked it up. When he was done, she was waiting.

'So now that I've managed to fit all that into one morning, and Tess will be back soon, can you do without me for the afternoon?'

'I'll miss you terribly,' he only half teased. 'Why?'

A shadow crossed her face. 'I want to head back to Waldron Park.'

'To look for Jonah.'

'I didn't imagine him, Connor! Besides, there's work to do out there.'

'Okay, okay. How about I come out later on this afternoon and give you a hand?'

'Sounds wonderful.' She placed a kiss on his lips. 'Bring a bag. I want to stay out there tonight.'

'Got it.'

A china doll in a floral dress, a music box, a scary book. But where to put them? He was coming. She knew he wasn't far away. She needed to keep them safe. A sound outside drew her attention from the movie playing in her mind. She slipped quietly from the bed and dragged on her robe before opening the door. The sensor light was on so something was out there. Two eyes in the garden, the swish of bushes as the little dog just on the edge of the light wagged her body excitedly.

'Molly?' she called.

Molly raced towards her, skidded into her leg, then charged off again.

'You are real! Come here!' She attempted to lure the pup back. She almost got a hand on her twice, but the dog kept bouncing around just out of reach.

'Mol — ly!'

Was that Jonah? Callie chased after Molly, who was heading down the trail to the river. She moved as quickly as she could, almost tripping over a patch of particularly uneven ground, trying to keep the dog in sight. It was definitely Jonah's voice calling. She needed to see him, to talk to him, to prove to herself both Jonah and Molly existed. Callie broke through the trees to the clearing, stopped dead and backed up.

Figures draped in thick black robes rose from the earth and torches of fire blazed, casting shadows across faces, adding flickering explosions of flame to eyes already mad with power.

As she backed into the protective cover of the trees, a circle formed, becoming a wall. From within something writhed and squealed. A sacrifice. The circle became movement, the chanting more urgent, more commanding. As they danced and swayed, one figure abruptly ceased, his head turning to stare into the trees concealing Callie. There was nothing in that featureless face but darkness. Then, as it found her, a wicked smile.

She took a cautious step back. Another. Another. Then turned and ran.

⋆ ⋆ ⋆

The shake of the bed and the distressed sound that came from Callie's throat woke Connor from a deep sleep. 'Hey, what happened?' he asked groggily.

'Sorry,' she said, rubbing her eyes. 'Just a weird dream.' She sounded breathless.

'Come on, lie down.' He offered his arm, hoping she might snuggle in. She did, and he wrapped himself around her, could have yelped as her freezing feet touched his legs. *Man up*, he thought and tightened his grip. She was cold all over and . . . damp? Must have been a bad dream if she'd sweated her way through it. How could she be so hot and cold at the same time?

Then she was pushing away.

'I need a drink of water.'

He switched on the bedside light. 'Are you sure you're okay? You're not sick, are you?' He stared at the sheets as she threw off the blankets.

'Callie, what's this?'

The sheets were smeared with wet dirt. Her feet were filthy. She stared at the mess, just as shocked and confused as he was.

'Did you go outside tonight?'

Her face lost all traces of colour. 'I thought it was a dream.' She looked at the window, then walked out to the lounge room in a daze.

He got up and pulled on some track pants and a shirt.

'What was? Hey — don't go out there, it's freezing!'

But she was already out the door. She stood so still, so silent. He got her robe and put it over her shoulders, stood shivering beside her in the cold air, wondering what was going on.

'Can you hear it?' she whispered.

'I can't hear anything. Come back inside.'

'*Listen*,' she urged.

He listened, and . . . yeah, he could hear something. He had to concentrate, but it was there. 'What is that?'

'Chanting. Jonah and his pup were out here. I followed them down to the river but couldn't find them. There was a procession of people in cloaks. They were chanting — wait!'

Like hell he was going to wait. Whatever was going on, he needed to get to the bottom of it. It wouldn't particularly surprise him if a bunch of fruitcakes were out here playing around, not with the history of this place — especially now Cliff had passed away. And if the kid was around, he wanted to see him for himself.

He caught a glimmer of light through the trees

430

as he crashed down the trail, but it faded from view as he got closer. He reached the river, gasping in lungfuls of night air. The light was gone. There was no one here, yet the chanting droned and reverberated as though from all around, the deep, macabre notes soaking into the darkness and adding weight to the heaviness of the night.

He searched the trees, shivering with the cold and the knowledge that something was very wrong.

'Connor!' Callie caught up with him. She tugged at his arm, just as out of breath and wild-eyed as he was. 'If what I saw wasn't a dream, we need to get out of here.'

'Shhh.' But the chanting had stopped, leaving silence. 'It sounded like it was coming up from the earth.'

'Jonah told me they come from under the ground.'

And damn if that didn't freak him out more than he'd like to admit. 'Get back to the car. I'm taking you to Calico Mountain for what's left of the night.'

★   ★   ★

'Sleepwalking?' Indy asked at breakfast. 'Really?'

'I used to do it when I was little,' Callie told Connor and Indy. 'I think maybe that's what I did last night. It was like a dream, but it was real. And . . . Cliff said he thought I was checking up on him some nights. I just kind of shrugged it off, assumed he was dreaming.'

431

'Is that really possible?' Connor asked. 'Unlocking and locking doors?'

'Absolutely,' Indy said. 'People have been known to complete loads of complicated tasks while asleep. Even drive long distances.'

Callie shivered. 'It's kind of creepy to think I've been wandering around out there, sound asleep.'

'You think?' Connor said.

'But that doesn't explain the chanting, or Jonah.'

'It doesn't make a lot of sense,' Connor agreed. 'I can't imagine a real child would be out there at that time of night alone.'

'But he wasn't alone. The robed figures . . . ' Callie said, remembering the fear that had overtaken her.

'It sounds creepy as hell,' Indy admitted, 'but I'm going to keep looking for a rational explanation. Eileen used black magic rituals to scare the group members into doing what they were told, carrying on a much older tradition out there. I think it would be naïve to automatically assume it wouldn't continue once she was out of the picture. If that's the case, I can't rule out Adam's involvement. Which means this could be the way to catch him. I'd like to put police in the cottage, put the place quietly under surveillance. I need eyes and ears out there so the next time anything out of the ordinary happens, we can swarm quickly. Any objections?'

'No. I don't think Paisley will mind either. But it's been more than a month since I heard the chanting before this.'

'That's okay. It probably means we don't need to panic, but it won't hurt to be prepared.'

'I'll clean out the cottage as soon as Paisley gets back. We were going to move into the house, anyway.'

Indy looked her over with concern. 'Just be careful out there, okay? Don't be out there alone after dark.'

'Won't be an issue,' Connor promised.

★ ★ ★

Callie went back to Waldron Park as soon as she'd finished work. It was almost a dare she'd set herself: *Go back, cope, don't think of monsters or robed demons or ghost children with cute puppies. Act like everything's normal. This is your home now.*

She was a little more uncomfortable when she noticed Ned at the house as she pulled in. He was just staring at her from the front steps. She wasn't sure what was worse, the times when he was sickly sweet or the ones when he was silent and broody. She wondered what he was doing here and decided against heading up to the house until he'd done whatever it was he needed to do and gone back to Calico Mountain. Connor would be here in a couple of hours. She'd hang around in the cottage, make some dinner.

She took her time in the shower, letting the hot water seep into her. She'd banged her hip fighting back the branches of an out-of-control liquidambar earlier and as she got out, she could already see the bruise colouring up in the mirror. As she reached for her towel, her eyes caught sight of movement in the window behind her. 'Hey!' she yelled, and spun around.

The window she'd opened a crack for steam was now open wide. Ned was standing framed in it, staring emptily at her like he had from the house.

She drew the towel a round herself, backed towards the door. 'What are you doing?'

'Just came to see if you'd changed your mind about us,' he said flatly.

'Get out!'

'Not in.'

'What? Just . . . leave!' She lunged forwards, slammed the window shut. Locked it. Then she went out into the main living area, saw he'd gone around to that window. 'Ned, this is not right. Please, leave me alone!' She reached for the window to close it and he grabbed it, tried to open it further. She struggled to close it, fear increasing with every breath as she fought.

'Need to come in, Callie. Need to make you understand.'

'What is wrong with you!' With one last, desperate shove she got the window closed and locked it. She moved quickly, locking the other windows and doors. He appeared in every one of them as she worked her way around the cottage, his expression cold and blank. When she finished, and he didn't look in the last window, she realised she couldn't see him anywhere. It was almost dark. The sensor light at the front door kicked in. Two shadows blocked the light

434

sliding underneath. Three knocks on the door, slow and rhythmical. *Bang. Bang. Bang.*

'Go away!'

'You really should change your mind, Callie.'

'I'm calling the police!' she threatened.

'How?'

How? What did he mean? A tapping on the window whose curtains were still open had her eyes shooting to it. Her phone was being knocked against the glass from the outside. He had her damn phone! She bit back a sob. What now?

'Connor's coming!' she yelled at him. 'He won't be long!'

'Not coming. Thinks you're heading back to him. Later.'

Oh God, he'd sent Connor a text?

'You can't go back to him, Callie. It won't end well.'

She tried to figure out what to do. Her gaze fell on her laptop. She ran to it, opened it up. 'Come on . . . '

As soon as the screen flicked to life she got in her password, opened messenger. She'd call —

No internet connection.

She slowly looked up. Ned was back in the window. Smiling.

She stormed over and ripped at the curtains, closing them, then went back into the middle of the room and slowly sank onto the lounge, trembling.

'Want to get married, Callie?' came from the vicinity of the front door.

'Please go away.' It came out as no more than

a whisper. 'Please. Please go away.'

'I'll protect you from the monsters, Callie.'

You are the monster, she thought, and she clutched her amulet as though the necklace could somehow make the situation better. She got up again, went to the kitchen, snatched the largest knife in the rack. If he came in, she'd use it.

Through the curtains she saw each sensor light around the house flick to life as he walked the perimeter. The first had only just gone off as he made it back, and it kicked on again. Then she heard the creak of the fuse box opening. Everything went off. She backed up in the darkness, squealed when she hit the wall behind her. She turned the knife around in her hand, held it out in front of her while her other hand felt around for obstacles as she tried to picture the layout of the room in her mind.

The door rattled. It was only a matter of time until he came in. She peeked cautiously through a slit in a curtain, saw lights on up at the house. There was a phone there. But how was she going to reach it?

She pulled on her jeans and a jumper, quietly unlatched her bedroom window; had it open an inch when his face appeared in it. She screamed, quickly locked it with clumsy fingers and staggered back. She turned in small circles in the centre of the room, overwhelming panic making it impossible to think. She only knew she had to get to the house.

She ran the floorplan of the house through her mind, tried to picture the exits. There were two back doors, no external stairways to the ground from the first floor. There'd been a phone in Cliff's room, another in the kitchen. The kitchen would be easier. She could run out the back if she needed to from there. Upstairs she would be trapped.

She needed a diversion.

She picked up a rolled pair of socks and tossed them at the window across the lounge room. They rattled the pane. When she heard footsteps on the patio moving fast, she pushed open her bedroom window and jumped out, shut it behind her and crouched low, trying to hear over the sound of the blood pounding in her ears.

The grevillea was sharp and spiky. There was no way to get through it silently.

She ran.

'Callie!' Ned called out. 'I see you!'

She didn't stop, didn't look back. She heard the sound of her own steps on the drive, heard his coming fast behind. Then she heard his raspy breathing, felt his fingers skim her shoulder blade. Her legs were burning, the soft skin of her feet cut by the sharp gravel. She couldn't breathe. She kept her eyes pinned on the front door and kept going. Reaching it, she slammed it behind her, knocking him back. He'd been so close.

There was an enraged growl, a pounding on the door. 'You're not being reasonable, Callie!'

She stumbled into the kitchen, almost pulled the phone from the wall in her attempt to get to the keypad. She'd only pressed the first two buttons when it was snatched from her hand and tossed aside. He grabbed a fistful of her hair. Oh God — it was happening again.

'We have to be together,' Ned growled in her ear. 'It's the only way. Understand?'

She nodded wildly, grimaced at the pain of her hair being ripped from her scalp. 'Okay.'

'It's just you and me now.'

'Okay, Ned. Of course.'

He kept his hand in her hair and marched her past the table. Her fingers wrapped around the rung of a kitchen chair. She got her other hand on it and swung it back over her head, crashing it into his. When his grip loosened she stepped out, swung again, sending him to his knees. Then she snatched up the phone as she got her legs under her and ran. She made it back to the foyer, saw the door under the staircase ajar and remembered it locked from the inside. It was the only choice.

She lunged at it, slammed it shut and locked it. Leaning against it she dialled 000.

'I need help. Please. My address is — '

Crash.

The door reverberated with the force of the blow and the phone fell out of her hands. Silence. Then his footsteps, moving away. Where was he going? She fumbled around on the floor, could have sobbed when she couldn't find the phone. If she didn't call quickly he'd just disconnect the line. There was a faint glow somewhere below her. A black rectangle that was somehow brighter than the rest of the space. Its location didn't make sense until she took a step, almost toppled when her foot found purchase much lower than it should have. *Stairs*. Of course there were stairs.

She sat on the top one, slipped down to the next, then the next. She closed her eyes, prayed, and continued silently down the stairs into the darkness.

★　★　★

'Guess I put my foot in it again,' Tess said. 'With the witchcraft stuff.'

'We didn't know,' Connor said, sitting on Tess's lounge in front of the television fighting Logan for the popcorn.

'Can't help but feel sorry for her,' Indy said.

'But she was the one who brought up Winston the ghost,' Logan reminded them.

'What was that about, anyway?' Indy asked. 'She said something about a séance in the asylum?'

'Caused a lot of trouble,' Logan said. 'The thing they supposedly let loose was named Winston after someone claiming to be a psychic medium said she'd channelled him. He was a bootmaker in life.'

'How do you know all this stuff?' Connor asked. 'We did grow up in the same house, right?'

'Yeah but you quit scouts a year before I did. We snuck into Willow Court on our Easter campout and Jacob Lancefield told us the stories.'

'I bet they were as accurate as the ones about

all his hot girlfriends,' Connor said. 'Every kid in town wanted to get a look in that place. I never thought about breaking into it though.'

'No. But you were always Mr Goody Two Shoes.'

'I object to that.'

'Of course you do. Anyway, the story goes a few of the night staff held a séance in the asylum. The supervisor walked in on them and they didn't have time to close the circle. Fast forward a few years and the staff are reporting weird music, things moving by themselves, apparitions and attacks. The people in charge called in three high-ranking religious officials to deal with it. How often do you hear about a government agency sanctioning a house cleansing?'

'Yeah. Right,' Indy said.

'Hey, it made world news. Even CNN was interested.'

'So Winston, huh? I wonder if he knows Jonah,' Connor said.

Indy's phone rang and she groaned. 'Work . . . ' Then she jumped to her feet. 'What? The house or the cottage?'

Connor's heart jumped in his chest. *Callie's cottage?* Was Callie hurt? In danger? Hell — had Adam turned up there after all?

'Call Detective Denham. I'm on my way.' Indy dropped her phone in her pocket and headed for the door.

Connor was on his feet too. 'What happened?'

'No,' Indy ordered firmly. 'Stay put.' Then she disappeared.

Every second was killing him. He couldn't

wait here to find out what had happened to Callie.

Then: 'Okay, that's long enough,' Tess said. 'Let's go.'

34

Another vicious attack at the door shook her thoughts. Desperately, she scanned the darkness. There were two tiny lights. The black glow she'd seen from the stairs had to be a computer monitor. She carefully crept closer and skimmed her fingers over the desk, searching for a mouse. Finding it, she slid it side to side. The screen came to life. The desktop lit up with a picture of her in the garden. From the glow of the screen she made out shapes in the room. Pictures. The walls were full of images of her, doing all sorts of things during the day and night in and around the cottage. There were some — *oh God* — from inside the cottage. One from a vantage point behind the lounge, a few of her in the bathroom, more of her sleeping.

'I'm coming in, Callie.'

She searched frantically around the room. There must be another way out. There was a narrow window, set high on the wall. Would she even fit through it? She pushed at a cupboard shrouded in pictures, hoping to move it under the window. It was incredibly heavy, noisy.

She jumped back. The cupboard had been placed in front of a door branded with hexafoils and other markings she didn't understand. A door to where? The cellar was underground. She pushed it open. The space inside was pitch black and stank of damp, stale air. Tentatively she reached out — felt nothing.

Another crash at the door was followed by the splintering of wood and a flood of light pouring down the steps and into the room.

With no other choice, she stepped into the space behind the door and closed it behind her, trying not to think of spiders or anything else that could be in there.

'Callie?' The footsteps on the stairs didn't seem to be in any hurry.

She couldn't feel walls around her. There seemed to be too much room. She eased one arm out, reached a half circle around her. Nothing. The cavity was large.

Then a light came on in the cellar and just enough penetrated the gaps between the door and the frame to give her an impression of a long line of brickwork and dust, a tunnel running parallel to the house. She scrambled to remember what Paisley had said. *There's an old tunnel that runs from the river beside the house right under the town to the asylum . . .*

Did that mean this could be a way out?

The door behind her was yanked open and steely fingers locked around her arm. 'There you are!'

She couldn't help the scream and fought wildly as Ned held on with a bruising grip.

'Don't want to be going in there,' he said patiently, though his voice had an edge from the effort of holding on. 'Best come out now, it's not safe.'

She'd take her chances. She twisted with renewed ferocity, got her arm free and lashed out hard. She heard more than felt the thud as her fist connected with his face, and he disappeared back through the doorway with an enraged growl. Callie moved out of reach, further into the gaping black hole, and felt around her. A few inches above her head her fingers grazed the rough scrape of brickwork. She stepped forward, arms waving, searching for a safe way. Though she wanted to run, she made herself go carefully.

A bone-aching cold seeped into her, and a musty odour that reeked of air too sour to safely breathe had her fighting back a gag that became a choked sob. She forced away the tears — she needed to see. Could she get lost down here? She told herself to *stay calm, stay calm* against the pounding of her blood in her ears.

A torch beam shone down the tunnel. She ran, one arm stretched to the side, skinning her fingers as she kept track of her path, the other in front of her in case she hit another wall. The side wall disappeared but by the time she'd stopped she'd hit it again. A second tunnel? Now what? Should she go back? Or keep going forward? Which way was out? She swallowed more panic, more dread as a beam of light momentarily blinded her.

'You can't run, Callie. You're only going to get yourself killed.'

Forward, she thought. If she started making turns she'd be completely lost. She ran, Ned's torch illuminating enough of the hazy tunnel for her to pick up speed. As the tunnel curved the torch-beam faded, then she wondered if her eyes were playing tricks on her or if the darkness ahead might have held a touch of light. And was the air getting easier to breathe?

The torch was directly behind her again. It lit up a wall ahead just when she would have crashed into it. She stopped. A dead end.

'No . . . ' Another sob broke from her throat as she realised she was trapped. She spun to face him. The torch was blinding. Ned's features were difficult to make out from behind its glare and what she could see only looked more terrifying in the unnatural highlights.

Something brushed her face. She swiped at it desperately. A leaf. She looked up, reached up, and her fingers tangled in a metal grate, feeling damp leaves and earth. She pushed desperately at it, was showered in debris as it shook in place. The steady beam of light became erratic as Ned picked up his pace.

Tears and dirt stung her eyes and made seeing anything impossible as she frantically shoved at the grate. It twisted, one end lifting as the other dropped down to empty its contents on the ground around her. Another shake and it fell heavily, smashing against her cheek, but she barely noticed the pain as she braced her hands on either side of the opening and attempted to pull herself up. It was too high, too slippery. She began sobbing in earnest as her trembling arms wouldn't do what she needed them to. She forced herself to take one deep breath, changed her grip, tried again.

Ned was right in front of her as she jumped, propelling herself up hard, her elbows locking over the edges of the hole. Trembling from the exertion, she tried to lift herself the rest of the way. But two large hands grabbed her hips and pulled.

'No!' she screamed. She kicked her legs, she twisted, but he was too strong. She was going down.

There was an 'Oof', as her foot connected hard with Ned's body. When his hands released their grip, she managed to get a foot on his shoulder and boost herself off it, to tumble out of the hole onto the wet earth.

Staggering to her feet, Callie took a few steps as she fought to drag enough oxygen into her lungs. Head swimming, she bent over and waited for the world to stop spinning.

There was a clinking sound, then: 'Callie!' Ned roared. 'Don't leave!'

It got her moving again. Where was she? She ploughed through some scrub and caught sight of the river, followed it. Almost immediately the ground opened up and she knew, even in the dark, where she was. Ava's memorial.

'Callie?' Another deep voice had her spinning again. Though the night seemed almost like daylight after the darkness of the tunnel she could only just make out the features of the man pointing a torch and a gun in her direction.

'Jared?' She stumbled to a standstill.

'Yep.' He rushed forward. 'What's happened to you?'

'Ned, he's — ' She swung around at the sound of heavy breathing behind her.

'She's mine!' Ned bellowed.

Jared dragged Callie behind him and tackled

Ned. Both went down. It only took a matter of seconds for Jared to have Ned flipped over, handcuffs in place.

More lights danced down from between the heavy trees, and footsteps crashed behind her.

'Jared?' Indy called out sharply.

'She's here! She's safe.'

'Callie!' Connor's voice. He hurtled down the trail and wrenched her to him. 'Are you all right?'

'Where did you come from, Connor?' Indy said.

'Where the hell do you think?'

'I could have shot you.'

'Or us, I suppose,' Tess said, appearing behind them with Logan.

Jared got to his feet. 'He's out cold.'

'Are you hurt?' Indy asked Callie. 'Where'd you come from?'

Even as she started to say it, Jonah's words finally made sense. 'Under the ground.'

35

Connor left Callie sleeping in his apartment and went back to the cottage to get some of her things. They'd been up too much of the night, then when they'd finally got to bed, the crack to her cheek had coloured up and she'd been restless, even with the painkillers. She needed to rest. Indy and a few other police were parked in the drive so he walked up to the house first, to check it out.

Indy spotted him coming, waved. 'How is she?'

'Asleep. Sore. What are you up to?'

'Gathering evidence. But we're wrapping up so . . . want to see?'

'Hell, yes.'

'Come with me. Just don't touch anything.'

He moved around police packing up and got inside, followed Indy down the stairs to the cellar.

'Holy shit.'

'You should have seen it before,' she told him as he stared in disbelief at the piles of photographs being put into boxes. 'They were strung up everywhere. Here's the tunnel entrance.'

'Is it really a tunnel?'

'Yep.'

'That's weird.'

'It's not the first tunnel or drain to be found

under New Norfolk. Some people will tell you they're all over the place. This one's interesting because there was always talk of a tunnel from the Willow Court asylum to the river that was used to transport convicts and mental patients deemed unfit to be seen on the streets, and at one stage even for bringing in contraband. A few years back something was detected running under Burnett Street and they thought they'd found it but it turned out to be a large, hand-built drain.'

'So this could be it. This goes all the way under the town?'

'We don't know yet. It's just a guess due to the direction it's pointing, Jared walked for ten minutes or so before he turned around and came back. We've got university people coming out to investigate. They're quite excited about it.'

'Can I take a look?'

'Sure. If we go left, it's only a couple of minutes to the river.'

Connor stepped in, his head mere inches from skimming the roof. A string of lights illuminated the way. It was freezing, it smelled damn ordinary and there was a definite creep factor. 'I can't even imagine,' he said, 'how petrified she must have been, down here in the dark, not even knowing if there was a way out while that bastard was chasing her.'

When Indy remained silent he took a good look at her face. 'What is it?'

'I should have been more vigilant.'

'What? Do you know something I don't?'

'I've never been comfortable with Ned's

449

fixations. You know that.'

'Indy, Ned has worked for us for twenty years — he was working for us as a teen and he's never, and I mean never, crossed any lines. I would have had him off the place in a heartbeat if he had. If we couldn't pick he'd go this far, how could you?'

'Because I'm trained to. And if he was ever going to devolve, it was now. The stressor was there: the loss of his father. Facing grief along with monumental change to what is perceived as the loss of a safe and ordered world is disastrous to a personality like that. The situation had red flags all over it. And I left her out here alone with him.'

'You didn't *leave* her anywhere. This is her home, she owns it. Ned shouldn't have even been here.'

'She bought it?'

'Bought Ned's share, yeah. She and Paisley are going to turn it into a bed and breakfast.'

'More disruption, more loss and uncertainty. No wonder he cracked.'

'What's going to happen to him?'

'He'll be remanded in custody while he goes through psychiatric assessment at Wilfred Lopes. It's a secure mental health unit for offenders.'

'What do you think will happen after that?'

'He'll end up there or in Risdon. He's not getting away without some sort of decent sentence. That shrine he had in that house to Callie was damning; it proves he's been stalking her, terrorising her, and she's not the only one. Kaicey, myself, and at least five other women had also been stalked, just not to the same extent. That shows a long-term pattern of behaviour. He had folders of photographs in the big cupboard Callie moved, and on his computer. Videos too. The thing with stalking — even basic voyeurism — is that once it escalates to the next level, perpetrators never go back. Unless they're caught, they only ever get worse.'

'What's that?' he asked, pointing to an area off to the side of the tunnel housing a collection of dark shapes.

'Ritual equipment. Some of this stuff looks a million years old but there's some other bits and pieces over there that have been used much more recently. Don't touch anything. We have to take it all out piece by piece for analysis.'

'This would explain the ghosts. The chanting would have echoed up out of the tunnel.'

'Right. Let's get out of here. The place stinks.' Then as they walked back towards the cottage, she said, 'I don't need to tell you to keep this quiet.'

'Of course not.'

'Okay. I'll see you at home.'

⋆   ⋆   ⋆

'I can't believe Ned would do that!' Paisley said from where she sat at Connor's dining table. 'I just can't.'

She'd been angry, upset, teary and feeling sorry for herself, and all Callie could think of at that moment was, *Poor Paisley*. Something else

451

she had to deal with. 'It happened. I'm sorry. But — '

'You're sorry?' Paisley laughed bitterly. 'Why? I told you he was harmless. I told you not to worry. I never thought — could never have imagined this. I know I haven't had much to do with him for a long time but Ned was always . . . Ned. I need to see him. I need to know why. Yell at him — God, I want to kill him.'

'Indy called a couple of hours ago to tell me he's in remand. He went in front of the magistrate around lunchtime and was denied bail pending a psychiatric assessment. I don't know the procedure for seeing him. Indy could tell you.'

'I'll talk to her. Damn, what now?' Paisley pulled her phone from her bag, sent Callie a look that had Callie instantly on edge.

'Ned? Why are you calling? Do you have any idea what you've done? Why would you do that?' She pulled a face that said she wasn't happy with his answer. 'You idiot! Do you really think you knew better? I'm sorry. I can't help you. There's nothing I can do.' Then: 'Say hi to Dad for me.'

'What happened?'

'The mentally ill defence was rejected. Because of the evidence against him, his lawyer decided he should change his plea to guilty, be remorseful and appeal for leniency or something. He's going back to court tomorrow for sentencing.'

'I don't have to do anything?' Callie asked.

'Doesn't sound like it.'

'Why did you make the comment about your dad?'

'He reckons he won't last in prison. Said we'll be spreading his ashes next. What am I supposed to do? Even if I could somehow snap my fingers and get him out, would I? He's dangerous. He's also my brother. It's not that I don't care, it's that I care more about what he did to you and what he could do to someone else. And I'm still so angry about it, it's not in me to be sympathetic. Not now. Maybe not ever.'

The door opened and Connor came through, followed by Indy and Jared. He crossed the room and gently lifted Callie's head, examined her face and placed a kiss on her lips.

'Have you been taking the painkillers?'

'Yep. Hi,' she said to Indy and Jared. 'Are you hungry? Do you want me to get you anything?'

'No, we're fine. Thanks.' Indy sat. 'Connor tells me you recently purchased a share of the property.'

'That's right. What's wrong?'

'We found some things in the tunnel. There's no doubt in my mind that whatever's been going on out there is human, not supernatural.'

'I didn't think Ned would want to be involved in any of that,' Paisley said. 'But after last night, I don't think I know Ned at all. I knew everything that used to go on affected Ned the worst. But I thought he was okay. Or I never would never have left Callie with him . . . ever.'

36

Connor spent his afternoon in the office. He figured he'd have to put in at least another couple of hours before he caught up, and to do that he'd need something decent in his stomach. He headed out in search of food and came across Indy coming into the guesthouse.

'Hey,' she said. 'All good?'

'Yeah. You're not working?'

'Just finished what's amounted to a fifteen-hour shift. Thought I might grab a — ' she checked her watch, ' — very late lunch.'

He grinned. 'And defensive about it.'

'Tired,' she said. 'How's Callie?'

'Refusing to take it easy. She's out at Waldron Park with Paisley. They're into a mass clear-out, while Jared's setting up more surveillance around the property. Sorry,' he added when his phone rang.

'Is that Connor? This is Adelaide. Your Callie came to see me the other day.'

'*My* Callie?' How did Adelaide know anything about him or their relationship?

'I need to see you. I know quite a few things you should hear. I'll be home around seven. Come then, please.'

He frowned when the phone went dead and put it down. 'Adelaide wants me to go and see her. She said, 'Your Callie.' How could she know about our relationship? I've never even met the

454

woman. Did Callie mention me when you were both out there?'

'I don't think so.'

'And she knew my number.'

'So she knows about the connection too. I don't trust this woman. In some way or another she's much more involved in this than she let on. I think I'll come with you.'

'Indy, it's one old woman. I'll be fine. Besides, she wasn't keen to talk to you. Maybe I'll get more out of her.'

Indy thought about that. 'I'll put a car at the end of the street, listen in. She might say something valuable that you miss. Another set of ears can be handy.'

When she put it like that it made sense. 'All right. Let's just hope she knows something worthwhile. I'll let Callie know I'll be late.'

★ ★ ★

Connor followed Indy's instructions and found the house with no trouble. A quick look in the rear-view mirror showed Indy pulling up just around the corner in the unmarked car. Another plain-clothed officer got out, gave Connor the briefest nod and strolled down the street. Their presence made him nervous. Made this feel like a big deal. *Just a little old lady*, he reminded himself. But if Indy believed that, she and another officer wouldn't be lurking quite so close on his heels.

Keen to get the whole thing over and done with, he opened the iron gate and walked up the

455

path. Before he got up the two steps to the front door, the woman he assumed was Adelaide opened it and beamed him a smile.

'Come in, come in,' she said warmly. 'It's lovely of you to come out here at such short notice.'

He stepped into a narrow hallway and turned left into a rustic kitchen and dining area.

'Take a seat. I'll pop the kettle on for some supper,' Adelaide said, then fussed around in the kitchen. Biscuits were meticulously arranged on a china plate, then she very slowly and accurately cut thin slices of sponge cake and placed them carefully on another plate.

'You really don't need to go to all this trouble,' Connor said after she'd been at it for several minutes.

'It's no trouble at all, dear. I don't get many visitors these days. Thank you for coming.'

Another few minutes of fussing with the tablecloth was followed by tea leaves and hot water going into an antique teapot, milk poured into a fancy jug, and a difficult decision over which tea cups and saucers to use including a discussion on where each set came from and the story behind the purchase of each. *She even talks slowly*, he thought impatiently.

Finally he was seated with — no arguing! — a biscuit *and* a slice of cake on a delicate china plate in front of him, while Adelaide strained tea into his cup.

'Would you like sugar, dear?'

Had his life depended on it he would have died before suggesting he did. No doubt that would be another ten-minute exercise, this time in selecting the finest cubes and arranging them into some sort of geometric perfection in a sugar bowl she would also dither over choosing. Or something.

Adelaide contentedly sipped her Earl Grey tea. 'Oh! Napkins!' she announced suddenly and got up to collect some, folding them carefully and handing him one.

'So what was it exactly you wanted to tell me, Adelaide?' he asked.

Adelaide carefully lowered her cup to its matching saucer, dabbed her mouth with her napkin and placed it very correctly back on the table. 'Before I tell you that, I'd just like to apologise for how dreadfully rude I was to Callie during her last visit.'

'I'm not sure she thought you were rude,' he said. 'But don't worry about it. If you could just — '

'But I do! Of course I do. I wasn't brought up to be rude. My darling old nan — Jonah and I were brought up by our nan — well, she wouldn't have approved at all. She was very prim and proper. Would have had our hides . . . '

Connor gritted his teeth as she prattled on, and glanced out the window. How long was this going to take?

'So you see, it's just that I was very surprised that she'd found me. And when Callie said Jonah had been talking to her, had brought her here, well, you just could have blown me over with a feather. Such a sweet boy, he was, such a tragedy. It's quite lovely to know he's still around.'

'It must be,' Connor said, finding it hard to remain polite when he didn't believe a word she was saying.

'So tell me, how's Callie getting on? Having some trouble out at the cottage, I hear?'

'The police are all over it,' he said. 'They're looking into everything very carefully.'

She nodded slowly, a smile sliding across her face. 'There have always been rituals held at Waldron Park. Eileen saw them simply as a way of controlling people, but those before her were much more serious about it. I'm not surprised there's ghosts out there. Do you know how it all began?'

Connor took a sip of tea — he hated tea — and resigned himself to her getting to the point. Slowly.

★ ★ ★

Callie read Connor's message. He was running behind — had something to do. Well, that made two of them. Paisley hadn't turned up either. She looked around the pretty pink bedroom she was tidying up. She'd thought she'd dreamt it with its pink-wallpapered walls, lacy canopy bed and assortment of little girl's things in the wardrobe. But she'd been in here. Cliff had been right, he'd seen her in the house. Had he realised she was sleepwalking? Was that why he'd had her padlock the cellar door? But why was she sleepwalking again when she hadn't in so long? And those dreams . . . why had they always ended so badly?

She walked to the window and looked out over

the trees to the river. It was so quiet. So still.

Twin headlights swung across the drive over by the house. Paisley's car. Callie left the window and walked downstairs to meet her.

'Hi. What happened?'

'It took a bit longer to get the groceries than I thought.' Paisley stretched and smiled. 'I still can't believe I'm down here for good. Did you get everything cleaned out of the cottage?'

'Pretty much. Jared's over there getting himself sorted out.'

'Then let's unload the food.'

It took a few trips. Callie was just unloading the last items when Paisley crashed into her as she turned around from the boot.

'Whoa. Are you okay?'

Paisley's attention was on the drive just beyond the car, so Callie put the bags down and stepped around her to look for herself.

'Jonah?' she called out in disbelief.

He was standing several feet away, completely still, carrying his dog. It wasn't moving. Then he dropped it. It fell, lifeless.

'He made me kill her. He made me.'

'Oh my God.' She'd already taken a step towards him when Jonah's head turned towards the house. The thump of Paisley's hand against her arm that turned into a biting grip stopped Callie, had her turning to look too. 'Adam,' Paisley whispered.

It was the same cloaked figure she'd seen at the river. There was no mistaking that. Same black floor-length cloak, same terrifying grin looking out from underneath the hood. Paisley was already backing up.

'Go into the house now, Jonah,' the cloaked man ordered. 'Wait for me there.'

'Yes, Dad.'

'Jared!' Callie called out, wondering if she'd make the dash to the cottage.

'Jared can't help you I'm afraid,' came Adam's taunting voice.

Her eyes went back to the cottage in desperation anyway, but Jared didn't emerge from it. What had Adam done?

'Run!' Paisley ordered under her breath, and disappeared into the darkness. Having little choice, Callie followed.

'Paisley, where are you going? Paisley!' Callie ran, tripping and sliding, desperate for breath as they reached the clearing. She stopped, stared. 'What the hell is all this?'

Jewellery hung from branches of trees on the edges of the circle. A ring, a gold necklace, an earring, a bracelet. 'Metals hold energy,' Paisley said in a strangely calm voice. There was no trace of the terrified woman of only seconds ago. 'Dale and Lisa, Orson and Mitch, Kaicey. They couldn't be here but a part of each of them is. We need them, we need the original circle.'

'We?' Callie asked, heart thundering in her chest. 'Why do we need them? I don't understand. Paisley, Adam's going to be here any second . . . ' But Paisley already knew that, she realised with sick certainty.

The shock rendered Callie incapable of thought, of movement.

Paisley picked up a bag, moved it out of the

trees and put it down gently. A knife similar to a letter opener slipped to the ground. 'Oops.'

Callie took one careful step back, then another. 'You led me here on purpose.'

'I had to, Callie.' Paisley's tone was resolute. 'This has been too long in the making not to go through with it.'

The chills just kept washing over her, wave after wave of icy, electrical currents across her skin that warned her to run. *Run.* But where? Where was Adam? And still, she couldn't quite believe it. 'Go through with what?'

Nothing about Paisley's calm face was reassuring. 'I'm sorry to put you through this. It's just something I have to do.'

Callie was grabbed hard from behind. 'Welcome home, Ava,' a voice rasped in her ear.

461

37

'Adelaide, I really do need to get going,' Connor said a little more impatiently. 'Why did you ask me here?'

She checked her watch, nodded. 'Goodness, time is getting away. You were interested in finding Adam, weren't you?'

That got his attention. 'Ah . . . if this is about Adam you really should be speaking to Indy.'

'I've always been a bit wary of police,' Adelaide said, taking another biscuit. He waited while she took a bite, swallowed, dabbed at her lips with her napkin. 'I just don't feel comfortable around them.'

'Okay. Then . . . why don't you tell me and I'll pass it on?'

'You can tell the police if you like.' She took another bite, another swallow, another dab. 'But they won't stop him.' She smiled, drew in a deep breath. 'He's smart and he's had a long time to plan all this. And he's dangerous, because he doesn't have a conscience. At least, no one's ever seen any trace of one. His parents joined the group hoping to drive the devil out of him, but exposing him to that darkness only made him worse. Once he witnessed one of those rituals he was completely fascinated. Wanted in. Eileen said no. Adam never did accept no very well. And if there's one thing you can rely on him to do, it's retaliate when he doesn't get his own way.'

'Respectfully, you don't know Indy. She'll stop him.'

'Did you know Ava was his sister?'

'Ava was Paisley's sister. And what has that got to do with anything?'

'Well, you see, Eileen Waldron had an affair with Adam's father. Adam's mother was understandably furious but she was one of us. It wasn't easy to walk away from that. It looked like she wouldn't. Then Eileen found out she was pregnant and that was it. Heather packed up and left. Ava was born a few months later.'

'So Adam killed his sister.'

'There was something about that child. Ava, I mean. Something innately good and kind. Bright. Adam hated her with a passion. He hated that his father doted on her, hated that Eileen favoured her when he wanted her approval so much. He hated everything about that child. Every chance he got, he'd try and hurt her.'

'I know what he did. Paisley told us.'

Adelaide shook her head sadly. 'When they dragged her from the river, Eileen just about broke in two. Never recovered. I wasn't surprised she took off. Weight of guilt and all that.'

'And you all covered it up and sent Adam to prison. Made the kids testify against him and now they're all dead. I hope you're proud of yourselves.'

'We did what we thought was best at the time. But yes, they're all dead. Marcie too. She really shouldn't have spoken to Callie.'

'He killed Marcie too?' And then, with another, bone-chilling thought, 'What exactly was she trying to warn Callie about? Is Callie in trouble? And Paisley?'

Apparently, that was funny. 'Paisley? Oh — no. Of course not! Paisley's his high priestess. His queen, if you like.'

His thoughts were all crashing in at once. 'I have to go.'

'Uh-uh!' Adelaide said, lifting a gun from somewhere under the table. 'You're just going to sit there, and we're going to wait this out. Adam will be along when he's finished.'

'Wait this out?' It wasn't easy to think when you had a gun pointed at you. Had stalling him been the goal all along? Stalling him from what? Callie. She was out there with Paisley. She had no idea. Indy was listening, he reminded himself. But she didn't know about the gun.

'We both know you're not going to let me go,' he said very clearly, 'so what's stopping you from shooting me with that gun of yours right now?'

'I'd prefer to wait. I'm enjoying the conversation and, well, guns are so noisy! In a quiet neighbourhood like this the shot might draw attention. I'll risk it though,' she said, 'if you try anything. Wouldn't you rather just wait for Adam?'

'Why would you protect him? How do you know he won't come after you?'

The smile she gave was devoid of any warmth. 'Because I'm his mother. I'm Heather Adelaide Mansfield and I'm raising his son for him.'

'Let me guess,' Connor said over the surprise, wondering why Indy wasn't hurrying up. 'Jonah.'

'His mother, Rowena, was Marcie's daughter.

Died giving birth to little Jonah. Such a tragedy.'

Anger shot through him. 'You're as sick as Adam! You made Callie think she'd been seeing a dead kid.'

'Adam made the photo up. Good, wasn't it?'

A knock on the door had her turning with a frown. 'Oh dear. Now that'll be Maya from next door. She's the only one who comes over at this hour. She's nosey, but lovely. A young single mother with two preschoolers who'll be orphans without her. I mind them for her occasionally. You're going to shut up, and I'm going to get rid of her. If she sees you, or hears you, I'll have to shoot her, and it will be your fault, understand?'

Gun behind her back, Adelaide opened the door just a crack. 'Hello, M — '

The door was kicked in with a blow that sent Adelaide skidding backwards across the floor. Indy rushed in, wrestled the woman onto her stomach and cuffed her.

'You're under arrest.'

When she'd read Adelaide her rights the other police officer came in and took over.

'You okay?' Indy asked him.

'Better than her. Nice kick.'

'We have to go. I can't get hold of Jared.'

They raced to the car with Indy calling instructions to another police car as it pulled up.

Indy sped, siren on, towards Waldron Park.

'Do you think Adelaide could be telling the truth about Paisley and Adam being in it together?' he asked her.

'There's no other way they could have orchestrated this.'

465

'Orchestrated what?'

'All of it. To gain control of Waldron Park. I think she and Adam have visions of picking up where Eileen left off. She's manipulated this whole thing: getting Callie down here, convincing her to tie up all her money in the place, opening a joint account with an enormous stockpile of Callie's funds to go into restoring it.'

'That was partially because Dale's parents were suing.'

'Who do you think convinced them to? And now it's all official — if anything happens to either Callie or Paisley, the other one gets the lot.'

Connor allowed that to sink in for a moment before slowly shaking his head. 'I don't believe it.'

Indy flicked her gaze from the road just long enough to shoot him an apologetic glance. 'I'm sorry, you know I can't always tell you details about the case. There are three things you need to know right now. The first is I believe Callie is Ava Waldron. Ava supposedly drowned when she was five years old. Her father, Bruce, disappeared right after the incident. Eileen made it a priority to get Adam behind bars, but Bruce didn't wait around for that.

'Callie was raised by her father following a car accident when she was five years old. Her mother supposedly died in that accident and Callie has no memory of it. The thing is, I can't find a coroner's report on either of those events. Paisley says she pulled Ava's body out of the water, Jared's father says they never recovered a

466

body. And it just so happens that Callie and her father turned up in the same small town Dale's family ran to in order to escape the fallout from the trial.'

'Even if that's true, I just can't see Paisley hurting Callie. She's protective of her to a fault.'

'To keep her on side, to make her grateful. The second thing you need to know is I believe Paisley is likely suffering from a hereditary mental illness.'

'Is that sort of thing genetic?' he asked. 'Besides, what would be the chances of having two children affected by mental illness in the same household? Ned was never completely right, we knew that, but Paisley?'

'Actually the chances are quite high, but Ned was adopted, remember? His problems are a result of mild Foetal Alcohol Syndrome. His mother was a teenager with a drinking problem that resulted in her making bad decisions, falling pregnant. Her family had money and they wanted the problem resolved. They paid Eileen and Cliff a lot to take him on.'

'And you think Paisley is suffering from what — schizophrenia? Why?'

'The average age of onset of schizophrenia in women is much later than men — around twenty-five to thirty. Paisley could have been developing the disorder for some time and not known it. You know she talks to her mother all the time, right? Won't tell us how to contact her?'

'Yeah. So?'

'Eileen Waldron died ten years ago.'

Connor's breath rushed out on a stunned

curse. 'Are you certain? How could Ned not know?'

'Absolutely. Apparently the split between Eileen and Cliff was incredibly nasty. When Eileen and Paisley left, Ned chose to stay with Cliff. Eileen made no attempt to contact him again — he'd made his choice and that was that. And I don't think Paisley is deliberately lying. I think that, regardless of whether or not she acknowledges Eileen is dead, Paisley genuinely believes her mother is talking to her.'

'What's the third thing?'

'Adam has been systematically taking out people who'd in some cases not only moved, but changed their names, their identities. Paisley told us her mother was the only one who kept track of everyone's movements so she could warn them when Adam got out. And Eileen's dead. So how did he find them, unless Paisley was in possession of the list and provided that information?'

'I can kind of see what you're getting at with Waldron Park. Paisley gets Callie to fund it, then something happens to Callie and she gets the lot. But why would she help Adam kill the others?'

'Because they stood there and did nothing. That's what she said. They could have helped that night, but they didn't. I don't think she ever forgave them for that. She wanted them to suffer.'

'But Ava didn't die. She knows that. How could she side with the monster and want to hurt her now?'

'I think she saw Adam as a means to an end

with the others. Payback. And look at this differently. What happened that night took a toll on her whole life. In many ways, it destroyed it. She may have loved Ava then but it's very possible that, over the years, that turned to resentment, even hate. Up until Dale's death, Callie's life had been close to perfect, while Paisley's life hadn't really gone anywhere. If she kills Ava now, she'll finally be the one who has it all. And you know what tonight is?'

'Should I?'

'It's the winter solstice. The longest night.'

38

The inky darkness glittered with orange and gold, threads of flame flickering all around, illuminating the edges of her vision. Her eyes focused in on stars while her head throbbed. Biting cold seeped into her skin and caused cramping from the pull of her extended arms and legs. They itched and ached from the tight ropes holding her still. A shadow loomed over her, blocking the stars. A black figure in a hooded cloak. An ugly, smiling face looking down at her from beneath it.

She dragged at her hands and found no give in the rope. Adam's finger traced the line of her cheek. She flinched, disgusted, as her heart hammered in her chest and fear clutched at her throat.

'Too bad you're my sister,' he said with regret. 'You always were pretty.'

She turned her head left, right, everywhere. It was the only part of her body that would move. She was on the ground. *In the circle. Oh God.*

'You know your mother used to hold séances and medium sessions in the cellar? They used to call things. Dark things.' He leant down until his lips grazed her ear. 'We're going to call them back, Ava.'

Callie choked back a sob. 'I'm not Ava! Let me go!' A rumble of thunder warned the change was moving in and a light gust of wind bothered the torches. 'You're sick! You think you'll get away with this? Even if you kill me, they'll find me, find *you*. You'll be back in prison, not playing make-believe!'

Adam grabbed her throat, those black eyes furious. 'They haven't got a thing on me! I laid low, waited more than a year to see if Dale would take the rap for Lisa's murder and you for his. Mitch, Orson and Kaicey had to be put on hold all that time. Different time frames, different states.'

'Same methodology. You kill the same way, and you only killed the ones who testified. They know it's you. They'll prove it's you.' Light-headed, she struggled to breathe against his painful hold.

He only smiled. 'Knowing it and proving it are two different things. Besides, you didn't testify against me, did you, Ava? Not that they'll find you. Not here.' His grip marginally slackened as he sneered. 'Have you heard the devils? Do you know why we lure them?'

She couldn't speak.

'Devils have the most incredible jaw strength. They'll eat a whole carcass. Demolish it. Bones and all.' He let her go.

The breath she dragged in was loud and painful.

Paisley knelt over her, traced something on her forehead in oil. Adam disappeared from her line of sight and reappeared with a knife. He pointed it around the circle, chanting.

'What is he doing?' Callie whispered.

'Casting the circle, summoning the spirits,'

Paisley murmured. She smiled gently and moved to the edge of the circle. She pulled out a doll, walked a short distance away to place it on the memorial stone. 'Front row seat, Mum,' she said, stroking the doll's hair. 'I told you I'd do it. And I will.'

As the doll sat on its perch, the fire reflected in its eyes and the wind tossed its hair. It looked alive; as evil as the act it was witnessing.

Adam crouched beside Callie again. She wanted to beg, but the words wouldn't come. He grabbed the neckline of her shirt, staggered back. 'What's this?'

'Dad's amulet.'

Crack.

The breath in Callie's lungs whooshed out as Adam fell on top of her. Paisley stood over him with a tyre iron dangling from her hand. His blood dripped onto Callie's throat, trickling to the ground as Paisley dragged him off her.

'Mum told everyone the amulet was magically charged,' Paisley said, working quickly to free Callie's hands, releasing them from their bonds before moving to her feet. 'That to harm the wearer was to forfeit one's soul. Crazy, right? She only made it up to stop anyone within the coven giving her any trouble. Apparently, Adam's psycho enough to believe it, which is why Dad wore it. Why he gave it to you.'

'I thought you were going to kill me!' Callie couldn't stop her teeth rattling as the tremors continued. She could barely make her legs work to stagger out of the way.

'I would never hurt you!' Paisley was already

472

dragging at Adam's heavy, prone figure.

'He kept calling me Ava.'

'Because you are. You think you sleepwalked your way to Ava's hidden things by accident? Dad even padlocked the cellar, because you wandered down there asleep once, got lost in the dark.'

'No. It's not *me*,' she insisted.

'He left you a share of Waldron Park, too. The wording in the will was 'To my children, and to Eileen's'. He wasn't your father, but Eileen was your mother. He didn't want to love you but he did. And then he met you again, and he didn't want to love you, but he did.'

'I'm not Ava! That didn't happen to me.'

'Your father, Adam's father, took you away. You were so little and damaged from what Adam had done to you that night, you didn't remember much of anything when you woke up. They worked out a story about a car crash and in time, your father made you believe it.'

'That *thing* is not my brother.'

'Well, not for much longer.'

The way Paisley said it had the panic building in Callie's chest again. 'What are you doing? Why are you tying him up like that?'

'He made me kill our dog and then he dropped you anyway. Didn't you ever wonder why you hated swimming so much? I could never get you in your own pool.'

Tears mixed with the rain. Her life had been a lie, just like Lisa had told her. She really was Ava. She couldn't process it. Not there, not yet. 'It's awful, Paisley. It is. But what are you doing?'

473

'I screamed. I screamed so loud the parents finally heard and I ran to the river. It was so dark, but your little pink pyjama top had snagged in the branches of the tree he'd dropped you from. The adults came. Mitch's mother was a doctor. She revived you and she and Mum fixed up the damage Adam had done. Your dad put you in the car and drove away. We were never to speak of it. Not ever again. But the hurt, the guilt, were always there. I was the big sister. I'd promised to look after you. But I let him take you. I let him trick me. We lost everything that night. Even you. So I promised Mum before she died that this time, when Adam came back, I would look after you. I'd do a better job.'

'Your mum is dead?'

'I hear Mum all the time. *Protect Ava, protect Ava.* I hear her, I see her. She won't leave me alone. This is the only way I know for sure he won't ever hurt you. It's the only way I can keep my promise.' When Paisley's eyes met hers across the flames they looked as wild as Adam's had.

More thunder, a giant clap of it this time. The wind picked up again, a violent swirl of it that rattled and bent the trees and pulled leaves from branches. Adam came to with a snarl, viciously throwing himself around in an attempt to get free. 'You bitch!'

'Stand back,' Paisley told her. 'Get out of the circle.' Then she lifted her hands, began to recite words Callie didn't understand. Adam's thrashing became wilder, more desperate. Vile words spilled from his mouth.

'You don't know what you're doing!' Adam cried out.

Caught up in the terrible ritual, Callie could have sworn it was unnatural, the way the wind tossed the flames, shook the trees. The athame glinted menacingly as Paisley turned it downwards over Adam's chest.

'You need to know,' Paisley said loudly over Adam's curses and threats, 'the night before Dale died, we'd gone out to see Lisa, but Adam had already killed her. Dale thought about calling the police but I reminded him everyone had gone to so much trouble to hide, to keep their locations a secret for so long. If we brought it all out in the open, Adam might find them. So he took the photos of Lisa just in case, for evidence, then we buried her. You'll find her just past the gate to the high paddock. That's why he was so filthy. It took hours. And he did hit that roo, he wasn't lying.

'I turned up with Adam just after he got back. I was going to take you away while Adam killed him. If you hadn't been fighting, Dale would still have died that day. But you were fighting, and at one point Dale looked up, looked behind me and I saw the panic. I knew he'd seen Adam. That's why he was so desperate to stop you going outside. I smashed through the glass door and sent you off to get cable ties. Then Adam came in and finished Dale off. It wasn't anything you did. You didn't kill him.'

'Oh my God.' Callie's pain cut through the horror, added tears to the rivulets of rain streaming down her face. 'You helped Adam kill Dale?'

475

'You have to understand, he'd stood there that night, the longest night, and watched me kill Pixie, watched Adam drop you in the water and did nothing — except run. He ran away with the others. And then he married you. Almost seven years older than you and he put a ring on your finger while you were still so young.'

'Paisley, I was twenty-three. I wanted to marry him.'

'He had no right! Do you know how difficult it was for me to work with him? I had to be close to you to keep an eye on him, but I hated him. I hated all of them.'

'Oh, God. There's more, isn't there?'

'When I knew Adam was going to be released the second time, I started going to see him. I told him the story about you being dead had been made up to keep you safe from him, that you were alive. That I'd bring you to him. All he had to do was kill the others. I told him with Dale out of the way I could convince you to sell up and invest in Waldron Park. Set it up so he could sacrifice you on the longest night and I would own this place outright. We'd run it like it used to be run. Of course, there's no real way that could have happened, but this is Adam. His ego tends to get in the way of common sense.'

Callie jolted from her shocked stillness when Adam reared up sharply against the restraints and hissed out more curses. Paisley looked towards the doll, its clothes saturated, its hair limp against its shining face.

'While he's alive, he'll cause death.'

Adam continued to swear, spit, struggle. His

476

eyes gleamed unnaturally in the flames that fought the chaos of the wind and rain. He reminded Callie more of an animal than a man.

'You need to know I was never going to let Adam hurt you. I wanted him to believe that, but it was never the plan.' Paisley dropped to her knees, athame raised.

'I know. Of course I know. Put the knife down. Please!' Callie begged.

'Stop!' Indy's voice rang out as several torch beams focused on Paisley. 'I can't let you kill him, Paisley. I'm sorry. I don't want to, but I'll have to shoot if you move.'

'The voices won't stop until he's dead! I need them to stop. I'm tired, I'm done. *I* need to stop. It's only right he dies like this. Condemned to hell.'

'You're not a killer, Paisley!' Callie cried. 'You're not one of them!'

'No, I am one of us.' She laughed harshly. 'And this is my responsibility.'

She plunged the knife down.

A shot rang out, was lost in a clap of thunder. Paisley got to her feet clutching her damaged shoulder and stared at Adam's lifeless body, the athame buried in his chest. She smiled serenely. 'It'll be okay now, Ava.' She retreated towards the river. 'You're safe. The house is all yours. Look after it. Don't ever let it be what it was. The ghosts have gone.' She stumbled back one step too far, and tumbled into the water.

'No!' Without thought, Callie leapt in after her. The cold, black confusion of the fast-moving water tossed her violently. As panic clawed at her throat, she managed to grab Paisley's wrist, fighting hard to reach the bank and find a low tree branch. As she clung to the branch and Paisley, the current pummelled her body, dragging and choking. It froze the blood in her veins and stung her eyes. She could feel herself slipping, but refused to let go.

As Callie's vision cleared for a moment she saw Paisley — the Paisley who'd been her friend — smile sadly. Then she clasped Callie's wrist with her free hand and pulled it off hers. She was swept away in an instant.

'No!'

Callie let go, becoming tangled in debris. Disoriented, she couldn't tell up from down. Her arms and legs floundered as her lungs exploded. This was the dream, the nightmare that had woken her so many times. Only this time, she knew, if the darkness engulfed her, there'd be no waking up.

A sharp clawing scraped at her arm, then a vice-like grip, a tight band across her middle. She fought it, reason lost to panic, until she felt the press of the warm body, the words in her ear.

'Callie, it's Connor. Stop fighting!'

Connor. She twisted in his grip, wrapped herself around him and held on, breathing hard as he somehow kept them above the raging water.

Then there were more hands pulling and hauling and she was on the bank, everything aching and stinging with cold.

'Are you all right?' He hovered over her, dripping and shaking.

'Yes.'

'I thought I'd lost you!' He dragged her into his lap.

'Bring the cars down!' Indy called. 'Get a search team on the river.'

'I couldn't hold her,' Callie choked out. 'She pulled away.'

'She didn't want to come back to face all of this,' Connor said, holding tight. 'In her mind, it was done.'

She clung to him as she sobbed, heartbroken.

39

'She wasn't a bad person,' Callie told Indy as they stood by her car in the driveway. 'She was just damaged.'

Indy's smile was sympathetic. 'I didn't shoot to kill, Callie.'

'I know. And I wouldn't have let her go. She made that decision. I want to bring her back here, bury her ashes at the memorial.'

'That shouldn't be a problem.' Indy turned and opened the car door. 'I have to get moving. Unfortunately, I've got reports to work on. I'll leave you to it.'

'Thanks. For everything.'

Once in the car, Indy lowered the window. 'Hey, don't forget dinner, okay? Thanks to you, we have a restaurant review to celebrate.'

Callie smiled, though it was shadowed. 'I'll be there.'

She waved Indy off and answered her phone as it rang. 'No,' she told her solicitor, 'I won't be giving them the eighty thousand. Tell the Johnsons that before they get a cent, I'll be countersuing over the nearly hundred thousand in loans from the business they've accumulated over the years. Yes, I have the relevant documentation. And of course, I'll be happy to drop my suit should they decide to drop theirs. You too, goodbye.'

That was satisfying. She silently thanked

Paisley for that victory.

Not ready to go inside, she wandered down the trail to the river and stood, absorbing the sights and sounds of the morning, watching the sun glance off the rippling water as it broke through the mist. Ducks paddled by, dipping their heads in and out of the reeds in search of breakfast. Long willow branches swayed and whispered in a hint of breeze that twirled the mist into pretty spirals.

A deep sadness welled in Callie's chest as she allowed her thoughts to return to Paisley, the sister she hadn't known she'd had, in her life for such a short time. So many emotions swirled inside her. How was she supposed to feel about the woman who'd destroyed so many lives, then died to defend hers? Three days had passed since that terrible night and she still couldn't decide whether to allow herself to grieve for her or not. But she could grieve Dale now, in a way she hadn't been able to before. He had loved her, and though his fate had been sealed long before either of them knew it, she could be grateful for the time she'd had with him. And that knowledge brought with it a sense of peace.

She swiped at her face briskly as twin tears fell. A branch snapped behind her and she spun.

'Only me,' Connor said, coming down to join her. 'Was that Indy in the drive?'

'Yeah, just catching me up with a few things. She had to go again.'

'I'll see her tonight.' He breathed in deeply, released it slowly. 'It's a beautiful morning.'

She smiled a little wistfully, turned back to the

river, and felt his arms come around her from behind. 'It is.'

'Thinking about Paisley?'

The tears threatened again. 'She could have been so much more, Connor. But she never really had a chance, did she? She had a mental illness, but lots of people live with mental illness. The childhood she had — it was so cruel and twisted. A selfish mother, an absent father and a purely evil sociopath who put her in a horrible situation. But again, kids grow up and, somehow, they deal. And she seemed to for so long, didn't she? All the time she worked with me and Dale, and I never would have guessed what she'd been through.' She paused. 'What she was doing.'

He rested his chin on the top of her head as he stared out over the river with her. 'We can't know how much she witnessed, can only imagine the psychological damage that sort of evil could cause to a child. At least Jonah will get some help now, a chance. The foster family seem very nice.'

'They are, and I'll be keeping in close touch with them. He's my nephew. I'm going to make sure he gets whatever he needs.'

'It was too late for Paisley, but maybe not for him.'

'I know what she did was terrible, and I don't think I can ever fully forgive her for letting Adam kill Dale, but I can't hate her. Is that wrong?'

'No, of course not. Indy thought she was pretending to care about you because she resented you. But she was wrong. Your sister loved you, and in her own twisted way, was protecting you.'

482

'I know. I hope she's found peace. Somehow.'

'So do I. I hope they all have.'

She crouched in front of the memorial stone, where the rosebush flourished with new growth, and touched its cold surface. She'd add a new plaque, for Paisley. After a moment Connor gently pulled her back to her feet and hugged her, then pressed his lips gently to hers.

'So . . . do I call you Callie or Ava?'

'I haven't been Ava since I was dropped in the water over there by a sociopath. I'll stick with Callie.'

'I guess you've got a lot to learn about your family.'

'I'm not sure I'm ready to tackle it yet.'

'Understandable. It's a hell of a lot to take in. Give it time.'

'And Ned, he'd have information, but I'll never speak to him again. He could have stopped all this. He knew.'

'And Indy's busily adding whatever she can to his charges.'

Callie nodded and looked up at the tower of the house, just visible above the trees. 'What am I going to do with this place? Run it on my own? I don't think I can.'

'You're the most incredible person I've ever met,' he told her, his hands sliding up and down her arms affectionately. 'If anyone can do it on their own, it's you. But you don't have to do it solo. Unless you want to.'

'Oh?'

'It might have slipped your attention,' he said, turning her to face him, 'but you have me.'

Her lips curved up into a warm smile. 'Do I?'

'I don't want to pressure you about relationships and the future, not when you've just been through all this and when you're still working out your past. And I know you're less than keen to think about ever getting married — '

She stopped him by pressing her lips to his and kissing him until the emotions, good and bad, seeped out of her and were replaced simply with him. 'Yes,' she whispered against his lips. 'When you get around to asking, it'll be yes.'

His lips spread into a smile. 'I've been getting around to it long enough. Consider your *yes* a binding contract.'

It crossed her mind, as he kissed her again, that there were many kinds of new beginnings, many paths in life that twist and turn and intertwine. She wondered at how many tragic ones could possibly have led her here, on a route to somewhere bright and full of promise.

'Did Indy talk to you about dinner?' Connor asked when he eventually lifted his head.

'Yeah.'

'And . . . you actually *want* to come this time?'

She bumped him playfully. 'We'll see.'

They started up the trail, hand in hand. And as their words, happy words, loving words, floated away from them, the first delicate petals of a solitary rosebud opened to embrace the new day.

Acknowledgements

Thank you to my readers, for your constant support and lovely correspondence. Special thanks to Tony Jones, Tangil and Fred Kinch, and Ange D'Bras who assisted with the criminal elements of the story. To my amazing critique partners Tea Cooper and Ann B Harrison, thank you once again for all your hard work. To Kathryn Coughran, who never runs out of time to help, and Shelley Jones for all that extra running around, I couldn't do it without you. As always, thank you to the whole sensational team at Harlequin. With a special thanks to Jo Mackay and Annabel Blay, to editors Alex Craig and Kylie Mason, and my agent, Clare Forster. And finally thank you to my family, for way too many reasons to list.

We do hope that you have enjoyed reading this large print book.

Did you know that all of our titles are available for purchase?

We publish a wide range of high quality large print books including:
Romances, Mysteries, Classics
General Fiction
Non Fiction and Westerns

Special interest titles available in large print are:
The Little Oxford Dictionary
Music Book
Song Book
Hymn Book
Service Book

Also available from us courtesy of Oxford University Press:
Young Readers' Dictionary
(large print edition)
Young Readers' Thesaurus
(large print edition)

For further information or a free brochure, please contact us at:
Ulverscroft Large Print Books Ltd.,
The Green, Bradgate Road, Anstey,
Leicester, LE7 7FU, England.
Tel: (00 44) 0116 236 4325
Fax: (00 44) 0116 234 0205

Other titles published by Ulverscroft:

THE ROADHOUSE

Kerry McGinnis

When aspiring actress Charlie Carver learns that her cousin Annabelle has died, she immediately leaves Melbourne to fly home to the remote family roadhouse east of Alice Springs. But after her mother suffers a heart attack and is airlifted out for life-saving surgery, Charlie is left to take the reins of the struggling family business, alongside friends old and new, including captivating local stockman Mike. The authorities declare Annabelle to have taken her own life, but when a woman's body turns up at an abandoned mine site, Charlie begins to wonder what else is being covered up, and why. Beginning a search for the truth, a perilous bush chase ensues that threatens her own life, causing her to wonder whether she ever knew Annabelle at all.

THE OTHER WIFE

Michael Robotham

Childhood sweethearts William and Mary have been married for sixty years. William is a celebrated surgeon, Mary a devoted wife. Both have a strong sense of right and wrong. This is what their son, clinical psychologist and recent widower Joe O'Loughlin, has always believed. But when Joe is summoned to the hospital with news that his father has been brutally attacked, his world is turned upside down. Who is the strange woman crying at William's bedside, covered in his blood — a friend, a mistress, a fantasist, or a killer? Against the advice of the police, Joe launches his own investigation with the help of good friend and ex-policeman Vincent Ruiz. As he learns more, he discovers sides to his father he never knew — and is forcibly reminded that the truth comes at a price.

55

James Delargy

Gardner's Hill in Western Australia is a sleepy, remote town. It is home to Police Sergeant Chandler Jenkins, who is proud to run the town's small, relatively untroubled station. All that changes when Gabriel stumbles in, covered in dried blood. Gabriel was picked up while hitchhiking, drugged and driven to a cabin in the mountains and tied up in iron chains. The man who took him was called Heath. Heath told Gabriel he was going to be his 55th victim. Gabriel managed to escape and run into town. The next day, a man who says he is Heath walks into the same station and tells the exact same story. Except in his version, he is the victim. And Gabriel is the killer. Two suspects. Two identical stories. Which one is the truth?

THE SPOTTED DOG

Kerry Greenwood

Corinna Chapman — baker extraordinaire, talented sleuth, stalwart friend and lover — is back! When a distraught Scottish veteran from Afghanistan is knocked unconscious, waking up to find his beloved ex-service dog missing, Corinna and her lover, Daniel, find themselves inextricably drawn into the machinations of a notorious underworld gang of drug runners. Corinna and Daniel need to pull together all the strings to find the connections between their wandering Scottish veteran, his kidnapped dog, a student dramatic society that's moved into Corinna's building, burglaries, and the threatening notes that begin to mysteriously appear in Corinna's apartment. Between her forays into danger, there is still time in Corinna's life for tender encounters, as the delicious aromas of newly baked breads, muffins and treats waft out of her bakery, Earthly Delights.